# NOW AND THEN, AMEN

A nun is found murdered on the steps of the Quality Couch, Sydney's classiest brothel. She was Sister Mary Magdalene, an idealistic young woman who had previously worked at a mission in Nicaragua. Detective Inspector Scobie Malone begins to be suspicious when he learns that her real name is Teresa Hourigan – the granddaughter of Fingal Hourigan, one of Sydney's most powerful businessmen, who is currently entertaining some influential Contras at his palatial home.

The trail leads Malone deep into Hourigan's past and exposes the secret the old man has kept since 1929: the reason he hurriedly left Chicago for Australia in fear of his life. It also threatens to destroy the absurd ambition he cherishes to see his son, Archbishop Kerry Hourigan, hold the highest office at the Vatican and be the first ever Australian Pope. But Kerry's violent anti-Communism has already led him to acts which will fatally endanger his standing at Rome ...

In *Now and Then, Amen* Jon Cleary has written another of his first-class novels of suspense, distinguished by the dry humour that has become his trademark. As Scobie Malone uncovers more and more political involvement in the Church and crime in Australian big business, past and present interweave in a skein of corruption that binds the old world to the new, the 'now' to the 'then'.

# JON CLEARY

# NOW AND THEN, AMEN

COLLINS
8 Grafton Street, London W1
1988

William Collins Sons & Co. Ltd
London · Glasgow · Sydney · Auckland
Toronto · Johannesburg

BRITISH LIBRARY CATALOGUING IN PUBLICATION DATA

Cleary, Jon, 1917–
Now and Then, Amen.
I. Title
823[F]

ISBN 0-00-223385-5

First published 1988
Copyright © Sundowner Productions Pty Ltd 1988

Photoset in Monotype Sabon by
Butler and Tanner Ltd, Frome
Printed and bound in Great Britain by
Butler & Tanner Ltd, Frome and London

*For Hamilton and Gerald,*
*the oldest of friends*

# Author's Note

Since the completion of this book the New South Wales Police Department has been re-structured into regional divisions. There is no longer a Homicide Bureau as such. No person, living or dead, is represented in this story. It was all written with mirrors.

J. C.

# ONE

## I

The murdered nun was found slumped, like an overcome voyeur, on the front veranda of Sydney's classiest brothel.

Scobie Malone was at home in Randwick, trying to catch up on the weekend's newspapers, when the phone rang. It was answered by Claire, his twelve-year-old, who, naturally at that age, thought all phone calls were for her.

'Daddy,' she said resentfully, throwing back her long hair just like an androgynous pop star when things didn't go as she expected. 'It's Sergeant Clements. Don't be long. I'm expecting Darlene to ring me.'

'Find a drain and fall down it,' said Malone, who hoped she wouldn't.

'You talking to me, Inspector?' said Russ Clements, then laughed. Clements was a big untidy man who professed to have a lugubrious view of the world but who couldn't stop laughing at himself. 'Sorry to spoil your day, Scobie. They've just found a dead nun outside the Quality Couch.'

'I'm not in the mood for bad jokes, Russ. It's a wet Sunday.'

'This'll be better than going to church.' Clements was an agnostic, though, like a good many others, he had arrived at that frame of mind more through laziness than determination. Then he apologized: 'Sorry. You've probably already been?'

'Not yet.' Malone was a lip-service Catholic who if he missed Sunday Mass didn't feel he was being singed by the fires of hell. Though he worked in a profession with a high

I

danger factor, he did not expect to die without at least a moment or two for a last-minute deal with The Lord. 'Okay, I'll meet you there in twenty minutes.'

Lisa came into the hallway as he hung up the phone. 'You'll meet whom where?' Lisa was Dutch-born and could sometimes be pedantic about her English. She was meticulous about saying *whom* when it was called for; she also, unlike most Australians, including her husband, knew the difference between *disinterested* and *uninterested* and sometimes sounded like a recorded English lesson. Malone, nonetheless, loved her dearly, grammar and all.

'Russ Clements. There's been a homicide.'

She made a face; she hated the thought of anyone's dying, even the deserving. 'Where?'

'Outside the Quality Couch in Surry Hills. A nun.'

'The brothel? What was she doing there? Demonstrating? Trying to convert the randy? No, I shouldn't joke. How long will you be? We're going to Mother's and Dad's for lunch.'

'Aaaagh!' That was from Maureen, the nine-year-old, and Tom, the five-year-old.

'That's no way to talk about Grandma and Grandpa.'

'But lunch is so *boring*. And Grandpa always wants us to listen to that boring *classical* music.' Maureen was a devotee of rock video clips. 'Let's all go with Daddy to the brothel.'

'What's a brothel?' said Tom, more innocent than his sister.

'No place for a five-year-old,' said his mother. 'Now all of you go in and tidy up your rooms. They look like brothels.'

'Gee, I better have a look!' Tom scampered into his room to broaden his education.

Lisa got Malone's raincoat and umbrella out of the hall closet and handed them to him as he came out of their bedroom pulling on his jacket. She looked at him with love and concern, wondering what their life together would be like if he were not a detective. He was a tall man, an inch over six feet, and he still had the build of the athlete he had once been; he had played cricket for the State as a fast bowler,

2

though she had never seen him play and would not have understood the game if she had. He was not handsome, but he had the sort of face that would not deteriorate with age but might even become better-looking as the bones became more prominent. He had shrewd blue eyes, but she knew that they could just as often be kind and gentle. She worried that his police work would eventually coarsen or embitter him, but so far it hadn't happened.

She kissed him. 'Don't get too wet. And I hope she isn't a real nun. Maybe she's one of those queers who dress up as nuns.'

'Maybe,' said Malone, but he had learned long ago never to have preconceptions about a murder case. There are recipes for killing people, but most murders are pot luck.

When he got into the car, a four-year-old Holden Commodore, in the driveway he looked back at her through the rain as she stood in the front doorway. One year off forty, she was still beautiful and looked younger. She still had some of her pale summer tan that showed off her blonde hair and even in the grey light of the dismal late March day her smile suggested sunshine. There was a composure about her, a serenity that was like a haven to him; he always looked forward to coming home to her. Even their home, a Federation house over seventy years old, was the right background for her; both she and it suggested a permanency in his life. He backed out of the narrow driveway, cursing that murders should happen on a Sunday, supposedly a policeman's as well as everyone else's day of rest.

Randwick was a sprawling suburb five miles from the heart of the city, spread out along the top of a ridge that looked down on the smaller seaside suburb of Coogee. The western side of the ridge sloped down to the famous Randwick racecourse and to the University of New South Wales, built on the site of a former racecourse. It was an area whose few wealthy residents had made their money from racing; some grand old homes survived, though most of them now had been converted into flats. Indeed, most of the area now seemed to be flats, many of them occupied by overseas students; Asian faces were as common as the wizened faces of jockeys and strappers had once been. It was somehow illustrative of the country that the State's largest university and the biggest racecourse should be separated only by a narrow road. Life was a gamble and no one knew it better than the elements in Randwick.

Malone drove in through the steady rain towards the city. Surry Hills had never had any of the wealth that had once been in Randwick. It was an inner-city area, once a circle of low sand-hills that had been built upon and that had been mostly a working-class domain for over a hundred and fifty years. It had also, over the years, been home to countless brothels, some of the locals joining them as workers. None of them had ever been as up-market as the Quality Couch.

It was situated in one of the wider streets on top of a ridge where a few plane trees had survived the city's atmosphere. It occupied two three-storeyed terrace houses that had been converted into one and refurbished at great expense. The houses had been built by middle-class burghers in the 1880s, tight-fisted men who had wanted to stay close to their factories at the bottom of the hill, and were now lying restlessly in their graves and regretting they had invested in softgoods instead of sex. The Quality Couch catered for well-heeled businessmen, many of them visitors from overseas; one girl was said to be able to sing fourteen national anthems in their original tongues. All its girls were expected to be at least bilingual, even if only in shrieks of ecstasy. Many of its clients were professionals, accountants and advertising men and one well-known judge who liked to perform wearing his wig and nothing else. It was also visited by assorted shady characters whose incomes were larger than their reputations for honesty and decorum. Malone had been in a raiding party when he was on the Vice Squad and the brothel had first opened for business; an arrangement had been arrived at with the

4

Superintendent in charge of the Vice Squad and as far as Malone knew there had been no raids since. Tilly Mosman, the madame, could never be accused of running a disorderly house. Her discreetly worded brochures, claiming the precautions taken to ensure that her girls were free of AIDS, might have been written by the Australian Medical Association, especially since at least half a dozen doctors were amongst her clients.

An ambulance was parked outside the house and with it were three marked police cars, several unmarked ones and the inevitable TV newsreel vans. A dozen or so local residents stood on the opposite pavement, some of them in dressing-gowns, all of them huddled under umbrellas. They looked more melancholy than curious, like mourners who had been called earlier than they had expected.

Malone nodded to some of the uniformed policemen standing around in their glistening slickers and went into the big house through the rather grand front door. The Quality Couch did not encourage its clients to *sneak* in; it prided itself on its open-armed welcome. There was, however, no welcome this morning for the police.

Tilly Mosman was in an expensive négligé and some distress. 'A nun! Jesus Christ, what sick bastard would dump her body on my doorstep?'

'This is Inspector Malone.' Russ Clements looked unhappy, but as he turned his head towards Malone he winked. He was not given to sick jokes, but there was some humour in this. 'Miss Mosman, the owner of the establishment.'

'As if he didn't know!' She looked him up and down, something she had been doing to men since she was fifteen years old. 'Hello, Inspector. You used to be on the Vice Squad, right? I never forget a face.'

'That's all I've ever shown around here,' said Malone and was pleased when he saw a small grin crease her face. Women, and men, were always easier to talk to when their humour improved. 'How was she killed, Russ?'

5

'A knife or something like it through the heart. The medics say she would have died instantly.'

'Anyone hear anything? A scream?'

'Nothing. Myself, I think she was knifed somewhere else and dumped here. The body's completely stiff, she's been dead a fair while.'

'When was she found? Who found her?'

'I did.' Tilly Mosman sounded more composed now, though she kept casting anxious glances at the police officers who were tramping in and out the front door. She was house-proud to a fault: 'Wipe your feet! This isn't a crummy police station!'

Malone grinned and looked around the entrance hall in which they stood. What looked to be elegantly furnished rooms opened off on either side and a staircase with a highly polished balustrade led to the upper floors. Peach-pink carpet covered the entire ground floor and the stairs and Malone saw the footmarks already beginning to appear on it. 'Careful, fellers. Treat it as you would your own home.'

The police officers stopped in mid-stride, looked at him, raised their eyebrows, then went back outside and wiped their boots again. Malone looked back at Tilly Mosman. 'They're not used to such elegance. On our pay all we can afford is linoleum. How did you find the deceased?'

'The – ? Oh, *her*. You really do call 'em the deceased?'

'Sometimes we call them a stiff. But never in polite company. How did you find her?'

'When I went out to get the milk.' She pointed to a small wire basket that held four cartons of milk.

There seemed something incongruous and amusing about milk being delivered to the doorstep of a brothel, especially one like this. He wondered what the milkman would get as a Christmas box... He was aware of the atmosphere of the house, despite all its discreet elegance. The most expensive sex in the country, except for that practised by women who married for money, took place under this roof. Milk was too

6

mundane for it: champagne should be poured on the Wheaties, if breakfast was served.

'What time was that?' he said.

'I don't know for sure. About a quarter to eight, I guess. She was just lying in the corner of the front veranda, behind one of my big pots, one of the shrubs. I thought it was some drunk at first. Or a junkie.'

'Had you seen her before? I mean, had she been picketing your place?'

'Why would she do that? Nuns never picket places like mine. They know what men are like.'

'Some men,' said Malone and grinned. She smiled in return; her mood was improving. 'What about any of your girls? Would they know her? Are any of them here?'

She shook her head. 'None of them sleeps on the premises, except those who have all-night clients. But they have to be out by seven.'

'You don't serve them breakfast?' *No champagne on the Wheaties?*

'No. Some of the men don't like it, but I insist. I don't like the place looking like a brothel all day.' Even as she spoke there was a sound of a vacuum cleaner somewhere upstairs.

'My wife feels the same way,' said Malone.

She smiled again. She was a good-looking woman in her late forties; when one looked closely one saw that the years and poundage had started to catch up with her. She had big, innocent-looking eyes, but Malone suspected that if she had a heart of gold she would give none of it away but would wait for the metal prices to rise. She had buried two husbands with no regrets and it would have been surprising, in her calling, if she had had a high opinion of men. She had an equally low opinion of feminists. She was, Malone guessed, a classic madame, a businesswoman with no illusions.

A junior officer came to Malone's elbow. 'They're taking

the body to the morgue, Inspector. You want to see it before it goes?'

'*It?*' said Tilly Mosman and shuddered.

'I'd better.' Even after all his years on the force he was still upset when he had to view a corpse. It was not so much the sight of the still, grey body, or even the ghastliness of the wounds of some of them, that affected him; he looked at the stillness of the dead, at the utter irrevocable finality of death, and grieved for the life that had once been there. Even in the most hardened, brutal criminals there had once been some spark of innocence, some hope on someone's part for a better fate. He looked at Clements.

'Have you identified her?'

'Sister Mary Magdalene. Yeah, I know. It sounds like a bad joke, putting her on Tilly's doorstep, and maybe that's what it's meant to be. But that's her name, all right.'

Malone went out and got into the ambulance. The young nun looked as if she were no more than asleep, though the pallor of death had already settled on her; she also looked remarkably young, though he knew that death, perversely, could sometimes do that. If she had suffered any pain when she had been knifed, it had left no mark on her face. She had a handsome rather than a pretty face; she looked as if she might have been strong-willed, though he knew that death-masks could be deceptive. She was dressed in a grey woollen skirt, a grey blouse and a grey raincoat; a narrow-brimmed grey felt hat with a cross on the band lay on the pillow beside her. Malone made a sign of the cross with his thumb on her forehead, then on his own. The Celt in him never left him alone.

He got out of the ambulance into the rain dripping from the plane trees and Clements crowded in beside him under his umbrella. 'You ought to look at her shoes, Inspector.'

Malone frowned, then looked at the smart black walking shoes and the brand stamped inside them. 'Ferragamo? They're –'

'Yeah,' said Clements. 'I dunno much about women's wear, but I know that brand. They're Italian, pretty bloody expensive.'

'What would a nun be doing wearing shoes like that?'

They went back into the house and Malone held out the shoes to Tilly Mosman. 'How much would a pair of shoes like that cost?'

She looked at them, raised an eyebrow. 'Ferragamo? Two hundred and fifty, three hundred dollars. Was *she* wearing them? Jesus, aren't they supposed to take vows of poverty?'

When he was satisfied that Tilly Mosman could offer them no more information, Malone went on into Homicide headquarters, taking Clements with him.

'There goes my Sunday. Lisa and the kids are going to walk out on me one of these days.'

Clements, damp and rumpled, like a big Airedale that had just fallen in a creek, sat slumped in the car seat. 'Why would they have dumped her body outside a brothel?'

'Had she been raped or anything? Molested?'

'Nothing like that. It's almost as if whoever killed her was looking for publicity.'

Despite the new multi-million-dollar Police Centre which had been opened recently, the New South Wales Police Force still had sections and bureaux spread all round the city. Homicide was on the sixth floor of a leased commercial building, sharing the accommodation with other, more mundane sections. Murderers in custody often rode up in the lifts with clerks and typists from Accounts.

The squad room took up half a floor and had a temporary look about it; Malone sometimes thought it was intended to give heart to the accused. He took off his raincoat and jacket, hung them on a coat-tree that had been 'requisitioned' from a murdered swindler's office, and slumped down in his chair at the battered table that was his desk.

'Righto, what have we got?'

Clements had produced his 'murder box', the crumpled old

cardboard shoe carton which, over the years, had been the repository of all the physical clues on dozens of murder cases. It was like a lottery barrel: some won, some lost. Clements sat down opposite Malone and laid out what he had on the table.

'Rosary beads – pretty expensive ones, by the look of them. The crucifix is solid gold – feel it.' Malone did, weighing it in his hand; it was something worthy of a Renaissance cardinal at least. He thought of his mother's rosary, no heavier than a string of rice grains. 'A handbag with some money in it, forty dollars and a few cents, a comb, a mirror, a key-ring with two keys on it, some tissues – the usual things from a woman's handbag.'

'Nothing else? How did you identify her?'

Clements dropped the items he had named into the 'murder box'; then, with clumsy sleight of hand, he laid a small black notebook on the desk. 'She had this hidden up in her armpit, under her jacket. As if she had been hiding it from whoever did her in.'

Malone picked up the notebook. 'Leather, not vinyl. This nun went in for nothing but the best.'

Inside the cover was her identification: Sister Mary Magdalene, Convent of the Holy Spirit, Randwick. Malone sat up: 'My kids go there! I've never heard Claire or Maureen mention her. I was there at the school concert at Christmas – Lisa and I met all the nuns.'

'Maybe she started in the new school year. When the kids went back in February.'

'Maybe. But Maureen would've mentioned her – she brings home all the school gossip, never misses a thing. She wants to come into Homicide when she grows up. She thinks we work like those fashion dummies in *Miami Vice*.'

'I'd drown any kid of mine who wanted to follow me.' A confirmed bachelor, he was safe from committing infanticide.

Malone went back to the notebook. It was new, perhaps a Christmas present three months before; it had very few entries.

There were three phone numbers and, on a separate page, a note: Check Ballyduff.

The top phone number was marked *Convent* and the other two were marked only with initials B.H. and K.H. Malone dialled the convent number. 'May I speak to Sister Mary Magdalene?'

'I'm sorry,' said a woman's voice. 'Sister won't be back till this evening. Who is this, please?'

Malone hung up. He did not believe in giving bad news over the phone.

## 2

He and Clements drove out to Randwick. He hated it whenever he was called to a crime in his own neighbourhood; it was as if his family were being endangered. The rain had stopped, but everything looked sodden and limp, particularly the people standing at the bus stops. When he and Clements pulled up at a red light near a bus stop, the five or six people there looked at them resentfully. Because his father could no longer drive, Malone's parents always travelled by public transport and he wondered what they felt towards those who could afford to travel in cars. His father, who still divided the world into 'us' and 'them', the workers and the bosses, probably felt just like those staring at him now. The natives had become surlily envious since the economy had worsened.

The Convent of the Holy Spirit was perched on the highest point of the Randwick ridge, with a magnificent view down to Coogee and the sea. The sun, it seemed, always came up first on the Catholics.

'You ever notice,' said Clements, 'how the Tykes always have the best bit of real estate in the district, no matter where they are?'

Tykes: it was a word for Catholics that had gone out of

fashion. But Clements, like himself, still clung to words from his youth.

'Five of the Twelve Apostles were real estate salesmen.'

'I thought they were all fishermen?'

'Only on Fridays. Anything to make a quid.'

The jokes were poor but they were part of the cement between the two men. They had started together as cadets twenty-two years before and though, over the years, they had been separated into different squads they had never lost touch. For the past three years they had been working in Homicide. Malone had gained a jump in rank, but there had been no jealousy on Clements' part. He was entirely without ambition, a bachelor who saw no point in burdening himself with responsibility in either his private life or his career.

They drove up the winding driveway to the cream buildings, dominated by the convent chapel, on the peak of the ridge. A young novice, looking bewildered and frightened when Malone introduced themselves as police officers, took them to the office of the Mother Superior.

Mother Brendan was a small woman, sharp-beaked, sharp-eyed and sharp-tongued; she believed in discipline, for herself and everyone under her. 'Mr Malone, you're here as a police-man, not a parent?'

'I'm afraid so, Mother.'

'Who's been playing up? One of our girls?'

'None of your students. We're making enquiries about Sister Mary Magdalene.'

She looked at him shrewdly; her bright eyes looked as if they might burn holes in her spectacles. 'So it was you who telephoned earlier? What's happened to her? Is she in trouble?'

'She's dead, Mother. Murdered.'

All the sharpness suddenly went out of her. She turned her face away and, in profile, Malone saw the trembling of her lips. Then she recovered and looked back at him. 'God rest her soul. This is dreadful –' Then she stopped, her bright eyes watering.

As gently as he could, Malone told her what had happened to Sister Mary Magdalene and where she had been found.

'Outside a *brothel*? Will that be in the newspapers? I have to think of our girls . . . No, I don't.' She had recovered some of her sharpness, her self-discipline. 'I have to think of Mary Magdalene. Whoever killed her had a sick sense of humour, wouldn't you say? I presume you know who and what the original Mary Magdalene was?'

'Yes.' The town bike: but you didn't say that to a nun. 'Did she ever tell you why she chose that name?'

'She was a rebel. She was quite frank about that. She joined us only two months ago – she'd spent two years in Nicaragua, with our mission schools there. She was a bit of a handful, a radical, if you like, but I put up with it. The senior girls called her Red Ned.'

Red Ned: he had heard Maureen mention her, but he had never asked who Red Ned was. He would have to pay more attention to school gossip in future.

'She never took her politics into the classroom and our girls absolutely adored her. They'll be heartbroken.'

'Her politics?'

'She was something of a Marxist. Not really, not in any party sense. But she had some pretty radical ideas. The young ones, when they come back from working in the missions, are often like that.'

'Were you?'

'I grew up in a different time, Mr Malone. We never questioned anything we were taught. Now I'm sorry that we didn't . . .' Then she looked as if she could have bitten her tongue. She turned her sharpness on Malone. 'Well, have you arrested her murderer?'

'No, not yet. So far we haven't got a single lead. Who was she? Where did she come from? Has she any family?'

'As far as we know, no, she had no family. She did her training at our home order in Ireland – we're an Irish order. She said she was born in England and brought up by foster parents – there always seemed to be a bit of a mystery about her. She went straight from Ireland to Nicaragua, then out here. We know very little of her background, but that isn't unusual in our vocation. A nunnery has just as many individuals as ordinary society. We're just less exposed to temptation, that's all. That's all I ever warn our girls against – temptation.'

'That's always been my downfall,' said Clements and looked surprised at the warmth of her smile.

'She had no friends in Sydney?' said Malone.

'Oh yes, she had friends – or one, anyway. Miss O'Keefe. She came here once on a visit. We all liked her and I gave Mary permission to visit her. She was supposed to be spending this weekend with Miss O'Keefe. They were going to the opera last night, I thought.'

'Where does Miss O'Keefe live?'

She looked embarrassed, an expression that sat strangely on her bright face. 'I don't know, exactly. Somewhere in the country. Mary had permission to stay with her last night at the Regent Hotel.'

Malone kept his face in place: the Regent was perhaps the most expensive hotel in the city. He nodded at Clements and the latter produced the items he had taken from the murdered nun and a plastic bag containing her shoes.

'Did Mary Magdalene have any money of her own?'

Mother Brendan shook her head. 'Not as far as I know. I queried her about those shoes and that rosary – they were presents from Miss O'Keefe, she said. I wasn't happy about such extravagance.'

'Can we have a look at her room? Is that what you call it?'

'They do nowadays. I still call it my cell.'

'Does it have bars on it?' he said with a smile.

'Only to keep out the outside world,' she said, but didn't smile. She knew where the dangers, and the temptation, lay.

It was a room bare of all but the essentials. A narrow bed, a small wardrobe, a chest of drawers, a table and chair, a prayer-cushion and a crucifix on the otherwise bare wall: even Ferragamo would have wondered what his shoes were doing in such a cell.

Sister Mary Magdalene's possessions were as meagre. Amongst them, however, were two items that aroused Malone's curiosity: a small photograph and a pocket diary. 'Who's the woman with Sister Mary?'

Mother Brendan looked at the handsome blonde woman in the rather flamboyant trenchcoat, her arm round the young nun. 'That's Miss O'Keefe.'

Malone flipped through the diary. The entries were brief, written with an impatient hand. 'Who is K.H.? There are two entries here. Meet K.H. at Vaucluse, 4 p.m. – that was for last Tuesday. Then there's another for yesterday – Meet K.H. same place 1 p.m. Did you give her permission to leave the convent last Tuesday?'

Mother Brendan frowned. 'She was supposed to have gone to the dentist. She's never lied to me before, not that I know of. She was always almost *too* honest.'

'Who's K.H. then?'

'I have no idea.'

'Let me see that notebook, Russ.' Clements handed over the black leather notebook. 'Here it is – K.H. and a 337 number.'

'That's Vaucluse way.' Clements was a lode of inconsequential information.

'May I use your phone, Mother?' Lisa would have been proud of him: *may*, not *can*. He was afraid that Mother Brendan might be an English teacher.

She led them back to her office, a big room that was obviously furnished to reassure parents that they were not committing their daughters to a prison. Two couches and the window-drapes were in colourful prints, though they didn't quite match. A bright Pro Hart print hung opposite what could have been a Neville Cayley painting of a colourful dove or the Holy Spirit in a fit of apoplexy.

15

Malone dialled the 337 number and a woman's voice answered. 'The Hourigan residence.'

'I'm sorry, I think I must have the wrong number. Which Hourigan is that?'

'Mr Fingal Hourigan. Or were you wanting Archbishop Hourigan?'

'No. I'm sorry, I do have the wrong number.' He hung up and looked at Clements. 'Fingal Hourigan. And Archbishop Hourigan.'

'K. H. Kerry Hourigan. That's the Archbishop.'

Malone looked at him gratefully and admiringly. 'Is there anything you don't know?'

Mother Brendan said, 'Archbishop Hourigan? His name came up one night at supper and I thought Sister Mary was going to blow her top. She got *so* angry ... But she wouldn't tell me why. She apologized and just shut up. He's one of *the* Hourigans, isn't he?'

'Yes,' said Malone. 'I think we'll go and see *the* Hourigan himself. Old Man Fingal.'

'Can we claim Mary Magdalene's body? I'd like to bury her with a Mass. Unless we can find Miss O'Keefe, we may be the only mourners.'

'I'll try the Regent,' said Malone.

# 3

There was no Miss O'Keefe registered at the Regent and no Sister Mary Magdalene. Clements, who had gone in to check, came out and got in beside Malone. It had started to rain again and taxis were banking up in the drive-in entrance to pick up departing guests. One of the bell-boys came along and looked in at Malone.

'The commissionaire says would you mind moving on, sir?'

'In a moment.'

'No, *now*, sir.' He was a bell-boy with ambitions to be a manager.

'Police,' said Malone. 'One of our few perks is parking where we like. We'll be moving on in a moment. G'day.'

The bell-boy thought for a moment, decided he held a losing hand and went away. Malone looked at Clements. 'I don't think Sister Mary Magdalene was as honest as Mother Brendan thought. Do you know where Fingal Hourigan lives?'

'No, but I don't think we'll have any trouble finding it. I've seen his place from the harbour, he built it about twenty years ago. It looks like a cross between a cathedral and a castle. There's probably a moat and a drawbridge on the street side.'

They drove out along the south shore of the harbour. Vaucluse was at the eastern end, rising up towards the cliffs along the coast. New money had moved in over the past couple of decades, but Vaucluse still smelled of old money; some elements were said still to offer pound notes instead of dollars to the local tradesmen. Down in the waterfront homes money probably never made an appearance at all: the rich didn't need it.

The home of the richest of them all had no moat or draw-bridge, but it did have a ten-foot-high stone wall. Inset in the wall were tall wooden gates that totally obscured the view from the street. On the gates were welcoming signs that offered the possibility of either life imprisonment or dis-memberment by guard dogs. YOU HAVE BEEN WARNED, said a final hospitable note.

Malone spoke into the intercom in a box beside the gate and a woman's voice answered. 'Yes? Who's that?'

'Police,' said Malone. 'We'd like to see Mr Hourigan.'

'Do you have an appointment?'

'Do I need one? I once got in to see the State Premier without an appointment.' He winked and grinned at Clements. It was still raining and they were huddled together under Malone's umbrella like over-sized Siamese twins.

It was two minutes before there was a buzzing noise and

the gates swung open. There were no signs of any guard dogs; presumably they had been called in. The grounds were not large, perhaps no more than two acres; but two acres of harbour frontage would buy fifty to sixty housing lots out in the western suburbs where the dreamers and battlers lived. Malone was apolitical, but lately he had begun to feel anti-capitalist.

The house was built of stone and had ruined the architect's career. Fingal Hourigan had wanted an Irish castle with the sun-catching aspects of a Mediterranean villa; what he had got looked like a drifting hulk in the Bay of Biscay. Cruising ferries on the harbour headed for it with their loads of tourists: it was the comic turn of their guided tours. The Japanese, being polite, didn't laugh but wondered why the Australians made fun of their rich; the Americans smiled indulgently but thought, what the hell, a man could do what he liked with his money; and the British, at least those who bothered to make the cruise, only had their opinions confirmed that the Australians, especially Irish-Australians, had no taste anyway. Fingal Hourigan, never a man to worry about public opinion, least of all British opinion, only kept adding to his castle-villa. The latest addition was a gargoyle brought from a ruined French abbey and now standing on a terrace balustrade and poking its tongue out at the tourists.

Malone had met Fingal Hourigan only once, nineteen years before when he had been temporarily assigned to the Fraud Squad. Hourigan had come out of that investigation smelling of roses, but Malone had only remembered the smell of the fertilizer that had been used. He had seen no money change hands, but three months later a senior officer at Police Head-quarters had a brand-new car.

Hourigan was smaller than he had remembered him, but perhaps that had something to do with his age; he was rumoured to have turned eighty. He had a handsome lean face, spoiled only by a certain foxiness about the pale-blue eyes; his hair was thick and silvery and he obviously took pride in it; and he had a smile that could be read a dozen ways. He was dressed in a dark-blue cashmere suit, a cream silk shirt and a blue silk tie, and he leaned on a solid-silver walking-stick. He was said to be the country's only billionaire, but he was too shrewd to confirm or deny it. There is nothing so frustrating for self-made men than to be kept guessing about another man's riches.

'I was just going to church.' He had a firm, mellow-toned voice, that of a much younger man. 'You're busting in, you know, Inspector.'

Malone apologized, careful of where he trod; another of the rumours about Fingal Hourigan was that he could pull more reins than a race-full of bent jockeys. 'I really wanted to see your son, Archbishop Hourigan.'

Hourigan showed no surprise. 'What about?'

'A murdered nun,' said Malone, hoping for some surprise this time.

There was none; the pale-blue eyes stared back at him. 'That's not a good subject for a Sunday morning. In any event, he's coming with me to say Mass.'

'I won't delay him too long. Perhaps he can say Mass for the dead nun.'

The pale-blue eyes didn't flash; they just seemed to go dead, became pale-blue marbles. He stared at Malone for a long moment, then turned and pressed a button on a table near him. Almost as if she had been waiting poised on one foot for the call, the housekeeper who had admitted Malone and Clements appeared in the doorway. She was middle-aged, plump, matronly and brusque, the sort Malone had seen around presbyteries: she would say the rosary while she shot the butcher for over-charging. She looked at Malone as if he should be shot for intruding on her master.

'Maggie, tell the Archbishop he has a visitor. A police officer.' Malone wondered if his ears were too acute: was there a warning in Hourigan's voice? 'And ring the church, tell them we may be a little late for Mass.'

'Will I tell 'em to be starting the Mass without His Grace?'
She had a brogue one could have sliced with a peat-shovel.

'No, they can wait. Ten minutes' waiting won't hurt them.'

The housekeeper went away and Malone wondered what
the local parish priest and his congregation would think of
being kept waiting. Australians never liked to be kept waiting,
not even by the Pope.

While he did his own waiting Malone covertly took note
of his surroundings. Hourigan, it seemed, was an eclectic
collector; the big drawing-room, one couldn't call it a living-
room, looked as if it had been furnished from a museum's
left-overs. There were Aboriginal bark paintings, Greek vases,
an Egyptian sarcophagus, a Celtic stone cross, a French
Impressionist painting and a Streeton landscape. The chairs,
tables and couches were dark and heavy, right out of the
middle of the worst of the Victorian period. A grand piano
stood in one corner, covered with an emerald-green silk shawl;
one could imagine a concerto being converted into a lively
Irish jig. It was what Malone's mother, who might have been
able to afford one of the chairs, would have called a 'nice
home'.

Kerry, Archbishop Hourigan, came striding into the room.
Malone's first impression was that he would *stride* everywhere, even down from the altar to give communion ('Here,
take this! Move on! Next!'). He was taller than his father, six
feet at least, and heavily built; he gave corporeal meaning to
the term 'a solid church man'. He had a plump, blandly
handsome face with the long Irish upper lip and eyes only a
little darker than his father's. His hair was thick, like his
father's, dark-brown and wavy and beautifully cut; he would
hate to spoil it by having to cover it with a mitre. He had an
air of arrogant authority about him that, Malone guessed,
made junior priests and altar boys wish they were Presbyterians. He might question the Pope's infallibility but never
his own.

'A police officer to see me?' He had his father's mellow-toned voice, but fruitier and better projected; he would never need a microphone in the pulpit, he would keep awake the dozers in the back pews of even the biggest cathedrals. 'A parking fine or have I crossed against a red light?' He was all smiles; Malone waited for a blessing. Then he sobered: 'No, Inspector, it's more serious than that, isn't it?'

'Much more, Your Grace. We're investigating the murder of a young nun, Sister Mary Magdalene. Your phone number – or rather, your father's – was in her notebook. She also had a date, or so her book said, with you yesterday at four p.m.'

All the colour, even the weight, seemed to go out of Kerry Hourigan's face. He looked at his father and shook his head as if he had been punched. 'Oh no! Not that girl . . .'

'Her?' Fingal Hourigan looked directly at his son; Malone and Clements might as well have not been in the room. 'When they said a murdered nun, I never connected . . . Holy Jesus! We'll have to have a Mass said for her soul!'

Malone was suspicious. How many nuns did Fingal Hourigan know? The Archbishop had collapsed into a chair and Malone, turning away from the old man, looked at him. 'How well did you know her, Your Grace?'

'Eh? Know her? I –' He took out a handkerchief and wiped his nose without blowing it. Malone recognized the ploy, had seen it a hundred times; it was a way of gaining time while the thoughts were put in order. Kerry Hourigan put away the handkerchief, but not before Malone had recognized it as silk. The Catholic religious seemed to be living well these days: Ferragamo shoes, silk handkerchiefs . . . Peter's Pence must be doing well against the devalued Aussie dollar. 'I didn't know her at all. She telephoned me, said she wanted to talk to me about something. She sounded rather – well, uptight, excitable. A lot of these young nuns are very militant these days. They want to change the Church, as if they have some right to take it over. Women are running amok.'

*I should have Lisa here with me.* Malone turned to Fingal

Hourigan. 'How did you know about her?'

'She came here to see my son and I told her she wasn't welcome. I showed her the door and she left.'

'Just like that? How did you feel about that, Your Grace?'

The Archbishop didn't look at his father. 'I didn't think it was very charitable.'

Hourigan didn't seem put out that his son was criticizing him in front of strangers. 'My son is a very charitable man. Sometimes he has to be protected from himself. Blessed are the meek, but not the militant, I keep telling him. We're sorry to hear of the young girl's death and we'll have a Mass said for her, but she is no business of ours, Inspector.'

Malone wished he were better educated in the Bible; but he could think of no apt quotation to answer Fingal Hourigan. 'So the girl was a complete stranger to you both, you know nothing about her?'

'That's what we just said. Now if you'll excuse us?'

'Inspector –'

Clements' diplomatic cough sounded like a bad attack of croup. Malone looked at him and the sergeant nodded towards the grand piano, at something Malone had missed in his quick survey. On the silk shawl stood a gold-framed photograph of a woman, a handsome blonde woman in what looked like an artist's smock. It was Miss O'Keefe, Mary Magdalene's friend.

Malone kept his surprise to himself, said carefully, 'That lady looks familiar, Mr Hourigan. Who is she?'

It seemed to Malone that Fingal Hourigan was just as careful in his reply; at least he took his time. 'She is my daughter Brigid. I don't know where you would have met her.'

'My mistake,' said Malone. 'I must have been thinking of someone else.' Then he looked at the Archbishop, who was still sitting in his chair. 'I remember reading in the papers that you are only here on a visit. When will you be leaving?'

'I'm leaving on Saturday. I'm going back to Rome.' Kerry

Hourigan stood up, regained some of his authority. 'I take it you won't be needing me again, Inspector?'

'Oh, I can't promise that, Your Grace. Police work is much like religion, I should think – we never know what the sinners are going to do. You won't be going to Rome, will you, Mr Hourigan?'

'If I decide to go, will I have to get your permission?'

'I don't think so. The last thing I want is to bring the Vatican down on my head.'

Fingal Hourigan abruptly smiled; his teeth were expensive and bright, but his smile was charmless, at least at the moment.

'You're Irish, aren't you? I've never known an Irishman yet who was a good copper. It's something in our make-up.'

'Some of us keep trying,' said Malone. He looked at the Archbishop. 'There has never been an Irish Pope, has there? But they must keep trying. Like us Aussies.'

The Hourigans looked at each other. Then Fingal said, 'Goodbye, Inspector. Watch the dogs on your way out.'

But the dogs were not in sight as Malone and Clements walked down the driveway to the tall gates. It was still raining and Malone wondered if they were the sort of guard dogs that only worked in fine weather.

'Like the dockers,' said Clements, who had his prejudices. Then he said, 'Did you notice the chill when you made that crack about an Irish Pope? I thought my balls were going to fall off.'

'I didn't mean anything by it.' As they got into the car the rain suddenly ceased and small patches of blue appeared in the low grey overcast; they were not sunlit and they reminded Malone somehow of Fingal Hourigan's eyes. 'There was a chill, too, when he mentioned his daughter.'

'Miss O'Keefe? I've got the feeling we've been listening to a pack of lies this morning. I wonder how many she'll tell us when we find her?'

'How much do we know about Fingal Hourigan?'

23

'I only know what I've read in the papers.'

'How much is that?'

Clements thought for a moment. He chewed on his lip, a habit he had had since childhood. Then he shook his head.

'Now you ask,' he said, 'I know bugger-all about him.'

# TWO

## I

Malone and Clements drove out to see Brigid Hourigan, also known as Miss O'Keefe. They had no trouble in finding where she lived: Malone rang an art critic whom he had met through Lisa.

'Brigid Hourigan? She lives at Stokes Point, got the sort of home no art critic could afford. She's one of the best artists we have, but for some reason she almost never exhibits here in Australia – maybe she thinks she would be trading on her father's name. All her stuff goes overseas and sells for big prices. She's very popular with European collectors. She sort of takes the mickey out of religious art, without being blasphemous, like some of these young smart-alecs who paint naked Christs with big derricks. You and Lisa thinking of buying something of hers?'

'On a cop's pay? Don't be blasphemous.'

As they drove north out of the city the sky had begun to clear and the promise of a beautiful autumn day had begun to assert itself. Malone loved the change of seasons; it was almost as if it gave him the opportunity to change moods. Summer had been a fine season twenty years ago, when he had been playing cricket; but it was not a term in which to be slogging through an investigation; tempers were always cooler in cooler weather. He longed for winter, which was not his season of discontent.

'You think Old Man Hourigan will have phoned Miss O'Keefe?' said Clements.

'If he hasn't, the Archbishop will have. Get the Irish and the Church together and even the confessional holds no secrets. So says *my* old man, a lapsed Irish Tyke.'

'My folks were Congregational. If they lapsed, they never knew.'

Stokes Point was a narrow strip of road and bush-surrounded houses on the eastern side of Pittwater, a wide stretch of yachting water twenty-five miles north of the city. The houses were a mixture, from old fibro weekenders to more expensive abodes by experimental architects. Brigid Hourigan's was the grandest on the point.

The garden surrounding it was lush and semi-tropical; it suggested lassitude, an indolent passion for laziness. It was not well kept; if there was a gardener he believed in letting nature take its course. The house, large and terraced, had a Mediterranean look to it; several marble goddesses stood on the terraces, their hauteur spoiled only by scarves of kookaburra crap. Everything looked slightly run down, like a scratched and faded painting left too long in the open.

A young Italian houseman greeted them at the big teak front door. He was dressed in sandals, black slacks and a white jacket buttoned to the neck. He was belligerently unwelcoming till Malone produced his badge, then he looked suddenly afraid. 'Does Signorina Hourigan know you are coming?'

'Possibly,' said Malone.

The houseman went away, glancing back at them over his shoulder as he went, and Clements said, 'Signorina? Somehow it doesn't go with Hourigan.'

The room in which they stood, though cluttered and untidy, had more taste to it than Fingal Hourigan's drawing-room. There were antique Italian and Spanish tables and sideboards, chairs that might have accommodated the broad bums of *conquistadores* and *condottieri*, heavy figured drapes that

26

suggested castles and *palazzi*. There were small pieces of statuary, but only two paintings, each in a richly carved frame. One was a Goya and the other was a Canaletto, but neither Malone nor Clements knew that. They both liked what they saw: neither painting had been done by a smart-arse.

Brigid Hourigan came into the room, the young Italian trailing her. She was dressed in a bright-red housecoat that threw colour into her face. She was younger-looking than Malone had expected; her photos did not do her justice. She was not strictly beautiful, but strikingly handsome, her thoughts hidden in her wide, heavily-lidded eyes which were much darker than her father's. She was, Malone guessed, a dark-minded Celt, one who would never be sentimental about Gloccamorra or Mother Machree. She held an expensive cut-glass tumbler of whisky in one hand and looked ready to toss it at Malone if he asked the wrong questions.

'I have some bad news, Miss Hourigan –'

'Yes?' She gave nothing away: he might have been telling her it was going to rain again.

'Your friend, Sister Mary Magdalene –' He waited for some reaction, but there was none. Bugger it, he thought, they *haven't* phoned her! What sort of men were Fingal Hourigan and this woman's brother, the Archbishop? He said gently, 'She's been murdered.'

The whisky in the glass shook a little, but that was the only sign that she was upset. 'Where? How?'

'She was killed with a knife. Her body was found outside a brothel in Surry Hills.'

'Oh Jesus God!' Then the reaction did set in; for a moment it looked as if she might collapse. The young Italian moved quickly to her, put his arm round her and led her to a chair. He looked in angry reproach at Malone, as if the latter should not have brought such news, but he said nothing.

Malone waited till Brigid Hourigan had recovered. Through the wide plate-glass doors of the big room he could see out over a broad terrace to the shining expanse of

27

Pittwater. The Sunday yachts, glad of the break in the weather, were already beating their way up from the yacht club moorings at the south end of the big inlet. A small dinghy went by close inshore, sailed by a couple of teenagers whose shouts and laughter came up clearly, almost derisively. He looked back at Brigid Hourigan, was surprised to find she had been weeping: he hadn't expected that of her.

'How did you know to come here?' She had the family's deep rich voice. A family conversation must have sounded like an oratorio.

'Mother Brendan, at the convent, told us about a Miss O'Keefe. Then we saw your photo in your father's house at Vaucluse. Didn't he phone you we might be coming?'

'My father and I don't communicate regularly.' She took a sip, a long one, of her drink.

'What about your brother, the Archbishop? Do you and he speak to each other?'

'Occasionally.' Then she seemed to realize that this interview might not be as short as she had hoped: 'I'm sorry. Won't you sit down?'

Malone and Clements lowered themselves into the big leather chairs; neither of them looked like a *conquistadore*. Australians can be heroes, but somehow never look heroic. Perhaps they are always afraid of being taken down a peg or two.

'Why the Miss O'Keefe? Did Sister Mary know who you really were?'

She hesitated, then said, 'She always knew. We just thought it better the convent didn't associate me with the Hourigan name.'

Malone wanted to ask why, but decided to leave that till later. 'Were you close friends?'

She nodded. 'I wish we'd have been closer. We might have been, if she'd lived.'

'Did she ever confide in you? Have you any idea why anyone would have wanted to murder her?'

'Not – murder her, no. But not everyone liked her opinions. She felt very strongly about certain things.'

'Such as?'

She looked up at the houseman hovering behind her and said, 'Perhaps the gentlemen would like some coffee or a drink, Michele?'

'Coffee,' said Malone, and Clements nodded.

'Refill that for me,' she said and handed her glass to Michele, who then went out of the room. 'I like my liquor. My brother, the Archbishop, preaches little sermons about it, but I think there are bigger sins. What do think, Sergeant?'

Clements was no authority on sin: 'Inspector Malone tells me you have to be a Catholic to know what sin is all about.'

'How true,' said the Archbishop's sister and looked at Malone. 'I've been surrounded by sin all my life. Or the condemnation of it.'

'Did Sister Mary condemn it?'

'My drinking or sin in general?' She shook her head and all at once looked sad and older. 'Teresa had more understanding than any young girl I've ever met.'

'Teresa?'

'Did I say that?' For a moment she seemed annoyed with herself. 'Yes, Teresa. That was her given name before she went into the convent.'

'What was her surname?'

'She was known in the order as Teresa French.'

Malone sensed the evasion. 'But French wasn't her real name. What was it?'

The Italian houseman came back with a tray on which were two cups of coffee, some biscuits and the refilled whisky glass. When the three had been served, he retreated to a corner of the room and stood there. His mistress made no attempt to dismiss him; she did not seem to think it odd that a servant should remain listening to her being interviewed by the police. But then servants in Australia, even immigrants, have always looked upon themselves as equals of their masters or their mistresses. Jack's as good as his master was part of the national anthem, though Jack was never prepared to accept arbitration on the matter in case the decision went against him.

Brigid Hourigan sipped her drink, then said, 'Hourigan.'

'Pardon?' said Malone, sipping the strong Italian coffee and trying not to make a face.

'Hourigan. That was her surname.'

Malone put down his cup, looked at the strong handsome face, saw the resemblance that had escaped him till now and said, 'She was your daughter?'

She nodded. 'Illegitimate, if you want to be bourgeois about it.' The second glass of whisky was loosening her tongue, though not thickening it; the voice was as rich and deep as ever. At the moment it was also sad and full of love and regret. 'It doesn't matter who her father was – he's dead.' And sounded forgotten. 'He was French – hence her fake surname. She was always religious, even as a child. I don't know why, unless she inherited it from my mother – though she never met my mother. Perhaps she was just atoning for my sins. I've always been a sinner,' she said without coyness or pride.

'Perhaps her uncle influenced her?'

'My brother didn't know she had become a nun till two years ago.'

'Did your father know?'

She shrugged. 'Perhaps. My father seems to know everything.' The tongue certainly was loose.

'Had she been seeing much of your brother? I mean since he got back to Sydney?'

'I don't know. She'd been pestering him – she told me that. And so did he. They didn't see eye to eye on much connected with the Church.'

'Anything specific?'

All at once she looked tired, ready to break. She put down her glass and the whisky splashed on her housecoat. Malone,

30

as so often, felt the sudden hatred of his job. He was continually bruising people, most of them innocent, as if the law compelled him to carry his bunched fist ready to hit them. He was not concerned with justice, that came later from other, supposedly better-educated people; but on the way to justice the law (and society) sometimes expected too much of men like himself and Clements. He glanced at Clements and saw that the big man had turned his head away and was staring out at the distant water.

'I'm sorry, Miss Hourigan –' In normal circumstances, he guessed, she would not bruise easily, if at all. Today, however, she had lost a child, her only one, and she had abruptly realized the depth of her loss.

Then she drew herself together; it was a visible effort. 'Why don't you ask my brother?' she said spitefully. 'The Archbishop has always had great regard for specifics. His sermons are full of them.'

'We'll do that. But we may have to come back ...'

She nodded and stood up, swaying a little. The Italian houseman hurried forward and took her arm. 'The signorina will have to lie down. Could you please see yourselves out, signori?'

They went slowly out of the room, he now with his arm round her, she with her head on his shoulder. Malone looked at Clements and the latter raised his thick, untidy eyebrows.

'Is that what servants are for?' said Clements softly.

'Why not?' said Malone. 'You miss out on a lot in an egalitarian society.'

'Egalitarian? You been reading the *Times on Sunday* again?'

The shallow joke camouflaged the pity they felt for the woman. It was not something they could confess to each other.

# 2

They drove back to the city under a now bright blue sky, against the Sunday morning traffic heading for a last day on the beaches before the weather turned cold. A convoy of three battered cars cruised by them, surfboards strapped to the roofs, fins sticking up like those of cruising sharks. At Brookvale the crowd was already arriving for today's rugby league matches, going into the ground with their club scarves and beanies and flags, like hordes of squires ready to set up the battlefield for their knights.

'Who do you think will win today? I've got twenty bucks on Manly.'

'Russ, is there anything you won't bet on?'

'I've never bet on the outcome of a case,' said Clements, looking sideways at him. 'You thinking of betting on this one?'

'With the Pope as the Archbishop's trainer? But I think we'll go and have another look at his form.'

When they reached the Hourigan mansion they had to go through a repeat routine. 'It's Inspector Malone again. I'd like to see the Archbishop.'

The intercom crackled with disapproval. 'Have you got an appointment with His Grace?'

'Just tell him I want to go to confession.'

There was another wait of a minute or two, then there was the buzz and the gates opened. The housekeeper was waiting for them at the front door, looking as unwelcoming as the first time. Malone had a moment of fantasy in which he saw her as one of the guard dogs, a Doberman with an Irish bark.

'What has a policeman got to confess?' she demanded.

'Where's your sense of humour, Maggie?'

'Mrs Kelly, from you. And I keep me sense of humour to meself.' And she would, like a family secret.

She led them this time not into the big drawing-room but into a library only slightly smaller. Or perhaps it was an office:

on side tables stood a word processor, a computer, a copying machine and a wire basket full of documents. But books lined the walls to the high ceiling and the titles there were as eclectic as the pieces out in the drawing-room. Fingal Hourigan sat behind a magnificent antique desk at which nothing less than a major armistice of war should have been signed. Or a papal bull.

Archbishop Hourigan sat beside the desk in a high-backed chair designed for the hierarchy, either ecclesiastic or commercial. Malone and Clements were motioned towards two lesser chairs. Malone had the sudden feeling that he was in an annexe of the Vatican, that at any moment the Swiss Guards might appear on the terrace outside the big french doors.

'Have you come to tell us you've found the person who murdered Mary Magdalene?'

'No, Your Grace. We're not much more informed than when we left here a couple of hours ago. Except that we've found out she was your niece. And your granddaughter, Mr Hourigan.'

Father and son looked at each other. There was sudden pain in the Archbishop's face, but his father's had no expression at all. Then Kerry Hourigan said, his voice unexpectedly hoarse, 'I suppose we should have told you that. But we were trying to protect my sister.'

'Oh? In what way?'

The Archbishop waved a hand: not helplessly but uncertainly. 'I really don't know. It was instinctive. My father doesn't like publicity . . .'

'You've had plenty of publicity, Your Grace. This past month you've been on TV, in the newspapers . . . How do you feel about that, Mr Hourigan?'

Fingal was still showing no expression. 'If it helps the Church, I have no objection. My son is a public figure.'

*So are you, mate.* 'Your daughter also doesn't like publicity.'

33

'So I'm told,' said Fingal, but didn't say who had told him.

Malone looked again at the Archbishop, who now seemed to have regained some of his composure. 'Why did you tell us earlier that you didn't know her?'

'I really don't know. I suppose I was just so shocked by the news. It was stupid –'

'Yes, damned stupid,' said Malone, feeling that for the moment he was in command here. But out of the corner of his eye he could see Fingal Hourigan, who would never let any situation get away from him. 'I understand you and Sister Mary didn't agree on certain Church matters?'

'They were generational differences.'

'What exactly do you do at the Vatican? I've forgotten what the papers said.'

'I'm the Director of the Department for the Defence Against Subversive Religions.'

'Subversive religions being communism, things like that?'

'Not only communism. The new Islamic fundamentalism. Certain other religions.' He had the smug certainty of someone who had got the word direct from Jesus Christ. Malone, a live-and-let-live Christian, the sort who turned the other cheek out of laziness, felt the intolerance he always felt when other people sounded intolerant. But maybe the others were more aware of the dangers ... 'There are enemies, Inspector.'

'Sergeant Clements is a Congregationalist – or was. Would he be part of the enemy?'

The Archbishop glanced at Clements, smiled, raised a hand as if he were about to bless him. 'I'm sure the Congregationalists aren't subversive, Mr Clements. Do they still exist?' His arrogance was going to be a handicap when he got to Heaven, but nobody has proved Heaven is full of humble citizens.

'Was Sister Mary subversive?' said Malone.

'Yes,' said her uncle emphatically. If he and his father felt any grief over her death it had been rapidly submerged.

34

'Did she disagree with anyone else besides you?'

'She would have disagreed with Jesus Christ himself,' said Fingal. He had the look and sound of a man who would have done the same himself, as an equal. 'She was looking for trouble.'

'Jesus Christ!' said Clements, but only Malone heard him.

'So she might have made some enemies?'

'You can be sure of that,' said Fingal, taking over from his son.

'In Nicaragua, maybe?'

'Possibly. There could be some Nicaraguans here. The country's full of people from everywhere these days.' He had been in Australia long enough to consider all late-comers as foreigners. He had the same antipathy towards the Aboriginal Australians, who were too foreign for him to understand. 'Why don't you look there, amongst the Latin Americans?'

'We'll do that,' said Malone. 'Were you ever in Nicaragua, Your Grace?'

The Archbishop nodded after a moment's hesitation. 'Some years ago, before the Sandinista Government took over.'

'And not since then?'

Again there was a slight hesitation, as if he were checking his memory, then he said, 'No.'

Malone looked at both of them, father and son. 'So you have no idea who might have killed her?'

Archbishop Hourigan looked shocked, or tried to look that way. 'Did you really expect us to? Good God, man, we don't know *murderers*!'

*I wonder what mortal sins you've heard in the confessional?* But Malone didn't ask that question. Whoever had killed Sister Mary Magdalene wouldn't be the sort to ask for absolution.

'No, I suppose not. It's never as easy as that – I mean for us police. Oh, your sister left us before –'

'You've been to see her?' said Fingal.

'Of course. Didn't you expect us to?' The look on the old man's face told Malone he had scored a point, but he didn't press it. He went on: 'We didn't have time to tell her the body is in the City Morgue. Mother Brendan, from the convent, was going to claim it, but she didn't know Sister Mary Magdalene was a Hourigan.'

'She was never that,' said Fingal Hourigan.

'Oh yes, she was,' Kerry Hourigan told him. 'She took Brigid's name by deed poll when she came home three months ago. I guess she hadn't told them that at the convent.'

The expression on the old man's face suggested that Teresa Hourigan had introduced AIDS into the family instead of just herself. He stood up and without a word walked out of the room, the silver walking-stick thumping once on the tiled floor of the entrance hall like a rifle shot.

'You must forgive my father,' said the Archbishop, pressing a button on the desk; somewhere at the back of the house a bell rang. 'He is a man of strong feelings.'

'He'll have plenty of practice with them,' said Malone as he and Clements rose. 'I'm sure we'll be back to test them.'

Mrs Kelly, all a-glower, swept them out of the house. 'You had no right coming here! They are decent gentlemen, both of them!'

'Maggie,' said Malone quietly and kindly, 'haven't they told you? Mr Hourigan's granddaughter, the Archbishop's niece, has been murdered.'

'Holy Mother of God!' She was suddenly flattened, turned to a cardboard figure in the frame of the big doorway. Then she frowned, as if she hadn't heard right. 'Who?'

'The young nun who came here yesterday. It was yesterday, wasn't it?'

She blessed herself, mouth trembling in a silent prayer. 'Yes. She came several times ...'

'Maggie!'

Fingal Hourigan stood behind her, a small figure of towering rage. The silver stick quivered like a lightning bolt; for a

36

moment it looked as if he might strike the housekeeper. Then, abruptly, there as an amazing change. The rage disappeared, gone as if a mask had been whipped off him; he smiled at Malone, tapped the floor with the stick as if seeking some rhythm. Mrs Kelly looked over her shoulder at him: she was unafraid of his temper.

'Someone around here should be praying for her, yes,' she said and pushed past him and disappeared into the house.

Malone looked directly at Fingal Hourigan. 'It would seem that someone around here isn't telling the truth.'

Hourigan smiled; but it was a challenge, not a friendly expression. 'The truth is a dangerous weapon, Inspector. It should be prohibited by law. Good-day to you.'

He shut the door in Malone's face.

# 3

Malone made it home in time that evening to go to six o'clock Mass with Lisa and the children. He sat in a back pew of the Sacred Heart Church in Randwick and listened to Father Joannes, the parish priest, drone on with all the old platitudes that were now brassy with usage. He came from the old school of priests and politicians who taught that everything had to be said thrice, as if the sinners and voters were criminally slow on the uptake. He believed in fear of the Lord and not love of Him. He was followed by a trio twanging guitars and singing a pop hymn whose words were as banal and meaningless as those heard on *Countdown*. Malone sat and wondered what he was doing here in this gathering, which, except for the guitars, might have been the same sort of service his mother had come to fifty years ago. He found himself wondering what Sister Mary Magdalene, the rebel, had thought of it all, she with the mud and misery of Nicaragua on her Ferragamo shoes. If, indeed, she had worn any shoes at all in that racked country.

Going home Lisa said, 'A bad day? You really look down in the dumps.'

'I always am when I have to work on Sundays.'

'Weren't they terrific hymns?' said Maureen, the rock video fan. 'They make Mass *interesting*.'

'Jesus,' said Malone quietly.

'Are you swearing?' said Tom.

'No, I was praying. Who wants to go to McDonald's for supper?'

'I'd rather go to Prunier's,' said Claire, who read the social columns of the *Sun-Herald*.

Malone looked at her. One day she would be beautiful and would probably be featured in the *Sun-Herald* herself; by then, he knew, he would have half-lost her to another man. 'Let's settle for McDonald's tonight.'

They all agreed to, including Lisa, the Dutch gourmet. 'Well, at least I shan't have to cook,' she said defensively. 'I'm like you, I don't like working on Sundays.'

The meal was the best spot of the day for Malone. He munched on his Big Mac and looked at his family and compared it to the Hourigans. We're happy, he thought, and what more can I offer them? Maybe dinner at Prunier's or Berowra Waters, but he was sure happiness wasn't an item on the menu at those restaurants.

They drove home and the children were put to bed. Then he and Lisa settled down to finish off the weekend papers. But first Lisa said, 'Do you want to talk about it?'

He knew what she meant. After fourteen years of marriage nothing had to be spelled out between them, not unless they were arguing and wanted to be defensive. They were compatible, but in the best of ways, by not being too alike. She had a natural patience; he had had to learn to wear his. Being a Celt, he had not been born a listener, but he had learned to be that, too; being Dutch, coming from the crossroads of so much historical trade, she listened to the bid before she made her counter-bid. Invariably she always left him with the feeling that he had lost all their arguments.

Tonight there was no argument. 'I've got a young nun, murdered, and two-thirds of her family don't seem to care a damn.'

'Who's the one-third who does care?'

'Her mother.' He explained the circumstances of the case. 'Old Man Hourigan doesn't worry me – he seems to be just a self-centred rich old bastard. But the Archbishop . . . I could have been telling him Martin Luther was dead, for all he seemed to care.'

'Do you think archbishops are so much different from other men?'

'They're expected to be. A little more charity and compassion . . .'

'You expect too much of people.'

'When did you become so cynical?'

'I'm not. It just hurts me to see you lose your illusions.'

'They were lost years ago, even before I met you.'

She shook her head, leaned across and kissed him. 'You're wrong. They're like your sun cancers – I don't think you'll ever get rid of them.'

Then the phone rang out in the hallway. She got up, went out and came back a moment later looking concerned. 'It's for you.'

'Who is it?'

'He wouldn't say.'

Malone got up, hoping this wasn't another call to duty, went out and picked up the phone. 'This is Inspector Malone. Who's that?'

'It doesn't matter who I am, Inspector.' The man's voice was soft, with a faint accent. 'We'll probably never meet. For your sake, I hope not. Take heed of my warning, Inspector –' The formality of the words brought a small grin to Malone's face, though he knew the man did not mean to sound humorous. 'It will be better for all concerned if you let the Sister Mary Magdalene case just rest. Let it die quietly.'

39

'Thank you for the warning, Mr – ?'

'No names, Inspector.' One could almost see the man smiling at the other end of the line.

'Righto, no names. But no deal, either. I don't drop murder cases, warning or no warning.'

There was a moment's silence; then: 'You will regret your attitude, Inspector. Good-night.'

The phone went dead in Malone's ear. He replaced the receiver and stood staring at the wall in front of him. It was not the first threat he had received; he could be afraid but not alarmed. When such threats were made he thought not of himself but of his family: they would suffer more than he, even if, or especially if, he were killed. But no archbishop would go *that* far . . . Then he wondered why he had instantly connected Archbishop Hourigan with the threatening stranger.

He went back into the living-room. This was home, his harbour: he felt safe here. The house, an old-fashioned one with gabled roof and decorated eaves, had been built at the turn of the century when houses had been built to last and tradesmen had taken pride in their work. It had survived the climate, termites, burglars, mortgages and the Malone kids. The Malones had bought it cheaply, because of its run-down condition, and Lisa had lovingly restored it. It was no castle, but it was a fort against the woes of the world, political door-knockers, Avon ladies and Jehovah's Witnesses.

But even now, at nine-thirty on a Sunday evening, there was a knock at the door. 'Don't answer it,' said Lisa.

He looked at her, curious at the fear in her voice: she was not normally like this. 'Why not?'

'I don't know,' she said lamely. 'I just feel . . . I don't know.'

This time there was a ring at the front door; whoever it was had found the bell. 'There's someone at the front door!' yelled Maureen, ever helpful.

Malone walked down the hall, switched on the outside light, opened the front door but kept the chain on. Through the screen of the iron-grille security door he saw a dark-haired young man in jeans and brown tweed jacket. He carried a black motor-cyclist's helmet in one hand, like a spare skull.

'Inspector Malone? I'm Father Luis Marquez.' He lifted the collar-peak of his open-necked shirt and showed the small cross he wore there. 'I'd like to talk to you. I'm sorry to break in on you like this —'

'What about?'

'Sister Mary Magdalene.'

Malone hesitated; he hated the intrusion of police work into his home. 'Can't it wait till tomorrow? At Homicide headquarters.'

'Please, Inspector —'

Malone hesitated again; then he unlocked the security door. He led the young priest through into the living-room and knew at once he had done the wrong thing when he saw Lisa's remonstrating frown. 'I'm sorry, darl. This is Father —?'

'Marquez,' said the young man. 'I'm Nicaraguan.'

He was almost as tall as Malone, olive-skinned, with high cheekbones, a flat straight nose and black eyes. His hair, too, was black and lay on his long head like a pelt. He was handsome and on other occasions he might have been aware of it; but tonight he looked only worried, perhaps even afraid. Or worse: a priest who had run out of prayer.

'Would you like a drink?' said Lisa. 'Or coffee?' She prided herself on her coffee, being Dutch; she would offer it even to a Brazilian or a Colombian. 'I make good coffee.'

Marquez smiled; it was a handsome smile, one that would have been devastating in either pulpit or bedroom. 'I haven't had a good cup since I came to Australia.'

'When was that?' said Malone as Lisa went out to the kitchen.

'Well, I'm lying, really. My mother makes a good cup.' Again there was a flash of very white, straight teeth. I'm being worked on, Malone thought. The charm was like a bribe. 'I came here fifteen years ago, when I was sixteen. My father had fought against the Somozas. As a young boy, fourteen years old, he fought with Augusto Cesar Sandino.' He paused, but Malone was unimpressed. He had never heard of Sandino. Then Marquez went on, 'He went on fighting, after Sandino was killed. But finally his luck ran out and we had to leave Nicaragua. We came to Australia. My mother was tired of soldiers everywhere, she said she wanted a quiet country where the sun shone and no one was afraid of the soldiers. It was she who chose Australia.'

'Is your father still alive?' Malone knew nothing of Nicaragua's history other than what he occasionally read in the newspapers. But ignorance of the world is not a crime; if it were, 99 per cent of the world would be behind bars. Ignorance was not bliss, either: not when it was brought home to you in your own living-room. 'Is he mixed up with Sister Mary Magdalene's death?'

'Mother of God, no!' The handsome face was suddenly strained. 'He's dead, he's been dead three years. And my mother – she's not mixed up in it! It's just me – and all because of Mary Magdalene. Well, no, that's not the truth –' He shook his head and his face slackened, seemed to age. 'I think I was just waiting for my conscience to come alive.'

'What parish do you belong to?'

'I don't belong to any, not a church parish. I'm one of the two R.C. chaplains on campus at the University of New South Wales. I'm supposed to look after the ethnic students.'

'Are there any Nicaraguan students there?'

'A couple, I think. There aren't very many of us Central Americans in Sydney. They're mostly *South* Americans – Chileans, Argentines, Uruguayans – most Australians think we all come out of the one pot, anyway. But I look after all of them, including the Mediterranean ethnics. Even the odd Catholic Turk – and they're pretty odd, I can tell you.' He smiled again.

'Have you been home to Nicaragua?'

'Once, a couple of years ago.'

'Are you a – what do they call them? A Sandista?' Like most of the natives, when he read a foreign word in a newspaper or book he usually ran all the letters together and came up with his own interpretation. It was a variation on the old English attitude: the foreigners of the world really should Anglicize themselves.

'Sandinistas. They're named after Augusto Cesar Sandino, the man my father fought with. No, I don't belong to them. But I guess you could say I'm sympathetic to them. But I'm not rabid about them, not the way Mary Magdalene was.'

Lisa came back with the coffee, sat down, became part of the interview. Malone didn't mind, not this evening. Normally he tried to keep her well removed from any of his cases, but tonight he was glad she was there.

'How did you meet Mary?'

Father Marquez sipped the coffee, nodded appreciatively. 'Very good.'

'It's Colombian,' said Lisa.

'My mother always uses it. Nicaraguan coffee is pretty terrible. Everything in Nicaragua is pretty terrible these days. That was what Mary was always on about. She spent two years there, you know, up in the mountains. She was captured by the Contras, but managed to get them to release her. She came to the University to talk about it. That was how I met her.'

'How did you know to come here?' said Malone. 'And why?'

'When I saw the news on TV tonight –' He stopped, stared at his hands for a moment. 'I couldn't believe it. Then I rang Mother Brendan at the convent. She said you were in charge of the case. She said your children went to the school and she gave me your address.'

'She had a hide,' said Lisa. 'You'd think private people like nuns would respect other people's privacy.'

'I'm sorry,' said Marquez, acutely embarrassed. 'I should not have come. Mother Brendan was only trying to help.'

43

Lisa poured herself a second cup of coffee, having drained the first in an angry gulp. She looked at Malone. 'Do you want me to leave?'

He grinned, not annoyed at her intervention; she had said only what he had thought. 'No, stay. If Father Marquez is used to dealing with the odd Catholic Turk, he won't be too upset by you. Now let's get down to brass tacks, Father. Why are you here?'

Marquez put down his coffee cup. 'Because I think I may be next on their list.'

Lisa sat very still and so did Malone; but it was an acquired habit with him, born of long practice in interviews such as this. 'Whose list?'

'I said there aren't very many Nicaraguans in Sydney – that's true. But there are some here, maybe a dozen or more, who are strong Contra supporters. When Mary came on to campus to talk to a group, they turned up out of nowhere and picketed her and abused her. It never got into the papers. Picketing is pretty common on campus and anyway the general public doesn't seem very interested these days in what students are on about. But the Contra supporters got pretty nasty.'

'Are you saying they could be her killers?'

'No, not them. But the people behind them – yes.'

'What people?'

'I'm not sure. Two of the top Contra men came into Sydney about three weeks ago, from Miami, I believe. They got here about a week after Archbishop Hourigan arrived. He came from Miami, too.'

'You'd better be careful here, Father. Are you saying the Archbishop is connected with the Contras?'

'I have no proof. But Mary Magdalene was certain he was. I went with her one night to a meeting he was addressing and she stood up and charged him with it.'

'I'm sorry she's dead,' said Lisa, 'but she sounds a real pain in the neck.'

'Most true believers are,' said Father Marquez gently.

'What did Archbishop Hourigan say?' Malone had never been a true believer in anything, though God knew he had tried.

'He just ignored her. He's so – so arrogant – it's impossible to describe –'

'I've met him.' But arrogance, like ignorance, is not a crime. If it were, certain Prime Ministers and State Premiers would have been declared habitual criminals. 'So Mary Magdalene never had any real contact with him?'

'Oh yes, several times. I don't know how –'

'She was his niece.'

Marquez had put forward his cup at Lisa's gesture of more coffee; both of them looked sharply at Malone and the coffee spilled into the saucer. 'She never mentioned that! Mother of God!' Marquez shook his head in wonder. '*That* was how she knew so much about him . . .'

'How much did she know?'

'She never told me everything – she always seemed to be holding something back. I don't think she entirely trusted Australia or Australians. She said we were too smug, too suburban to care passionately about anything. Some of us might care about rain-forests and wetlands and the killing of kangaroos, but we didn't care about *people*.'

'She didn't think of you as a Nicaraguan?'

'She said I'd been here too long, I'd been brainwashed, that the sun and the beer had got to me. She was a bigot, in her own way.'

'I'm beginning to dislike her,' said Lisa.

'No, don't,' said Marquez quickly. 'She was just, I don't know, too *caring*. I go to the convent occasionally, to talk to the classes. The girls in her classes adored her. She just had this, I suppose you'd call it Marxist, thing about Nicaragua.'

'Are you a Marxist?'

'Me? God, no! I've only voted twice in my life and both times for Malcolm Fraser – and I don't think God has forgiven me.' Again there was the smile. The girls at the convent, Lisa thought, might adore him, too. 'No, you can be for the Sandinistas without being a Marxist.'

'What about the Archbishop?'

Marquez laughed. 'He's even further to the right than Pius the Ninth.'

'He was before my time.' Malone had always had difficulty in remembering popes' names and their numbers. 'Did Mary ever mention her grandfather, Fingal Hourigan?'

Marquez shook his head. 'The rich old guy – he's her grandfather? God, he's worth *millions*!'

'He's a billionaire,' said Lisa. 'I'd mention my grandfather if he was in that bracket.'

'No, she never said a word about him. She never said anything about her family at all. I really didn't know her that well at all. I just *liked* her. And I think she liked me.' Then he looked at both of them defensively, as if they might have made the wrong inference. He's aware of his looks and his appeal to women, Lisa thought. 'I don't mean there was anything like *that* . . .'

'Who are the men you think might want to kill you?' said Malone.

Marquez hesitated, then said, 'I don't know who they are, but I'm sure there are some ex-Somoza men here in Sydney. The Somoza dynasty ran Nicaragua as if they owned the whole country – which, I guess, they did in a way. The last President, Anastasio, is dead, but his gang still hang on, running the Contras and trying to raise money wherever they can. Mary thought that was why the two guys came in from Miami. Their names are Paredes Canto and Domecq Cruz.'

Malone jotted down the names, asking for the correct spelling. 'You think they are the ones threatening you?'

'I don't know, to be honest. I've had two phone calls, one last week after I'd been to the Archbishop's talk with Mary, the second one this evening. The man spoke to me in Spanish. He had a Nicaraguan accent like my father's – in Central

America the accents are quite distinct. He mentioned my father – he knew all about him. He said they knew about my association with Mary Magdalene and just to forget her or I'd regret it.'

'Are you afraid?' said Malone, testing him.

'Yes,' said Marquez without hesitation or embarrassment. 'I'm not a guerilla fighter, Mr Malone. I was on Mary's side, but I wasn't carrying any gun for her. She knew that and sometimes she couldn't understand it, especially since I was born in Nicaragua and what had happened to my father there. He was tortured by the Somoza National Guard... But we came out here to start a new life. I became a priest because I wanted to preach peace – I believe in a loving God, not a wrathful one ...'

'Are you asking for police protection? I don't know that I can arrange that, not at this stage. How did you get here tonight?'

'I have a motorbike.'

'Were you followed?'

Marquez looked surprised. 'I don't know. I didn't think to look. I'm not used to this, Inspector –'

'You'd better be more careful, for the time being anyway. You're pretty vulnerable on a motorbike.'

'University chaplains can't afford cars. We're the bottom end of the totem pole – I think we're supposed to be symbols of poverty to the students.' He smiled again, bravely this time, Malone thought. He found himself liking the young priest and didn't blame him for being afraid. Bravado was another form of heart disease.

He showed Marquez to the door. 'I'll want to see you again – I'll call you at the Uni. If you want to get in touch with me, if these blokes call you again, phone me at Homicide.' He lowered his voice. 'Don't phone me here.'

'I understand, Inspector.' Marquez lowered his own voice. 'I'm sorry I intruded. It won't happen again.'

Malone switched off the light in the hallway behind him

and waited while Marquez went out to his motorbike, put on his helmet, started up the bike and rode away with a wave of his hand. Malone waited to see if any car pulled out from the kerb in the quiet street, but none did. He re-locked the security door, closed the front door and went back to the living-room.

Lisa was waiting for him, the tray of coffee cups and the pot ready to be taken out to the kitchen. 'It's got worse, hasn't it?'

'Much worse,' he said, but didn't tell her about the threat he had received just before Father Marquez had arrived.

'How do these things ever start?'

He grinned. 'Original sin,' he said, but he doubted if even Father Marquez or Archbishop Hourigan believed that. 'It may have started yesterday or it may have started years ago.'

# THREE

## I

It had indeed started years ago, in Chicago in 1929.

Seamus (Jimmy) Mulligan chose a St Valentine's Day card from the rack in the drugstore. Mae, who had the same name as his boss's wife, was a girl who was full of romance; she often told him that, lying on her back under humping customers, she dreamed she was being made love to by John Gilbert or Ronald Colman. It didn't annoy Jimmy that she didn't dream of him. He never dreamed of her.

He pocketed the card and envelope without paying for it and went to the drugstore's pay phone. He dialled a number and while he waited for it to be answered he looked out at the dreary afternoon. Snow was falling, looking as unreal as he always found it; like falling souls, his mother used to describe it and blessed herself with a flurry of fingers. He hated Chicago in the winter, but so far he had never made enough money to go south for the freezing season. He had money in the bank, but he was a careful man: he would never splurge it on a long vacation. Not unless he knew suckers at the vacation spot who would finance it.

The ringing at the other end stopped and a rough voice said, 'Yeah? Who's dat?'

'Jack O'Hare,' said Jimmy, who always used Irish aliases; he was not romantic, but he was superstitious. It was bad luck to deny your heritage: that son-of-a-bitch St Patrick would send the snakes after you. 'Is your boss there?'

49

There was a grunt at the other end, then Moran came on the line. Jimmy in his mind's eye, which had 20/20 vision, could see the big morose Irishman at the other end. The battered face, as intelligent-looking as a drummer's travel-bag, would be screwed up as its owner tried to concentrate. George 'Bugs' Moran hated talking on the phone, where he couldn't glower at the other man.

'What you got, Jack?'

'Al Brown's had another consignment of booze come in from Detroit. I got it right off the boat.'

'Where's it at?'

'Ah, Mr Moran, you know I never tell you that. I oughtna be telling you where I got it from, only I thought it'd make you feel better.' Moran hated the man from whom the liquor had been hijacked. 'It's all yours, Mr Moran, a whole truck-load for fifty-seven bucks a case. Old Log Cabin label, the best. The Mayor himself drinks it.'

Bugs Moran took his time, as he always did when asked to give any subject some thought. He had inherited the leadership of the Dion O'Banion gang by default. Vincent Drucci, who had taken over from O'Banion himself, who had died of a surfeit of bullets, had suffered that most ignominious death for a gangster: he had been shot by a single policeman, a travesty of justice in gangland's eyes. Moran, with the mantle of leadership thrust upon him, had, like certain Vice Presidents in the same situation, stumbled around in the dark. When he had finally collected his thoughts, which weren't many, he decided that bootleg hijacking would be the best way of using his talent, which was mostly muscle. He chose to hijack the shipments of the Capone gang, a decision that showed his Irish idea of logic.

'Okay, I'll take 'em,' he said at last. 'Bring the truck to the usual place tomorrow morning, ten-thirty.'

'Cash on delivery?'

'Aint it always?' said Moran, who prided himself on certain concessions to honesty.

50

'You'll be there? I don't wanna deal with any of your stooges, Mr Moran. You know me. It's always between the principals.'

'I'll be there,' growled Moran and hung up.

Jimmy Mulligan turned up the collar of his Irish tweed overcoat, the best that Donegal could weave, pulled down the brim of his grey Borsolino hat and went out into the grey, freezing day. He had never liked Chicago in any season, from the day he had been brought here as a six-months-old baby from Ballyseanduff in County Kerry; for the first five years of his life he had suffered from colds, croup, bronchitis, influenza and a constantly running nose that had earned him the nickname at school of The Drip. But, as his father had told him, Chicago was where the money was to be made, so long as you didn't worry about scruples.

'Only the rich can afford scruples,' Paddy Mulligan had said, 'and they had to be unscrupulous to get rich.'

Paddy Mulligan had come to America in 1890. He had tried to get a job with Tammany Hall in New York, but all the good jobs were already taken in that hive of political patronage. He had come west to Chicago and been taken on by John 'The Bath' Coughlin and Michael 'Hinky Dink' Kenna, two God-fearing, church-going scoundrels who ran the First Ward; he had become a devout Democrat, though he had never bothered himself with the party's national policy or image. He had gone back on a visit to Ireland in 1904, met, courted, married and got pregnant Cathleen O'Farrell. He returned to Chicago and she followed him a year later with young Seamus, already dribbling at the nose.

Jimmy grew up, got over his chest ills, wiped his nose and joined his father in the First Ward. But politics didn't offer enough for an ambitious eighteen-year-old. He began doing odd jobs on the side. He invented the term 'feasibility consultant', putting it under his name on printed business cards, and equally ambitious but minor gang leaders began paying for his advice. He did no killing, never carried a gun; he just

51

advised on the feasibility of an assassination, the risks and potential in a new bootleg territory; he was the forerunner of one of today's flourishing professions. He came to the attention of Dion O'Banion, Hymie Weiss and Vincent Drucci, three wise men looking for a wiser one, but he always remained his own man. Working for men as disparate as those three, he had to be his own man if he was to survive.

Then he had been called in to do a job for the Big Fella himself. Al Capone's liquor was being hijacked; he suspected it was being done by Bugs Moran, but he was not certain. Could Mr Mulligan infiltrate the Moran gang?

'I can give it a try, Mr Capone. Moran don't know me – he never met me when I did a job or two for o'banion. I'll try another name and see what I can do. Is it okay if I lose a consignment of booze, maybe two, just to get the proof?'

'Sure. I'll get it back, one way or the other.'

So he had been working for Capone for a month and every day he was coming to realize that no one remained his own man while working for Capone; or ever would be again. Consultants, more than any other businessmen, should be aware of their own expendability.

So on this February day in 1929 he walked uptown, with the wind behind him, to the Metropole Hotel on South Michigan. Snow covered his shoulders like his mother's shawl; but his expensive hand-made shoes were dark with slush. Winter lashed, poked and scratched at him; the North Pole let him know it was just a suburb of Chicago. He pined for sunshine and warmth, for Florida, which he had never seen, or even for that home of ratbaggery, California, which he had only read about. He would go out there and make love to Billie Dove or Lil Tashman, two classy dames.

He turned in to the Metropole Hotel, glad of its warmth. He walked across the big lobby to one of the private elevators, nodded hello to the house detective who stood outside it, and got the elevator boy to take him up to the second of the two floors occupied by the Capone mob. Each floor was more heavily guarded than the White House; occupancy here was not guaranteed by the voters. In any event, who would be bothered bumping off Herbert Hoover?

Jimmy Mulligan got out of the elevator, looked down at his soaked shoes in disgust; he should have worn his two-toned galoshes. He took off his overcoat and straightened his silk tie against the stiff collar of his Sulka shirt. He had once heard a newspaperman describe him as 'natty' and the description had haunted him ever since.

'Mr Mulligan to see Mr Brown,' he said to the chief guard, two hundredweight of lard and a few dimes' worth of brain.

'Al ain't here.' Capone was still referred to as Al Brown, a *nom de guerre* he had adopted when he had first come west from New York; he was also known as the Big Fella, a compliment he appreciated though he did not like to be addressed as such to his face. He positively hated to be called Scarface, even behind his back. 'He's down to the other place. He expecting you?'

Mulligan nodded, only half-attentive to the big hoodlum. He was always fascinated when he came up here, or to the floor below. Capone rented fifty rooms in the hotel; this was the powerhouse of his empire. Politicians and judges and police officers came here to pay their respects and to be paid off; Sunday morning was pay-day and the supplicants came straight here from Mass, their souls clean if not their hands. The senior ones got in to see the Big Fella himself, in Suite 409–410, where he sat beneath portraits of his three heroes, George Washington, Abraham Lincoln and Mayor Big Bill Thompson. There he burdened them with little homilies on the dangers of being in the limelight, an illumination the politicians couldn't live without, and how he longed for respectability, the dream of every mother for her son. Mrs Capone had raised five sons and four of them had become gangsters; even her only daughter had married a gangster. If Mrs Capone had been praying for respectability for her

53

family, she had been facing the wrong way. The fifth son had left home in 1919, gone out to Nebraska and become a law officer, a blot on the family honour.

Today was a slow day: there were only whores, gamblers and bootleg liquor salesmen on the two floors. But this was Monday and the smell of Sunday's power still lingered; it was like snuff in Jimmy Mulligan's nostrils. Some day he would have power like this, but in a warmer climate.

'Call the other place and tell him I'm coming,' he said, practising authority, and the hoodlum, recognizing someone higher up the brain scale than himself, made a gesture that almost looked like a salute.

Jimmy put his hat and overcoat back on, went out of the hotel into the grey day that now seemed lighter because the snow had settled in thickening banks. He walked two blocks down to 2145 South Michigan, his feet freezing in his soaked shoes. He paused outside the doctor's office, admired the respectability of the name-plate on the door: Dr A. Brown. He pressed the bell-button and was admitted. The Metropole Hotel might be where the power lay, but this was where the money was. And Jimmy Mulligan was as fascinated by money as he was by power.

There were people waiting in the reception room, but none of them, Mulligan knew, would be patients. Not that they were a healthy-looking lot; they had the look of men and women who rarely, if ever, saw sunlight; their livers and lungs would resemble a brown string-bag. The prescriptions they were waiting for were cheques or bills.

Mulligan was admitted at once to the surgery behind the reception room. The back wall was lined with shelves, on which were rows and rows of bottles of various sizes, all containing coloured liquids. These were Dr Brown's medicines, his panaceas and elixirs: samples of all the liquors supplied by the man behind the desk. Who was Dr Al Brown himself, the Big Fella, Alphonse Capone.

'Mr Mulligan –' The relationship between the two men

was always formal. There was very little difference in their ages; each of them had ambitions to be a gentleman. 'You made the arrangement we talked about?'

'It was like selling candy to a sweet-toothed idjit,' said Mulligan. 'The brains in that outfit wouldn't make a decent breakfast. Greed turns intelligence into a headache.'

Capone looked around at the four other men in the surgery. 'Don't you guys wish you had Mr Mulligan's education?'

'I had no education,' said Mulligan modestly. 'An hour a day in the public library, that was all. Emerson on Monday, Thoreau on Tuesday . . . I've also read Machiavelli,' he added with touch of his forelock to Mr Capone's Italian heritage.

'I've heard of him,' said Capone, impressed. His four henchmen nodded, thinking he was probably some educated hood from New York or Detroit. 'So Moran is expecting the shipment tomorrow?'

Mulligan gave him the details. At the same time he was observing Capone, as he always did when he met the crime boss. The big jowly face with the two three-inch scars down the left cheek and the thick lips was not a friendly one; the smile could be pleasant, but the dark eyes never seemed to match it. The thick fingers sported diamond rings and the gold watch on the fat wrist was a reminder that time could be expensive. The silk-and-mohair suit was a little flashy for Mulligan's taste and so were the grey spats above the small, almost dainty shoes. But Capone owned an empire and emperors have to have the right clothes. A little vulgarity never hurt, since 99 per cent of the peasants were themselves vulgar.

'What do I owe you, Mr Mulligan?'

Mulligan had already got his payment, though Capone didn't know that. 'I'll leave that to you, Mr Capone. Ours has been a gentleman's agreement.'

Capone smiled: even the eyes seemed to have some mirth in them. 'You trust too much, Mr Mulligan. Ain't you ever been double-crossed?'

'Once.'

'You kill the guy?'

Mulligan shook his head, 'There are other ways, Mr Capone.' He had betrayed the double-crosser to the police; but it would not be politic to tell that to the Big Fella. 'You're not a double-crosser.'

'No, you're right, I ain't.' He had all the assurance of an emperor. 'That's what fucks me about Moran. Two grand for your trouble, Mr Mulligan, that okay?'

'Three, Mr Capone,' said Mulligan and was aware at once of the stiffening attitude of the four henchmen in their chairs against the walls.

But Capone was relaxed, just smiled again. 'They told me you was ambitious. You hoping some day to make the sorta money I make?'

'Maybe.' Mulligan knew he was treading on ice much thinner than that out on the shores of Lake Michigan, but he could not resist the thrill of it. 'I ain't aiming to compete against you, I ain't that dumb. But there are other cities ... I'm fascinated by power, Mr Capone, and you gotta have money to have that.'

Capone nodded, still relaxed: this Irishman would never be a real competitor. 'That's right. I'm king of this city, of the State too, and I only got that because I got the dough. I could be king of America, if it wasn't for the fucking Government.'

'I'm sure we'd all vote for you,' said Mulligan, who hadn't voted in his life.

'Sure,' said Capone, who knew a liar when he sat in front of him. 'Okay, go through to the back room. Mr Guzik will fix you up. You want it in cash, right?'

'Is there any other form of currency?' said Mulligan. 'Goodday, Mr Capone. May your empire increase.'

'It ain't getting any easier,' said the crime boss. 'The fucking Government's starting to take itself seriously.'

'Ain't it always the way? Power corrupts, absolute power corrupts absolutely.'

Capone pondered that for a moment, then nodded. 'Who said that?'

Mulligan could not remember, but he never admitted ignorance. 'Leonardo da Vince.'

'Us Italians,' said Capone, though he always claimed to be 100 per cent American, especially when talking to Immigration. 'We got it all figured out, right?'

'You certainly have,' said Mulligan and thought, But wait till us Irish come into our own.

2

Next morning, St Valentine's Day, at 10.30 Jimmy Mulligan sat in his car fifty yards up the street from the S.M.C. Cartage Company's garage at 2122 Clark Street. His car was a 1928 black Chevrolet tourer, an inconspicuous vehicle that was the opposite of Mulligan's dream, an emerald-green Duesenberg, the sort of car that should be driven only in bright sunlight. The Chevrolet's side curtains were up against the biting wind and Mulligan sat hunched down behind the wheel.

Clark Street was a good site for a massacre, an urban substitute for the Badlands. It was an ugly narrow thorough-fare of small stores, apartment buildings that looked like eroded cliffs, gas stations where only shabby, rundown vehicles stopped, and the occasional narrow-fronted ware-house that hinted at secret stocks behind their locked doors. The street's inhabitants, blue-collared and hopeless, wel-comed any sort of excitement as long as they were not harmed personally. On this cold, windy, snow-swept morning the street was virtually deserted.

At a few minutes before eleven o'clock Mulligan sat up as he saw the big black tourer come down the street. It drew in to the kerb just north of the cartage company's garage and five men got out, three of them in police uniform. Wonderful,

57

thought Mulligan. Only an Italian, a Machiavelli, would think of sending killers dressed as cops.

The five men went into the garage. Mulligan waited, face pressed against the micre window in the Chevrolet's side curtain. Then, out of the corner of his eye, he saw the three other watchers on the opposite side of the street. He turned his head slightly, then abruptly slid down in the seat. The three men on the other side of the road were Bugs Moran and two of his bodyguards.

'Holy Jaisus!' said Mulligan, who, like all Irishmen, was given to prayer when in need of help. Holy Jesus had one ear continually turned for yelps for help out of Ireland.

Moran, equally Irish, had been late for his appointment. There was a burst of gunfire from the garage, then silence, then several more shots, as if *coups de grâce* had been effected, though none of those involved or watching would have called them that. The police report would later say that over a hundred bullets had been fired, including fourteen into the body of one man who, as he lay dying, insisted to the police, 'Nobody shot me.'

Mulligan did not bother to count the shots, even if his ear had been sharp enough and his National Cash Register mind nimble enough. He heard only one shot and it seemed to him that it was destined for him, though it might take a day or two to hit. He lifted himself up in the seat and saw the three 'policemen' come out of the garage, herding the two civilians ahead of them with their hands up, a nice pantomime that Mulligan admired even as he felt close to vomiting with shock. The five men got into the Packard tourer and drove off at a sedate speed. He swivelled his gaze to the other side of the street, but Moran and his bodyguards were already gone. They would not have seen him, but that did not matter. They would know who had set up the massacre and that it had been intended Moran should be part of it.

Mulligan started up the Chevrolet and started south, then

58

east. He finished up on Lake Shore Drive, though later he would not be able to remember how he had got there. He parked the car and sat in the freezing tent of it, while the snow, coming in across Lake Michigan, piled up to obscure the windscreen. It didn't matter that he couldn't see the other side of the street. He could see the future.

He had been too smart, but not smart enough: he hadn't allowed for bad luck, a Celtic fate. Banking on Moran's demise, he had already sold the supposedly hijacked truckload of liquor to a man from Kansas City; if Capone had queried where it had gone, he would have blamed it on the dead Moran. But now ...

He started up the car, got the snow off the windscreen and drove home to his one-bedroom flat just off Prairie Avenue, on the South Side. He lived five blocks from the Capone family home, but he had always kept his private address as private as possible; his business card put him at a downtown hotel, where the day and night clerks took all messages for him. Now he had to find a new address, one far from here.

He packed three suitcases, taking time to pack them neatly; on top of his folded clothes he put the brass-framed photo of his dead mother and father. He had no brothers or sisters; his nearest kin were cousins in Ballyseanduff in County Kerry. As he was going out the door he saw the envelope and card on the table: he had forgotten to send Mae her St Valentine's greeting. He had already written in the card: *To Mae, my favourite hump.* He thought a moment, then he put the card in the envelope and addressed it to Mrs Mae Capone.

On his way out he dropped the envelope in the mail-box on the street corner. Then he put the suitcases in the Chevrolet and drove to his bank. He drew out his entire bank balance, including the 3,000 dollars he had deposited the day before: 28,869 dollars. Then he got back into the car and pondered where he should head. For one moment, out of sentiment for his mother and father, he thought of going back to Bally-seanduff, his birthplace; it would be a good place to hide while he planned his future. But the Winter Country, as its Roman conquerors had called it, was not inviting: he had had enough of winter. He started up the car and drove south, not sure where he was going but knowing that he was not looking for the sun but for safety.

Eight months later he landed in Australia. His name now was Fingal Hourigan and he was determined to found an empire, maybe not as evil as Capone's but just as rich.

He could see the years stretching ahead of him like a golden road. Like all of us, though, he couldn't see those whom he would meet along the way.

# FOUR

## I

Commissioner John Leeds was the neatest officer in the New South Wales Police Department; Assistant Commissioner Bill Zanuch was the second neatest. Sitting opposite them, hunched down as if he had been flung into his high-backed chair by an Opposition front-bencher, an unlikely political happening, was the untidiest politician in the country, State Premier Hans Vanderberg.

'It's no good turning your good eye to skulbuggery.' He was also an untidy man with a phrase.

'No,' said Zanuch and looked at his chief to see if he had got the meaning of what the Premier had said. Leeds just looked imperturbable, which was the only way to survive a meeting with The Dutchman, as he was called.

'Something's going on and I don't want to know anything about it,' Vanderberg went on.

'Are we talking about Archbishop Hourigan?' Leeds guessed that they still were, but the Premier did have a habit of going off at tangents that might have been lunatic in a less devious man.

'Who else? His old man, Fingal, was on to me first thing this morning, half-way through my porridge. That bugger of yours, Malone, is causing more trouble.'

'He'd only be doing his job.' Leeds hadn't yet read the summaries that were always waiting on his desk for him each morning. He and Zanuch had been here at the State Office

Block for a nine o'clock appointment; Vanderberg, who knew better than any of his ministers how to handle power, was his own Police Minister. 'Is he handling that nun's case, Bill?'

Zanuch nodded. He was a vain, handsome man whose ideal world would have been lined with mirrors; but he was a good policeman and hoped some day to be Commissioner. He looked at the Premier, the man who appointed commissioners. 'I can have him taken off the case.'

'No,' said Leeds. 'I'll talk to him first. What's Fingal Hourigan's complaint, Hans?'

Vanderberg had watched the split-second encounter between the two senior policemen; he got secret enjoyment out of watching the same sort of rivalry in his Cabinet. He believed in a divided world, otherwise politicians wouldn't be necessary. He rolled the end of his creased, twisted tie round one finger; it was a tie that had been presented to him by a country cricket team. He hated cricket, but even cricketers voted and you never knew who counted in marginal seats. Fingal Hourigan certainly counted. Any man who gave $100,000 every year to the Party, even if he didn't vote Labour, had to be counted and listened to. The Dutchman had no scruples, only common sense, a more valuable political gift. He liked to think, however, because politicians like to think there is some good in themselves, that he had one or two more scruples than Fingal.

'Malone has been making a nuisance of himself with the Archbishop. He's been out to the Hourigan place twice.'

'Bill can talk to him, ask him why.' Leeds looked at Zanuch. 'But don't take him off the case. Not yet, anyway. It's no good for morale if we keep interfering.'

Zanuch smoothed down his already smoothly lying tie. It was a Police Force tie, but in silk, not polyester. He was in civilian dress this morning, while Commissioner Leeds was in uniform; somehow, and Zanuch was smugly aware of the impression, the Commissioner looked the odd man out amongst the three of them. Zanuch knew how much politicians disliked uniforms. Nothing catches the eye like medals, braid and bright buttons and politicians hated losing the voters' eye. So he always did his best not to upstage the Premier. Upstaging his own Commissioner was another matter.

'We can't have Malone stirring up another of his hornets' nests. He never knows when to be discreet.'

'I'd have thought that was a good thing in a police officer,' said Leeds, though he didn't believe it. Lately he had found himself wanting to disagree with his senior Assistant Commissioner on anything the latter proposed.

'Discretion never hurt anyone, John,' said Vanderberg, who had hurt more people in more ways than could be counted. 'The Archbishop will be going back to Rome at the end of the week. Just hold off till he's out of town. We don't want to upset the Catholics.'

'I thought you were one,' said Leeds.

'Only on Sundays.' A non-voting day. 'Every other day in the week I'm as ecumenical a bugger as you can find. I was out at a Muslim mosque the other day. Malone should be a Catholic, with a name like that. You'd think he'd back-pedal.'

Leeds stood up. 'I'll talk to him,' he said flatly, neither promising nor denying.

He waited for Zanuch to rise; he wasn't going to let his junior remain with the Premier. Zanuch hesitated, then decided on his own discretion: he stood up. The two police officers nodded to their political boss and went out, Leeds leading the way.

Vanderberg grinned after them. He had come to Australia from Holland immediately after the Second World War; he had mastered local politics but he had never really become Australian. He still saw the locals with a stranger's eye, but a knowing stranger: he was the con man who could make himself sound and look like the natives. He had a European sense of superiority, but he was too wise ever to let it show. He got his way by letting the local elements, the white

Aborigines, try out their superiority on each other.

He reached for his intercom. 'Miss Parsell, get me Fingal Hourigan on the phone. He's waiting to hear from me.'

## 2

'You're at it again, Scobie,' said John Leeds.

Malone sighed inwardly; he knew the signs. 'Another complaint, sir?'

'I've just come from seeing the Premier. It seems that this time you're harassing the Catholic Church. What's your version?'

Malone told him, briefly. He and the Commissioner had been involved in other cases, though at opposite ends of the totem pole, as Father Marquez would have said, and he knew he could speak frankly, although always with respect. Leeds did not encourage 'mateyness', the national weakness in labour relations. He was a sympathetic boss who protected his men against outside interference; but he was the boss. One who could be talked to: 'Archbishop Hourigan's name just keeps cropping up. I'm beginning to think Sister Mary Magdalene was murdered because she was harassing him.'

'I hope you haven't been making a statement like that to anyone? That's an explosive charge.' He hadn't meant a play on words: on serious matters he was a very serious man.

'I haven't mentioned it to anyone, sir.' Except to Lisa, in bed last night, and she was beyond the Commissioner's authority.

Leeds put his hands flat on the almost-empty top of his desk. Police desks were notorious for their wild fungi of paper; but the Commissioner's could have been that of the abbot of a monastic order, one not given to illumination. 'Do you have enough evidence to bring him in for questioning?'

'No, sir. I have some other leads I want to follow up.'

'Such as?'

'I was threatened over the phone last night. So was Father Marquez.'

Leeds's fingers tensed on the desk top. 'I don't like that sort of thing happening to my officers. Nor to priests,' he added as an ecumenical afterthought. 'That alters my view of the case.'

'This isn't going to be an easy one,' said Malone. 'I'm aware of the clout I'm up against.'

Leeds allowed himself a smile. 'Clout has never worried you before. Just be careful. And don't make any arrest until you've checked with me through the usual channels.'

'If I have to, do I go and see Archbishop Hourigan again?'

Leeds pondered a moment, lifted his hands to form a steeple in front of his chin, emphasizing the image of an abbot. 'Use your discretion. In which, I'm afraid, I have very little faith.'

Malone grinned: there was an empathy between the two men despite the difference in rank. 'I've mellowed, sir.'

'Famous words that didn't last. Good luck.'

Malone went out through the outer office, aware of the stares of the secretaries. Junior officers like himself were rarely called before the Commissioner unless accompanied by a Superintendent or above. There had, however, been two or three cases over the past few years in which the Homicide detective and the Commissioner, had, through political circumstances, worked in closer contact than was normal. The two men shared certain secrets, an intimacy which is always the subject of envy in any organization. The secretaries looked at him, then rang the typing pool, who would make carbon copies of the envy and spread it amongst the Assistant Commissioners and Chief Superintendents, who all had their own secrets but none shared with the Commissioner.

Russ Clements, who destroyed secrets by sharing them with everyone, even some criminals, was waiting when Malone got back from Administrative Headquarters. He sat with his 'murder box' in his lap, looking as if waiting for the manna of clues to fall into it. 'There's not much to go on.'

'There's a little more,' said Malone and told him about Father Marquez's visit last night and the phone threats.

'We can check those guys from Nicaragua. I've got a good contact in Immigration.' He lifted the phone, rang a number, spoke to someone and sat waiting, smiling at Malone with anticipation. 'When computers work, they're a great invention . . . This is against all the rules, Immigration has a strict code of confidentiality. But the world would stop dead, wouldn't it, if we all stuck to the rules?'

'I didn't hear a word you said,' said Malone, pious as one of the less tempted saints.

Clements's grin widened, then he listened to whoever was on the other end of the phone. He scribbled down two names and an address. 'Thanks, Stan. You want anyone run in or a ticket fixed, give me a ring.'

'You're a crooked cop,' said Malone as Clements hung up.

'Ain't it a help, though?' said Clements and looked at his piece of paper. 'Their full names are Francisco Paredes Canto and Max Domecq Cruz. In Spanish, as I remember it, you use the middle name as a surname. Nicaraguan-born, but they were travelling on US passports. They gave as their address the White Sails Motel at Rose Bay. That would be less than a mile from old man Hourigan's house.'

'What reason for their visit?'

'Tourists, but that doesn't mean a thing. Remember those two Mafia guys who came in to have a look at the poker machine racket? They were tourists. But Immigration has nothing on file against Paredes and Domecq.'

Malone took his time with his thoughts. 'Can you get anything on them from the FBI?'

'We could try. But since the CIA are supposed to be backing the Contras, you think the FBI are going to help us?'

'From what I've heard from Joe Nagler in Special Branch, the FBI and the CIA aren't exactly buddy-buddy. They go their own way, just the same as we do out here with the Federals. Try your luck.'

Clements ferreted around in his desk, an unlicensed refuse dump; Malone, a reasonably tidy man, was sure that, buried in its drawers, were the remains of old homicides, old lunches, perhaps even a fossilized limb or two. But Clements knew his way around his own garbage. He came up with what he sought, a tattered schedule of world time. 'It's seven o'clock Sunday night in Washington. Do the Yanks work round the clock and at weekends?'

'Let's try them.'

Clements went away to fax a message to the FBI and Malone settled down to getting his notes in order for his preliminary report. He could feel the undercurrent of anger in himself at the political interference in the case; he had half-expected it but not so soon. Nobody, it seemed, cared about the dead nun; she was already garbage. But no, that was unfair: Brigid Hourigan cared. He looked at the paper in his typewriter: without guiding thought, his fingers had tapped out, *Who cares?* and underlined it. Don't get angry, he told himself; angry policemen never see things clearly. This was a case where he could already see the fog creeping in, the political fog that obscured so much political work in this State. Take it easy, he said silently, keep your eyes and your feelings wide open. Keep the courage of your suspicions, let's see whose side The Lord is on, the Archbishop's or the nun's.

Clements came back. 'It's gone off. While we're waiting, I'm going back to Tilly Mosman. I'm still puzzled why the girl was dumped on her doorstep.'

'Who owns the Quality Couch?'

'I've got that –' Clements looked at his notebook. For all his lumbering, seemingly careless style, he was a methodical policeman, one whose mind was always two jumps ahead of his appearance and other people's impression of him. 'Tilly has the lease on the house, but she doesn't own it. It's owned by Ballyduff Properties, they own both sides of the whole street. Guess who owns Ballyduff Properties?'

67

The coincidences in this case were too tight. 'Fingal Hourigan?' Clements nodded and Malone said, 'I'm glad it's not the Catholic Church. We don't want to take them on.'

'Taking on Fingal Hourigan can't be much better. But I don't think he'd be in the brothel business, not even the up-market stuff. He's way beyond that now.'

'Start digging into his background, see what you can come up with. In the meantime, who's claimed the nun's body?'

'Her mother. They're doing the autopsy today and releasing the body tomorrow for burial.'

'That's quick. No inquest?'

'There's a special one today – guess who pulled strings? I'm due out there in half an hour. It'll be the usual – murder by person or persons unknown.'

'Has Tilly been called?'

'I'm picking her up. Then I'll go back with her and talk to her girls.'

He went away to pick up Tilly Mosman and take her to the inquest; Fingal Hourigan, it seemed, could have court schedules altered.

Malone settled back to clear up his paper-work. He sometimes wondered how much paper-work the modern criminal had to do. White-collar crims probably did much more than the average cop, but they rarely, if ever, committed homicide and so were outside his bailiwick. The law had been invented to protect property and Malone, protecting people, sometimes thought he was working in the slums of the law. But he knew for whom he had the greatest contempt.

The fax to Washington was answered in two hours; someone in the FBI headquarters must be working round the clock, including weekends. But then crime in the US, according to the Sunday newspapers, was a round-the-clock event, a murder a minute . . . All that paperwork!

When Clements came back from the Quality Couch, Malone handed him the message and the two photos. Clements read the message, then said, 'How do the Yanks let guys like that into their country?'

Francisco Paredes Canto and Max Domecq Cruz had been personal aides to the ex-chief of the National Guard. Each of them had been charged with three murders in Nicaragua, but the cases had never come to court. They had been present at the massacre of forty Indians who had been demonstrating against a particular landlord, a crony of then President Anastasio Somoza Debayle, but no charges had been laid against them. They had fled Nicaragua when the Sandinistas had come to power and had been granted US passports two years ago. Their names were linked with a major anti-Sandinista guerrilla movement based in Honduras and their principal source of income was thought to be from a connection with a drug ring in Colombia. The FBI had no proof of any of the charges.

'I think the FBI suffers from politics the same way we do, only more so,' said Malone.

He studied the two photos. Paredes was a handsome grey-haired man; the hair was thick and wavy and glistened like oiled iron. He had a thin moustache of the sort that had long gone out of fashion, and eyes and a mouth that would promise nothing if there was no dividend in return. He was sixty, according to the FBI report, but was lean and looked in fine condition. Domecq was younger, forty-two, dark and saturnine, but running a little to fat. He looked like a successful gambler, the sort who would be at home in any casino anywhere in the world.

'You pick up anything out at Tilly's?'

'The girls heard and say nothing.'

'Did they have any Spanish-speaking clients Saturday night?'

'A couple, but the girls said they were regulars, young guys with plenty of money to flash around. How do these Wogs manage it?'

'Russ, you're getting to be a racist in your old age.'

Clements nodded morosely; then abruptly grinned. 'I'm starting to understand bigotry. You can actually enjoy it if you put your mind to it.'

'Well, don't get too bigoted about these Wogs from Nicaragua. Be objective about them. Do we go and pick them up for questioning?'

'I think I'd like nothing better,' said Clements, trying not to look bigoted and not succeeding.

Malone gratefully put away his unfinished paper-work and he and Clements drove out to the White Sails Motel in Rose Bay. It was on New South Head Road, the main artery from the city out to the south head of the harbour. It had no view of the harbour or the white sails that decorated the waters on most days; but it looked clean and respectable and reasonably expensive. As it should in Rose Bay: the suburb itself was clean, respectable and more than reasonably expensive. It would never have seen itself as a haven for suspected political murderers with links to an international drug ring. It harboured one or two white-collar criminals, but they could not be condemned till they were caught. Rose Bay might have its bigotry, but not against its own kind, the white-collared black sheep.

The manageress of the White Sails came from over the hill, from Bondi and its beach. She was a strawberry blonde, a colour that went incongruously with her deep tan. She had hung on to her figure, her only good feature. She had lain in the sun for years; she had the skin one would love to sandpaper. Malone had met her sort before: the girls always hanging around where men hung out, at surf clubs and rugby clubs and pubs, all their femininity lost in trying to be 'one of the boys'.

'You'd love a beer, wouldn't you?' she said as soon as Malone and Clements had identified themselves.

'No, thanks,' said Malone, to Clements's disappointment, and showed Miss Allsop, as she said she was, the photos of Paredes and Domecq.

'Oh, those South American guys. No, they're not here. They checked out on Sunday.'

'In a hurry? I mean, how long had they booked in for?'

'They'd paid up till tomorrow. They just said they'd decided to go on to Melbourne and I gave 'em a refund. Anything wrong with them? They seemed real nice. I went out to dinner with one of them last Thursday. Mr Domecq.'

Malone was not surprised and was a little sad for her; on her dying day she would be looking for some man to take her out to dinner. 'No, we have nothing serious on them, just routine stuff. Did Mr Domecq tell you anything about himself?'

'Just about life in Miami. He said he was in the import business there.'

'Did he say what?' *Drugs, for instance?*

'No, he was a bit vague. This and that, he said.'

'What was he like?'

'You mean how did he treat me? Oh, he was a gentleman, up to a point –' That was all she expected of men; she gave the impression she would be disappointed if men were gentlemen all the way. 'I like Latin men, they have something about them.'

'We're both Scandinavians,' said Malone. 'No hope for us. What about Mr Paredes?'

'He seemed to be the senior partner, if you know what I mean. He kept very much to himself. He had a sorta, now I come to think about it, a *cruel* look to him. But he was always polite. And they were always beautifully dressed, both of them, real sharp.'

'If they come back here, give us a ring, will you? But don't let them know.'

'Oh, it's like that, is it?' All at once she looked knowing, though she knew nothing.

Malone nodded and winked and she gave him a smile that invited him back. She stood at the doorway of her small office, an autumn girl in an autumn day, and waved to them as they drove away.

'I hope the bastard gave her a good dinner,' said Clements.

'I hope that's all he gave her. Do you ever feel like her, being a bachelor?'

'It's different being a man.' But Clements sounded neither convinced nor convincing.

They stopped at a phone box and Malone made a call to the Hourigan mansion. 'May I make an appointment to see Archbishop Hourigan?'

'No,' said Mrs Kelly, belligerent as ever. 'He's at the cathedral all day today. There's a special Mass at five o'clock and he's preaching the sermon.'

'What's the special Mass for? Some saint's day?' *St Fingal, maybe?*

'It's a Mass against *The Threat of Communism*.' She sounded as if she were reading from some pamphlet, all capitals and italics.

'Will you be there, Mrs Kelly?'

'No, I've got the house to look after.' She knew the priorities and the dangers. Communism was not likely to strike in Vaucluse.

At five o'clock Malone was at St Mary's Cathedral, alone but for about a thousand worshippers. Either the fame of Kerry Hourigan as a speaker had spread wider than Malone had anticipated or there was a greater fear of the threat of Communism than he had imagined. In the last year or two conservatism, never far below the surface of the Land of the Easy Going, had started to rise like methane gas from some marsh hidden beneath the beaches and the sports ovals. The congregation this evening looked ready for a crusade, so long as they weren't taxed for it. Malone could not control his cynicism even in church.

The Mass was a straightforward one, though the hymns were sung with more fervour than Malone remembered and the words sounded martial. Then Archbishop Hourigan climbed into the pulpit like an overweight pilot into a fighter-bomber. Malone had thought of him in the drawing-room of his father's house as urbane, sophisticated, low-key. In the pulpit this evening he was another man, all brimstone and rhetoric. He carved the air with his hands like a man slashing his way through the entire Soviet Presidium; he thumped every Marxist since Karl himself into the pulpit railing with a bunched fist. The chill air in the cathedral began to warm up under his harangue and the response of the congregation; Malone looked up at the huge vaulted ceiling, waiting for battle flags to flutter and fall, but a lone pigeon, disturbed by the unusual fervour, was the only sign of movement there. Communism got a going-over that it had not experienced since the days of Hitler and Franco, and Malone looked up again, waiting this time for the roof to open and the Lord Himself to come floating down. Malone had once attended a Billy Graham revival meeting, looking for pickpockets helping themselves to worldly goods while the born-again Christians were in a state of spiritual ecstasy and ready to give away everything but their children. The American evangelist had been like a bronchial crooner compared to the bellicose wizard up there in the cathedral pulpit.

Then Archbishop Hourigan called for donations to the cause. Baskets were passed round; money and cheques fluttered like manna into them. The Archbishop, a man of the financial as well as the spiritual world, had come prepared; for those with credit cards there were appropriate slips of paper. American Express and Diners Club could now pay your heavenly dues. The baskets were taken up to the altar, Kerry Hourigan gave a blessing of thanks and the celebrant priest came back to finish Mass. It was an anti-climax and Malone, a rebel but still an old-fashioned Catholic in many ways, wondered what The Lord, as the Host, thought of being on the lower half of the vaudeville bill.

When it came time for communion, he went up to the altar. He hadn't been to confession in at least three years, but he took advantage of the new philosophy of conscience: he didn't *feel* a sinner. But then, he guessed, neither had Stalin. He stood in the line waiting to be given the Host by Hourigan and was surprised when he saw Father Marquez up ahead of him. The celebrant priest, two other priests and the Archbishop were all giving communion; Malone had positioned himself to be in the line for Hourigan and so, it seemed, had Marquez. The young priest stood in front of the Archbishop; Malone, only four behind in the line, waited for some reaction from the prelate, but there was none. Marquez took the wafer and walked away; Hourigan's eyes did not follow him, not even for an instant; they could have been complete strangers to each other. Then it was Malone's turn.

He chose the old-fashioned way of lifting his face for the wafer to be put on his tongue rather than having it placed in his hands. He looked straight at the Archbishop and said quietly, 'I'd like to see you after this, Your Grace.'

'The Body of Christ,' said Hourigan and for a moment his hand shook.

'Amen,' said Malone and went back to his seat and prayed, not for himself but for his family, as he always did.

When Mass was over he got up and moved across to where he saw Father Marquez still sitting. He sat down beside him. 'Was that the sort of stuff that upset Sister Mary Magdalene?'

'Not that so much – that was pretty much bulldust tonight. No, she used to argue with his specific accusations about the Sandinistas, about their atrocities against the Church and the *campesinos*. From what my father used to tell me, I don't think they're any worse than the Somoza gang was. Maybe nowhere near as bad.'

'Did he recognize you as a friend of hers?'

'I don't know.'

'Can you hang on a minute? I'd like him to meet you.'

Father Marquez looked uneasy. 'Do I have to?' Then he saw the look of reproach on Malone's face and he nodded. 'Yes, I guess so. I owe Mary that. Okay, I'll wait.'

Malone went round to the vestry. Kerry Hourigan was in there in the middle of an admiring throng; the Cardinal, the head of this archdiocese, stood in the background like an umpteenth Apostle. He was a modest man, part of the wallpaper of the Church, and Hourigan, wearing the aura that Rome alone gives, knew it. Then the Archbishop caught sight of Malone and the light in his eyes, if not the aura, dimmed.

He detached himself from the almost blasphemous adoration; Communism, tonight, was responsible for more sin than it knew of. He crossed to Malone, who stood against a wall like a wooden effigy that hadn't been blessed.

'Not here, Inspector. Can't you see I'm holding court?' The arrogance, Malone guessed, would never be dimmed.

'Is that what it is, Your Grace? I thought it was a meeting of NATO.'

Hourigan smiled. 'You love your little joke, Inspector. Meet me at the rear of the cathedral, in one of the back pews. No one will interrupt us. They'll think I'm trying to convert you.'

It was Malone's turn to smile. 'You didn't do that from the pulpit. I don't think you'll do it in a back pew. Ten minutes, or I'll come back and start showing my badge. Your New Right friends here are supposed to be all for law and order.'

Ten minutes later, almost on the dot, the Archbishop came down to the back pew where Malone waited for him. He pulled up sharply when he also saw Father Marquez.

'A friend of your niece's,' said Malone. 'He won't be staying. I just thought you'd like to meet him.'

'I've seen you before, haven't I?' said the Archbishop.

'Possibly, Your Grace,' said Marquez. 'But I was usually in Sister Mary's shadow.'

'She'd have had the world in it if she'd had her way.'

Here we go again with the rhetoric, thought Malone. 'Father Marquez is Nicaraguan. He's had two death threats since your niece died.'

Hourigan was resting a hand on the back of a pew; Malone saw it tighten grimly. 'I'm upset to hear that. One tragedy is

75

enough. I hope you are being very careful, my son.'

'Oh, very much so, Your Grace. Inspector Malone is seeing that I get police protection.'

He may be politically innocent, Malone thought, but he's a shrewd young bugger. Hourigan nodded and said, 'Let's hope we have a quick end to this dreadful business. I'll pray for your safety.'

'Thank you,' said Marquez, but didn't sound reassured. 'I must go now, Inspector. I'll be in touch. Good-night, Your Grace. That was an interesting sermon tonight.'

'You agreed with it?'

'I doubt if it would go down with those I have to work with,' said Marquez and turned on his heel. 'Good-night.'

Hourigan looked after him as he disappeared out the big doors. 'The young are so blind, aren't they?'

'So are some of the middle-aged,' said Malone.

'Meaning me or thee?' said Hourigan with a smile. Then he said, though not aggressively, 'Are you a Communist sympathizer, Inspector?'

'Not that I'm aware of, Your Grace.' It was as if they were using their titles of rank to draw up the battle lines between them; there was a hint of mockery in the voice of each. 'I've probably seen more sin, or anyway the results of it, than you have. I'm not sure any more that everything is cut and dried. Which was what you were preaching tonight.'

'Communism is still the biggest threat to the world, bigger than all the health threats, the economic recessions . . . Out here in Australia you just don't know what's going on in the rest of the world.'

'Sister Mary Magdalene knew what was going on in Central America. We think that was why she was silenced.'

That silenced Hourigan for the moment. He sat surrounded by the huge silence of the cathedral; it was empty now but for the small figure of a warden putting out the last of the candles on the main altar at the far end of the great church. He was always affected by an empty church, especially a

76

cathedral; he found less peace in it than when it was filled by an overflowing congregation. The bare pews, the vaulted ceiling reaching towards God, the stillness of the air, all of it troubled him. Solitude is no place for a reluctant conscience.

In his heart he believed that religion was a philosophy, something he had never confessed to any confessor. He had been born two centuries too late; since there was no Voltaire these days to debate with, he had chosen to exhibit fervour and faith, as tonight, instead of reasoned argument; the latter never caught the public eye. He had been immodestly ambitious ever since he had first entered the seminary; he had chosen a career, not a vocation. The celibacy had worried him at first, but he had in time become accustomed to it, though sin occasionally lingered in the groin. Yet he loved The Lord and His ways; it was just that he expected The Lord to compromise. He had had no ambition to be a saint, he had just wanted to be a cardinal. It was his father, the make-believe Catholic, the sinner who knew no sin, who had raised his sights. He had chosen as his path his own war against Communism, a philosophy that sometimes masqueraded as a religion.

At last he said, with no hint of arrogance this time, 'Are you accusing me of the murder of my niece, Inspector?'

'I didn't say that. But I think you know more about her and her death than you've told me.'

'You came to communion this evening, but are you a true Catholic?'

'Sort of.'

'What does that mean?'

'I have my doubts about certain things. But I didn't come here to make my confession.'

Hourigan nodded. 'No, I suppose not.' He looked up and about him, then back at Malone. 'Do you know what this edifice represents? It's the Church in stone, the monument to God. I'd stand outside there and defend it with my life if someone tried to burn it down. That's how I feel about the

Church as a whole.' He believed what he said; or tried to. But he sounded convincing, at least to his own ears.

'Let's stick to Mary Magdalene. I don't think she was trying to burn down the Church, neither this cathedral nor the Church as a whole.'

'The people she believed in, the ones she worked for, are trying to do just that. Not only the Church but the whole of democracy, too. You live in a fools' paradise here in Australia. If we don't stop the spread of Communism we are dead, Inspector. Dead!' His voice rose and he thumped the back of the pew in front of him. 'My niece was a menace. So are the religious like her, the ones with their Marxist views and their contempt for the Church's authority!'

'Simmer down,' said Malone quietly. 'The Marist brothers told me never to raise my voice in church, except to sing a hymn. We were taught never to ask questions, too. Your job, and the priests', might have been easier if we had been taught to ask questions. But I didn't come here to debate the threat of Communism with you. All I'm interested in is who killed Mary Magdalene. Did you ever visit Nicaragua while she was there?'

'You asked me that. I told you – no.'

'So you did. What about Honduras? I believe that's next door.' At school geography had been his favourite subject; he knew where the world was, unlike most of his countrymen. 'When were you last there?'

Hourigan hesitated. The lights in the cathedral had been dimmed and it was almost impossible to read his expression. At last he said, 'I was there three months ago.'

'Did you know your niece was in Nicaragua then?'

'Yes.'

'Did you try to see her?'

'I sent for her. She was brought to Tegucigalpa. That's the capital.'

'Brought?'

'Perhaps I used the wrong word there.' He sounded

uncomfortable. 'Escorted. She had to travel through dangerous country getting out of Nicaragua.'

'And what happened?'

'We had a debate – an argument, if you like. She was a stubborn, reckless young girl. Like her mother,' he added, then looked quickly at Malone, as if regretting having said that. 'It's a family trait.'

'It must come from your own mother. I've never heard your father described as reckless.'

The Archbishop looked at him with a shrewder eye. 'You're not a dumb cop, are you, Inspector? You know much more than you show.'

'We're just like priests, Your Grace. It doesn't pay to show you're a know-all till you're at least a bishop. Did you threaten your niece?'

'Threaten her? I'm not a violent man.'

*I wouldn't put money on that.* 'Threaten her with excommunication, anything like that?'

'No.'

'Why did she come back to Australia then? I mean if you saw her in Honduras three months ago, then it must have been immediately after that that she left for Australia. Who ordered that?'

'I have no idea.' He turned his head, faced Malone directly. The challenge might just as well have been spelled out. *Prove that I did.* 'Now you must excuse me. If he's on time, and he always is, a most un-Irish thing, my father is waiting for me outside.'

He stood up and Malone followed him. They both genuflected; Hourigan crossed himself, but Malone didn't. They walked down the side aisle, passed a stone bowl into which the Archbishop dipped his hand and crossed himself again.

'You don't believe in the power of holy water, Inspector?'

'I'm afraid not. I told you I had doubts. But if it upsets you –' He put his hand in the bowl, then crossed himself with the water. His mother would have been pleased to see him do that: she threw holy water around like a religious market gardener.

'It doesn't upset me, Inspector. Symbols have their uses, but true faith can survive without them.'

'You have true faith?'

'Oh, absolutely.' He smiled, turned it into a deep chuckle. 'It's a pity you and I are on opposite sides.'

'I didn't know we were.' Malone chuckled, too, just to show he was joking. But the Archbishop, looking at him sideways, almost fell down the wide steps in front of the cathedral and Malone had to grab his arm. 'Steady there, Your Grace, I'm no Communist.'

As they reached the bottom of the steps a dark Rolls-Royce drew up at the kerb. It was a Phantom V, the biggest model, and Malone knew there were only one or two in the whole of the State. A uniformed chauffeur jumped out of the front seat, came round and opened the rear door. A light came on and Malone saw Fingal Hourigan sitting in the back seat. Beside him was a handsome, olive-skinned, grey-haired man.

'Good evening, Mr Hourigan,' said Malone. 'And it's Mr Paredes, isn't it?'

It was not such a wild guess, and he knew, as a policeman, that shots in the dark sometimes hit home. Even if they didn't, they could cause the target some uneasiness. Paredes's chin came up as if he had been clipped there.

Fingal Hourigan leaned forward. 'Good-night, Inspector. Who our friends are is none of your business.'

The Archbishop stepped by Malone and got into the car, putting his bulk down on the jump-seat. The chauffeur closed the door, went round, got in and the car silently drove off. Malone looked after it, then turned and looked back up at the dark towers of the cathedral.

'Don't fall down,' he told the stones. 'You'll outlast me.'

# FIVE

———————————————

## I

Sydney in the 1930s reminded Fingal Hourigan, ex-Jimmy Mulligan, very much of Chicago. Its police and politicians could be bought, though not its judges. There were criminal gangs, but they were amateurs compared to the Chicago mobs; they knew nothing of organization. Australians, it seemed, had a sardonic attitude towards being organized, especially their criminals. There were, of course, sections of the population that *were* organized: political parties, trade unions, returned soldiers, certain crooked trainers and jockeys. By and large, however, the voters preferred to think of themselves as individuals, resentful of being told what they should do, and nowhere was that more apparent than amongst the criminal elements. Though certain crims admired Al Capone from afar and dreamed of imitating him if Prohibition ever came to Australia, none had yet shown his organizational ability. They spent their energies in sly grog selling, prostitution rackets, some uncoordinated bank hold-ups and assorted razor slashings amongst themselves. They were a poor lot, proper descendants of the convict gangs of the past, and Fingal Hourigan decided to have nothing to do with them.

He landed in Sydney on Wednesday, October 30, 1929. In America it was still Tuesday, October 29, and investors and bankers were airborne, like wingless hang-gliders, as they leapt from high windows, the thump of their landings adding

81

to the tumult of the Big Crash. The Sydney newspapers featured the Panic on Wall Street, but the thumps were heard only faintly down in the Antipodes; America's troubles, said the locals, were not ours. Fingal, recognizing fools when they stood in a crowd in the street, got off the ship and instantly started buying property.

His first purchase was a hotel, a pub, in Paddington, a working-class inner suburb. It had taken him only a week to see that Australians, like the Irish, were natural-born drinkers; unlike the Irish, who could blame their drunkenness and misery on the English, the natives had no excuse. In summer they did blame the heat, but in winter they drank twice as much. Fingal saw the market and moved into it. It was noticeable that three out of five hotel owners had Irish names, proving that some smart Irishmen had got out of the Ould Country.

Five months after Fingal's arrival he was startled to read that there was to be a referendum in the neighbouring State of Victoria on the introduction of Prohibition; if the notion spread, his hotels, for he now had two, would soon be out of business. Liquor was not to be sold except for medicinal and sacramental purposes, which presumably meant doctors and priests would constantly have temptation on hand. Fingal at once sent a large donation to the Prohibitionists, assuring them, under an assumed name, of his fervent support. If Prohibition was introduced into Victoria he would move down there and become the bootleg king of Melbourne. Unfortunately for his dreams, the Prohibitionists lost overwhelmingly. The winning margin equalled the number of drunks who voted, though all the pubs were supposedly closed on that Saturday. It was suggested they had had access to the medicinal and sacramental supplies. Fingal did not mind the loss of his donation. He always backed both sides in any contest.

The Depression at last began to settle on Australia; though, since there was a height restriction of 150 feet on local buildings, no one was jumping out of windows. There was no point in attempting suicide if it might mean no more than one's being crippled. Violence broke out between striking workers and scabs; the police, caught in between, flailed in all directions with their truncheons, often knocking out each other. The Labour Government of the day brought in what it proudly claimed was a tough Budget, increasing company tax to 6 per cent; blood boiled in the Union Club and other hotbeds of business conservatism and some saw the end of the world looming up. There was talk of marching on the madhouse that was Canberra, the national capital, but since all the banner-makers were flat out supplying the striking and unemployed workers, that idea was abandoned. Newspapers advised readers how to live on £1 a week, ignoring the fact that on £1 a week no citizen, if he had the strength to crawl to the newsagent's, could afford to buy a newspaper. A cold miserable wind blew through the voters, even in summer, though no one suffered as much as the poorer elements of the northern hemisphere. Starvation, somehow, tastes better in the sunshine: or so the well-fed, volunteer charity workers tried to tell the hungry.

Fingal Hourigan didn't suffer at all. Besides his hotels he now had a widening starting-price betting network; SP bookies had been at work since the first convict had tried to out-run the pursuing soldiers, but Fingal was the first man to organize them into a chain. He also bought up closed-down factories and shops, using his profits from the bookmaking; he bought three more hotels, all of them in good situations. In the course of buying the Windjammer Hotel near the Woolloomooloo docks he met Sheila Regan.

She was behind the bar when he walked into the pub, an ethereal-looking girl who looked as if she should be pulling holy water instead of beer. She was pale-skinned, had blonde hair and dark-blue eyes that said she believed all that the world told her. She was a saint, up to her knees in her father's foaming ale and lager, an unwelcome steadying influence on the hard drinkers from the wharves across the road. Paddy Regan kept her out of the bar as much as possible, but this day he was short-staffed and she had volunteered to be a stand-in barmaid. She stood at the end of the long bar and the drinkers, afraid of conversion, crowded together at the other end.

Fingal walked in, took one look at her and fell in love. He had never been a romantic, never had a girl who walked soft-footed through his dreams. He had had girl-friends, but he had always thought of them as the Drainage Board, there to get the dirty water off his chest. Marriage was a fate that, like cancer or an honest living, never crossed his mind. He had never contemplated the possibility of loneliness: money and possessions would always be the best company. Then he met Sheila.

'I am looking for Mr Regan,' he said and was surprised that he sounded breathless.

'He is my father.' She had a voice that should have been in a choir, singing the softer, more seductive notes. 'What are you selling?'

'I'm not selling, I'm buying.' Somehow he managed to sound unaggressive; he couldn't bring himself to bruise this vision. 'Your father is expecting me. I'm Fingal Hourigan. At your service,' he added, getting his breath back and deciding to be a little flourishing in speech and gesture, something she never got from the dockers.

She smiled: was he wrong or was it a knowing smile? But the eyes were still as innocent as those of a convent novice. 'I'd love to visit Ireland, Mr Hourigan.'

He blinked: had he missed something? 'Pardon?'

'You offered your services, Mr Hourigan. Oh, here's Dad. Be careful of him. He's a hard man for a bargain.'

She gave him another smile and floated away, making way for Paddy Regan. He was a thin, red-faced man with thick wavy hair and sharp bitter eyes, the very opposite of his daughter's. Sheila's looks had come from her mother, a dark-

84

haired beauty who had run away with a sailor from the S.S. *Mariposa* when it had docked across the road. She was now in Long Beach, California, living with yet another sailor, though, to be fair to her, he too was from the Matson Line. She was not promiscuous, she wrote her daughter.

'I've thought about your offer, Mr Hourigan,' said Regan in a voice laced with the best of his hotel's stock. His breath was an advertisement for what he sold, if you were a drinker who bought through your nose. 'It's not enough, not by a long chalk.'

'Mr Regan,' said Fingal, one eye watching Sheila pulling beer for the cautiously suspicious drinkers at the other end of the bar. 'I know your financial position down to every penny owed. I will pay you cash, notes in your hand, no cheques, and we'll alter the bill of sale any way you want to fool your creditors.'

'Cash, eh?' Regan pulled them each a beer, peered into the amber looking for a green light of advice. 'I owe something to the brewery, you know.'

'Indeed I do know. You owe quite a lot. Leave that to me.'

'I'm attached to the place.' Regan looked around him. He was attached to it because, wifeless, he was now afraid of the outside world. Out there were too many sober villains who would take him down. It didn't seem to occur to him that he was standing across the bar from one of them. 'Would you want me to stay on and manage it for you?'

Fingal looked along the bar at Sheila, who now stood watching him. She was silhouetted against a window on which a brewery advertisement was painted: a Walter Jardine rugby league forward looked ready to leap out of the glass and rape her. He said, 'I'd like to consult your daughter on that.'

Regan did not look surprised; he was a weak man who acknowleged that women, or anyway *his* women, always had their own way. 'Be careful, Hourigan. She's a hard girl for a bargain.'

Fingal smiled; how could such an ethereal beauty drive a bargain? 'I once made love to the queen of an African tribe. She sold me the tribe in the morning.'

'Don't waste your mullarkey on me, Hourigan. I'm Irish, too. Are you planning to make love to my daughter?'

'Not yet,' said Fingal. 'Only when it is honourable to do so.'

Sheila advised him to buy the hotel and to engage her father as manager, but not to let him keep the books. He asked her would she go out with him.

'I was wondering when you'd get around to asking me,' she said.

He had been talking to her for less than five minutes. He put her forwardness down to her innocence. 'Where would you like to go?'

'To the fights.'

He blinked again: she was full of surprises. But he took her to the fights that night, sat at the ringside in the old Stadium and watched Jack Carroll chop an American import to pieces and, out of the corner of his eye, watched the angel beside him leaning forward with all the blood-lust of a half-starved lioness. When he took her home he tried a chaste good-night kiss and was instantly devoured by lips, teeth and tongue that burnt him: even her teeth seemed hot.

A month later Fingal proposed to her and she accepted him. 'On condition that you will take me to Ireland for our honeymoon.'

'I'll take you to the moon itself, if you wish,' said Fingal, both feet off the ground as he made love to her, not honourably.

'Ireland will do,' she said. 'Now roll over, it's my turn on top. I've just finished reading *The Perfumed Garden*.'

'Does your father know?'

'No, he thought I was reading the *Annals of Mary*.'

'You look so angelic. How can you be so wanton?'

'It's my mother in me. Don't worry, I go to confession

every Saturday – I can see the priest's hair standing on end through the grille. Don't expect me to be wanton on Saturday nights.'

'Sunday to Fridays all right?'

'Every night, three times a night. Oh, I do love you, Fingal!'

Which she did; and he her. They were married on the January day in 1933 when, on the other side of the world, Adolf Hitler became Chancellor of Germany. Both events appeared in the *Sydney Morning Herald*, though the Hourigan announcement was only a paid advertisement in the 'classifieds' column. The general public paid little more attention to Hitler than they did to Hourigan; they were about to declare war on England, whose fast bowlers were hurling cricket balls at the heads of Australian batsmen. The Empire looked ready to fall apart and local weddings and foreign politics were minor events.

Fingal, as promised, took Sheila to Ireland for their honeymoon. She fell in love with the misty, gentle countryside, but said she wouldn't like to live there. He then took her to Italy and in St Peter's she fell on her knees with a force that he thought would crack them and prayed for half an hour without lifting her head; then they went back to the Hotel Hassler and made wanton love for the rest of the day. He took her to Germany and she fell in love with the countryside of that country. But he was not a pastoral lad and the Irish fields and the German forests made no impression on him. But he went to a Nazi rally and watched, fascinated, while Hitler mesmerized his audience. Capone had had power, but never like this. He dreamed for a moment of capturing an audience back home like this, of 50,000 voters standing up at the Sydney Cricket Ground and shouting, '*Heil* Fingal!' But he knew it would never work, that if ever he was to have power in Australia it would not be through rhetoric. The natives back there were too laconic, they would always suspect the orator.

Sheila wanted them to go home through America; she might

be a hard woman with a bargain, as her father had said, but she knew how to spend her husband's money. Fingal, however, said they had to hurry home: he had to go back to making money. The truth was that he was afraid to go anywhere near the United States. Al Capone, in and out of jail now, hounded by the US Treasury, was still a force and, as Fingal well knew, he was not a man to forget a treachery. America, and particularly Chicago, was to be avoided like the rock of Scylla, a Greek dame he had read about in the Chicago Public Library.

Eighteen months later, back in Sydney and having watered *The Perfumed Garden* till it was overgrown and had become weedy, as had Fingal, Sheila decided she wanted a child and took out her diaphragm. Nine months later, to the day, she gave birth to Kerry Seamus. She said that was enough children for the time being, as if she had given birth to a litter; she wanted to learn to be a mother, something her own mother had never been. Three years later she decided it was time for another child and she became pregnant with Brigid Maureen. When it came time for delivery it was a difficult birth and Fingal, who still loved her dearly, almost went out of his mind with the fear that he would lose her. She survived and so did the baby, a bawling, brawling infant who entered the world fighting everyone in sight; it was rumoured that when the doctor slapped her to bring her to life, she slapped him back. Her four-year-old brother hated her and she, from some primeval instinct, even before she had her eyes open, hated him.

And then, slowly but steadily, Sheila came to hate Fingal. It began in ways that, at first, he didn't quite catch. There would be a barbed remark about his preoccupation with money; women, he had once told her, knew nothing about the making of money. Then she began to complain about the way he made his money; he turned his back on that argument, because he would never discuss with anyone how he did that. That was how it had been in Chicago with Capone and the other gang-leaders, including the Irish: money matters were no concern of the women.

Then she began to have what she called 'a marital headache'; it always seemed to coincide with an ache in his groin. At last he discovered the reason for her turning away from him, figuratively and in bed. She had given up reading *The Perfumed Garden* and turned to the writings of St Teresa of Avila.

'She's atoning for the sins of her mother,' said Regan.

He was still managing the Windjammer Hotel, living above the premises and staring each morning across the road to the wharf where his errant wife had waved goodbye as she had fled with the American sailor. He never visited the Hourigans in their home in Bellevue Hill and he was slowly drinking himself to death, though at Fingal's expense.

'How are the babies?'

Fingal brought the children down once a month in the big Buick he now owned; but Sheila never came. 'Always on their knees. She's teaching them to pray, even the baby.'

'There's something wrong with us Irish, Fingal. We put too much money on prayer. What does she want to do with the boy? Make him Pope?'

Fingal nodded seriously. 'She actually said that yesterday. I think she's going out of her mind, Paddy.'

'The same thing happened to her ma when she ran away with the Yank.'

In the spring of 1939, two days before Hitler marched into Poland and the world fell into the second war to end all wars, Sheila went completely out of her mind. Fingal was never able to explain to himself or, later, to his children why she did so. She was put away in a home and Fingal engaged a succession of housekeepers and nannies to look after the children; none of them could stand the pious little brats, let alone love them, and none of them lasted longer than six months. The home became no more than a house: love, like world peace, had gone out the window. Fingal turned to making more money,

89

which could be loved without fear of rejection.

The war was kind to Fingal Hourigan. He made money on the black market, in war industries, in property. When the Japanese shelled a harbourside section of Sydney in 1942 he bought up half of Vaucluse from residents fleeing to the Blue Mountains west of the city. He made substantial donations to war comforts funds and in return was rewarded by ladies on the fund committees who couldn't give fleshly comforts to their absent husbands. He made no committed alliances, however. He was still in love with Sheila: not the pathetic deranged woman in the private mental home but the ethereal-looking girl who had smiled at him in a hotel bar long ago.

The war ended and there was no bigger victor than Fingal Hourigan. He had sold out his starting-price business and now he was on his way to being respectable: if being in business where no criminal charges could be made meant being respectable. He indulged in insider trading, though the term was not yet invented; in tax evasion, a legitimate if not honourable pursuit; in mortgage foreclosures, only dis-reputable if pursued against elderly widows; and cheating any Government department, a national sport. He had raised skulduggery (or skulbuggery, as a later acquaintance would call it) to an art.

## 2

In 1948 Kerry, who was then fourteen, came to him and asked for a man-to-man talk. They had never been close, more like uncle and nephew, and there was a certain constraint between them that had always obstructed any confidences.

'Is it about sex? Don't the Jesuits teach you about that?' Kerry, for the past three years, had been attending St Ignatius' College as a boarder. It was an expensive school and it had been chosen for him by Sheila before she had gone round the bend from sex to religion.

'No, I know all about that. I found one of your old books when I was home for the holidays.'

'What book?'

'*The Perfumed Garden.*'

Fingal didn't disclaim ownership. 'It's a book on acrobatics. Go on.'

'I want to be a priest.'

'*The Perfumed Garden* brought that on?'

Kerry laughed, something he rarely did in the company of his father. Fingal looked at him, liking the sound; Kerry was a big boy for his age, already as tall as his father, and the laugh came up from his belly. Fingal grinned, sat back in his chair and relaxed.

'Actually, I want to be a cardinal.'

'I think fourteen-year-old cardinals went out of fashion when the Popes stopped having bastard sons. Who gave you the idea of being a priest?'

'Mother.'

Once a month Kerry and his ten-year-old sister were taken by the current housekeeper to see their mother. Sheila had occasional lucid stretches – 'some women do,' said her now totally alcoholic father, locked away in his room above the Windjammer bar and no longer managing the hotel – and she spent those moments giving advice to the children on how to avoid the wicked ways of the world she had left. Fingal, carefully guarding the memory of the girl he had once loved, never went near her. He paid the bills and sent her expensive presents and flowers every Friday, but that was the extent of his concern for her.

'She ought to know better,' said Fingal. 'Are you religious, pious, full of faith, all the rest of the bulldust?'

'Yes, I think so. You do good in the world, if you're a priest.'

'And if you're not? You think I'm not doing any good in the world?'

'I don't know. You never tell me or Brigid anything about

what you do. You make a lot of money, and that's all I know.'

There's no need for you to know, thought Fingal; better that you don't. His interests were so wide now that no one who worked for him, not even his accountants, knew the full extent of his holdings or his pursuits. Only this year, after several years of legitimate business, he had slipped back to the criminal side, lured by the money available. He had recently taken over the gold smuggling racket between Hong Kong, Bombay and points west; Sydney was the half-way house, the exchange point, and he now owned the ships that brought in the gold. Taking charge had involved the elimination of certain opposition, though they had never known who *their* opposition was. Crooked cops had taken care of the elimination, though they never knew who paid them. One competitor, a businessman as well-known as Fingal, had held out, but he had been disposed of by being thrown off the back of a ferry one night into the harbour; the two thugs who had done the job had never known who paid for their services. The body had been recovered, half-eaten by a shark, and the coroner had put death down to suicide brought on by worry about the deceased's health. There had been a big funeral attended by politicians and prominent businessmen, including Fingal Hourigan. He had sat in a back pew of the Anglican cathedral, listened to the eulogies, hidden his smile and added up what the gold smuggling would bring him each year. It would be several million pounds at least. More than even the most venal cardinal would ever make.

'That's *my* religion,' he said. 'Making money is what makes the world go round. Not love or prayers.'

'Don't you believe in God?'

'No, But don't tell the Jesuits – they'd be here on my doorstep as soon as you mentioned it. You believe in God, if you like, but I don't need Him.' In his mind he used the pronoun with a lower case *h*.

Kerry looked worried. 'He could strike you dead for that. Aren't you afraid?'

He had been afraid ever since he had left Chicago nineteen years ago, afraid that some day Capone, or someone sent by the Big Fella, would catch up with him. That is, until a year ago, when Capone, racked by syphilis, hatred for the Internal Revenue men and regrets for his lost empire, died in Florida of an apoplectic seizure. Fingal had said a prayer that day, but no one had heard it, probably least of all The Lord.

'No,' he said. 'Fear is for cowards. Are you a coward?'

Kerry thought about it, then said, 'I don't think so. I'm like you, Dad, in lots of ways.'

'Except about religion. Go away and think about wanting to be a priest. I won't say no if you're stuck on it, but don't expect me to give you my blessing.'

Kerry grinned and his father grinned in return: they were growing closer. 'That would be sacrilege, Dad.'

'Sure. Don't tell the Jesuits.'

Kerry left him then and he sat in his living-room in the house in Bellevue Hill and looked down towards the harbour, where he could see one of his ships heading for Hong Kong and another shipment of gold. The house was more than large enough for him and the children and the housekeeper, but it was still too small: the memories of Sheila crowded him. He would build another house, one down on the water at Vaucluse. He began to dream of a castle, something that Al Capone had never owned.

When Brigid came home on a weekend pass from Rose Bay Convent, another expensive school, Fingal took her into the Hotel Australia for lunch. It was the first time he had taken her out alone and she looked at him with a sceptical eye far too experienced for a ten-year-old.

'Why are you doing this, Daddy?'

'I've been a neglectful father. You and I should get to know each other better.'

She played with a chocolate éclair. 'I don't know anything at all about you, Daddy. You've never told us anything about where you came from. Do Kerry and I have a grandfather

93

and grandmother, I mean from your side?'

'No. Some day I'll tell you about myself, when you're older. I was an adventurer.' He changed the subject. 'Did you know Kerry wants to be a priest?'

'No. He's like you, he never tells me anything about himself.'

'Do you want to be a nun?'

'Hell, no!'

'Do they teach you to swear at Rose Bay? Still, I'm glad to hear it. You're too pretty to be wasted in a convent.'

'There are pretty nuns. You don't have to be ugly to be a nun. I just don't want to be one, because I want to grow up and be an artist.'

'Are you any good?' He had never seen any of her work, not even any of her schoolwork. I'm a terrible father, he thought, but would only have given himself a hernia if he had tried to dredge up any guilt.

'The sisters say I'm very good. They don't like what I draw, but that's because they're old-fashioned.'

'What do you draw?'

'Naked men and women,' she said, and suddenly he saw Sheila in her.

She was a remarkably pretty child, with her mother's eyes, but there were already hints that the prettiness would fade and some day there would be a strong-boned handsome woman in her place.

'You can hold back on those. Wait till you leave school and I'll send you to an art school, a good one.'

'I want to go to Paris and live with Pablo Picasso.'

'Paris is no place for a young girl, especially with Picasso. Stay at home and marry a rich young man in Sydney. You can still be an artist.'

'It wouldn't be as much fun. I think I'm like you, Daddy, in lots of ways. An adventurer.'

Perhaps they were right, perhaps there was more of him in them than he saw.

Paddy Regan died in January 1950 from a surfeit of hops and lost hopes. A month later Sheila died; there was a wild happy look in her eyes, as if she had caught sight of The Lord in the moment before He took her. She was buried privately and there was no announcement in the newspapers. Fingal did not look at her when she was laid out in her coffin; she was a stranger, he was not burying his old one true love. The children cried, but with fear more than grief. Two deaths in a month: it was too much for children to be faced with such mortality.

A month later Kerry entered the seminary to study for the priesthood. He still wanted to be a cardinal, an ambition he did not confess to the monsignor in charge. Brigid showed promise at school of being a talented artist; she had given up drawing naked men and women, a retreat greeted with relief by the nuns. She still dreamed of going to Paris and living with Picasso, a dream she did not confess to the mother superior.

Fingal Hourigan went on making money. Then in 1955 he took into his employ Jonathan Tewsday, a crook as devout as himself.

# SIX

## I

Brothels are like parliaments: no one there ever believes the intentions of the rest of those present. Not even when the police come calling.

'I never expected it of you, Inspector. You've come back for a pay-off.'

'Why would I do that, Tilly? I'm not on the Vice Squad.'

Tilly Mosman looked at him dubiously. 'Why did you have to come back now? It's the girls' rest period.'

'Better now than when they're working. I don't think your clients would be too happy if I'm sitting on the end of the bed asking the girls questions.'

Malone had gone from the cathedral back to Homicide, picked up the fax photos of Paredes and Domecq and come here to the Quality Couch. Tilly Mosman had invited him in, but reluctantly.

'They go back to work at eight. Have you eaten? You can have supper with us. It's only light. The girls don't like to work on a full stomach.'

Malone grinned. 'Theirs or their clients'?'

'No crudity, Inspector, I don't allow that.'

Tilly Mosman prided herself on her taste; it was what distinguished her establishment from similar ones around town. As Malone followed her through the downstairs drawing-room into the small dining-room at the back of the house he noted the expense and good taste. Even the nudes in the paintings on the silk-hung walls had a look of class about them, high-priced whores who posed only for the best painters. The two Vietnamese maids who were emptying the ashtrays and cleaning up after this afternoon's trade did not look like Saigon bar-girls; dressed in demure black uniforms with white lace aprons, they would not have been out of place in a Point Piper mansion. To which Tilly Mosman some day aspired.

Half a dozen girls, dressed in cotton wraps, their make-up removed, sat around the dining-table eating quiche, salad and cake. They looked up as Malone entered and all of them sat very still. 'It's all right, girls,' said Tilly. 'It's not a raid. This is Scobie Malone. He's come to ask questions about that poor nun they found outside yesterday morning.'

The girls relaxed and two of them moved aside to let Malone sit between them. They piled his plate with food, like good wives, then offered him a glass of mineral water. 'Tilly never lets us drink wine when we're at work, says it clouds our minds,' said one of them. 'As if it mattered.'

She was a naturalized redhead, a pretty woman who might have been twenty-two or thirty-two; she had probably looked this age at sixteen. She had a husky voice, cultivated as part of her trade, and a smile with a touch of malice in it. For which Malone couldn't blame her.

'Is this all there are of you? Six?'

'There are eight others. They go home to feed their hubbies or put the kids to bed.'

Malone took the two photos out of the manilla folder and laid them on the table. 'Any of you recognize either of these men?'

The photos were passed around, like severed heads; the girls looked at them dispassionately. No matter what they might think of their own menfolk, if they had any, here in this house men were just livestock, bulls who paid. Malone knew that he could not have chosen sharper eyes or sharper memories.

'Yes,' said a girl sitting opposite him. She was a mixed-blood, part-Chinese, part-European, part-something darker; she was beautiful in a striking way and Malone wondered how long it would be before some well-heeled client took her away from the Quality Couch. He felt the attraction of her and decided he would not tell Lisa where he had been tonight. 'I've entertained him two or three times. Three.'

She pushed one of the photos back across the table and Malone looked down at Max Domecq Cruz. 'What about the other one?'

He looked around the table, but all the girls shook their heads. They all looked interested and ready to help and even a little afraid: if a nun could be killed on their doorstep, why not one of them?

'Sergeant Clements was here and you girls told him you had only two Spanish-speaking clients Saturday night.'

'This man didn't speak Spanish,' said the girl opposite him. 'He said he was an American.'

Malone looked at Tilly Mosman, keeping to protocol: 'Can I take her into another room?'

Tilly nodded. 'Go ahead, Dawn. Don't upset her too much, Scobie. She has to go back to work.'

The girl led him out of the dining-room and into a small, exquisitely furnished side-room. Malone, conscious of all the elegance around him, wondered what the bedrooms upstairs were like. There had been a time when he had been almost totally unaware of his surroundings, when rooms were only furnished by the people in them, but Lisa had educated him to an appreciation of couch and table and drape. She had, he'd told her, also educated him to an appreciation of mortgage.

'Is Dawn your real name?'

'No. Why do you want my name?'

'Righto, we'll forget it for the moment.' He did not want to antagonize her; after all, she was entitled to some privacy if she demanded it. In an hour or so she'd have precious little. 'What was this man's name?'

She arranged herself on a love-seat and gestured for him to sit next to her. The face-to-face seats had been designed for lovers; it was also an ideal arrangement for an intimate interrogation. Malone was surprised that he felt uncomfortable sitting so close to the girl. She was even more beautiful now that he had time to look at her closely; her skin was flawless and he could not find any of her features that was out of proportion to the others. Every gesture, every line of her body hinted at sensuality: he felt the attraction of her again and wished he had not sat down so close to her. The perfume she wore was thick in his nostrils, accentuated by the nervous heat of her body.

'Is this what they call a love-seat?' She nodded, and he grinned and added defensively, 'I should buy one for my wife and me.'

She smiled, showing beautifully even white teeth. 'Nobody's ever said that to me. Nobody ever mentions their wife in this place, it's taboo.'

'What did our friend talk about? What was his name?'

'Sebastian. Raul Sebastian. He never told me much at all about himself. Just that he lived in Miami.' She had put her arm on the division between them; her hand rested on his upper arm. It was an unconscious movement, a trick of the trade that she performed automatically. 'I think he's genuinely keen on me. He asked me if I'd like to go and live in Miami.'

'You could do better than that.'

'Here in Sydney? Don't be silly. There are several guys who come here who say they're in love with me, but none of 'em would marry me. All his friends would know where he picked me up.'

'Why'd you go on the game then?'

'The money, what else? I'm lazy, too lazy to move somewhere else and start again. All I can hope is that some day I'll finish up with my own house, like Tilly.'

He looked at the lovely waste of her. Nature had made her perfect, then left her to her own devices. Or men's vices. 'How did Sebastian come here? Do they come in off the street or are your clients recommended?'

'Oh, recommended!' She looked at him indignantly; she had her standards. 'We're the top of the class.'

'I'm sure you are. Sorry. Who recommended Sebastian?'

'I don't know. Tilly takes care of all that. But I don't think she'll tell you.'

'Let's try her. Will you get her for me?'

'I'm here,' said Tilly Mosman, appearing in the doorway. 'I was eavesdropping. You're a nice man, Scobie, but my policy is, Never trust any man. Dawn is right – I'm not going to tell you who recommended Mr Sebastian.'

Malone stood up, relieved to be away from the side of Dawn. He had always been a faithful husband; was he at last developing the seven-year itch? 'Trust me this time, Tilly.' He told her who Sebastian really was. 'He's connected with the murder of Sister Mary Magdalene in some way, I don't know how. You don't want to be an accessory after the fact.'

Tilly looked suddenly worried and a frown cracked the flawless face beside her. The women looked at each other, then Tilly said, 'Is he dangerous? I mean would he come back and, you know, hurt Dawn or me?'

'I don't think so. If he comes back, get in touch with us – I'll have men here within two minutes.' The Police Centre was only a few blocks away. 'Who recommended him, Tilly?'

She hesitated, jealous of her standards. Then: 'Sir Jonathan Tewsday.'

Malone kept his eyebrows in place. 'Is he a client of yours?'

'Not now.'

*So he once was.* Malone had met Tewsday only once, years ago when he had been a young detective-constable on the Fraud Squad; he had also then met Fingal Hourigan for the first time. The Squad had been unable to lay any charges against Tewsday or Hourigan; both men had gone on to be ornaments of the Establishment, all tarnish scrubbed away by their wealth. It was said that Tewsday had bought his knighthood, but it would not have been cheap; the dead Premier who had sold it to him had never believed in bargains. It was also said that Fingal Hourigan, the bargain hunter, Tewsday's boss, had refused a knighthood because there was no discount.

'What did Sir Jonathan say about Mr Sebastian?'

'That he was a gentleman who paid his bills in cash. I take credit cards, but I prefer not to.'

Malone grinned. 'What do you put it down to?'

'I call it telex charges. It's a form of communication, isn't it? So's what my girls do.'

Malone looked at Dawn, who smiled lazily. He said, 'Was he a gentleman?

Dawn shrugged, but offered no comment. Then Tilly said, 'He paid his account each night, though he made what I thought was an ungentlemanly remark. He said the devalued Aussie dollar gave him a cheap roll in the hay. None of my girls is a cheap roll in the hay, no matter what the dollar's valued at.'

She had her pride and so did her girls; Dawn gave a slow nod to emphasize what Tilly had said. Malone nodded in reply: he respected any professional, even some crims.

'Righto, let me know if he calls again.'

'You're not going to get in touch with Sir Jonathan?'

'Don't worry, Tilly. If I do, he won't know how I got to him.'

'I'd like to believe that . . .' She knew the power of powerful men, both good and bad. 'Don't call again, Scobie, not unless you have to.'

He smiled, knowing the brush-off wasn't personal. He went through to the front door and Dawn, a good hostess, accompanied him. She put her hand on his arm; he felt the effect of her perfume and her attraction. 'All the girls would like you to find who murdered that nun. Some of us are religious, in a sort of way.'

'Sure, Dawn. Take care of yourself. And don't go to Miami.'

She kissed him on the cheek, looked unafraid but lazily so. Bed, he guessed, was her natural habitat.

'I'll probably never get away from here, not till I'm Tilly's age. When I get my own house, come to the opening.'

'I'll do that. Can I bring my wife? Good-night, Dawn.'

As he went out to his car, a hired stretched limousine drew up at the kerb. Six Japanese men got out, two of them with cameras strung round their necks, stood for a moment as if gathering their courage or their potency, then went into the Quality Couch, like tourists looking for Aussie souvenirs. Malone wondered if they would pay by credit card, if they would think the over-valued yen would give them a cheap roll in the hay.

He went straight home, suddenly feeling worn out. Enough had been done for the day; Sir Jonathan Tewsday could wait till tomorrow, Tuesday. The skies had cleared and he drove home through a beautiful autumn night. He pulled the car into the garage beside the house, got out and, before going inside, stood and looked up at the stars. He had read in the newspapers that a new supernova had just been discovered, the death of a star 170,000 years ago. He looked for it and found it, a tiny bright explosion south-west of the Southern Cross. He had always been interested in the stars, ever since he had been a small boy; not as an amateur astronomer nor as a carnival astrologer but as a dreamer. What a way to die, he thought, 170,000 years ago and only now the word was out. All deaths should be like that, so that those who loved the deceased would themselves be dead before the grief began. He wondered if Brigid Hourigan was sitting beneath the stars tonight and grieving for her daughter.

He went into the house, took off his jacket and dropped it over the back of a couch. Lisa kissed him, then, ever neat, picked up the jacket to put it away on a hanger. She lifted a sleeve and smelled it. 'Arpège?'

'Russ Clements is wearing it.'

'You're holding hands with a detective-sergeant?' She led him out into the kitchen. 'Your dinner's in the oven.'

'I've eaten.' He hadn't eaten much, but he had a sweet tooth that was always hungry. 'What's for dessert?'

'I thought you'd had it,' said Lisa, taking a Dutch apple cake from the oven. 'Maybe mousse Arpège?'

He mock-winced. 'You can do better than that. If you must know, I had dinner with the girls at the Quality Couch. I had a girl on either knee and they fed me with a silver spoon. I think both of them were naked, but I'm not sure. I was too interested in what they were telling me.'

She cut a wide slice of apple cake, put whipped cream on it and pushed it across to him. Then she sat down opposite him and smiled. 'The day I think I can't trust you, I'll walk out. It wouldn't be that I just couldn't stand losing you to some other woman, it would be that I'd be so disappointed. I could never believe in anyone again if I couldn't believe in you. Now eat up.'

'You really know how to give a man an appetite.' There was a lump in his throat; and an oxyacetylene burn of guilt in his breast. He would never be able to tell her about Dawn, the whore of all men's dreams. He clasped her hand, glad that the children were in bed: this was not a family moment. 'I love you. I'll buy you a gallon of Arpège.'

She squeezed his hand, lifted it and kissed it. Then, aware of the worry in him, she said, 'What did the girls tell you that was so interesting?'

Should he burden her with his worries? But who else was there to confide in? Russ Clements, of course; but Russ couldn't hold his hand. So he told her and as always saw the sympathy in her face. How could he have looked at the girl in the brothel, who would be worn beyond sympathy for anyone but herself?

'I think I'm opening a can of worms bigger than tiger snakes.'

Yesterday: a cathedral and a brothel. Today: what?

'How about a visit to a cemetery?' said Clements, as if reading his mind. 'Sister Mary Magdalene is being buried this morning at Northern Suburbs. There's nothing in the papers. I got that from the morgue.'

The forensic report had been on Malone's desk when he came to the office this morning. It said that the killing of the young nun had been a professional job: 'The knife used, I would say, was one designed for killing, possibly the type used by military Special Services or something like it. The knife was driven into the heart at exactly the right angle to a depth of eight centimetres. Death would have occurred within two seconds. Very professional.' One could feel the cold admiration of the writer.

On the way out to the cemetery Malone told Clements about his visit last night to the Quality Couch. 'I think we'll pay a visit to Sir Jonathan.'

Clements looked at him dubiously. 'Scobie, we're opening up –'

'I know. A can of tiger snakes.'

'That wasn't what I was going to say. But –' He nodded, then bit his lip. 'Yeah, you're right. Tiger snakes, taipans, pythons, the bloody lot. Not to mention the Pope.'

'He'd thank you for that, in there in the snake-pit. I don't think we have to worry about him.'

'I dunno. You Tykes have got the influence.'

'Is Tewsday a Catholic?'

Clements shrugged. 'Does it matter, if he's a mate of Old Man Hourigan and the Archbishop? They're all in bed together.'

It was a cool day, the wind coming off the mountains to the west with a whisper of winter. The cemetery struck Malone as being like all others, hectares of loneliness: the dead never kept each other company, no matter what the living intended.

The gravestones, like tablets planted by some minor Moses, stared at each other with messages written by the living for the living: the dead beneath them were beyond any communication. Some of the gravestones were fancier than others, ornamented with marble angels, marble wreaths and a shower of marble snow; but they, too, were messages from the living to the living. Wealth, or the manifestation of it, should never be buried, unless one were an Egyptian king.

There was some evidence of wealth, though not of the Ptolemys, in the parking lot: a silver Rolls-Royce and the latest Jaguar, a bright-red model that stood out like a fountain of blood in the monochrome of the cemetery. Clements pulled the unmarked police Commodore in beside them and got out. Standing apart from the two expensive cars were a small mini-bus and a motor-cycle. Clements made a note of the number-plates and Malone once again nodded in appreciation of the methodical efficiency of the big yobbo.

Further over were half a dozen other cars and three television vans. The reporters and cameramen had already moved over towards the open grave where Sister Mary Magdalene was to be buried; they had the grace to keep apart from the small group of mourners around the grave. The cameramen, however, already had their inquisitive cameras pointed at Brigid Hourigan: no one any longer was entitled to private grief.

Father Marquez was saying the last prayers, his voice sometimes choking. Around the grave there were half a dozen uniformed schoolgirls; Mother Brendan and a younger nun; Brigid Hourigan and her manservant Michele; and a portly, bald man who had the look of an expensive physician. Sir Jonathan Tewsday, however, revived only sick companies, though he was known to have killed off as many as he had cured.

Malone wondered who had invited Father Marquez to say the prayers. When the young priest had finished, his face as sad as Brigid's, the gravediggers moved in as the mourners moved away. Malone felt a touch of unaccountable grief; then he knew he was looking into the future, praying against the burial of his own children. As he turned away he saw the headstone on the neighbouring grave: Sheila Regan Hourigan, 1913–1950. Mary Magdalene was being buried beside her grandmother and Malone wondered why her grandfather and her uncle hadn't attended.

He moved across to Father Marquez. The young priest was still looking down into the grave and he started when Malone touched his arm.

'Oh, Inspector – I didn't see you. I'm glad you came. I was going to phone you later.' He turned away for a moment to give a sad smile to the schoolgirls as they filed past; through their tears they looked back at him soul-stricken. Mother Brendan harrumphed softly and pushed them on, but the young nun paused. 'Yes, Helena?'

Sister Helena, on a better day, would have been plain and cheerful, good company; today she was just plain, her face turned to suet. 'Did you get the letter?'

'Yes. I was just about to tell Inspector Malone about it. This is Sister Helena. She found a letter addressed to me under Mary Magdalene's mattress. It could have caused a scandal . . .'

'I knew it wasn't a love letter – Mary wasn't the sort.' Sister Helena herself might have been, in other circumstances. She was still a schoolgirl, which was a reason she would always be popular with the girls she taught. 'I must be going. There's Mother Brendan cracking the whip.' There was just a faint crumbling of the suet; her energy could never remain far below the surface. 'Nice meeting you, Inspector. Find the devil who killed her!'

Then she was gone and Father Marquez looked after her. 'You see? I told you everyone loved Mary who knew her.'

'Did you?'

Marquez smiled, shook his head. 'Not that way. Here's the

letter. I sort of wish I hadn't read it. There's more in there than I want to know.'

Malone took the letter. He read it, his face showing nothing of his reaction. 'Can I keep it? Why would she have written it d'you think?'

'Sure, keep it, I don't want it. I don't know why she wrote it – unless she thought she was in danger. But she doesn't say anything about being afraid. You don't seem surprised by what's in it?'

'Not surprised, no. But I'm like you – there's more in it than I'd rather know.' Russ Clements had come up to stand beside them. Malone introduced him, then handed the letter to him. 'Read it, Russ, then put it in the murder box.'

He said goodbye to Father Marquez and walked back to the car park. Brigid Hourigan stood beside the red Jaguar, complementing it with the rich blue cape that she wore. Jonathan Tewsday stood beside her, holding her wrist as if taking her temperature.

'I didn't expect you, Inspector,' said Brigid. She had been weeping, but there were no tears now. Her blonde hair was wrapped in a blood-red turban that offset the cloak; she was a ball of style, if a little theatrical. Malone preferred it to the usual mourner's black; at death there should be some challenge that life went on. 'Is this police duty?'

'In a way. Sometimes the murderer turns up, fired by a sort of final curiosity.'

She looked at him with interest. 'You'd know more about the psychology of that than I would.' Then she looked around her; it was difficult to tell if she was mocking him. 'Did you see anyone you suspect?'

'No.' So far he hadn't looked at Tewsday. As casually as he could, he said, 'Your brother the Archbishop didn't come?'

'No. He was afraid there might be some publicity.' Her voice was sour.

He could go all the way to Nicaragua, unafraid of the Sandinistas and their guns: so the letter had said. He could not come to his niece's funeral because he feared reporters and their cameras. 'So far you've kept the Hourigan name out of the papers.'

'Not me, Inspector.' She looked at Tewsday with a smile as sour as her voice. 'Sir Jonathan and my father have done that. Do you know Inspector Malone, Jonathan?'

'I don't think I've had the pleasure,' said Tewsday, exhibiting a convenient memory. 'I take it you're in charge of this awful case. Any clues so far?'

'A few. I think we'll know before the end of the week *why* she was murdered.'

Michele held open the door of the Jaguar and Brigid was about to get into the car. She paused. 'Will you let me know, Inspector? I'm entitled to know.'

'Of course, Miss Hourigan. We'll be in touch again, anyway. There are more questions we want to ask you.' Out of the corner of his eye he saw Tewsday lift one of his chins.

Brigid nodded, then got into the car. Michele closed the door gently after her, got into the front seat and drove the car away. Malone wondered if Brigid always rode in the back seat or whether, today, she too was afraid of publicity.

'A remarkable woman,' said Tewsday. 'Talented and beautiful and headstrong.'

'Her daughter seems to have been something like her. Headstrong, anyway. I'd like to ask you some questions, Sir Jonathan.'

There was the sudden roar of an engine: Father Marquez had kick-started his motorbike. He pulled on his dark-visored helmet, waved a gloved hand to Malone, then wheeled the bike round and sped off as if getting away in some religious grand prix.

'Who is the priest?' said Tewsday.

'A friend of Sister Mary's – her closest friend, possibly.'

'The young – they're so different from my day.'

'You don't have children?'

'Three daughters. When do you want to ask me those questions, whatever they are?'

'Now.'

'Here? This is hardly the place.'

'Are you going back to town? Maybe I could ride back with you?'

'You're intrusive, aren't you, Inspector? Has anyone ever told you that?' He had the sort of voice that had been cultivated as he had gone up in the world; he sounded as if he were juggling his vowels, fearful that he might drop them and squash them.

'It comes with the job. I'm naturally shy.'

'That isn't what I've heard.' Then Tewsday realized his mistake; he lowered the lids on his large pop-eyes. 'Get in.'

Malone signalled to Clements to go back into town without him. The chauffeur, a muscle-bound man who bulged even through his grey uniform, smiled at Malone. 'Mind your head as you get in, sir. A lot of people think these cars are higher than they are.'

'Especially people who travel in Holdens,' said Malone.

He got into the Rolls-Royce. It was a Silver Spur, a later model than Hourigan's Phantom, but it did not have the other's cachet. Tewsday evidently knew his place in the corporate garage.

Tewsday settled back in his seat as the car moved off. He was of medium height but looked shorter because of his bulk. He had a florid complexion and a voice to match: both had come with the indulgences of wealth. He was one of the leading financiers in the country and he knew it and would never be modest about it. He had character, most of it bad, but no one had ever proved it so.

He pressed a window-button and they were cut off from the chauffeur. 'So what are your questions, Inspector?'

Malone nodded at the chauffeur on the other side of the glass panel. 'An American as your chauffeur?'

'Isn't Australia supposed to be a melting-pot, just like America was?'

'I didn't think Americans migrated here to take menial jobs.'

'There's no shame in starting at the bottom, Inspector. I did. I presume you did, too?'

This wasn't going to be easy. He decided to attack at once. 'Are you raising money for Archbishop Hourigan?'

'Raising –? You mean for some Catholic charity? I'm not a Catholic, Inspector.'

'I don't think the Archbishop is really interested in charity. Not from listening to him preach last night at the cathedral. No, are you raising money for his crusade against the Contras in Nicaragua?'

Tewsday laughed, a rich sound, richly cultivated; Malone wondered if he spent half an hour each day in vocal exercises. 'Contras? Good heavens, man, what have they got to do with us? Australia doesn't invest in Central America. We have more bananas here than we can eat.'

'Then what is your association with Mr Paredes and Mr Domecq? What do they have to sell besides bananas?'

Tewsday turned away and looked out the window. The Rolls had pulled up at a traffic light. Standing beside them was the convent mini-bus; the girls who had been at the funeral stared out at them; two of them said something to each other, their mouths opening silently behind the glass like those of pretty goldfish. Sister Helena, who was driving the mini-bus, turned and smiled at Tewsday.

'Nuns,' he said, face still turned away from Malone. 'I'll never understand them.'

'Did that include Sister Mary Magdalene?'

The car moved off again; Tewsday waved some plump fingers at the mini-bus, then looked back at Malone. 'She was a nuisance to her uncle, the Archbishop, but you probably know that.'

'Was she a nuisance to Mr Paredes and Mr Domecq? What's

their connection with you, Sir Jonathan?' Malone kept his tone conversational; it was difficult to be too confrontational sitting beside Tewsday in the latter's luxury. 'Better that you tell me. I'll be taking them in for questioning some time today.'

Tewsday was fiddling with a ring on his left hand; it was a broad gold band with a black opal set in it. On the wrist of the same hand there was a gold watch; a gold cuff glinted on the cuff of the shirt. Over the years he had learned a certain restraint, but he was a man who would always advertise his wealth. All he lacked was power: his boss had that.

'I think you had better ask Mr Hourigan, the Archbishop's father, about that. I run Mr Hourigan's companies, but in the end I am still only his employee.' It hurt him to admit it: his chins seemed to quiver.

'What about Ballyduff? That's the company that owns the freehold on the Quality Couch. Do you think it was just coincidence that Sister Mary Magdalene's body was found there?'

'I have made money on coincidences, Inspector, so I'd never bet against it.'

That was no answer, but Malone let it pass. 'Do you know anything about a company named Austarm? Sister Mary mentioned it in a letter.'

'Who to?'

'To a friend. Do you know anything about it?'

Tewsday looked out the window again, then back at Malone. 'It's a small company in our overall group. I don't think I've ever visited it. It's somewhere in the bush, Moss Vale, I think.'

'What does it make?'

'Small arms, maybe larger stuff. I don't really know. There are over fifty companies in our group, Inspector. There are group managers within the larger organization. They run their own bailiwicks.'

'And all you're concerned with is the profit and loss?'

Tewsday didn't miss the mild sarcasm. 'At the end of the financial year, Inspector, that's all that counts. And I'm responsible for it.'

'Why did you come to the funeral this morning, and not the uncle or the grandfather? Are you responsible for funerals, too?'

It was rude and Malone knew it, but Tewsday had to be shaken out of his set jelly. The plump face flushed and Tewsday sat forward as if he were going to shout to the chauffeur to pull up. His mouth opened, then closed, and he sat leaning forward, breathing heavily; for a moment Malone thought he had had some sort of attack. Then slowly he relaxed and sat back. A hide like his would never burst under apoplexy.

'You're everything I've heard about you, Malone. Intrusive, insulting . . .'

*Who have you been listening to?* But Malone didn't ask that. He sighed and said, 'If people were more co-operative, I wouldn't need to be like that. Let's cut out the bull, Sir Jonathan. I'm looking for who murdered a young nun, who, as far as I can tell, had more good points than she had bad ones. She had compassion and she cared about people worse off than herself and some bastard killed her for being that way!' He couldn't help the heat that had suddenly appeared in his voice.

Tewsday shook his head, looked more composed now. 'It was not like that, Malone. Not like that at all. But I'm not the one to tell you all about it.'

'What about Paredes or Domecq?'

'You might get somewhere with them.'

'Where do I find them?'

Tewsday hesitated, then said, 'They're staying with Mr Hourigan and the Archbishop.'

Malone had the feeling that Tewsday had said too much and knew it. But he was protecting himself; one could see him hastily building the wall round himself. They rode the rest of the way in silence. At last, when they had crossed the Harbour Bridge and were sliding into the central business district, Tewsday said, 'Where would you like to be dropped?'

'Anywhere will do. It's time I had a think walk.'

Tewsday looked at him curiously. 'Arnold Bennett?' Malone looked at him blankly and Tewsday explained: 'He was an English novelist, before my time, but I read him and other dead writers. Howard Spring, J. B. Priestley, Hugh Walpole, Maugham. I'm an old-fashioned man. Bennett used to go for what he called think walks when he had what they call writer's block.'

'I've never read him. I guess I suffer from policeman's block. I got the expression from my wife.'

'Don't tax yourself. Stay in the car. Gawler can take you where you want to go.'

The car drew up outside Ballyduff House, a seventy-storey glass-and-granite monument to Hourigan enterprise. Tewsday got out, ignoring yet obviously conscious of the curious stares of the passing citizens: princes, especially unroyal ones, like to be acknowledged. That the reaction of the local elements would be more resentment than admiration didn't worry him.

'Good luck with your problems, Inspector. I think you may have quite a few.'

Malone watched him cross the pavement and go into the building, leaning back against the weight of his stomach, his top chin lifted arrogantly. Malone settled uncomfortably back into the luxurious leather of the seat, feeling that the first of the tiger snakes had just got out of the opened can.

He pressed the window-button and the glass slid down between himself and the chauffeur. 'Your name's Gawler?'

'Yes, sir. Gary Gawler.'

'I'd like to go to Homicide. It's up in Liverpool Street. You're American?'

'Yes, sir. I saw the tourist advertisements with that guy

113

Paul Hogan and I decided to give it a try. Give it a burl, as you Aussies say.'

'What did you do in America?'

'Oh, this and that. I'll move on to something else after this, I guess. But Sir Jonathan is a good man to work for.'

'I'm sure he is. Where did you come from in the States?'

'Chicago. Which end of Liverpool Street, sir? I'm afraid I've never had to drive Sir Jonathan to Homicide.'

# SEVEN

## I

When Fingal Hourigan first met Jonathan Tewsday in 1955 he should have recognized a young man as ruthlessly ambitious as he himself had once been. He was a real estate salesman, a junior one at that, and he would not have been selling the Hourigan home in Bellevue Hill had his boss not been knocked down by a car.

'A woman driver?' said Fingal.

'Yes, sir. His wife.'

'Deliberately?'

'I don't think so. Evidently she got Reverse mixed up with Drive.'

'They're all the same,' said Fingal, who had never allowed Sheila to drive, even before she had become deranged. 'Tuesday? The second day of the week?'

'No, sir.' He handed Fingal his card. 'Some day I hope it will be as well-known as your own. With all due respect.'

Fingal was unimpressed. 'Okay, sell this house and find me another. One with a water frontage.'

Jonathan Tewsday sold the Bellevue Hill house within two days for seven thousand pounds above Fingal's reserve price. The profit was a drop in a bucket to Fingal, but he took note of it; profit was always profit, especially when it was tax free. Within the week Tewsday had come up with a waterfront property at Vaucluse that, he said, was going for a song.

'I don't write songs, I write cheques,' said Fingal. 'How much is it?'

'Thirty-two thousand pounds.'

Fingal went out to Vaucluse to inspect it, bought it, then said, 'Knock down the house. I'll build my own.'

Tewsday all at once caught a glimpse of Fingal's wealth; in the 1950s no one paid a small fortune for a property, only to knock it down. Then and there he decided that, somehow he was going to attach himself to Fingal Hourigan's wagon. He never over-estimated anything (except, of course, prices promised to prospective house sellers), least of all his chances; but, even though young, he was not myopic about the future and could take the long view. He knew that, sooner or later, he could be of use again to Fingal Hourigan.

The opportunity came six months later. There were no commercial developments in the eastern suburbs, where Tewsday operated, that would interest a man of Fingal's investment scope. Tewsday looked across the harbour to North Sydney; he needed a telescope, but he saw all he needed to see. The northern end of the Harbour Bridge promised to lead to a twin city to the main business district on the south side; already the smart developers were moving in. Without his boss's knowledge, Tewsday took a thirty-day option in the firm's name on a row of houses just off the northern approach to the Bridge. Then he went to the offices of Bally-duff Holdings in a building not far back from Circular Quay. It took him three days to get into Fingal's office. While he waited he wondered why such a wealthy company should headquarter itself in such an old unattractive building. He was not to know that it was another manifestation of Fingal's fear, still with his memories of Chicago, of being too conspicuous. The building of the castle at Vaucluse would be an example of conspicuous anonymity, but it would be the first break-out from his long-held fear of the ghost of Capone.

At last Tewsday was shown into Fingal's office. Fingal

looked at this persistent young man for the first time; that is, *really* looked at him. He saw a man in his mid-twenties, hair already thinning, stomach and a second chin already developing, a fastidious dresser who wore expensive English shoes: Fingal always started his scrutiny from the feet up of anyone who interested him. This Jonathan Tewsday had eyes the colour of sultanas, well suited to his puddeny face; his mouth had all the flexibility of a veteran con man's. Fingal decided at once that he couldn't be trusted, so he listened to him, for he believed that trustworthy men never made money as fast as the other kind. Though he did not make the admission to himself, they were vultures of a feather.

Tewsday, for his part, was examining the man he hoped would soon be his employer; or, eventually, his partner. He was a dreamer, though he would give dreams a bad name. Fingal was now fifty years old, but looked at least five or six years younger, despite the streaks of grey now appearing in his thick brown hair. He had virtually lost his American accent and when it did occasionally surface people put it down as Irish. He was soberly but expensively dressed; he had acquired a patina of conservative success. Or successful conservatism, which was of greater value in the Australia of that decade. The new rich did not wear white shoes and tycoons had not yet taken to wearing gold chains; new money tried to look like old money from the feet up. His office complemented his own appearance, all dark panelling, brass lamps and leather chairs; the paintings on the walls were sober Australian landscapes, not a bushranger nor a bared breast in sight. Fingal might have been a Supreme Court judge or the Governor of the Commonwealth Bank. But Tewsday, who had done his homework, knew he was sitting opposite a man as rapacious and unscrupulous as himself. It made him feel good.

'You have ten minutes, young man. Get started.'

Tewsday opened his brief-case, an English leather one bought three mornings ago at Kitchings: he, too, knew the value of looking conservatively successful. 'Mr Hourigan, have you looked at the possibilities for development in North Sydney?'

'Yes,' said Fingal unencouragingly, though he had not.

Tewsday didn't miss a beat. 'Then you know the difficulties of dealing with a suburban-minded council that doesn't know the value of a bribe?'

Fingal smiled; but only to himself. 'What have you got in mind?'

Tewsday told him, producing the sketch plans he had commissioned with an architect friend. 'This row of ten houses overlooks where the new freeway will run. There is room there for a twenty-storey office block, plus half a dozen shops.'

'Are the houses owner-occupied?'

'Only two. The rest are tenanted.'

'Is it zoned for commercial development?'

'Not yet. But if the price is right, it can be. I can guarantee that.'

'What's in this for you, Mr Tewsday?'

'I want to come to work for you, Mr Hourigan. Five thousand pounds a year, plus expenses, to start with.'

'Nobody starts as high as that with me. You have a lot of *chutzpah*.'

It was a word that Tewsday had never heard up till then; the European Jews who would one day be a force in the country's economy had not yet shown the local natives what *chutzpah* was. But Tewsday not only had an eye for opportunity, he had an ear for meaning and he caught it. 'Mr Hourigan, you wouldn't have appreciated me if I'd come in here and under-valued myself.'

'What are you besides a smart-arse who can buy and sell real estate?'

I'm never going to love this man, thought Tewsday; but he had never believed that love made the world go round. 'I'm that rare bird, an accountant with imagination.'

Fingal this time allowed his smile to show. 'Mr Tewsday, I don't employ accountants unless they have imagination. You'll have some competition. I'll give you a six months' trial. Three thousand a year and expenses, supply your own transport, take it or leave it.'

'Those are coolie's wages, Mr Hourigan.' He took a risk with his *chutzpah*.

'Then you'd better get used to dim sims and fried rice.' Fingal pressed a button on his desk and almost immediately the door to the outer office opened and a secretary stood there. 'Miss Stevens will show you out. You can start Monday, report to Mr Borsolino. You'll get on well with him – he's an accountant with imagination.'

Tewsday stood up, closing his briefcase. 'I haven't said I accept your offer, Mr Hourigan.'

Fingal looked up at him. 'You came in here with your mind made up to accept the job no matter what I offered you. It's only because you're so keen that I'm giving you a trial. But you'll have to learn to be less transparent, Mr Tewsday. You'll never get anywhere in business by laying yourself out like an open book. Any imaginative accountant will tell you that an open book is just asking for trouble. Good-day.'

When Tewsday had gone, Fingal got up and walked to the window of his office. He looked out past one or two buildings that partly obscured the view of the harbour, across the water to North Sydney. He should have moved in there sooner; but money had been so easy to make here south of the harbour. Beginning with the wool boom during the Korean War, during which he had bought his first merino sheep stud, money was becoming more manifestly visible than at any time since the 1920s. A new young, aggressive breed of developer was beginning to emerge, some of them refugees from post-war Europe. The old refugee, from Chicago, had to stay ahead of them. The number of upstarts was growing, smart-arses who had no respect for tradition. He had little time for it himself, but one could always call upon it as a last resort.

Jonathan Tewsday reported the following Monday to Robert Borsolino, a slightly older smart-arse who knew a younger one when he presented himself. 'What am I supposed to do with you?' His imagination didn't run to making use of juniors; they might depose one. 'Did Mr Hourigan say?'

'I'm to be left to my own devices.' Fingal had said no such thing, but Tewsday knew that middle-level executives, especially ones not much older than himself, did not go to the chairman and managing director and query his reasons for his directives. 'Or vices, as the case may be.'

'Don't be a smart-arse,' said Borsolino. He was a thin, dark-haired man with a very thin veneer of good temper. 'Three thousand a year, eh? Prove you're worth it.'

Tewsday went over to North Sydney, picked up the deputy-mayor and brought him back to the south side of the harbour to lunch at the Hotel Australia. Bill Oodskirt, the deputy-mayor, was flattered; his usual rendezvous for such dealings was the fish café at Crows' Nest. He was a short, fat little man with plastered-down red hair; he was a butcher by trade and, stripped, would have gone unnoticed in his own shop window. His collar was too tight and he was constantly tugging at it, as if he were choking.

He choked when Tewsday offered him a thousand pounds. 'This is highly unusual, Mr Tewsday.' He meant that he had never before been offered more than a hundred pounds, but Tewsday deliberately misunderstood him.

'Mr Oodskirt, you're worth it, every penny of it. You have the influence in Council, I know your record. You vote and two-thirds of the Council vote with you. All you have to do is have this section of Rogers Street zoned for commercial development.'

'We've been thinking about it,' said Oodskirt, who always liked to find excuses for his venality and corruption. 'Yes, we've definitely been thinking along those lines.'

'Of course you have!' said Tewsday, showing enthusiasm for his victim's imagination. 'Sydney is going to be the New York of the South Pacific and North Sydney will be a major part of it. And you'll be a part of it, too.'

'It's a lot of money,' said Oodskirt, having a sudden attack of guilt, something he couldn't explain, since he'd had no previous symptoms.

It was not a lot of money, if one took the long view. Tewsday knew that within ten years the site would be worth ten times the present price; it took imagination to see that far ahead and calculate such a sum, but Tewsday could feel it in his bones. Oodskirt, on the other hand, though he cut up bones every day in his shop, had no imagination. He never saw further than next week and the next envelope under the table.

'As I said, Mr Oodskirt, you're worth every penny of it. A little more claret?'

'Don't mind if I do.' Oodskirt's collar suddenly seemed to have got looser. He sat back, a big shot whose worth was appreciated. 'Better than the old Porphyry Pearl, isn't it?'

'Indeed it is,' said Tewsday, who wouldn't have drunk the cheaper wine if he had been dying of thirst. He was already a wine snob, for which no breeding is necessary.

The following week the Rogers Street block was zoned commercial. The week after that Tewsday bought the ten houses in Ballyduff's name, withdrew the option money and paid it back into his former employer's agency account. His former employer knew nothing about the withdrawal and the re-deposit till a month later when he received his bank statement. By then he knew there would be no catching Tewsday.

A month later Tewsday was sent for by his new employer. 'You've bought us a parcel of trouble, young man.'

'I don't understand –' For once Tewsday couldn't finish a sentence.

'The two owner-occupiers in those houses in North Sydney

121

have moved out. The rest, the tenants, are staying put. On top of that, squatters have moved into the two houses the owners have vacated.'

'I don't think we have a problem, Mr Hourigan. The courts will evict them.'

'Borsolino says that could take twelve months or more. Furthermore the Commos in the unions are taking up their cause. That feller Nev Norway has got into the act. You know him?'

'I know of him, Mr Hourigan. I've never met him personally.'

'I met him once, right after the war. He'd turn this country into a Soviet republic, if he had his way. He has no time for capitalists like you and me.'

Tewsday was flattered to have already the same status as his boss. 'Everyone has his price, Mr Hourigan.'

'I doubt it with Norway. Try your luck, but never mention my name. You're on your own. Fall on your face and you're fired.'

Tewsday went down to see Nev Norway, at his union's offices not far from the Darling Harbour wharves. He didn't wear his new Richard Hunt suit or his suede shoes; he went in an open-necked shirt, the collar worn outside his jacket in true working-class style, and a pair of his father's old leather shoes that he dug out of a family trunk. Both his parents were dead, glad to have gone to their graves to escape from a son who had disappointed them by showing an interest in nothing but making money and who, on his father's death bed, had told the old man that he had voted Liberal in the last elections.

'You'd have known my dad,' said Tewsday, flattening his vowels, dropping the accent he had been cultivating. 'He was a tally clerk down there on the wharves. Any Day Tewsday, they used to call him – he'd go out on strike any day you called him.'

Nev Norway was not taken in by his visitor's appearance or his accent; this kid was a toff, or aspired to be one. Norway himself was not built to be a tailor's dummy; he was almost as broad as he was high and had a face to match. He was famous for his red cardigan, worn in all weathers; it was rumoured that Lenin, on a secret visit to Australia in 1904, had been present at Norway's birth and swaddled the new-born babe in his own cardigan. He was shrewd, had a dry sense of humour and was as ruthless as his Russian idols had been. It was said that he had wept for two days when Stalin had died, though no one had actually witnessed that incredible collapse.

'Are you here to join the union?' His humour could be sardonic.

'No, I'm here to talk progress, Mr Norway.'

The union boss suspected anyone who called him Mr Norway; only the enemy, the other bosses, the capitalists, called him that. 'Who do you represent, Mr Tewsday?'

'Ballyduff Properties.'

'Fingal Hourigan's lot? Get out! You're wasting my time.'

Tewsday didn't move. The union boss's office was a cubby-hole, made even smaller by the piles of pamphlets stacked in each corner: Norway was notorious as the most prolific pamphlet-writer since St Paul, a comparison he found odious. The walls were decorated with posters, all of them threatening: non-Communists were made to feel they were being attacked from all sides. Tewsday, no coward, was undaunted. The pursuit of money has created as many heroes as patriotism.

'Mr Hourigan has nothing to do with this. This is my baby.' His vowels had rounded again. 'I want you to withdraw your support for the tenants and squatters over at North Sydney. In return we'll make a substantial donation to your union's funds.'

'*We?* I thought you said Fingal Hourigan had nothing to do with this? You look as if you couldn't make a donation to the church plate. If you go to church ...'

Tewsday didn't. 'I'm not a church-goer, Mr Norway. I'm a man of the world, like you. Those people over at North Sydney can't stand in the way of progress. We wouldn't be getting rid of them if we weren't sure they could get accommodation elsewhere.'

'Where, for instance?'

'There'll soon be plenty available out west. Mount Druitt is being developed, lots of cheap housing –'

'Out in the bloody backblocks? Would you move out there, get your arse frozen off in winter and the top of your head burnt off in summer? No bloody fear, you wouldn't! Get out, you young arsehole, and shove your money up it! Your old man must be spinning in his grave, no matter what day it is!'

'You're making a mistake you'll regret, Norway –'

The union boss got up from behind his desk, moving with surprising speed, came round and grabbed Tewsday by the scruff of his neck and the seat of his pants. It was an old-fashioned technique, the headlock had not yet come into style, but it was effective. Tewsday, before he could struggle, was tossed out the office door and landed on his hands and knees in the narrow dusty hallway in front of four hefty wharfies come to pay their dues.

'He was trying to sell me a subscription to the *Catholic Weekly*,' Norway told them.

'Never!' said the wharfies and threw up their hands in horror; they were taking Workers' Education lessons in drama. 'Shall we throw him down the stairs?'

'Not a bad idea,' said Norway, grinning. 'Not head first, but. He might chip the woodwork.'

So Tewsday finished up down in the street, battered, bruised and bewildered as to what to do next. Things, over the next couple of weeks, went from bad to worse. Norway, who had friends amongst the older industrial reporters on the city's newspapers, got the right sort of publicity for his campaign on behalf of the tenants and squatters: the little Aussie battlers who were being tossed out on to the streets in the name of Progress. Television had not yet arrived in Australia, that would not come till next year, so there were no two-headed demons to record the banners and the parading pickets and the squatters perched on the roofs of their houses like pugnacious pigeons.

Tewsday stayed out of Fingal's way, meanwhile planning his own campaign. He had never gone in for thuggery; real-estate deals, up till now, had never required more than slick words and envelopes under the table. But the situation, or rather his own, was now becoming desperate. He went to certain rugby union clubs where, even though *union* was in their title, he knew there was no love for trade unions. He enlisted a dozen rugby front-row forwards, all of them famous for their thuggery on the field, everyone a capitalist or hoping to be, and sent them over to North Sydney to confront the wharfies who were now picketing the houses. They lost the match twelve-nil: there was no referee and they hadn't expected to be met by pick-handles. The tenants and squatters sat on their front verandas or stood on their rooftops and cheered as the battle went on. Next day the *Daily Telegraph*, contradicting its industrial reporter, ran an editorial on union brutality. All the rugby league, soccer, Australian Rules, tennis and cricket-following readers nodded their heads in agree-ment, mistaking the union blamed.

Tewsday was now at his wits' end; which, since his wits ran in circles, was not as desperate as it sounds. He went to a night club in King's Cross and spoke to the bouncer on the door. The Cross in those days was not a focus for sleaze and junkies and drug-ridden prostitutes. There were prostitutes, but they were all female, mostly clean and just trying to make an honest living; there were spivs and crooks, but they didn't mug one in the street; and there were the odd one or two professional killers who didn't charge an exorbitant fee. The night-club bouncer, a giant named Jack Paxit, was not a killer but had a friend who was.

'Who you want done? *Him?* Jesus, sport, that's asking for trouble. It'll cost you.'

'How much?'

'It'll take two blokes, I reckon. So me mate'll have to get a helper. Six hundred quid.' A fair price: inflation was not a worry in those days.

'Five hundred.' Tewsday could not forget his real-estate training, it was natural for him to bargain.

'Six hundred, sport, take it or leave it. I gotta get my cut.'

'Can I trust you to forget I ever came to you?'

'Sport, you're the Invisible Man. You ever see that fillum with Claude Rains? I was just a kid . . . I never seen you, sport, never heard your name. When you want it done?'

'As soon as possible.'

Two days later Nev Norway disappeared and to this day nobody knows where he went.

Fingal had conveniently taken himself out of the country during all this. He had gone to Hong Kong, renewed acquaintance with some of his old gold-smuggling contacts who, like himself, were now looking for less dangerous pursuits. In partnership with them he started buying up what little land remained in Hong Kong. From there he had gone to Japan, but the Japanese had defeated him with their bland politeness and smiling masks. He liked to recognize the taste for larceny in the eyes of those he took as partners, but the Japanese had the gaze of neither larcenous nor honest men: blank eyes seemed to look right through him. He came back to Sydney convinced that they would some day rule the world. They had lost only the shortest of wars, the military one.

On his first day back at the office he was driven into the company garage in his three-year-old Jaguar Mark VII. As he got out of the car he saw Jonathan Tewsday drive in in a Jaguar XK 120. He dismissed his chauffeur, then walked the length of the garage to accost Tewsday.

'Is that car yours? How can you afford it?'

'It's second-hand, Mr Hourigan. I'm paying it off.'

'Get rid of it. If my shareholders find out you're driving something like that, they'll think I'm over-paying you.' Since his holding company owned 40 per cent of all his public companies, he had no respect for his shareholders, but, like tradition, they occasionally had their uses. 'See me in my office at ten sharp.'

Tewsday, brimming with resentment but keeping the lid on, presented himself to Fingal sharp at ten o'clock. Was he going to be sacked? Already he was thinking of other companies where he could present himself. He was not yet a general but he had the makings of one: he went into nothing without making sure of a good line of retreat.

Fingal wasted no time in preliminaries: 'What's happened to Nev Norway?'

'I have no idea, sir,' said Tewsday and succeeded for a moment in assuming a cherubic look, albeit that of a fallen one.

'You didn't arrange his disappearance?'

'No, sir. He had plenty of enemies, including the Government down in Canberra.'

'You think Menzies had him got rid of?' Fingal laughed, a sound as dry as a bedouin's cough. 'The Prime Minister doesn't have people bumped off. He's subtler than that. They get postings to Washington or somewhere. He's dead, isn't he?'

'The Prime Minister?'

'Don't be a smart-arse, son. You'll never hold your own with me. Norway.'

Tewsday hesitated, then nodded. He knew he was on a cliff-edge and for the first time he felt the vertigo of the unconfident. 'I've heard that, sir.'

'Where'd you hear it?'

He lied, 'From one or two reporters on the papers, industrial roundsmen. And a crime reporter.'

Fingal looked at him shrewdly. He knew this young man was crooked, but he would never have suspected him of arranging a murder. All the young, and old, murderers he had known back in Chicago had been as obvious as if they had worn badges or had been cast in their roles by Hollywood. Since coming to Australia he had had to employ murderers only once and his go-between then had been a lawyer who had looked as murderous as some of the clients he had defended. The lawyer had since conveniently died and Fingal now felt safe from any connection with the murder. He would have to watch any possible connection with the disappearance of Nev Norway.

'Have the police been to question you?'

'Yes, sir. I could tell them nothing.'

'Were they satisfied with that?'

'I think so.' Tewsday was beginning to feel a little easier. If he had been about to be sacked, it would have been over by now. Fingal Hourigan would never slow down the guillotine.

'Have you got rid of the tenants and squatters?'

'Not yet. I think I can arrange that in a week or two.'

'Don't kick 'em out in the street. Buy up some cheap flats somewhere and move them there at our expense.'

'Do we need to go to that expense, sir? It's only a matter of a few days – they've lost the guts to fight since Norway disappeared –'

'You'd better learn something about public relations if you want to keep working for me.' Fingal had never worried before about public relations, particularly in business; all of a sudden he had been bitten by that most debilitating of bugs, an urge for respectability. Or anyway to be outside of any police questioning. 'Buy the flats and move them. Talk to Borsolino about writing 'em off against tax – he'll find a way. No publicity, if you can avoid it. Let this whole thing die down as soon as possible.'

'What about the houses? How soon do you want them knocked down?'

'Leave it as long as you can. The papers won't come back to the story. Let the architects get all the plans for the new building done and then we'll knock the houses down.'

Tewsday stood up, knowing he was safe. 'I'm sure all this will turn out satisfactorily, Mr Hourigan.' He sounded smug, a tone no employer should ever condone.

Fingal didn't. 'Get rid of your car, get a Holden or something.'

'Of course, sir.' Tewsday swapped smugness for obsequiousness, another mistake. Only kings, presidents and prime ministers can suffer it.

'Don't crawl,' said Fingal. 'And in future, no murders, understand? This is a reputable company.'

'Yes, sir,' said Tewsday, this time neither smug nor obsequious, just afraid. This tough old bastard would always have the edge on him.

Next day Tewsday sold his XK 120, at a profit. A month later Fingal took delivery of his first Rolls-Royce, a black Silver Cloud. It made him more conspicuous than he wanted to be, but, he told himself, he had to have a car worthy of the castle he was having built at Vaucluse. It certainly put all the other cars in the Ballyduff garage in their place.

Two months later the houses in North Sydney were knocked down. The event made none of the newspapers, not even any of the trades unions' news bulletins. Occasionally, when news was dead, references would be made to the disappearance of Nev Norway, but nothing ever came of them. In the atmosphere of that period a dead Commo, even a murdered one, got no more sympathy than a live one. Fragments of what might have been a red cardigan had been picked up in their nets by fishermen off Coogee beach, but they didn't report it to the police; people were always tossing their garbage and old clothes into the sea. The tenants and squatters who, no matter how indirectly, had been the cause of Norway's disappearance, settled down in their new flats, went on being little Aussie battlers, though one or two turned traitor by having a good word to say about Ballyduff Properties.

A year later Jonathan Tewsday was running his own small development division in Ballyduff. He had sold his second-hand Holden and ventured to buy a new Rover; Fingal made no comment. The two met only once a month, when Fingal presided over a management meeting, but Tewsday was now just one of the team. The only contest between the two men was their search for respectability.

Then in September 1956, at the launching of Fingal's new television station, Tewsday met the Hourigan siblings, Kerry and Brigid, for the first time.

## 2

Television had just been introduced to Australia and Fingal, putting together a consortium of merchant bankers, indus-trialists, radio executives, plus two writers, two producers and two elderly actors to add a touch of the arts, had applied for a television licence and been granted one. Within two years he would have disposed of all his partners, the artists getting the chop first, and then would have, as a newspaper owned by a failed rival bidder would say, a licence to print his own money.

Television was such a new toy that the launching of the new station enticed Kerry along to one of his father's business functions. He got leave from the seminary and, picked up by Brigid in her new MG, was driven out to Carlingford in the western suburbs to the new complex.

'How's the Jesus business going?'

Brigid was now almost seventeen, looked twenty and had had no trouble getting her driver's licence. She was beautiful, sexy-looking enough to have had Picasso, had he seen her, dropping his brushes and his pants at first sight of her. She had just started art classes with an old local artist who had once been as gamey as Picasso but no longer had any lead in his pencil.

'I hope you don't talk like that about me to your friends.' Kerry was now twenty-one, big, beefy and handsome, ideal clay for the cardinal he still hoped to be.

'I'll never understand you, Kerry. You're no more religious than I am. Oh, you may not go in for sin and all that, but you don't have a true vocation.'

She had inherited her father's shrewd appraisal of men. She had also, unfortunately, inherited her mother's passion for them; or, rather, what they offered her. She had been expelled from the Rose Bay Convent after being found in a garden shed with one of the young gardeners; that suburban Mellors had been the first of half a dozen lovers as the junior Lady Chatterley had moved on up the social scale. She was a sinner, but she would never be repentant, least of all to her brother the trainee priest.

'Are you running away from the world?'

'No.' He would have to be patient with her; she had guessed the truth, or anyway the half-truth, of him. Already he knew that he would never be able to suffer the duties of a parish curate or priest; the hoi-polloi flock would have to look for another shepherd. 'It's useless trying to explain a vocation to someone who doesn't have it. It's not the same as under-standing your predilection for sin – I understand that.'

'My predilection for sin! God, you're already talking like an archbishop!'

She couldn't have given him higher praise. 'Keep your eye on the road. I don't want to have to give the two of us Extreme Unction.' At the seminary they taught him to think in Capitals, as if God were a grammarian.

'God,' she said, though He was only a very casual acquaint-ance nowadays, 'how could I have had you as a brother?'

Fingal, spending the consortium's money, had spared none of it to make the television complex the best in the country. Huge and lavish, it seemed like an affront to the small fibro and timber cottages that surrounded it, the homes of the little Aussie battlers who would look to it for their escape from

131

their drudgery and their debt worries. Fingal knew the venture could not fail; better to spend the money now while the pound still had value. Nowhere in the world were television station owners going broke. BHN Channel 8 was a gold mine standing in landscaped gardens.

As they drew into the parking lot Kerry heard the music coming from a nearby building. 'What on earth is that?'

'They're putting on a separate party for the staff who are going to work here. None of them know anything, but they'll all be experts within a week.' She was repeating her father's opinion.

'No, I mean that awful music.'

'Oh God, what sort of stuff do you hear in the seminary? That's rock and roll, the new music. It sounds like Bill Haley and "Rock Around the Clock".'

Kerry shook his head in wonder. 'Whatever's going to happen to Guy Lombardo?'

The party for the executives was more sedate. The only music was the humming of praise for the opportunities that lay ahead. Jonathan Tewsday, the most junior executive there, stood in a corner and sipped champagne, Australian, of course, since Fingal, seeing further opportunities, had just gone into vineyards. When the sexy-looking pretty girl came in with the young novice priest, Tewsday knew she had to be saved.

When the priest left the girl, Tewsday went up to her, taking two glasses of champagne with him. 'To help you relax.'

'Oh, I'm relaxed, all right. But my father won't let me drink alcohol in public.'

'Who's your father?'

'The chairman, Mr Hourigan.'

Though he had never met or even seen photographs of them, Tewsday now recognized the young girl and the priest. These were the Hourigan heirs, never spoken of by the chairman, never discussed by his executives; but always there in the background, the sometime future bosses. 'I'm Jonathan Tewsday, one of your father's junior executives. Are you at university?'

'No, I'm an art student.'

'What do you paint?' He knew nothing about art and had no interest in it. Endorsement and sponsorship of the arts had not yet become fashionable in the commercial and industrial world; money was still being spent only to make money. Art, and artists, should be self-supporting.

'Naked men, mostly. I'm going to specialize in portraits of penises.' She was learning the youthful pleasure of being outrageous; later she would recognize that outrageousness was the last resort of the untalented. So far she was not certain how much talent she had.

He clenched his scalp, holding on to his already thinning hair. 'Will there be a living in it?' As if, in her circumstances, that mattered.

'Do you think I need to care?' she said, reading his mind. She had already dismissed him as the sort of young man in whom she would never show any interest. Plump and sleek as a young seal, one for whom appearances would be an abiding preoccupation, the urge for riches oozing out of him, he was everything she currently despised. Her father's riches allowed her to be comfortably and snobbishly idealistic, some-thing else she would grow out of. 'Oh, this is my brother Kerry. This is Mr Tewsday, a junior executive.'

She moved off on that insult and Kerry smiled uncomfort-ably. 'Don't take any notice of her, Mr Tewsday. Underneath, she's really a very nice kid.'

'Are you being charitable because you're her brother or because you're a priest?'

'Oh, I'm not a priest yet, just a trainee. Like you as an executive.' Kerry, too, could toss an insult: he and Brigid were not their father's children for nothing.

Tewsday wanted to ask him why any young man in today's world, so full of opportunity, would want to be a priest; but such a question, he guessed, would be another insult. He knew as much about religion as he did about art.

'Do they let you out much? I mean to parties like this?'

'Oh, they don't make us live a monastic life, if that's what you mean. They like to expose us to temptation occasionally, just so's we'll recognize it.'

'There's plenty here,' said Tewsday, looking around. 'Wine and women.'

'I'm not tempted,' said Kerry, smiling.

'Where will you finish up?'

'When I'm ordained or later on? The Church is just like working for my father. You don't shoot to the top in a rush. I'm patient.'

Tewsday all at once recognized another man with ambition; it surprised him, because he thought all clerics were supposed to be humble. 'You'd like to be a bishop or something?'

'A cardinal, actually,' said Kerry, smiled and walked away.

Tewsday looked after him, then looked across at Brigid, holding court to several of her father's more senior executives. Even so young, she was the best of all flirts, an arrogant one: men like to be trampled on before, as they think, they conquer. The senior executives, Don Juans in their own imagination, middle-aged fools in the eyes of their watching wives, jostled each other to catch her attention. Tewsday turned and saw Fingal Hourigan watching the group. The look in the old man's eyes told him that each of the senior executives had been put on probation. He looked for pride in the old man's face, but there was none, at least not in his daughter. That only showed when he looked across the room at his son. God damn! thought Tewsday: by the time I get to the top in this corporation, I'll have a cardinal as a chairman.

Fingal had taken the monsignor in charge of the seminary to dinner at the Union club. He had joined that conservative establishment last year as part of the consolidation of his respectability; there had been one or two demurs from some of the elderly, stuffier members, but no one had black-balled him. The committee would have preferred a new member whose family could be traced back, preferably on the land or one of the more respected ways of making money; they would not have wanted the tracing to go back too far, for fear that a convict ancestor might have been unearthed; the rattle of chains in a family closet had not yet become a patriotic jingle. At least a man with no family line had no skeletons visible. And he did have money, lots of it, something that was now beginning to have a respectability of its own.

The monsignor was not out of place in the club, even though a Catholic; he came of an old moneyed family and it showed. 'A nice Burgundy, Mr Hourigan. We're producing some fine wines in Australia these days.'

'Do you use them on the altar?'

'Of course.' The monsignor was a cheerful man, only occasionally depressed by the classes he taught. A radical student would have brightened his life, but the seminaries, like the universities of the day, seemed full of conservative youth. He wondered what the coming decades would bring. He had read the new English play, *Look Back in Anger*, and he wondered if, when the play came to Sydney, he should take his classes to see it. 'Why did you want to see me? Are you going to make a gift to the seminary or is it just about Kerry?'

'You're a smart man, Cliff. Okay you'll get your gift. Now what about Kerry? How's he making out?'

'The smartest one I've had in years. We are taught – and teach – not to be fulsome. But I have to say your son is brilliant. He is very sound in theology, history, all that, but he is positively brilliant at administration. He is bishop material, if ever I've seen it.' The Burgundy had made him fulsome.

'Nothing more than a bishop?'

'Ah, that is in God's hands,' said the monsignor and smiled, because he knew it wasn't.

'How do we influence God then?'

'Pray, Fingal, pray. Are you good at that?'

'I'm good at anything I put my mind to.' But he wouldn't know how to start praying.

In the closed room of his mind he had begun to have megalomaniacal dreams. If Kerry had been American-born he would have made him President. Something like that was happening now in the United States; word had reached him of Joseph Kennedy's campaign to have his eldest surviving son nominated as the next Democrat presidential candidate. But, since Kerry was Australian-born and Australia amounted to nothing in the world politically, he had begun to dream of other empires. And so had come, as an extension of Kerry's own ambition, which he recognized now was genuine and strong, to the idea of an Australian-born Pope. So far he had not mentioned the idea to Kerry. He looked across the table and wondered if, half-jokingly, he should mention it to this worldly cleric. But no: the monsignor would treat it as a joke. So would the rest of the Church. The Italians, who ran the Church and thought they had a God-given right to the Papacy, would laugh, then scratch their heads, wondering where Australia was. No Pope had yet found it.

'Can you save him from the backblocks when he's ordained?'

'It'll be out of my hands, Fingal. But I'll do my best to recommend him to some admin. office. I don't think he's cut out for weddings and christenings. I'm not myself, especially christenings. Many's the time I've wanted to hold the squawling brat under the water, instead of splashing him with it.'

Kerry was ordained in 1962. Brigid, rebelling against her father, wheedling money out of her trust account by sleeping with one of the trustees, one of her father's lawyers, had left for Paris in late 1958. She had kissed her father goodbye, the first time she had kissed him in six years.

'Don't be angry, Dad. You have Kerry to fuss over.'

'I don't fuss over anyone.'

'No, that's not true.' Certainly not over her. She had been only fourteen when she had recognized the tribal sign: the son was the one who counted. 'But some day you may be proud of me. I'm a good artist and I'm going to be much better.'

'I'll never understand you,' Fingal had said.

'I don't think you understand *women*. You've never talked about her, but did you ever understand Mother? What made her mental? You?'

'Never!' he said fiercely. He would never have done that to the golden-haired girl who still occasionally slept with him in his dreams. 'It was in her genes. I didn't know when we married, but her grandmother went mad when she was only twenty-five.'

'Then I might go mad, too?'

'I doubt it.' He looked at her, sane, confident and seemingly invulnerable. He loved her, but he couldn't show it. The Irish do share a few characteristics with the English; sometimes he wondered if he were Anglo-Irish instead of pure Irish. He had the piratical inclinations of the English. 'You're a Hourigan through and through.'

'No insanity there?'

None that he knew of; but perhaps his ambition for his son was a form of insanity. Brigid went off to Paris, wrote home twice a year and told her father and her brother nothing. Then she came home for Kerry's ordination.

Fingal threw a reception afterwards in the castle on the waterfront at Vaucluse, where he had been living for the past five years. As if having a new priest for a son were some sort of protection, he invited the half a dozen women he had been sleeping with for the past ten years. They were youngish widows, divorcees and one career woman, a TV chat show hostess. None of them had known of the others, but, with that instinct that is more highly developed in mistresses than in wives, risk always heightening the senses, they recognized the up-till-then unknown competition as soon as they saw it. Fingal greeted each with a peck on the cheek and nothing more, stood safe between his son and daughter, the Church and Art.

'My son, Father Hourigan. And my daughter Brigid, home from Paris and living with Picasso.'

'Unfortunately not,' said Brigid, wondering which one of the women was her father's regular bed-mate.

It was an early summer day and the reception was being held in the garden of the big house. It was an Italian-style garden, all stone balustrades and clipped hedges and pebble paths, a proper setting for a young priest destined eventually for the Vatican; but none of the guests, not even the seminary's monsignor, caught the significance. Only the guest of honour's sister saw it.

'Has Dad booked you into the Vatican yet?' she said when she and Kerry were alone.

'Aren't you pleased I'm a priest?'

She bit her lip and for a moment looked as if she might weep. He was shocked; he had never seen her cry, not even as a child. He knew nothing of the childhood tears in the lonely bedroom.

'Of course I am. It's what you've always wanted, isn't it?'

'Ever since I got the vocation for it.'

She looked at him out of the corner of her eye. 'You really do have a vocation?'

'I really do,' he said, and out on the harbour there was a sudden flash of sunlight, as if God had fired a warning shot.

She looked down at the garden from the terrace where they stood. 'There should be a maze.'

'Do they have mazes in Italian gardens?'

'Didn't Machiavelli invent the maze?' She had no idea if Machiavelli had, indeed, ever been in a garden of any sort; but she had just spent almost four years in Paris and learned the French trick of answering questions with a question. Then below her she saw a face she recognized, though the scalp above it had widened. 'Why, it's – I've forgotten your name. Friday, Saturday? The junior executive.'

Tewsday, thirty now and almost bald, came up on to the terrace as Kerry left his sister and went into the house. 'Not any more – a junior executive, that is. Jonathan Tewsday.'

'Of course! Is there a Mrs Tewsday and lots of little days of the week?'

She hadn't changed in her attitude towards businessmen. An independent income is the best support for an artist's standards; idealism flowers beautifully when watered by a trust fund. She would never need the likes of Jonathan Tewsday.

She was still beautiful, but had become a flamboyant dresser; if her brother ever became a cardinal, it would be a race between them to see who caught the eye. She was dressed in black-and-white chequered knickerbockers, white silk shirt and black-and-white chequered cap, with a red silk scarf tied to the handle of her black handbag. It was her *Jules et Jim* look, but Jules and Jim and Pierre and Yves and Roger and Daniel had all been left back in Paris where, like Fingal's mistresses, they did not know of each other.

Tewsday thought she looked terrific, but wouldn't have walked down the street with her. He knew nothing about women's fashion, he was too intent on his own wardrobe. 'I've learned about Art since we last met. Let's go out to dinner and talk about it.'

'All right,' she said on the whim that was part of her mother's bequest, 'let's go now.'

'Do you want to change?'

'Why? Don't you like this?'

'Love it,' he said and hoped they wouldn't be seen by anyone he knew. 'Do we have to ask your father's permission to go?'

'Never do that,' she said. 'He delights in saying no.'

Fingal, who could see in a dozen directions at once, saw them go. He had come to appreciate the worth of Tewsday, but never gave him any verbal encouragement, just promotion and a salary increase; which was all Tewsday craved, since

139

praise wasn't bankable. He had distinguished himself the previous year when there had been a massive credit squeeze throughout the country. Ballyduff had been awash with liquidity and Tewsday had gained an audience with the chairman. He had brought a list of companies that, unknown to the general market, were on the verge of bankruptcy and ready for takeover. Fingal, though he had said nothing, had been impressed by his junior's inside knowledge. He had also had inside knowledge of the extent of the newly discovered iron ore deposits in north-west Australia, the biggest ever found, and he suggested early investment there. Fingal, after having them checked, had given him the go-ahead on all the suggestions. Tewsday was on his way, a young man to be watched, as business circles said, and no one watched him more closely than his executive chairman. He was not to be encouraged too much, especially by the chairman's daughter.

'Don't worry, Dad,' said Kerry, coming to stand beside his father. 'Brigid can look after herself.'

'It's him I'm worried about,' said Fingal, but that wasn't true. He wanted no one in the corporation admitted to the family. An outsider, once admitted, might want to know the secrets of the family.

Brigid stayed in Sydney a month on that visit. She went out with Jonathan Tewsday three or four times and went to bed with him once; not out of any attraction to him or liking for him but out of her own sexual hunger. She was at a loose end, something she confessed to no one, hardly even to herself. Her development as a painter seemed to be standing still and, almost as bad, her one sustained love affair, with Jules, who was married, was petering out. The future, which for the young is tomorrow, had begun to look like a washed-out fresco.

She went back to Paris, determined not to confess failure to her father, and Kerry, certain of success, taking the long view, went into a desk job with the Catholic Education Office. Tewsday went back to making money for Ballyduff and Fingal sat in his chairman's chair and waited patiently for the future, in which he was certain he would have a controlling interest.

# 3

Brigid took up again with her married Frenchman, a lawyer who specialized in divorce and large settlements. But he was only a *cinq à sept* lover; he would not leave his wife, who was as rich as Brigid and, when she put her mind to it, a far better cook. In February 1963 Brigid discovered she was pregnant. Trying to force her Frenchman to leave his wife and at least live with her, if not marry her, she refused to have an abortion. Jules the lawyer declined the invitation, all at once honourable towards his wife, an occasional French habit. Brigid went to London and had her baby on the National Health, a choice that was a subconscious thumbing of her nose at the *bourgeoisie*, her lover and her father, neither of whom would ever understand her rebellious nature. Teresa was born on November 22, 1963, a terrible day in history. Brigid wept for her, hoping it was not an omen.

She did not see her father and brother again till Teresa was two years old. Fingal came to London occasionally in that period, but Brigid contrived to be somewhere on the Continent when he was there. She did it out of perversity, another of her mother's bequests; but she also did not want Fingal assuming a proprietary interest in Teresa, though it was difficult to see him as a grandparent, especially a doting one. She had not told him directly of the child's birth, but had mentioned (confessed?) it in a letter to Kerry, who had written back and told her how delighted he was for her sake, if that was what she wanted.

Then the two Hourigan men came to Europe together, Fingal to do business in Germany, Kerry to attend a short course in Rome. They met in Zurich, Brigid coming there from Lerici, in Lyguria, where she now lived.

'You didn't bring the child?' said Fingal.

'I wasn't sure you'd want to see her.'

He wasn't sure himself, but, 'She's my granddaughter.'

'And my niece,' said Kerry, trying to sound avuncular or anyway espiscopal, which is much the same thing.

'What would you have done with her if I'd brought her? Played kitchy-koo with her? Neither of you are child-lovers – you make W. C. Fields look like Santa Claus. You'll meet her eventually, but I wasn't going to bring her here and display her like some toy doll. She's not my toy, she's my child.'

They were having lunch in Fingal's suite in the Baur au Lac, looking out on the lake. She had noticed that Kerry took the luxury for granted; though a priest, he was still his father's son. Luxury, so far, had not concerned her. Her trust allowance allowed her to live very comfortably and she had that reassuring backstop that the children of the rich always have, family money that would pay for any emergency. So far she had not had to call on her father for help and she hoped she would never have to.

'Are you living with anyone?' said Fingal.

'No.' An Italian writer came down from Milan every second weekend to stay with her, but that couldn't be called *living* with anyone. 'Are you?'

Kerry was the one who looked shocked, not Fingal. 'What sort of question is that!'

'It's all right, Kerry,' said Fingal. 'I asked her the same question. She has a right to throw it back at me. No, I'm not, Brigid.'

'Why did you never marry again?'

'Because I'm still in love with your mother.' It was an amazing admission from him: he had never mentioned the word *love* in their hearing. Both of them waited for him to go on; but he had said enough. 'Do you want sweets?'

'No,' said Brigid, 'I want you to talk about Mother, what she was like before . . .'

'That's a closed book.'

'You obviously haven't closed it, not entirely.'

Fingal sat silent, suddenly withdrawn, and after a moment Kerry said quietly, 'I think we'd better leave it, Bridie.' It was the name he had called her as a child.

Brigid felt she had almost entered a half-closed door; or rather, the closed book that had been their father's life. She had felt on the verge of *knowing* him at long last, but he had shut her out once again. She decided, then and there, that it would be for the last time.

She went back to Lerici, to the delightful village on the Gulf of La Spezia where she was renting a villa once owned by the Baroness Orczy, where that lady had written *The Scarlet Pimpernel*. Brigid looked down over olive groves, across the village to the old castle high on the point; beyond it was the arm of the gulf that reached round to Portavenere. She had tried painting the landscape and the seascape, experimenting with the interpretation of light, but her brush, she knew, was lifeless. It only came alive when she painted *people*, but even with them as subjects she was finding it difficult to have something to say. Mostly, she sat in the sun on her terrace and took delight in being a mother as Teresa continued to grow.

Three months after her return from Zurich, someone turned up on her doorstep; but he was no pimpernel, even though he carried a bunch of primroses. Tewsday had always been heavy-handed in his courting.

'I was in the neighbourhood, so I thought I'd drop in.'

'The neighbourhood? In Lerici?'

'Well, not Lerici, exactly. Genoa, actually. Your father is buying into a shipping line and he sent me over to look into it.'

'Did he tell you I was living here?' She knew he would not have.

'No. You know your father, he never tells anyone about his family. No, I dropped in on Kerry in Rome.'

'Dropped in again?'

'Well, not dropped in, exactly. Bumped into, actually. I met him at the airport. He was going back to Sydney and I was changing planes to go up to Genoa.'

'Where are you staying?'

'Well, actually –' He was still out on the terrace, had not yet been invited inside. He stood back and looked at the villa. 'I was hoping it was big enough for you to have a spare room for the night. Oh, who's this? One of your servant's children?'

'No, she's mine,' said Brigid flatly and made no attempt to introduce the $2\frac{1}{2}$-year-old Teresa. 'Well, come in.'

It was a Thursday and the Italian writer was not due till tomorrow night. Tewsday took her to dinner that evening in the Albergo Shelley and across the zabaglione and the last of the Tuscan wine he said, 'Kerry told me about your villa and *The Scarlet Pimpernel*. You're like the Pimpernel himself, so damned elusive.'

'You read it?'

'Oh, I used to be a great reader.'

'Shelley lived here in this house, before it became a hotel.' The great reader looked blank. 'Percy Bysshe Shelley. The poet. Byron lived down there, at the Casa Magni. He used to swim across here to visit Shelley.'

'Ah, I never read much poetry. Queers, were they?'

She took him home then, but not to her bed. He tried to get into it, but she kicked him out. 'What about your wife?'

'I'm not married, for God's sake!'

That surprised her. She thought he would be well married by now, smug and snug with a businessman's wife in a businessman's home, the kids, born or unborn, already registered for Cranbrook or Ascham schools, their lives mapped out like business charts.

'Brigid – listen – I want to marry you!' His voice was loud in the bare-walled, marble-tiled bedroom.

She fell back amongst the pillows laughing till she gave herself a stitch. He stood at the end of her bed in his pyjama trousers, Richard Hunt's best silk, the long hair along his temples standing out: his plump face looked like a moon about to fly off in a fury. It is not true that there is no fury like a woman scorned; Congreve, who said that, had never been spurned by a man. Tewsday came close to murder that night. All that saved her was that he did not have the courage to strike the blow himself, there were no thugs to do the deed for him. He had been rejected before, but he could not stand being laughed at. From that moment on he hated her; had he loved her, he might have reacted differently. But he loved only three things: money, success and himself. He stamped out of her room, out of the house, out of Italy, went back to courting success and money. He did not need to court himself: that love was consummated every time he looked in the mirror.

Back in Sydney, meanwhile, Father Kerry Hourigan made his first mistake as a priest. He had been moved from the Catholic Education Office to be an assistant to the Bishop-Coadjutor, a man so renowned for his misogynism that he made St Paul look like Don Juan. A newspaper columnist rang the Bishop's office and asked for a comment on Australian women's apparent hunger for the Pill, which they were swallowing at twice the rate of women elsewhere. Kerry answered the phone, said, 'Perhaps they think they're jelly-beans,' and hung up.

It was a harmless, facetious remark; but the columnist that day was short of material. He rang a well-known chain of confectionery shops, asked its opinion of the relationship between the Pill and jelly-beans, then wrote his column. The next day the LOLLY WAR BETWEEN CATHOLIC CHURCH AND DARREL LEA was the joke of Sydney.

Kerry was sent for by the Bishop-Coadjutor and exiled to the bush. 'I have no time for women, but I'm not prepared to be made a fool of because of them and their lust.' He was as purple-faced as his shirt-front.

Fingal got in touch with the monsignor at the seminary, who managed to get him a meeting with the Cardinal, a man known as Cement Crotch because of his habit of sitting on the fence on all controversial matters. The Cardinal was sympathetic, but said he couldn't over-rule the Bishop-Coadjutor.

Kerry was sent to a country town as curate to an old Irish priest who drank beer by the gallon, coached the local rugby team, understood the sins of those who crowded his confessional and gave them lenient penance, and who preached against Communism with all the fire and rhetoric of an old-time evangelist. Kerry hated life in the country town, hated the Saturday evenings in the confessional, but the old Irish priest, unwittingly, put him on to the cause that would lead him to Rome. The Vietnam War was warming up, the Domino Theory was a constant catch-cry in editorials and the Threat of Communism was now more important than the possibility of defeat at cricket by the West Indians or the Englishmen. Kerry had discovered the torch he had to carry into the future.

Brigid wrote to him to commiserate, in a mildly sarcastic way, on his having to go out and wash away the sins of the Great Unwashed. She mentioned, in passing, that Jonathan Tewsday had paid her an unwelcome visit and had reduced her to hysterics by asking her to marry him. *It was not just him*, she wrote, *but the thought of marrying any businessman just breaks me up. I can't imagine anything more boring . . .*

Kerry didn't share his sister's jaundiced opinion of businessmen; they certainly weren't as boring as farmers. He did not, however, like Jonathan Tewsday, whom he had now met several times and he would certainly not want him as a brother-in-law. He wrote his father a weekly letter and in one of them he mentioned Tewsday's visit to Brigid and his proposal of marriage.

A day after receiving the letter Fingal sent for Tewsday. 'Pack your bags. I'm sending you to Wellington.'

'Wellington, *New Zealand*? But that's Antarctica!'

'Then you'd better take a fur coat. You're taking over our office there and I'm bringing Parkinson to Sydney.'

'I'd like to know what I've done to deserve this, Mr Hourigan –'

'You've stepped out of line,' said Fingal.

Tewsday knew at once what he meant. 'I think my private life is my own affair, Mr Hourigan –'

'Not when you try to link it with mine.'

Fingal had thought long and hard last night whether he should get rid of Tewsday altogether. He recognized the social as well as the business ambitions of the younger man; not that he concerned himself too much with his own social status, but he knew that Fingal Hourigan's son-in-law would always be in demand for the big social occasions. He also knew that there was no risk that Brigid would take Tewsday as her husband; she, too, was without social ambition. Tewsday's crime was that he had dared to think of himself as Fingal's son-in-law.

Tewsday pondered a moment, then said, 'I think I'll resign, then.'

Fingal remarked the half-hearted threat. He was tempted for a moment to accept the resignation: he wanted to drive the knife deep into the smug young man. He was, however, a businessman and he could never shut out business, not even to feed his spite. Tewsday was the up-and-coming young man in Sydney's, if not the country's, business world. He would be grabbed by any one of half a dozen other corporations, and Fingal would never give a competitor the time of day let alone his most valued protégé. Yet Tewsday had to be taught a lesson.

'A year in New Zealand will give you time to think about it. There's nothing else there to do.'

Tewsday, for his part, did not want to leave Ballyduff. He knew he could walk into any other corporation in town and virtually write his own ticket. There was, however, no other corporation in town, or indeed the country, which showed the potential to dominate the national scene as Ballyduff undoubtedly would in the next five years. Tewsday had developed the long view into an art; tomorrow was next year, the day after, five years hence. If he stayed with Ballyduff, put up with the year's exile in Wellington, he would be running this company before he was fifty years old. In his late forties, amongst the greybeards then running most of the country's corporations, he would be the Young Turk.

'Just a year?'

'That will depend on what you do with the possibilities there. There must be *something* that can be developed there.' Fingal never looked in the direction of New Zealand; to him it was just a northern suburb of Antarctica. The national religion was rugby, there were fifteen Apostles called the All Blacks, and New Zealand racehorses always won the Melbourne Cup. He sometimes wondered why, like Tasmania, it was on the map. He was not alone in his myopia in Australia. 'You can leave on Friday.'

So Jonathan Tewsday went to New Zealand to do his penance. He did not beat his breast or order sackcloth from Richard Hunt's. He did, however, take the long view on his growing hatred of the Hourigans. Some day they would all pay.

# 4

Tewsday returned to Sydney and the headquarters of Ballyduff in September 1967, bringing back with him a pregnant wife. She came from one of the most socially acceptable families in New Zealand, a pioneer clan that had produced some of the finest merino wool in the world, though not from family members; two of the country's leading bankers; a Cabinet minister; and three All Blacks. The family didn't think much of the Australian who had no interest in sheep or rugby, but the daughter of the clan, a good-looking girl named Fiona, had a mind of her own and, like her husband-to-be, a long view. She knew she could never be an All Black, would always be a second-class citizen, always in the shadows in the Land of the Long White Cloud, so she took the opportunity to escape to Australia where, she had heard, women were learning to break free of their chains. She also loved Jonathan, though she sometimes wondered why. She consoled herself that she was probably not the first woman who had had doubts about her one true love. There is no evidence that she was blind in love after she dipped into the fruit.

Tewsday, with that sleek confidence of the unabashable, moved back into Ballyduff as if he had never been away. Fingal gave him no special welcome, did not even bother to mention his stay in New Zealand. He had done his exile term, had brought back a wife and so settled his social course and, most importantly, had trebled the investments and profits of the New Zealand subsidiary. Tewsday had also multiplied his hatred of Fingal Hourigan, but was prepared to bide his time for his revenge.

Kerry also came back from exile. His talents, the archdiocese soon realized, were too great to be wasted in the bush; the farmers could be relied upon to find their own way to salvation. Word of his understanding of and passion against the threat of Communism had got back to Sydney. He was what was needed in Rome, where there was a new crusade and where, said the Cardinal, separating national pride from religious expediency, there were not enough Australians.

'You're on your way,' said Fingal. 'Now don't bugger it up by making any more facetious remarks. Stick to Communism – you can never be facetious about that. Will you want any more money?'

'I'd like something comfortable in Rome. I don't want to have to share accommodation with some other recruit from overseas – Lord knows whom I might get.' Kerry would always look for creature comforts; he had no wish to be compared with St Francis of Assisi, poverty was for the birds. 'Perhaps you could buy one of the old *palazzi*, say it was your Rome *pied-à-terre*, and I could live in it.'

149

Fingal smiled, 'You sound just like you did when you were fourteen years old. Show a little modesty for a start. We'll get you a small flat, something that won't make the bishops or even the monsignors envious. We'll get you a car, too.'

'A Lancia,' said Kerry, who, had he been a disciple, would never have followed The Lord on foot.

'A Fiat *cinquecento*,' said Fingal, who had a better sense of the value of modesty.

'I'll never fit into it.'

'Just shrink your ego, that's all you need to do.'

Kerry went to Rome, where Brigid came once to visit him with her new lover, a Communist Party official from Bologna. The two men got on well together, much to the chagrin of both of them and the amusement of Brigid; each recognized in the other a man constrained by the austerities of his beliefs. Brigid took them out to dinner at the Grand Hotel, fed them lobster and pheasant and wild strawberries from Sardinia and had a wonderful time, since she was the only one not troubled by conscience. She did not bring Teresa to Rome and Kerry made only a polite enquiry about his niece.

On her return to Lerici Brigid broke up with her Communist lover, who wanted her to paint pictures of social significance. With Teresa and an Italian nurse she left Italy for London to throw herself into the last years of the Swinging Sixties. She was surprised to find that she now envied Kerry, began to wish she had some vocation of her own. Romance, or lust, call it what one liked, was no vocation.

Fingal, meanwhile, was discovering his own loneliness. He had enough acquaintances to fill in what empty hours he had; but he had no friends and, despite his bouts of loneliness, wished for none. He also had no desire for romance; but lust still troubled him. A young whore named Tilly Mosman satisfied him there.

He had taken a small apartment in the medical specialists' street, Macquarie Street, in a building where all the other suites were occupied by doctors. If he were seen entering the building, which happened every Thursday in the early evening, it would be assumed that he was visiting one of the doctors. He and Tilly were never seen together; she was always waiting for him in the apartment when he arrived and always left after him. She already had a discretion that was advanced for her years.

'Do you have any other clients?' said Fingal, being indiscreet.

'No,' she said, lying.

'Is this what you want to do for the rest of your life?'

'No, I'd like to own my own house, a high-class one, the best in town. I've been reading the business pages in the *Herald*. They say that service industries are going to be the big thing.'

He smiled. 'This is a service industry? Well, yes, I guess it is. If I financed you, would you ever mention my name to anyone?'

'Have I done that so far?'

'I don't know. Have you?'

'No. What would you do to me if I did?'

'I think I'd have you killed.'

'You wouldn't!' She started up in the bed, suddenly afraid of him for the first time.

'No,' he said; but, he thought, he probably would have to have it done. He would have to give up a lot of pleasures when he became the Pope's father. Though by then he would be beyond all *this*. 'When the time comes, I'll see what we can do about setting you up in your own establishment. But not yet – you're too young.'

'That's what I'd like to be – the youngest madam in the country.'

He couldn't blame her; he had been just as ambitious at her age, even younger. 'We'll see, we'll see.'

In 1969 Australia discovered nickel. Holes suddenly appeared all over the Outback; some of the most worthless land on the planet became as valuable as a building site on Wall Street. Companies sprang up like financial weeds; ordinary men, and women, in the street rushed to fertilize the weeds with their savings. Mining shares rose from ten cents to a hundred dollars almost overnight. Entrepreneurs, a word most Australians had never heard of up till then and certainly couldn't pronounce, came out of the scrub, the desert and the woodwork of one-room offices in the cities and became millionaires as fast as one could say, No Capital Gains Tax. It was the gold-rush of the nineteenth century all over again, except that it took place on the stock exchanges of the nation.

Tewsday floated a new mining company for Ballyduff and Fingal let him have his head. But Tewsday made one of his rare business mistakes. In the rush to beat the competition to the bonanza, he only cursorily checked the so-called mining experts who came to him for backing. Bundiwindi Mining turned out to have much less nickel content in its ore than the 'experts' had claimed.

The Fraud Squad called at Ballyduff headquarters and asked to see Mr Tewsday. The two officers were shown into his office: Inspector Zanuch and a young detective-constable whose name was Maloney or something like that. Tewsday, who had always had the potential, had grown into a snob, a man who failed to recognize inferiors, even in his own organization.

'We were duped, Inspector.' He decided to be utterly frank, he laid his case on the table like a saint pleading guilty to over-zealousness. 'We relied upon those we thought were honest experts.'

'They've fled the country, Mr Tewsday.' Zanuch was already the second-best dressed man on the force, a conservative dandy who matched the man opposite him. Alongside them Detective-Constable Malone looked like a vagrant who had wandered into the wrong room. 'We estimate they've made a quarter of a million dollars each, all tax free, which should buy them a nice hideaway somewhere. That, as they say, leaves you holding the baby.'

'You surely don't think a corporation like ours would be a knowing partner in a conspiracy to defraud? Or, indeed, that I would be?' He had been made a Commander of the British Empire in that year's Honours List: the Empire no longer existed and he commanded nothing, but CBE meant something after one's name, even if most of the natives weren't quite sure what it meant.

Zanuch looked at Malone. 'Constable Malone has dug out some interesting facts, Mr Tewsday. Perhaps you'd like to hear them?'

Malone took out a notebook. 'On November the first last you hosted a lunch at the Wentworth Hotel in a private dining-room. You told a group of bankers and stockbrokers that you personally had been to inspect the mining leases in Western Australia, to wit, the Bundiwindi leases, and that you had then gone on to Perth and seen the ore samples tested for the nickel content you claimed, to wit, eight per cent. The true content was a non-commercial one per cent, is that not right?'

'Where did you get that information?'

'From two of the stockbrokers and one of the bankers present. And from one of the geologists on the leases – he said you'd never been near Bundiwindi.'

Tewsday looked at the young detective. He was tall and well-built, a ramshackle dresser, someone Tewsday felt he didn't need to remember; the police force, he guessed, was full of these nondescripts. 'What makes you think I'd risk my reputation by concocting anything like those men have alleged?'

'Greed?' said the nondescript.

Tewsday gave him a hard, second look then. 'That's an indiscreet remark, Constable. You may live to regret it.'

Inspector Zanuch said, 'We have a good deal of evidence, Mr Tewsday. I suggest it might be a good idea if you got in touch with your lawyers.'

Tewsday sat very still, even his plump hand lying like a

dead starfish on his desk. He was barely into his forties now, but he had looked middle-aged for the past five years: this had been the destined portrait of him and he had been growing into it since he was in his mid-twenties. He had a plump pink-marble look to him and, unless he lost weight, one had the impression that the marble wouldn't age any more. There was, however, a crack in the marble at the moment.

'I think I'd better have a few words with someone.' He stood up. 'Will you excuse me for ten minutes? My secretary will get you some coffee.'

'Can we trust you, Mr Tewsday?' said Zanuch. 'Maybe Constable Malone had better go with you.'

'No.' Tewsday's voice was hard. 'I'll be back, Inspector. I don't run out.'

There were two large offices on this floor, his own and that of the other joint managing director. On the floor above, having the space to itself, was the office of the executive chairman. This was accessible without appointment only to Tewsday and the other managing director. Fingal Hourigan had never been a gregarious boss and now he had become almost monastic.

He looked up in irritation as his long-time, long-suffering secretary, Miss Stevens, a durable, patient woman, showed Tewsday in. 'What's the matter?'

'We're in trouble,' said Tewsday and told him about the Fraud Squad's visit.

'Is what they say true?'

'Up to a point.'

'Jesus!' Fingal sat back in his high-backed chair. His hair was iron-grey now, but touches of white were showing through. 'How many times have I told you to cover your tracks? You'll never learn, you youngsters. Did you go over to Western Australia to inspect the leases?'

'No. I took the word of our two experts. You met them, we agreed they looked on the up-and-up. I found out after they'd bolted that there was only one intersection that showed eight per cent, but it would have yielded nothing commercial, it was so narrow and shallow.'

'Well, whatever happened, we've been left holding a crock of shit.' When he was wildly angry some of the old Chicago street argot slipped back on to his tongue. 'You can carry it.'

'You okayed the float, Fingal.'

'Have another look at the prospectus. You won't find my name anywhere on it. But yours is, with that big flash signature of yours.'

The two men stared at each other; the war between them would never end. Fingal had not allowed the enmity between them to blind him to Tewsday's business talent: he had promoted him as he had deserved to be. As a balance and a threat he had created a joint managing directorship: Borsolino, Tewsday's sour rival, occupied that. Tewsday, for his part, had stayed on at Ballyduff, riding out the occasional rude rebuff, because he was on course towards his ambition, some day soon to be chairman and chief executive of what was now one of the five largest corporations in the country. Ballyduff was a battlefield, but no campaign medals would be issued. Both men kept their hatred of each other very private.

'It won't reflect too well on Ballyduff,' said Tewsday.

Fingal reflected on that. 'Okay, I'll see what I can do. Go back downstairs, tell those cops you'll talk to them in a couple of days when you've seen our lawyers. Stall 'em. Handle 'em with kid gloves – you're good at that.' He wanted to say *greasy* kid gloves, but restrained himself. 'I'll get in touch with Joe Redford.'

Tewsday left him, drew on kid gloves and went downstairs to stall Zanuch and Malone. Fingal got up and walked to one of the big windows of his huge office. This new Ballyduff House had been up only a few months; here on the sixty-ninth floor, one floor under the boardroom, where he also ruled, he was king of the city. Here, if he so wished, he could piss on the citizens from a great height. He was already the richest man in the land and in his pockets he had enough politicians to form a party of his own.

Joe Redford was one of them. He was the conservative Premier of the State, a politician who knew he and his party would be tossed out at the next elections. He was in his late sixties and his last hurrah, feathering his nest as fast as he could pick up the necessary. From his window Fingal could look south and almost directly into the window of the Premier's office. He walked back to his desk, picked up the phone and talked to Redford on a private line for ten minutes.

Two days later a senior officer called in Inspector Zanuch and said the case against Bundiwindi Mining would be dropped. Zanuch argued, but only half-heartedly; he could sense corruption, even though he couldn't smell it. Three months later the senior officer was driving a new car, one that seemed expensive for a man on his salary. The Premier's wife had $50,000 deposited in her bank account by Sugarcane Properties, a company registered in Queensland and used by Fingal for such donations. Tewsday emerged unmarked, except for this further debt to his enemy.

# EIGHT

## I

The letter had said: *My uncle came to Nicaragua last November, a month before I left to come home to Sydney . . .*

Mary Magdalene knew exactly where she was, even though the windows were boarded up. She had been to this village several times, though not in the past six months. The Contras had been in control of this mountain area for that long and the Bishop in her own region had forbidden any of the priests, nuns and lay workers to come near any of these villages. No one had expected the Contras to come down out of the mountains on a kidnapping raid.

The village where she worked was on a small lake below a tangle of low mountains. She had set up the school when she had arrived here two years ago; she was assisted by a part-Indian nun, Sister Carmel, and an American lay worker, Audrey Burke. There was a two-room schoolhouse, built of adobe by the villagers, and a two-room hut where the three women lived. A lean-to kitchen had been built on the outside of the hut. It was all very primitive, but then everything, she had learned, was comparative. Audrey, however, brought up in a *House and Gardens* kitchen and who thought a micro-wave oven was essential to survival, was of the opinion that humility as taught by Christ could sometimes be a drag.

It was Audrey, a thin pretty girl from Kansas City, who had come running in to say there were soldiers in Jeeps at the end of the village's main street. Mary Magdalene had gone out of the schoolhouse into the bright sunlight and the first thing she saw was the mineral-water vendor running down the street, pushing his rattling cart ahead of him. 'They've taken Señor Caracas and his children!'

José Caracas was the village's principal employer. He owned a coffee plantation and also grew corn and wheat for the neighbouring markets. His father had been a Somoza supporter and had fled to the United States when the Somoza regime was toppled. José had stayed on and made his peace with the Sandinistas. Because he treated his employees with respect and good wages and because they had not complained against him, his holdings had not been seized; the Government was a silent partner, in return respecting his ability to run a successful commercial venture. His three older children were at school in Managua, the capital, but his two youngest came here to the parish school, another toleration by the Government.

'Where's Father Roa?' Mary shouted, but the mineral-water man rattled on past her at full speed.

'He's gone into Esteli,' said Audrey.

'Damn! He's never around when we need him.' Father Roa, old and a drunk, had given up the ghost, if not the Holy Ghost, and no longer cared about his flock. They could find their own way to Heaven where, he hoped, he would be waiting for them, young again and sober.

'Why would the soldiers be taking Señor Caracas?' Audrey was not qualified as a teacher or, indeed, for anything. She had turned up out of nowhere one day, fresh-faced and fresh with that American enthusiasm that Mary Magdalene found endearing and exasperating at the same time. They were always so *optimistic*. 'It must be a mistake.'

It was a mistake, all right; they were not Government soldiers. Mary looked up the street and saw now that the few villagers who had been out in the midday heat had disappeared into their homes. Out on the lake two flat-bottomed boats that had been about to come in had turned back and now stood offshore. Four Jeeps, crammed with Contras in camouflaged green battle-dress, were coming down the narrow street; behind them she recognized the battered old Oldsmobile that was José Caracas's only relic of the family's lost affluence. The small convoy came to a halt in front of the school.

'Go back inside.' He was a young lieutenant with a soft wispy beard and hard dark eyes.

'Where are you taking Señor Caracas? Leave the children with us.' She had come out without her hat and she was squinting in the bright reflection flung up from the red dust of the road.

'Go back inside,' he repeated. 'It's none of your business. You outsiders are a pain in the ass.'

'What's the difference between us and the other pains in the ass, the Americans who are working with you?' Mary was glad that it was Audrey, an American, who asked the question.

Sister Carmel stood quietly in the background, as if trying to lose herself in the thin shadow flung by the overhang of the school's roof. Mary could not blame her: Carmel would have to remain here, no matter which side won the civil war. If an old Spanish-blood priest did not want to fight, who could blame a part-Indian nun if she chose to be neutral? God Himself hadn't yet made up his mind whose side he was on in this war-racked country.

'Leave the children with us,' said Mary doggedly. 'Where's their mother?'

Half a dozen parakeets, like small green missiles, suddenly took off from the strawberry tree beside the schoolhouse. The lieutenant turned his head sharply; all at once he looked nervous. Then he looked back at Mary, but said nothing. The three soldiers in the Jeep behind him, mere boys, looked sheepish. Mary stared at them, then wheeled and went up the line to the Oldsmobile. It was a convertible, but the top, ragged and patched, was up against the midday sun. Two soldiers were in the front seat and José Caracas was slumped in the back seat, his arm wrapped protectingly round his two small daughters.

'For your own sake, Sister Mary, don't interfere.' He was a small, jovial man; or had once been. All the joviality had gone and had left just a shell. He wore a white shirt and white trousers, but they were dirty, as if he had been dragged through the dust, and there was a large patch of blood on the shirt. He looked at Mary with glistening frightened eyes and she realized with a shock that he was weeping. 'They have killed my wife.'

The two children shuddered and he wrapped his arms tighter round them.

'It was an accident,' said the young soldier behind the wheel. He, too, looked sheepish, like the soldiers in the Jeep at the front of the column. He believed in his cause, but he hadn't expected to kill women. 'She was trying to protect the children and the gun just went off.'

Mary put her hands on the side of the car and leaned forward, feeling sick and faint. Rose Caracas had been a friend, a quiet plump women who was the right complement to her thin, jovial husband; there had been nothing in her life but him and her children. One heard of deaths every day in this country, but this was the first death of a friend.

She had not come here originally to take sides in the war, political or military. The order had been working here in Central America for over a hundred years, not always in a non-partisan way; in the 1920s it had been known by the locals as the Little Sisters of United Fruit. Over the past two years, however, the younger nuns, more politically aware than their older sisters, had begun to question their own neutrality. Rome might lay down its edicts, but Rome knew little, if anything, of the pain and bewilderment in these red-dust, green-tangled hills. One prayed to God for advice and, if He didn't strike one down with a bolt of lightning, one took it as approval of what one was doing. She was sensible enough, however, to run indoors whenever an electric storm had struck. She had never run away from the Contras.

She straightened up. 'Leave the children with me, Señor Caracas. I'll take care of them till you return.'

'No.' The young lieutenant had come up from the front of the convoy, treading quietly in the dust as if to ambush her. 'Damn you, Sister, get into the car! You're coming with us!'

He swung open the door of the car, grabbed her roughly and thrust her in before she could resist. Audrey came running up, yelling, and attacked the lieutenant, throwing both fists at him at once in the way women do. He took hold of one of her wrists, stepped aside and pulled her head first into the side of the car; some American instructor had taught him unarmed combat. Audrey's head hit the car with a horrible thump and she slid down into the dust and lay there.

'Drive on!'

He ran ahead, jumped into the leading Jeep and the convoy took off at once. Mary Magdalene scrambled up from the floor of the Oldsmobile, looked out over the side and back at the inert figure of Audrey still lying in the middle of the roadway, with Carmel, taking sides at last, running towards her.

Caracas moved over in the back seat and Mary slid on to it beside him. She took one of the children from him and cradled her in her lap. 'There, Teresa, we'll be all right. We'll be all right.' But the little girl looked at her with no faith at all.

Ten minutes later the convoy came to an abrupt halt. The lieutenant came back to the Oldsmobile and Mary and Caracas were both blindfolded with dirty bandanas. Then the convoy moved off again and travelled for another hour, climbing all the time. Once it stopped, not moving for ten minutes or so; Mary heard the clatter of a helicopter and guessed that the convoy must have pulled in under some trees to hide from a Government Mi-24. They must have been well hidden; the helicopter cruised up and down the road, then swung away and was gone out of earshot in a moment. The convoy moved on, then at last stopped; Mary, blind but not deaf, knew they had arrived in some village. She was feeling car-sick from the constant twisting and turning of the road and from the smell of the bandana tied round the upper part of her face: it was like having her face buried in someone's armpit. Teresa was taken from her arms and Mary herself was led, gently, by the young driver, out of the car and into a house. It was a *campesino*'s house: she could feel the dirt floor under the crêpe-soled boots she wore.

The young driver took off the bandana. She rubbed her eyes and blinked at him, standing there in his embarrassment. 'What are they going to do to us?'

'I don't know, Sister, not you, anyway. They're going to take Señor Caracas and the children across the border.' He lowered his voice. 'Don't make the lieutenant angry, Sister. He might kill you.'

She looked at him with horror, not believing him. But he was deadly serious; she could see the horror in his own face. He was part-Indian, but he didn't have the mask that the full-blooded Indians could sometimes wear.

'Why would they want to do that, for God's sake?'

'Not *they. Him.* He's a fanatic, Sister.' He couldn't understand fanaticism, that was something that wasn't in the printed-in-the-USA army manuals. His face had started to change; he was putting on the mask. Perhaps, she thought, they never lose it, that the Spanish blood in him can never crumble it. But then, she remembered, there was also a Spanish mask, something that had come out of Africa with the Moors long ago. She began to feel something that had been creeping into her for the past six months, that she might never feel at home in this country. The young driver said, 'What's your name? Are you an American?'

'Sister Mary Magdalene. No, I'm not American, I'm a mixture. Irish-Australian.' She didn't add French: her father, her mother had told her, was dead and best forgotten.

He shook his head, puzzled. 'I just don't know what you're

doing here,' he said and left her wondering the same thing. Doubt is no comfort, no staff: she was suddenly afraid. She took out her beads and began to pray, but she had, too, doubts about the efficacy of prayer.

They kept her in the room for another two days; having abducted her, they didn't seem to know what to do with her. Several times she heard arguments outside the house; she recognized the voice of the lieutenant, angrier than the other voices. It was cold at night and the one blanket they gave her did not keep her warm. They brought her meals twice a day: chicken, beans and rice; at least they were not going to allow her to starve. The young driver brought the meals, still friendly and concerned for her; but when she asked what had happened to Señor Caracas and the children, the mask came down, he was suddenly Indian. The war, she guessed, had become much more complex than he had been led to believe.

On the second day she stood in front of the closed door, barring his way. 'Where am I? I'm in Telgalpa, aren't I? I heard someone say the name.'

She knew the village, a collection of whitewashed houses, rusting tin sheds and a small pottery factory clinging to the side of a mountain; one wondered why it had been built in such a precarious position and outsiders, coming to it, always looked as if they were in a hurry to depart before the whole lot slid off down into the valley below. A dilapidated church, like one of God's hovels, stood at the end of the main street, dominating the one flat space in the village, the Plaza di La Señora. The whole village looked on the verge of ruin, yet somehow it had survived earthquakes and, she guessed, it was now surviving the war.

The driver hesitated, then said, 'We'll be going soon, back over the border.'

Here in the mountains the border was only a line on a map, a figment of the cartographers' imagination. 'Are they going to take me with them?'

'I don't know. Just don't make the lieutenant angry.'

But the lieutenant didn't come to see her, not till the third day. Then he opened the door and stood there with a big man in what looked to be army tans and a windbreaker. 'Here she is,' the lieutenant said angrily, as if he resented the newcomer's presence.

'Leave us,' said the big man. He looked around the small room, then said to Mary in English, 'Let's go outside.'

'You can't do that!' The lieutenant's anger grew.

The big man looked at him with contempt; or so it seemed to Mary. 'Don't tell me what I can or cannot do, lieutenant,' he said in poor Spanish. He stood in front of the other man and gestured to Mary. 'Come along, Sister. Let's get some light on all this.'

She followed him out of the house and up a dirt path between narrow terraces of corn. They came out on to a terrace where so far nothing had been planted and he gestured to her to sit down on the low stone wall that held up the terrace above it. A laurel tree threw some shade over both of them and she was able to look at him without squinting. On the way up here, after three days of darkness in the house, she had been almost blinded by the bright sun and had stumbled several times.

The big man sat down on the stones beside her and gazed at her steadily for almost a minute. Then he said, 'I'm Archbishop Kerry Hourigan, your uncle.'

She felt suddenly faint; she swayed and he put out a hand to steady her. In the two years she had been in Nicaragua she had come to expect the unexpected; but this was beyond her imagination. One's uncle, one she had never met, did not drop out of a clear blue sky, no matter how closely he might be connected to God. She recovered and told him what she thought.

He smiled. 'I'm glad to see you have a sense of humour. That's the Hourigan in you.' He had no idea who her father was, Brigid had always kept that secret. If he had known, he would not have remarked on it: his opinion of the French in

164

the Vatican was that they had no sense of humour, only malicious wit. 'But this isn't a humorous situation... Damn it,' he said, suddenly irritable. 'Why are you working in this damned country? They're Marxists.'

'Not the *campesinos*, not all of them. I'm not working for the Government, I'm working for the Church.'

'You know what the Holy Father thinks of priests and nuns who work in a Marxist system.'

'Does that include Poland?'

'Poland is different,' he said, realizing he was up against another Hourigan, no matter who her father had been. The Hourigans always had minds of their own: no one knew that better than he. 'You're helping the system here. I've heard the reports on you.'

'Reports? Who's been taking notice of me? I'm not important enough. All I do is teach in my village school and assist the local priest. Sometimes I help the doctor when he comes to visit the village. What are you doing here, anyway? Does the Cardinal in Managua know you're here? Did he send you to rescue me? Or to tick me off? Is he the one who's got the reports on me?' She was angry that she might have been spied upon, possibly by old Father Roa.

Kerry Hourigan shook his head. 'I'm not supposed to be here. I came in over the border from Honduras – I came here only because of you.' He was lying, but The Lord didn't punish you if you lied in His cause. If He did, Hell would be fuller than it was. 'You're an embarrassment, my child.'

*My child*: God, how she hated being addressed like that! The Church seniors always put one down: the father figure gave them some protection. 'To you or the Church?'

'Both. Go home, Mary –'

'I don't have a home, Uncle. I've never had one, except the convent.'

'That was your mother's fault. She should have brought you home to Australia. It's criminal that you and I have never met till now, that you've never met your grandfather.'

'I regret it. I've often wondered what you and Grandfather were like – I mean, when I learned who you were. I was sixteen before she told me . . . She only told me after I decided I wanted to be a nun. She never took me back to Australia when she'd go – I'd be left in a boarding school in England or Switzerland.' All at once she was bitter. 'Home is my school down in my village, it's where I've been happiest. That's where I want to go back to.'

'Your mother is back in Australia now.'

'I know. She writes to me every week – I think she's starting to feel guilty . . .'

He was exasperated with her, yet felt sorry for her. She was not his responsibility, that was her mother's; yet he was not without a sense of family duty, he was the one here on the spot. He was just not accustomed to taking care of an individual, he had been trained for bigger responsibilities.

He had come to Honduras with Francisco Paredes Canto and Max Domecq Cruz to talk to the local Contra commanders. With the drying up of American supplies, the guerrillas were looking for a new source of arms. He had the money and the contacts, but he had wanted to assure himself that everything he paid for would reach the Contras. His father did not believe in his money, or any part of it, being hijacked. The venture had to be not only successful but secret: there were certain people in the Vatican who would have his head if they knew what he was up to. He was supposed to be in the United States raising money for the Defence Against Subversive Religions.

Yesterday he had heard about the young nun, Sister Mary Magdalene, and he had known at once who she was. The Contra chiefs in Honduras didn't want her; there had been too much trouble in the past over what had happened to foreign missionaries. They could not leave her fate to the lieutenant in Telgalpa; they knew his reputation. Kerry Hourigan, conscience overcoming his zeal, had volunteered to talk to her, though he had not mentioned his relationship to her.

Now he was regretting his fit of conscience. It was all very well to have a conscience, but, like lust, it should be kept under control.

'If you go back there, what will you do?'

'The same as I've always done. Teach the children.'

'Teach them what? The ways of The Lord or the ways of Karl Marx?'

She laughed: it was a harsh sound coming from such a young throat. 'Oh Uncle! When did you last get down to the level of someone like the *campesinos*? When did you last hear the confession of an ordinary worker? Or the mother of six or seven kids?'

Oh, how simple-minded were the young. Did they really think only the poor could arouse compassion? None knew better than he the agonizing sins of the rich.

'I'm not a Marxist,' she said. 'All I do is listen to their troubles.'

'They have plenty of troubles under the Sandinistas.'

'Are you for the Contras?'

'Yes,' he said almost defiantly. He had no ambition to be a closet martyr; if he was going to sacrifice himself for The Lord, he wouldn't mind headlines. If Judgement Day should prove to be a low-key occasion, he wouldn't attend. But, of course, it was easy to be outspoken here in these mountains; secrecy was still necessary back in Rome. He backed off a little, in case, by some chance, she had a line to the Cardinal in Managua, who, he knew, had a line to Rome: 'Let's say I'm against Marxism. It is the evil of the world.'

'I wouldn't know,' she said simply. 'The world doesn't count for much in my village.'

He looked away from her, out over the valley to the opposite ridge. He saw a flash of brilliant green, as if someone had thrown a huge long emerald down into the valley: it was a *quetzal*, the most beautiful bird in the New World; he had an eye for beauty and it made his heart ache to see it. Then he saw a King vulture drop down out of the sky and alight on the roof beam of the church in the square; he watched it, fascinated by it and repelled. He had seen it in Indian carvings, beautiful yet ugly; somehow it was symbolic of this region. He turned his face away from it, his ear now caught. A big *higuera* tree stood opposite the church; a boy came out from under its shade carrying a transistor radio turned up full blast; an American voice was belting out a rock-'n'-roll song. The vulture took off from the roof of the church as if its ear, like his own, had been offended; it flapped away on black and white wings till it was just a speck on the far side of the valley. No, he thought, I couldn't work here, not at her level. He looked back at her.

'You can't stay here.'

'Here? I don't want to – I want to go back to my village.'

That wasn't what he had meant: he had meant here in Nicaragua. The missionaries always finished up on the wrong side if they stayed long enough; they never saw the whole picture. 'All right, you can go back to your village.'

She looked almost like a *campesino*: scuffed and worn boots, a shapeless skirt, an unpressed shirt, short straggly hair that looked as if she had cut it herself. He was a fastidious dresser, something he had inherited from his father, and he detested anyone, even nuns, who didn't try to keep up appearances.

'Thanks, Uncle. What about you?'

'What about me?'

'Are you coming down to Managua to see the Cardinal?'

'I don't think President Ortega and his Government would welcome me. No, I'm going back to Rome. I think it would be better if you didn't mention that I was the one who arranged your release. The Sandinistas might get the wrong impression.'

'About you or me?'

She had no respect for his rank; he wondered what respect she gave to her superiors in the Order. But then she was not family-related to her superiors: perhaps she saw himself and her only as uncle and niece. 'Both of us. God bless you, Mary.'

'You too, Uncle.' Then suddenly she smiled and put out her hand. 'I'd like to meet you in other circumstances. We could have some ding-dong arguments. Just like you and Mother used to have.'

'God forbid!' But he smiled; in other circumstances he might have come to like her. 'Keep up the good work.'

*... But that was a hypocritical remark if ever I've heard one*, said the letter to Father Marquez. *A month later I got an instruction from the Order in Ireland that I was being transferred to Australia, that I had done more than my fair share of field mission work. Two years! I've met nuns and priests who have been in the field for thirty or forty years ... It was easy to guess who had applied the pressure. Ireland always does what Rome tells it ...*

## 2

'Here's the letter.' Clements lifted it out of the murder box. 'What do you want done with it? I mean, do you want to show it to the Archbishop?'

'Not yet. The holy bastard has been stringing me along. He said he'd seen her in Honduras, that she'd been brought out of Nicaragua to Tegal – whatever the capital is. He was *in* Nicaragua – doing what?'

Malone had been dropped outside Homicide by Tewsday's chauffeur. He had stood on the pavement for a while, wishing he had had his 'think walk'. His mind was still muddied. He had more questions to ask, of the Archbishop, of Fingal Hourigan, of Paredes and Domecq, if he could find them. He was not, however, going to go off half-cocked, like a conservationist's gun.

'Why do I expect Archbishops to be the soul of truth?' said Clements, the non-religious.

The phone rang and Malone picked it up. It was Father

Marquez, sounding breathless, as if he had run to the phone at his end. 'Inspector? This is Luis Marquez. Holy God, you know –' He paused to get his breath; for a moment Malone thought he had quit and gone. Then he came back, his voice more under control: 'I've just had another threat. The same guy, Inspector.'

'What did he say?'

'He wanted to know what was in the letter I gave you.'

Malone racked his memory, trying to remember the scene at the cemetery. 'You're sure it was the same man? He spoke to you in Spanish?'

'It was him, all right. He couldn't have been there, Inspector, I mean at the cemetery. I was scared – I'm even more scared now – and I kept looking around to see who was watching the burial. If he saw us, he must have been some distance away, watching us through glasses. Or someone at the funeral saw me give you the letter and told him.'

That thought had already occurred to Malone. 'I'll check up on that angle.'

'Inspector, I'm really scared. I didn't want to get into all this. And now . . .'

'Easy, Luis. Where are you – at the University? Do you live alone there?'

'Yes, I have a room here. I eat in the canteen.'

'Can you go and live in some church presbytery, I mean where you'll have company?'

'I guess so. I can go up to Randwick. If I explain to them . . . But for how long? And I don't want any of them dragged into this. The parish priest up there is a pretty conservative old stick . . .'

'Do you have to stay at the University for the rest of the day? Yes? Righto, I'll send a man out to keep you company, then he can escort you up to the presbytery at Randwick. His name is Detective-Constable Graham.'

Malone hung up, then sent for Andy Graham. The latter arrived, as usual all enthusiasm; Malone felt he should have been a football cheer-leader instead of a cop. He was tall and overweight and had a rather vacant, good-looking face behind which a brain was growing that would one day, perhaps too late, be shrewd enough to temper his enthusiasm. Malone explained what he wanted him to do.

'Right!' said Graham and Malone was relieved when he didn't punch the air. 'Let's hope the bastard shows up, right?'

'Right,' said Malone and hoped the Spanish-speaking bastard would never put in an appearance. 'Just stick close to Father Marquez till you leave him at the presbytery this evening. What are you? Catholic?'

'No, a Methodist. The Uniting Church.'

'Don't get into any argument. Be ecumenical.'

'Right!'

And Andy Graham went off, metaphorically punching the air, the flap of his holster already undone under his jacket. Clements grinned at Malone.

'He should transfer to the mounted section. He'd have jumped on his horse and galloped all the way to Kensington. I felt like shouting Hi-ho, Silver!'

'We're getting old, Russ.' Then he looked down the big room and added softly, 'We're just about to get older. Or anyway *feel* it.'

Chief Superintendent Danforth was lumbering towards them, nodding to the other detectives as he passed them, making a royal progress, though there was nothing regal about him.

'Inspector –' He wheezed down into a chair, both vocally and physically; the chair looked and sounded as if it might collapse beneath him. He might once have been athletic, but that was long ago; he was within a year of retirement and he was wheezing his way towards it, careful not to exert himself. As long as Malone had known him he had been slow-moving and slow-thinking, one of the last of the old school who had risen in the ranks on seniority and not merit. 'You're on this murdered nun case? What's the progress?'

Malone glanced towards the murder box; Clements had slipped the letter back into it and put the lid on the old shoe-box. 'Not much, Chief. You know who's involved.'

'Oh, indeed I do. Definitely.' Danforth ran a beefy hand over his short-back-and-sides. He was a man from the 1950s: he had stopped still in time. He had once been corrupt, but the new regime had put paid to that; he had had sense enough to realize the gravy train had run off the rails and he had been lucky to escape. 'I think you are biting off more than you can chew, Scobie.'

*Scobie*: that meant this was going to be a man-to-man talk. Malone looked at Clements and the latter took the hint and rose. 'I'll see that Andy Graham has got away.'

Danforth waited till he and Malone were alone, then he moved his chair closer to the latter's desk. They were separated from the other detectives in the big room by several empty desks; none the less, he lowered his voice conspiratorially. 'Scobie, it's not going to be worth all the trouble this will cause. You're going to be up against the Catholic Church.'

'Did they tell you that?'

'Who?'

'The Church.'

'Not directly, no. But you know how much clout they have in this State. Half the MPs are Tykes. So's the Premier. He's never going to give the Church a kick in the bum.'

'I haven't pointed a finger at the Church. I've got a murdered nun and her uncle's an archbishop. That's all.'

'It doesn't stop there, and you know it. There's the nun's grandad.'

'Has he been talking to you, Harry?' Let's keep it man-to-man.

'Not directly, no.'

'Tewsday, then? Sir Jonathan?'

Danforth sat back, ran his hand over his head again, as if putting all his thoughts together under his grey thatch; Malone had the image of a hand of not very good cards being put in order before being played. 'We don't need any names. Walls have ears.'

Malone strangled the laugh that started in his chest; he managed to nod soberly. 'Righto, no names. But we know who we both mean.'

Danforth nodded in return, just as soberly. 'There's too much influence, Scobie. You could never beat it. You could find yourself in charge of the traffic branch out at Tibooburra.'

Tibooburra was in the far west of the State; it had a population you could gather in a single schoolroom. Malone played his own best card: 'The Commissioner is in on this, Harry. I have to report to him.'

Danforth ran his hand over his head again, this time a little worriedly. 'The Commissioner, eh? How did he get into it?'

Malone wasn't going to tell him that. Danforth was obviously the Hourigan, or Tewsday, man in the department. 'I think you'd have to ask him that, Harry. He doesn't take me into his confidence.'

Danforth nodded, still worried. 'Yeah, yeah, I'll do that.'

Then the phone rang and Malone picked it up.

'Inspector Malone? We talked the other night.'

Malone recognized the voice from its faint accent. 'Go ahead.'

'Inspector, the young woman has been buried. Let her rest in peace.'

'Oh, she'll do that, all right. She's the only one who's going to have any peace.' He could feel himself getting angry: first, the threat to Marquez, then Danforth trying to apply pressure and now this.

The voice hardened, though it remained quiet. 'Be sensible, Inspector. We don't want to do anything you'd regret.'

'Are you threatening me –' he took a wild chance. '– Mr Domecq? Or is it Mr Paredes?'

There was silence for just a moment; the man, whoever he was, was used to thinking on his feet. 'You have the wrong names, Inspector. Don't be too smart or –' But he didn't finish the threat.

Malone held on to his temper, aware of Danforth sitting opposite him, both ears strained. 'Whoever you are, let me tell you something. This isn't Latin America. Nobody threatens the police in this country.' At least not since the bushrangers' day; or in a shoot-out. But not over the phone: it was un-Australian. 'Go back and tell your boss, whoever *he* is, that it won't work. If anything happens to me, the whole of Homicide will be down on you and you'll be up shit creek. That's an old Aussie expression. I don't know the Spanish for it, but your boss might translate it.'

He slammed the phone down and looked at Danforth. The Chief Superintendent pursed his lips in a silent whistle. That last message of mine was for you, too, Malone thought; and knew that Danforth had got it. Danforth at last said, 'You'll report that to the Commissioner, I take it?'

'Of course. You know how he feels about his men being threatened.'

'Yes. So he should. Definitely.' Danforth nodded, almost too eager to agree. 'They made a mistake there.' He stood up, wheezing. 'Well, think about what I said, Scobie. It was just between you and me, you understand?'

At least he had the grace not to wink, thought Malone. 'Sure, Harry. I appreciate it. You had my best interests at heart. Definitely.'

'I always had my men's interests at heart. That's how I got to be Chief Superintendent.' He lumbered away, elephantinely smug.

Clements came back as soon as Danforth had disappeared. Malone told him about Danforth's attempt at pressure and of the threat over the phone. 'I'm beginning to wish my leave was due. I'd like to go bush somewhere with Lisa and the kids.'

'Are you going to back off?'

'Would you expect me to? But I'm not sure where the hell

174

to go next. I think it's just as Tewsday told me – Old Man Hourigan is hiding Paredes and Domecq. I've checked with Immigration and they haven't left the country, not unless they went out on different passports to the ones they used when they came in.'

'Let's get a warrant to search the Hourigan place.'

'We'd never get one. He'd pull enough strings to make a shark net.' He looked out the window, at Hyde Park green and peaceful in the autumn sun. 'It's a nice day. D'you feel like staking out the Hourigan mansion? Just sitting in your car and making out your bets for Saturday?'

Clements made a face. 'I can think of things I'd rather be doing. I'd better take someone with me, in case I fall asleep. Are you staying here?'

'I'll be here all day. I've got to finalize the report on the Lloyd case.' The Lloyd case had been a double murder in a family; the murderer, a son who had killed his mother and sister, was in custody and had confessed. It was an open-and-shut case, the sort that made police work easy. If investigating murder ever was easy: Malone hoped he would never become as callous as that. 'When I get that out of the way, my desk is clear.'

'You want to bet?' said Clements.

Malone worked till five o'clock, when his desk was as clear as it would ever be; he would never achieve the barren neatness of the Commissioner. Clements, sounding bored, called in to say there had been no movement in or out of the Hourigan place, not even a delivery man. Malone told him to pack up and go home, then he did the same himself.

As he was leaving his desk a call came in from Andy Graham. 'Inspector, I'm just taking Father Marquez up to Randwick. You want me to stay with him there, too?'

'I don't think so, Andy. Just tell him not to go out tonight. You or someone else can pick him up again in the morning.'

He went down, got into his Commodore and drove out into the peak-hour traffic. He was almost home in Randwick, looking forward to the comfort of Lisa and the children, when he decided to drive on the extra half-mile to the church. Father Marquez might like some comfort, too, though Malone was not sure that he could give any.

He arrived at the church just as Andy Graham, in an ummarked police car, pulled up in the parking lot and deposited the young priest. Graham said good-night and drove off with his usual haste.

Marquez looked after him. 'He drives like one of those Grand Prix drivers. It's the first time I felt I should have been wearing my crash helmet in a car.'

'He's our traffic cops' favourite target.'

'He's a ball of energy, isn't he? He told me he did a year in Arts down at the University, but couldn't stand the slow pace. I gather he used to breeze through a millennium of history while everyone else was plodding through a decade.'

The young priest sounded talkative, as if he were nervous. Malone said, 'Where's your motorbike?'

'I left it down on campus.' He looked at Malone in the dim light of a street-lamp outside the parking lot. 'I appreciate what you're doing, Inspector. But how long is it going to go on?'

The parking lot had once been the extensive grounds of an old house that had belonged to one of the district's best families. Now the house was a community centre, the whole area surrounded by tall, thick ficus trees. The church was on the south side of the parking lot, its steeple piercing the night sky. The lights were on in the church and a few people were arriving for evening Mass, most of them elderly. The young were too busy, who needed to demonstrate his faith seven days a week, for God's sake?

Malone looked around at the shadows. They suggested a menacing silence, despite the noise of the traffic out on the busy street. He abruptly felt uneasy: *we're targets side by side, just waiting to be hit.*

'I'll walk you down to the presbytery.'

At that moment the car swung into the parking lot. It

came in slowly, its headlamps sweeping across the large two-storeyed house as it turned and came towards Malone and Marquez. It was moving slowly, as if the driver was looking for a vacant spot away from the half-a-dozen other parked cars. Malone, blinded by the headlamps, stepped to one side and Marquez followed him.

'It's probably one of the old ladies,' Marquez said. 'They shouldn't be driving at night –'

Then the car was opposite them. Malone caught a glimpse of the driver, but he couldn't tell whether it was a man or a woman; he or she seemed to be wearing a balaclava or a ski helmet. Malone did, however, see the shotgun come up; the driver drove with one hand for a moment. Then he took both hands off the steering wheel and pumped the gun. Malone fell down, rolling away, but Father Marquez caught the full force of the blast. He seemed to jump backwards, hit the parked car behind him and fell in a contorted heap. The assassin's car accelerated, swung right with a squeal of tyres and drove out on to the street. It went straight across the north and south streams of traffic, causing a louder screech of tyres and several nerve-shuddering bangs of crashing metal, and down a narrow street opposite. Malone had scrambled to his feet, but he caught nothing that would identify the car except that it was dark and medium-sized.

He dropped to his knees beside Marquez; but as soon as he touched the young priest he knew he was dead. Then someone was running across from the front of the church: Malone stood up and recognized Father Joannes, the parish priest.

'I heard the shots – Oh, Holy Jesus!' He was a burly man in his sixties, one who had spent all his early years in bush parishes and had helped in the physical labour of building his churches. He was old-fashioned in his theology and moral approach, but he was practical and tough-nerved. 'I'll get an ambulance! Are you all right?'

'I'm okay, Father. You stay here with Father Marquez –

177

say some prayers. I brought my own car, not a police one – I don't have a radiophone in it.' Other people were now coming across from the church, some of them approaching apprehensively. 'Where can I find a phone?'

'There's one in the community centre. It's open – the cleaners are in there.'

Malone ran across to the old house, feeling weak in the legs, found a phone and called Police Centre. 'Get the local boys up here – I want the parking lot cordoned off. Get in touch with Sergeant Clements – he should be at home – and tell him I want him here on the double. And Constable Graham. Get an ambulance here, but tell 'em the man is already dead.'

'What about the car, Inspector, the one that got away?'

'No description – I missed it.' He hung up and stared at the hand still on the phone. It was shaking like an old man's with palsy. Then he felt his knees beginning to tremble and he leaned against the wall in front of him.

'You all right?' A cleaning woman stood beside him, her hand in the middle of his back, her broad blunt face wrinkled with concern. 'Here, sit down.'

He straightened up, shook his head at the chair she pushed towards him. He clenched his fists, trying to force the nervousness out of them. He had felt shock before, but never like this. He looked at the phone, wondering if he should call Lisa, wanting to hear the reassuring sound of her voice; then he decided against it. He wanted to be fully in control of himself before he spoke to her. What was happening to him must not be allowed to touch her or the children.

The police from the local station arrived within two minutes; the ambulance was only three minutes behind them. The parking lot was filling up with spectators, most of them from the church: this was more interesting than Mass. Some of them bent their heads in prayer and crossed themselves as Father Marquez's body was lifted into the ambulance. Father Joannes, ashen-faced in the glare of the cars' headlamps, which had been switched on to shed more light, came across to Malone.

'Why? He rang this morning and said there was some trouble he wanted to avoid –'

'It had to do with the murder of Sister Magdalene, from the convent. Father Marquez was an innocent victim – they should never have touched him –'

'Who's *they*?'

This was no place to tell him; if ever he was to be told. The early evening was busy: the glare of the headlamps, the flashing roof-lights of the police cars and the ambulance, the dark figures moving restlessly in silhouette, the shriek of tyres as the traffic out in the street pulled up to see what was going on. Three cars had crashed into each other when the killer's car had cut across the traffic streams; they had been pulled into the kerb and two tow-wagons had already arrived like four-wheeled vultures. The Moreton Bay fig trees loomed against the night sky like dark clouds underlit with green and there was a touch of damp in the air, as if rain was building up to drown out the whole scene. It would be a good thing if it did, Malone thought.

'I'll explain some other time, Father,' he said, wanting to get away before the media reporters arrived. 'But you don't have to worry. They won't be back.'

'I hope not,' said Father Joannes and blessed himself. 'I can't keep up with what goes on today.'

'Neither can I,' said Malone, but he knew they were speaking in different contexts.

Russ Clements and Andy Graham arrived within ten seconds of each other. The media vans and cars were right on their tail. Malone gave Graham instructions: 'The local sergeant seems to have got everything under control – let him handle the reporters.'

'What about Father Marquez's family?'

'There's only his mother, I gather. Let the local police handle that, too.'

'I'm glad you're not asking me to do it,' said Graham, all enthusiasm suddenly unconscious. 'That's a bastard of a job. Do we try and trace the killer's car?'

'Scout around locally, see if it's been abandoned – it might have been a stolen job. He used a shotgun – he got off five or six shots, I didn't count.'

Graham went off, still showing no enthusiasm; he knew as well as Malone that he had virtually nothing to work on. Malone turned to Clements, who was studying him carefully.

'He meant to get you too, didn't he?'

'I think so.'

'It knocked the shit out of you, didn't it?'

Malone looked at his hands; they had stopped trembling. 'How did you guess?'

'I know how I'd feel if it was that close – shotguns aren't like hand-pieces. Half-a-dozen times I've seen the damage it can do. The older we get, the sight doesn't get any better. You want to go home? I'll take over here.'

Once again Malone felt the warm, if unstated affection that Clements felt for him; the big man was as upset as himself at how close he had come to being blasted. He had shut his mind at how Father Marquez had looked. He had seen him only dimly in the shadow of the car where he had fallen; when he had come out of the community centre and the cars' headlamps had been switched on, he had not gone near the body. But in his mind's eye he knew the terrible damage that had been done to the handsome young priest and, unless he could keep that eye shut, he knew the lasting unnerving effect it would have on him. And Clements, too, knew it.

'No,' he said, 'I'm going out to Vaucluse to talk to Archbishop Hourigan.'

On the way they stopped at a public phone-box and Malone rang Lisa. 'You'll hear it on the radio – they may even have it on the seven o'clock TV news. Father Marquez has been shot. He's dead.'

There was a gasp; then Lisa said, 'Are you all right?'

'Why shouldn't I be?'

'I don't know. I – Were you with him?'

It would be in the papers tomorrow morning. 'Yes. But I'm okay. I'll be home in an hour or so. What's for dinner?'

She knew him too well. 'Don't start acting casual. You've got no appetite. Take care, darling.'

She hung up and in his mind's eye again, that weakness that always makes us vulnerable, he saw her close her eyes and lean against the table on which their phone stood. In the background would be the noise of the children, but she would be deaf to them. But then, he knew, she would recover and take up again whatever she had been doing when he had called. Married to him, she had become a woman for all emergencies.

It started to rain as he and Clements drew up outside the Hourigan mansion. Parking was always easy here; the Vaucluse elements had their own off-street parking. Malone got out and crossed to the intercom on the big gates. Mrs Kelly, the warden, answered. 'What would you be wanting this time? Mr Hourigan isn't receiving visitors.'

'The police are never visitors, Mrs Kelly. We're just gate-crashers.'

He waited patiently; she was gone almost five minutes. Two dogs came down the driveway and barked savagely at him on the other side of the tall gates. Then the intercom crackled again; her voice sounded like broken glass being rattled in a tin cup. 'You're lucky he's such a gentleman. Come in when I've put the dogs away.'

There was a further delay, then the gates swung open. The

first thing Malone saw as he and Clements walked up to the house was the red Jaguar parked in the driveway. Michele sat behind the wheel, his head laid back as if he were asleep.

Mrs Kelly was waiting for them at the front door. 'Don't keep Mr Hourigan too long. He's going to a dinner, a business dinner.'

No mourning period here, not whilst there was more money to be made. Fingal Hourigan was in black tie and dinner suit, looking like a crafty penguin, an emperor who, given the chance, would have made money out of Antarctica. His daughter Brigid, still in the crimson turban she had worn to the funeral and a blue woollen dress, was seated at the grand piano, the keyboard open in front of her.

'I hope this isn't going to become a regular habit, Inspector.' Hourigan was a frank host; in one's eighties, politeness only wastes valuable time. 'What's it about now?'

Malone told him bluntly, watching both him and Brigid. The old man showed no expression; Brigid dropped her hand, made a discordant thump on the keyboard. 'Both Father Marquez and I had threats over the phone today. I'd like to interview Mr Paredes or Mr Domecq. Are they staying here?'

'What makes you think they have anything to do with what you've just told me?' He was still standing, leaning on the silver walking-stick; he made no gesture for them to be seated. Behind him Brigid had quietly closed the keyboard lid and stood up.

'I'll tell you that, Mr Hourigan, when I've talked to them. Are they here?'

'No.'

'Yes,' said Brigid. 'They're in the study. I'll get them.'

She had to pass her father to go out of the drawing-room. He put up the walking-stick, blocking her way. 'You've just made me out a liar.'

'That's what you are, Dad. I didn't make you one.'

She pushed the walking-stick aside and went on out of the room. She moved with dignity and grace, Malone remarked, almost queenly. The Hourigans, no matter where they had come from, had learned the touch of class that arrogance gives.

Fingal looked at Malone. 'Do you have daughters, Inspector? They're much harder to handle than sons.'

'Even when the son is an archbishop?'

Fingal ignored that, looked at Clements. 'What do you do, sergeant? Just stand in the background?'

'Most of the time, yes,' said Clements. 'Sometimes you learn more that way.'

Then Fingal looked at them both, his bright-blue eyes glinting in the light of the expensive lamps surrounding him; he was afraid of shadows, there were all those gathered in his past like a black storm. 'You're a couple of smart-arses.'

'We try,' said Malone.

Then Brigid came back into the room with Paredes and Domecq. They were better- and more prosperous-looking then their photos had shown. Both of them were immaculately dressed in navy-blue mohair, their white shirts with the starched collars reminding Malone of a fashion he had seen in old magazines. They had the air of men prepared for any situation.

'This wasn't my idea that you should meet Inspector Malone,' Fingal told them.

Paredes smiled politely, looking unperturbed. 'There is nothing to be concerned about, Mr Hourigan. Back in the States we are always being interviewed. The FBI, Congressional committees... It is the lot of political refugees.'

Malone had met this ploy before: be frank, lay everything out in the open. Well, *almost* everything. 'Mr Paredes, did you ever meet Sister Mary Magdalene?'

Paredes glanced at Brigid, who had gone back to sit at the piano. 'Miss Hourigan's daughter? Never. A dreadful tragedy... We came here today to pay our respects to Miss Hourigan.'

'What about you, Mr Domecq? Did you ever meet her?'

'I never had the pleasure. If she was as charming as her mother ...' He gave Brigid a gambler's smile, all charm and challenge under the dark moustache. She gave him no smile in return. She had opened the keyboard and now she struck a note, one that sounded curiously flat.

Domecq's voice was the one Malone had heard over the phone. 'Where were you this evening, Mr Domecq? Say three-quarters of an hour ago?'

'Why, I was here.' Domecq looked surprised; or feigned it. 'I was upstairs, having a bath.'

'I can vouch for that,' said Fingal. 'You're barking up the wrong tree, Inspector. You're also being bloody insulting. I think I'll have a word with your superiors.'

'I think you already have, Mr Hourigan. He passed on the word this morning. But maybe you'd like to have a word with the Commissioner? I'm working directly under him.'

Fingal said nothing for a moment, then he nodded his head in appreciation. 'You are a smart-arse.'

'I'm glad to hear that,' said Brigid from her place at the piano. She looked as if she might at any moment start playing, perhaps some martial music. 'I'm relying on you, Inspector, and you too, Sergeant, to find out who murdered my daughter. Nobody else seems to care.'

Most other mothers, Malone thought, would have broken down at that. But Brigid Hourigan was in control of herself; whatever turmoil of grief and anger was going on inside her, none of it showed on the surface. Malone recognized an ally, though he wondered how much she, being a Hourigan, would demand of him and Clements.

'I might have cared more if you had brought her home sooner,' said Fingal. 'I hardly knew the girl.'

Malone felt suddenly uncomfortable; behind him he sensed that Clements felt the same way. Even Paredes and Domecq looked as if they wanted to be gone from the room. Family tensions were the smallest of wars, understood by everyone and the wounds felt accordingly.

184

Brigid seemed to sense the others' embarrassment; she changed the subject. 'Did Father Marquez have any family?'

'Just his mother, as far as I know.'

'I must call on her – I feel we owe it to her. If it had not been for Teresa . . . I think I need a drink. Where is the liquor kept, Dad?' Evidently she didn't know her way round her father's house.

He hesitated, then nodded towards a flamboyantly inlaid bureau. 'In there.'

She went to the bureau, pulled at a handle and the whole top opened up to expose two shelves of cut-glass decanters and expensive glasses. 'How cute! Where's the ice – in the bottom drawer?'

It was: the bottom drawer was a shallow refrigerator. Fingal realized that none of his visitors, least of all his daughter, was impressed; or if they were, not in the way he had intended. The bureau would be thrown out tomorrow. He had begun to weaken: he could be made to look small. And all because of his daughter.

Brigid took her whisky straight, except for one ice cube. She held the glass up to the men enquiringly, but they all shook their heads. Then, still moving with dignified grace, she went back to the piano stool. She looked at Paredes and Domecq with calm hostility.

'Both of those young people died because of what you two gentlemen are trying to do.'

'You are mistaken, Miss Brigid,' said Paredes, as calm as she. 'Our visit to Australia has nothing to do with Nicaragua.'

'Bullshit,' said Brigid without raising her voice; somehow she even made the word sound dignified. 'They are here, Inspector, with my brother the Archbishop to raise money for their precious Contras. Teresa told me all about it.'

'You are treading on dangerous ground here,' said her father. 'You're committing slander.'

'Dad –' She smiled, took a sip of her whisky. 'When I was growing up, our house stank with slander. You never had a good word to say for anyone, even the nuns who taught me. If Señor Paredes and Señor Domecq think I'm slandering them, let them sue me. They have two good witnesses, *police* witnesses. Would you speak for the plaintiffs, Inspector?'

The interrogation had been taken away from Malone, but he didn't mind. 'I don't think so, Miss Hourigan. But as your father says, you're treading on dangerous ground.'

She caught the warning; but she seemed careless of the risk she was running. She looked into her glass and, with her face turned downwards, Malone saw the tears glistening on the long eyelashes. The grief in her was about to burst out.

'Mr Paredes, Mr Domecq,' said Malone, 'I'd like you to come with us. We have some questions – I think it would be better if I didn't ask them here.'

'Do you have a warrant?' said Fingal.

'It's only for questioning, Mr Hourigan. But if you want to make an issue of it, I'll see the Commissioner . . .'

Fingal stared at him, then he turned to the two Nicaraguans. 'Go with him, Francisco. I'll have my lawyer there as soon as possible.'

'I'd like your son to come with us, too,' said Malone. 'Where is the Archbishop?'

There was no smirk; but there was a flash of triumphant satisfaction on the shrewd old face.

'You've missed him. He left for Rome an hour ago.'

# NINE

'You can go in my car, Señor Paredes,' said Fingal Hourigan;
then abruptly changed his mind: 'No, I'll need it. Try our
police cars – they're comfortable enough.'

The change of mind was abruptly rude; but Malone,
amused, saw the reason for it. Fingal, at this stage, wanted
no public connection with the Contra agents; the Hourigan
Rolls-Royce would be too obvious an advertisement. Let
Paredes and Domecq travel in a slum for tonight.

On the ride in to Homicide Domecq looked bewildered: as
if, in what had seemed like Heaven, God had turned out to
have no influence. 'Don't you know who Señor Hourigan *is*?'

'No,' said Clements dead-pan into the driving mirror, 'who
is he?'

Malone, half-turned in the front seat, saw Paredes smile
thinly. This isn't the first time he's ridden in the back of a
police car, Malone thought; the older man was a veteran of
many and varied situations. Interrogating him was not going
to be easy.

He said something in Spanish and Malone said, 'Speak
English, Mr Paredes. It will make it easier for you.'

'In what way, Inspector? You're not threatening us, surely?
I just told my friend we are in the hands of honest cops. It is
only a matter of adjustment.'

*That's the way we seem to be going on both sides in this
case*; but he was not going to tell Paredes that. Maybe the

Nicaraguan had already guessed it. He looked as confident in the back of the police car as any Police Commissioner.

Clements pulled the car up in front of the Remington Rand building. 'I thought you might like to take 'em in the front entrance, Inspector. I'll put the car in the garage.'

Malone got out and waited for Paredes and Domecq to follow him. He was not sure that he wanted to see any reporter idling his time up on the sixth floor, but if one should be there and ask embarrassing questions, could he be blamed if the reporter made the wrong inference from the evasive answers?

There were, however, no reporters visible. As they had come in across the pavement to the front door of the building, four young men had passed them. One of them made a *moue* of his lips and blew a sour kiss to Domecq, who glanced in puzzlement at Malone.

'He thinks you're a cop,' said Malone. 'The gay district starts just up the street.'

'You have a gay community here?' Paredes sounded as if he found the thought distasteful; behind the sleek conservative look was an old-time Latin macho man. 'A district?'

'Oh, we're up with everything here. We're not as behind the times as you seem to think.'

When they got out of the lift on the sixth floor both Nicaraguans looked around them, as if not believing where they had been brought. '*This* is Police Headquarters? A private office block?'

'No, this is just Homicide.'

Paredes smiled, still looking around him. 'And you say you're not behind the times?'

'Remington Rand sponsor us,' said Malone. 'Next year IBM are taking us over. Or is it the CIA? You'd know about them, wouldn't you?'

'The CIA? Never heard of them.' Paredes smiled again, but Malone could see that, for the first time, the Nicaraguan looked unsure of himself. Malone decided to push him a little more off-balance.

'Who made the decision to threaten me and Father Marquez?' he said bluntly. 'You or Mr Domecq?'

'I have no idea what you are talking about.' Paredes had recovered; the acting was perfect.

Malone looked at Domecq. 'We have a tape of your last call, Mr Domecq. You probably know that voice-prints are as good as finger-prints, they're just as incriminating.'

Malone's own acting was perfect. So was Clements's, who had just arrived: he didn't even blink at Malone's bald lie. Both men, however, knew they would be marooned like shags on a rock if, or rather when, Domecq asked for a copy of the tape.

They were saved by the belle. She came walking down the aisle between the desks; the other detectives in the big room stopped work and turned to stare after her. She wore a revealing cocktail dress, with a matching shawl thrown over her shoulder; she was blonde and glamorous, but she also looked business-like; she gave the impression that she would be business-like even if she were naked. But she would never be any man's whore.

'Inspector Malone?' She had a pleasant voice, made only slightly artificial by the fluting vowels taught her at one of the more expensive eastern suburbs schools. Malone privately thought of it as the Ascham accent, easily acquired by the poor but socially ambitious just by standing outside the school gates and listening to the mums waiting for their daughters. 'I'm Zara Kersey.'

He recognized her now, if only from her photos which were a constant feature in the Sunday newspapers. She was known to the society columnists as the Queen of the Freeloaders; no charity ball, no gallery opening, no fashion launching was complete without Zara Kersey. A widow, she had once been married to a lawyer who, suiciding, had finished up at the bottom of the harbour with the load of tax evasion schemes he had devised and for which he was to have been prosecuted. She had been left three children and no money; that was when she had taken up freeloading. She had also taken up her husband's shattered practice; she had a law degree that she had never used up till then. Now, seven years later, she was one of the most successful commercial lawyers in Sydney. Malone wondered why Fingal had sent her and not a criminal eagle.

'Mr Hourigan sent me to represent and advise you,' she told the two Nicaraguans.

Domecq almost fell over himself to show his appreciation; he would have followed a skirt into Hades. Paredes, however, was not impressed. 'I am accustomed to lawyers looking less – seductive?'

She flicked a finger at the low-cut silver dress she wore. 'Take no notice of this. I've just come from a party to launch a new perfume.' She held out a wrist to Domecq, the ladies' man, and he sniffed at it like a bloodhound doused with a bucketful of clues. 'Like it?'

'Let Sergeant Clements have a sniff,' said Malone. 'He's been seduced by half the girls on the perfume counter at DJ's.'

Mrs Kersey withdrew her arm and was suddenly brisk. 'Is there any charge against my clients, Inspector?'

'None so far. We're just having a little get-together.'

'I've heard of you. You're supposed to be a hard nut to crack.'

'Just non-seduceable, that's all,' said Malone.

It seemed to him that she would be above using what had once been called womanly wiles; but he was in no mood for a skirmish between the sexes. She was a lawyer and he was a cop and he wanted no gender differences. He had a natural sympathy for women, but he was uncomfortable with them as opponents. He had always been glad that women had never played his class of cricket.

'Your clients don't have to talk, but it might pay them to listen to some of the questions we have to put to them.'

'Questions such as what?'

Malone looked at Paredes. 'Are you doing any business

with a company called Austarm?'

Paredes looked at Zara Kersey and she said, 'Austarm is a perfectly legitimate business, Inspector. I myself drew up its articles of association. It makes small arms. It supplies the Australian Army, if you are looking for credentials. What's the relevance of that question?'

'Relevant to what, Mrs Kersey?'

She had made a mistake; but she had got out of worse traps. 'You're not interested in legitimate business deals.'

'If they're legitimate, Mr Paredes won't have anything to hide. What are you buying?'

Paredes hesitated; then, on a nod from Zara Kersey, he said, 'Rifles and machine-guns.'

'Austarm is one of Mr Hourigan's companies, a subsidiary of Ballyduff Holdings?'

'Correct,' said Mrs Kersey.

'Is there an export licence for these arms?' said Clements, and Malone looked at him gratefully. Clements always had a good practical question buried away amongst his notes.

'Yes. Mr Hourigan has arranged that.'

'I'm sure he has,' said Malone, wondering which conduit Fingal had used to make the connection in Canberra. 'But why him and not Sir Jonathan Tewsday? He runs Mr Hourigan's companies, doesn't he? Is Archbishop Hourigan involved in all this? Is he the one who's arranging the finance?'

'Where did you get such an outrageous idea?' Zara Kersey, too, could act.

'From a letter his niece wrote to a young priest, Father Marquez. He was murdered tonight.'

She had apparently been briefed before she got here; she showed no surprise. 'Neither my clients nor Mr Hourigan and the Archbishop had anything to do with murder.'

'The murderer tried to kill the Inspector too,' said Clements quietly.

That shocked Mrs Kersey. 'I wasn't told that! I'm sorry, Inspector ... Well, now I can understand your prejudice ...'

'I'm not prejudiced,' said Malone, though he knew he was. Clements's quiet remark had brought back the event of an hour ago with shattering clarity. He could feel himself trembling inside, as if his very foundations were about to give way. He was silent for a moment, gathering some control, then he said, 'I'm just curious. You're not a criminal lawyer, but you must be used to entanglements in your own field. This one is chock-a-block with entanglements. And –' his voice hardened, though it got no louder – 'I'm going to get to the bottom of it! If that's being prejudiced, then that's what I am!'

'There may be cross-connections, Inspector – life is full of them, as you well know. But there is no evidence of any connection on the part of my clients with the murder of the priest and the attempt on your life.'

'The Inspector says he was threatened by Señor Domecq,' said Paredes. 'He says he has a tape of the telephone call.'

'Is that so, Inspector?' Zara Kersey gave Malone a hard stare. 'You'll let us hear it, of course.'

'No.'

'Why not?'

'You'll hear it when we lay charges against Mr Domecq.'

'You're bluffing, aren't you, Inspector?'

'No more than you, Mrs Kersey.' He looked at Domecq, changed tack: 'When you came out of the Quality Couch last Saturday night, did you bump into Sister Mary Magdalene? Had she followed you there?'

'The Quality Couch?' Domecq tried to look as if he were being questioned about a bedding store.

'The brothel in Surry Hills.'

Paredes and Zara Kersey looked sharply at Domecq; he just sat very still, a gambler who had been dealt a very bad hand. It was obvious that Paredes did not know his colleague had been to the brothel; anger darkened the older man's face, but he said nothing. At last Zara Kersey said, 'You don't have to answer that question, Mr Domecq. It may incriminate you.'

'He was at the Quality Couch last Saturday night,' Malone told her. 'He's already been identified.'

'You'll produce the witness or witnesses?'

'When the time comes. Well, Mr Domecq, what about Sister Mary Magdalene? Was she outside the brothel when you came out Saturday night?'

Domecq's head was bent, as if he was ashamed of having been in a brothel. Or maybe, Malone thought, he's afraid of Paredes. The latter's silence was more threatening than an outburst of anger.

At last Domecq lifted his head. 'She wasn't there – at least, I didn't see her. I told you – I never met her.'

'Not even at Mr Hourigan's house? She'd been there.'

'We never met the young lady,' said Paredes, his voice gravelly.

'Did you ever meet Father Marquez?'

'No.'

'Were you with Archbishop Hourigan when he was in Nicaragua last year? Oh, we know he was there, all right. It was in the letter I told you about.'

Paredes hesitated, then nodded. 'Yes, we were with him. We flew down with him from Miami.'

'But you didn't meet Sister Mary, his niece?'

Again the hesitation, then: 'We saw her only from a distance. I tell you, Inspector, we had nothing to do with the death of this young woman! Why should we kill an innocent girl like that?'

'I don't know. Why should Mr Domecq threaten me and Father Marquez?'

'You're making unfounded charges, Inspector,' said Zara Kersey flatly. She stood up, wrapping the silver shawl round her shoulders with an extravagant fling. 'I think you have taken up enough of my clients' time. Unless you care to produce a warrant or make some sort of definite charges, we'll be leaving.'

Malone said nothing for a long moment; then he stood up.

He looked at Zara Kersey, not the two Nicaraguans. 'It looks, then, as if we'll have to bring Archbishop Hourigan back from Rome. He seems to be the key to this whole mess.'

'I'll tell Mr Hourigan.'

'If you don't, I'm sure someone else will. Good-night, Mrs Kersey. I don't think that perfume you're wearing has much future. It's already wearing off.'

She wasn't offended; she had become that much of a lawyer. She just smiled and shook her head. 'You're just not a ladies' man, Inspector.' Unlike Domecq who, bouncy again, as if he had found good cards at the bottom of the deck, had offered her his arm. 'You'll be hearing from me again.'

'I'm sure I will.' Then he looked at Paredes. 'And from you, too, Mr Paredes? Or Mr Domecq?'

The older Nicaraguan just stared at him, then turned on his heel and followed Domecq and Zara Kersey down between the desks and out of the big room. The other detectives looked after them, then turned towards Malone.

'She has a lovely arse, Scobie. How come you get all the cases with good-looking birds!'

'Anyone can have this one,' said Malone, but under his breath.

'What do we do now?' Clements looked lugubrious, ready to throw in the towel.

'I shove my neck out.' Even in his own ears it sounded like suicidal bravado.


2


'Daddy, why do people kill each other? Especially a nun?'

'If I knew that, Claire, I'd be the smartest cop in the world.'

'Well, I gotta admit,' said Maureen, the TV addict, 'Sonny Crockett in *Miami Vice* is puzzled, too, sometimes.'

'I'm glad to hear it. I'm tired of being compared to those two over-dressed smart alecks.'

'Smart-arse is the word,' said Maureen, who occasionally sneaked a look at ABC telemovies, where language was freer.

'Not in this house it ain't,' said Malone.

He was in the girls' bedroom saying good-night to them. When he had arrived home they had just finished their home-work, had their baths and got into bed. Tom was already asleep in his room, dead to the world and its cares. Malone, very much alive to its cares and worn out by them, had hoped for a quick good-night kiss, but as soon as he had walked into the room he had seen that Claire was troubled. It turned out that the murder of Sister Mary Magdalene had been the talk of the school yesterday and today and then this evening, on the TV news, there had been the story of the killing of Father Marquez.

'She didn't teach our class,' said Claire. 'She taught Year Eleven and Twelve. But she was always fun to be around when we were playing netball. Sometimes she'd play – she was pretty rough, a real tomboy, you know?'

'Why did they call her Red Ned?' asked Maureen.

But he wasn't going to get into politics, not tonight; the day had been political enough and tomorrow would be worse. 'It's time you went to sleep.'

They lay on their pillows looking at him. Claire, blonde and promising to be beautiful, with a composure that was old for her years; Maureen, dark and vivacious, with his mother's long Irish lip and plenty of the cheeky lip he himself had had as a boy. All his and Lisa's and to be protected. But he knew, better than most fathers, how difficult it would be to shelter them, even against the possibility of murder.

Lisa came to the doorway. 'It's late, girls, and Dad's tired.'

'Is it any use saying prayers for Sister Mary and Father Marquez?' said Claire.

'It's always worth saying a prayer for anyone. I say them all the time.'

'Who for?' said Maureen, who had confessed to asking questions of the priest in the confessional.

'You. Claire and Tom. Dad. Everyone.'

'God, I didn't know you were so *holy*!'

Lisa switched out the light and led Malone out of the room and down to the kitchen, where his supper was on the table. 'Steak and kidney pie.'

'You always know just what a man needs. How do you do it?' He sat down and she poured him a glass of red wine from a cardboard cask. He raised the glass to her. 'I'm glad I'm home tonight.'

'So am I.' She poured herself a glass and sat down opposite him. 'Were you close to Father Marquez when he was shot?'

He hesitated, then nodded. The wine in her glass shook; then she put it to her mouth and gulped, as if it were medicine she was loath to take. He watched her carefully, waiting for some tears; but he should have known better. She lowered the glass, looked at him steadily. 'How close to him were you?'

'Let's talk about something else –'

'No!' She spilled some wine, but ignored it: she who was so careful of any crumb dropped or food splashed by the children. 'Let's talk about what happened tonight! Did they try to kill you, too?'

'I don't know,' he lied. The meat in the pie was already in small chunks, but he applied himself to cutting the chunks even smaller. He picked up a piece of kidney, chewed on it, hardly tasted it. 'The point is, I'm here, safe at home.'

'For how long, though? Safe, I mean.'

She looked around the kitchen, as if she were trying to imagine it as a bunker. It was her pride, all quality timber and copper and brass; a combination fridge and freezer, a double-oven stove, a Swedish dish-washer: it had been their biggest extravagance in their renovation of the house, but he had never begrudged her a penny of it. He had realized after he had married her that, despite her education, her wide travels and her successful career as a government private secretary and then in public relations, she was a *hausfrau* at heart. She was an almost perfect mother to the children, a wonderful lover to him in bed, but it was from this kitchen that she ran her life, the children's and, as far as the Police Department would allow, his.

She had put down the wine, no longer able to taste it. Almost automatically she now reached for the salt cellar and sprinkled salt on the red stain on the tablecloth.

The refrigerator suddenly started up: the sudden humming seemed to bring all his nerves together in an electric shock. 'Darl, for Christ's sake – I'm all *right*! If they meant to get me tonight, they won't try again –'

'Why not?' She lifted the tablecloth, put a paper napkin under the stain.

'Because it won't help their cause –'

'Who's they?'

He sighed, pushed his plate away. 'I wish I knew. I'm going round in bloody circles on this one. The only constant is Archbishop bloody Hourigan stuck there in the centre of it all ...'

'What if they come *here*?' She looked around her again, as if she meant *here*, this kitchen, not the rest of the house. 'I don't want any threats against Claire and Maureen and Tom ...'

'Do you want me to get you police protection?' He hated the thought, but it had to be faced.

'No. Well – I don't know ...' She stared at the red stain on the tablecloth. 'It looks like blood, doesn't it?'

'Stop it!' He had never seen her like this before. 'No, it doesn't. Blood goes darker ... Christ Almighty, why am I talking like this? Look, I'll get on to Jack Browning, the sergeant down at Randwick. We'll work something out. The thing is, I don't want a police car parked outside the house twenty-four hours a day.'

'Neither do I.' She had slumped forward, but now she straightened up. 'Finish your dinner, there are poached pears for dessert. An empty stomach's not going to do you any good. Are you going to arrest Archbishop Hourigan?'

'He's gone back to Rome.'

'What are you going to do then?'

'I'm going after him, if they'll let me.'

# 3

'No!' said Assistant Commissioner Zanuch emphatically. 'The idea is ridiculous!'

'I agree,' said Chief Superintendent Danforth, who never disagreed with his superiors, not now, so close to retirement and his superannuation.

'Let's hear your reasons, Inspector,' said Commissioner Leeds.

The four of them were in the Commissioner's office at headquarters. Malone had put in his report, a copy to each of his superiors rising in rank; it was unusual for a daily report to go direct to the Commissioner, but neither Zanuch nor Danforth had remarked on it. They knew their places in this particular case. Malone had been sent for a half-hour after he had filed his report and, five minutes into this room, he had asked for an extradition warrant against Archbishop Kerry Hourigan.

'Because I don't think we're going to get anywhere in this case without him. He's the key, sir.'

'It's too hot,' said Zanuch. 'We'll get our arses burned off.'

'That only happens if you sit on something,' said Leeds. 'I don't think we can sit on this one. Apart from the two murders, I'm bloody angry at the attempt on Inspector Malone's life!' He was too cool to show obvious anger, but the tension in him was apparent. He clenched a fist, the knuckles showing pale, but refrained from thumping his desk with it. 'For that reason alone, I'd like the Archbishop back here in Sydney so that we can question him.'

'It's not going to be easy,' said Zanuch, backing down. 'I

don't think it's possible to extradite anyone from the Vatican. Even the Italians can't get anyone out of there.'

'I'm afraid the Assistant Commissioner is right,' said Malone when Leeds looked questioningly at him. Clements, the non-Catholic, had done some homework. 'They treasure their own – I read that somewhere. The Pope makes his own judgement about his sinners – I read that, too.'

'What sort of books do you read? said Danforth, who read none. Then he saw the Commissioner's cold look and he ran a hand over his head, searching for another thought: 'What's the point of going to Rome, then?'

'I think we can scare him into coming home. He and his old man don't want a fuss. And neither do those Contra blokes, Paredes and Domecq.'

'Do you think those are the two who ordered those murders?' said the Commissioner. 'You don't come out and say that in your report.'

'I don't have any evidence, sir. None that would stand up in court. For all I know, it could have been Old Man Hourigan.'

He glanced at Danforth out of the corner of his eye as he said that. The big beefy hand went to the top of the short-back-and-sides, but there was no thought there at the moment. But Malone knew there would be before the morning was out, even if Fingal Hourigan had to put it there.

'You sure as hell have some wild ideas,' said Zanuch; then he looked at Leeds. 'What's the Premier going to say about this? He'll have to have a say in it, won't he?'

'Oh, I never thought he wouldn't,' said Leeds, unperturbed. 'I'll just let Inspector Malone argue his case before him.'

He looked at Malone and smiled his cool smile. Bugger it, thought Malone, why don't I transfer to something easy like Traffic or Public Relations?

# 4

In the Commissioner's car going down to the State Office Block, Leeds said, 'This is a messy one, Scobie.'

'I'm thinking of applying for a transfer out to Tibooburra.'

'You think there aren't any politics out there? Scobie, if ever you finish up in my job –'

'God forbid, sir.'

Leeds grinned. 'I think the chances are very slim. But if ever you do, you'll find out that police work is about fifty per cent politics.'

'I know that, sir, even at my level.'

They got out of the car outside of the tall black building at the corner of Macquarie and Bent. Malone wondered if any of the Premiers who had occupied the offices in this government building had ever been embarrassed by their address. He knew that the incumbent Premier wouldn't be: he had been bent all his life.

He was in a bent, bad mood this morning. 'Holy Jesus, John, bursting in on me like this! I'm Police Minister, but do I have to be worried by every little thing that goes wrong? Hullo, you're Malone, aren't you?' He never forgot a name: voter, friend, enemy. 'Oh Christ, it's not the Hourigan affair, is it? My secretary just said you wanted to see me, it was urgent ... What's up now?'

'I want Inspector Malone to go to Rome and bring back Archbishop Hourigan.' Malone was grateful for the way the Commissioner phrased the suggestion; he wasn't going to put one of his junior officers out on a limb on his own. Not in this room, where the toughest axeman in the country reigned. 'An extradition order won't work, so it'll have to be by persuasion.'

'Stand-over stuff, you mean?' Hans Vanderberg might mince a phrase, but he never minced a meaning. 'You think the Vatican will put up with that?'

Leeds looked at Malone, the Catholic, assuming he knew

more about Vatican history. But Malone had never been interested in the Vatican till now; he was the sort of Catholic for whom it and its ruling were too remote. There were other ways to Heaven; or so he occasionally hoped. He had read bits and pieces about the intrigues and influence of the popes and cardinals; he knew that in the past some of them had used the gun and pike as much as the cross. He didn't fancy his chances, but he would ask Lisa to pray for him. She seemed to be praying for everyone else.

'I'd like to try my luck, sir,' he said.

'It'll cost money,' said the Premier, who had spent millions on memorials to himself; he was known not only as The Dutchman but also as the Human Foundation Stone. 'How do you cops travel? Economy?'

'Overseas, I think he should go business class,' said Leeds.

'Jesus!' said Vanderberg. 'Haven't you heard a penny saved doesn't make a pound look foolish?'

'No,' said Leeds and wondered if anyone else had.

The Dutchman grinned. 'If you were one of my Ministers, John, you'd be on the back-benches in no time. Well, all right, Inspector, you can go to Rome, but for Christ's sake, keep it discreet. Are you discreet?'

Malone didn't look at his Commissioner. 'I try to be, sir.'

'Well, try your hardest in Rome. No publicity, you hear? You run into any of them *papapizza*, whatever they call 'em, them Italian photographers, you turn and run, okay?' Then he looked at Leeds. 'What are you going to do with the Archbishop when you get him back here?'

'That depends on how far Inspector Malone gets with his interrogation of him. We have to get to the bottom of this, Premier. This could get much bigger. If a firm in this State becomes a major supplier of arms to the Contras in Nicaragua –'

Vanderberg sat up. 'You didn't say anything about that!'

'I was saving that for the final argument,' said Leeds and told him about Austarm.

201

'Holy Christ!' God the Son was being called upon so frequently, Malone wondered whose side He was on. Maybe all the odds were not with the Archbishop. 'Can you smell the stink? We'll have every lily-livered group in the country, the anti-war mob, the Mothers for Peace, the Greenies, they'll all be out there in Macquarie Street demonstrating!'

'Not the Greenies, surely.'

'They'll join any bloody demo!' The Dutchman had never found a vote amongst the conservationists, so he couldn't be expected to be fair-minded about them.

'Are you in favour of the Contras?' said Leeds mildly.

'Christ, I'm in favour of no one!' Which was true; excluding himself, of course. 'Foreign policy's no concern of mine. Nothing that happens outside Sydney Heads has ever won or lost a vote for me. Who's this crowd – Austarm?'

Leeds looked at Malone and the latter said, 'They are one of Fingal Hourigan's companies.'

The Premier's head shrank into his shoulders, he sank down in his big leather chair. He looked like an ancient turtle that had just found major cracks in its shell. 'Jesus, what other bad news have you got?'

Leeds couldn't resist a small smile. 'I think the sooner we get the Archbishop back here, the better, don't you?'

On the way back to headquarters Leeds smiled. 'You can have a week in Rome, no more. I'll have Mr Zanuch arrange your ticket and expenses – it'll come out of the Special Fund. If anyone wants to know where you are, you've gone on compassionate leave. Do you have a sick grandmother who lives somewhere out of Sydney? Tibooburra, maybe?'

'I'll have to tell my sidekick, Sergeant Clements. He can keep his mouth shut. What about Superintendent Danforth?'

'I'll attend to him.' One knew that he would: the Commissioner had no time for the veteran detective.

Malone wondered if he should tell the Commissioner about Danforth's connection with either Hourigan or Tewsday; but what proof did he have? He decided to remain quiet. Fingal

Hourigan or Tewsday would learn no more from Danforth than they would know from the Archbishop in Rome as soon as Malone landed there.

'Is your passport in order? Good. Leave tomorrow, on Qantas. The sooner we get this over and done with . . .' Leeds looked at his junior officer. 'How do you and I get ourselves into these situations, Scobie?'

'I don't think it's our fault. If human nature were different, it wouldn't happen.'

Which, of course, is the explanation for History.


# 5

Next morning Lisa drove Malone to the airport. He had said goodbye to the children, all of whom wanted to know why they couldn't go with him – 'It's business.'

'Who with?' said Maureen. 'Mussolini or the Pope?'

'Mussolini's dead and the Pope is travelling somewhere – he's never home these days.'

'Neither are you,' said Claire.

'I'll bet he takes his wife and kids with him,' said Tom.

'The Pope doesn't have a wife and kids. He doesn't know how lucky he is.' But he pressed Lisa's hand as he said it.

'That's enough,' said Lisa. 'Kiss Dad goodbye. Maybe he'll bring you back an Italian T-shirt or something.'

'Yuk,' said Claire, already rolling herself into a ball of style. 'Italian is *last* year.'

'What's this year?'

'Japanese.'

'I'll come home via Tokyo. Hooroo. Take care of Mum.'

'I don't think I'll be a policeman,' said Tom. 'Always leaving your wife and kids.'

'Who's been coaching you? Get off to school before I arrest the lot of you.'

When the children had gone to school, Malone and Lisa

went to bed. 'I hate goodbyes at airports,' she said.

'They wouldn't let you do this at Mascot. Not even in the VIP lounge.'

'Ah, that's nice. I love you. Be careful.'

'You haven't stopped the Pill, have you?'

'I don't mean *that*. In Rome, stupid. Oh yes!'

Then they both forgot Rome and danger and politics. Here in each other's arms was the safest place in the world. Love isn't blind, but it can provide a merciful fog.

At the airport Clements was waiting for them. 'Thought I'd come out and see you off. Wish I were going with you.'

'Why don't you go instead of him?' said Lisa.

Clements looked at the two of them, then bit his lip. 'Like that, eh? Have I turned up in the middle of a domestic situation? When I was in uniform, I always hated those sort of calls, a domestic situation.'

Lisa kissed him, which did something towards making his day. 'I wish you *were* going with him. I'd feel happier.'

'Keep an eye on her and the kids, will you, Russ?' said Malone. 'The boys at Randwick are going to be dropping by, but Lisa doesn't want a car parked outside the house all day and night.'

'Changing the subject,' said Clements, 'look who's just checked in.'

Zara Kersey, looking like an advertisement for travel out-fitters, the Vuitton luggage brand-new and discreetly obvious, was standing at the first-class counter. She turned, saw Malone and smiled at him.

'Isn't that Zara Kersey?' said Lisa, who, disdainfully, never missed the social pages of the Sunday newspapers. 'How do you know her?'

'She's Fingal Hourigan's lawyer.'

'Is she going to Rome?'

'Probably,' he said gloomily. The word had already been got to Fingal Hourigan and the battalions were being drawn up. 'The Swiss Guards will probably be out to meet her.'

'She'll probably to able to accommodate them. I think I'd better come with you.'

'What about the kids?'

'Let Russ look after them. I wonder what perfume she wears – Arpège?'

'I think I'll leave you two,' said Clements, grinning. 'Look after yourself, Scobie. My old Congregational mum says you can never trust the Pope.'

'It's not him I'm afraid of. Look after Lisa and the kids, Russ.'

They shook hands, then Clements lumbered away. Lisa said, 'I wish I had a sister to marry him. He'd make a wonderful uncle for the kids.'

'Two cops in the family? You'd worry yourself stiff.'

They went up to the Qantas private lounge, poured themselves some coffee and sat down. Then Zara Kersey came in, looked around and saw that the only vacant seat was next to them. She looked at Malone enquiringly and after a moment's hesitation he shrugged and nodded. She came across, sat down and arranged her body and legs like a model and smiled at Lisa.

'I'm sorry to intrude. Husbands and wives should have a special section set apart for them. You *are* Mrs Malone? I'm Zara Kersey.'

Malone got up and went to get her some coffee and Lisa said, 'How did you know I was Mrs Malone?'

'Oh, he has that look. A happily married man.'

Lisa looked across at Malone at the coffee bench, then back at Zara Kersey. 'How do you know? I don't think I've ever noticed.'

Mrs Kersey smiled. 'Come on, Mrs Malone. Wives notice *everything* about their husbands. Especially anything they themselves are responsible for.'

Malone came back with the coffee. He had noticed that most of the men in the lounge had turned to look at Zara Kersey, but she had the knack of seeming unaware of their stares. Now Malone realized that the men were also looking at Lisa and suddenly he felt that simple-minded pride that all men feel when in the company of beautiful women amidst a group of envious men. He sat down, all at once relaxed. He knew who was the more beautiful of the two women, and she was his. He should have been disgusted with his smug possessiveness, but love is a form of possession.

'Seems we're going to Rome for the same reason, Inspector.'

'I guess so, except that we're on opposite sides. You're lucky to get away, aren't you? I thought you were the busiest lawyer in Sydney.'

'There are degrees of busy-ness, Inspector – you know that. When the Commissioner calls, do you tell him some Superintendent has first call on you? What are his priorities at home, Mrs Malone?'

'Oh, the children and I are a long last,' said Lisa, but she held his hand to show she was still in the race. 'What's it like working for a man as powerful as Mr Hourigan?'

'Exhilarating. Demanding. He thinks all women should be slaves.'

'You'll feel at home, then, in the Vatican.'

'I doubt it. I think your husband and I are going to be the odd ones out in Rome, even though we're on opposite sides.' Then their flight was announced and she said, 'Are you travelling first, Inspector? Perhaps we can sit together, if Mrs Malone doesn't mind?'

'He's in business class,' said Lisa. 'That's what he's on – business. Have a nice trip, Mrs Kersey.'

They smiled at each other like ice queens: Mary of Scotland and Elizabeth of England might have shown the same warmth towards each other. Zara Kersey got up and left and Malone sniffed the air.

'She's not wearing Arpège. You think I'm safe?'

Lisa held his hand all the way down to the passport control gates. There she kissed him and clung to him. 'If it gets dangerous, come home at once. Nothing is worth losing you.'

'Are we talking about Mrs Kersey?'

'You know we're not!' she said angrily; then softened and kissed him again. 'Ring me every day. Reverse the charges if you can't put it on expenses.'

'Make it short and sweet. It's a dollar-eighty a minute – I looked it up.'

'Tightwad.'

He left her with an aching regret, as if he were leaving her for ever. He was sometimes amazed at the depth of his love for her; but he knew from experience that the human heart had never been fully plumbed. In its depth could be found all the slime of human nature; but that was not all. Love went as deep as anything else, or everybody was a lost soul. He had only vaguely thought it out, but he believed it.

At Singapore Zara Kersey sought him out as he walked up and down the splendid transit lounge. When he had come through some years ago, the new Changi terminal had not been built; now it was one of the palaces of travel, the wayside station, the coach-stop raised to the luxury level. But outside it, he had read, in the city itself the hotels were empty, the stores uncrowded, the economy shaky.

'I thought you'd be in the duty-free shops,' she said.

'I'm not a shopper, never have been, even back home.'

'I love shopping, but not for bargains.' She said it without snobbery. 'Scobie – do you mind if we drop the Inspector and Mrs Kersey bit? – what do you want with the Arch-bishop?'

'Some answers, that's all.'

'That's all? You're not planning an arrest?'

'Is his old man expecting one? Zara –' he wondered what Lisa would think of this sudden intimacy, '– I don't think you realize what a mess you've landed in. I'm not sure of the proportions, but this is a bloody sight more than the murder of a nun and a priest.'

'But they're *your* interest, aren't they? You're just Homi-cide.'

'Sure, but this looks to me like a case of murder just being the stone in a pool.'

She looked at him with friendly amusement. 'You can be quite literary, can't you?'

'It's my wife's influence. What's that perfume you're wearing?'

'Poison, by Dior. Two drops and men have been known to fall dead at my feet.'

He grinned. 'My wife inoculated me just before she kissed me goodbye.'

'You're a nice man, Scobie. It's a pity we're on opposite sides.'

# TEN

## I

When the plane landed at Fiumicino airport there were no Swiss Guards to meet Zara Kersey. There was, however, Captain Aldo Goffi to meet Malone.

'Your Commissioner, Mr Leeds, met my chief, General della Porta, at an international conference of police. They are friends, by letter. Commissioner Leeds called the General and explained the situation. We understand your visit is *sub rosa*. Do you speak Italian?'

'*Ciao* and *arrivederci*.'

Goffi was an amiable man in his middle forties, thin and hollow-cheeked, his uniform sagging on him. He looked sad and experienced; on the drive into Rome Malone recognized the scars of police work. 'Are there politics in this, Inspector?'

'Sort of.'

'Ah, wouldn't it be splendid if all police work were just a shoot-out between the goods and the bads? Like in the old John Wayne films. I think I should have been a cowboy sheriff, a spaghetti Wyatt Earp. Where are you staying?'

'There wasn't time to book me in anywhere. What can you recommend that's cheap?'

'Is your police force as tidy with money as ours? Yes? Then I know a good *pensione*, run by a cousin of mine.' He smiled, showing big crooked teeth. 'Everyone has cousins in Italy.'

Malone had never been in Rome before. He had been abroad twice, once on a direct police trip to and from London, the other on a cheap excursion world trip with Lisa on their honeymoon; he had won $12,000 in a lottery and blown half of it on the trip. Rome had not been on their itinerary and now he looked out at the Eternal City with that scepticism that those of Celtic descent, bruised into cynicism by invaders, have about places other than their homeland. He would have been surprised to find that most Italians felt the same way, though for different reasons. After all, the Renaissance had been only yesterday.

The *pensione* was in a side street near the Forum. The cousin and his wife, Signor and Signora Pirelli, were of a size and disposition: they were built for laughter and Malone, a man of dry mirth, could see floods of it ahead. 'You like Italian food?' The signora rolled about with laughter, as if she had cracked a joke.

He always thought Italian food was for gummy gourmets; he liked food one could *chew*, a good steak or lamb chops. But: 'Love it, signora. That's why I've come to Rome.'

The Pirellis went off laughing and Goffi, a lugubrious man compared to them, said, 'You'll need a little sleep, eh? You must have jet lag. But General della Porta would like to see you this afternoon at four o'clock. He thinks you should see him before you approach anyone at the Vatican. He has his contacts there.'

'Cousins?'

Goffi smiled, shook hands with him; Malone, a modest man, was relieved when the captain didn't kiss him on both cheeks as he had his cousin. 'You and I are compatible, Inspector. I shall pick you up just before four.'

Malone slept till three, got up, showered, ate the fruit, cheese and bread that Signora Pirelli brought him and was waiting downstairs in the narrow entrance lobby when Goffi arrived at ten to four. 'The General is most un-Italian – he likes everyone to be punctual.'

'A man after my own heart.'

Goffi had a driver this afternoon, a ghost from the long-dead Mille Miglia; he drove through the Rome traffic as if the cars were no more than phantoms. Malone, a poor passenger even at dead slow, held his breath and kept his feet buried in the floor of the car. Goffi sat beside him relaxed and eager for compliments for his native city.

'You like Rome?'

'What I've seen of it,' said Malone, eyes glued on the impenetrable traffic ahead at which the driver was hurtling the car. 'Do you fellers ever have any accidents?'

'Not many,' said Goffi. 'And it's always the other driver's fault. Is that not right, Indello?'

'Yes, Captain,' said the driver, turning round and taking both hands off the wheel. 'All the time.'

Somehow they reached the Via del Quirinale and *carabinieri* headquarters. As they got out of the car Malone, legs shaking, looked back at the huge building that dominated this hill. 'What's that?'

'The Quirinale Palace. The President of the Republic lives there.'

'So close to police headquarters?'

Goffi caught the inference. 'Politics and the police go together, Inspector. Hasn't it always been the way.'

Malone grinned. 'I think you are going to be a great help to me, Captain.'

'It will be a pleasure.' Goffi's big ugly smile softened his gaunt face.

He led Malone into the big bleached ochre building that was *carabinieri* headquarters and up some wide stairs to the first floor. General della Porta's office made Commissioner Leeds's back home look like a closet; it was fit for the President of the Republic, if he wished to move from next door. The tall walls, separated from each other by what seemed to Malone a small ballroom, held aloft an elaborately carved ceiling. Tall narrow doors, two pairs of them, opened out on to a small balcony that overlooked the square below and the city beyond. Seated with his back to the doors, behind a huge desk, was a man who fitted the room. General Enrico della Porta had the look of a man who thought he should be commanding armies instead of a police force. He had a strong handsome face, if a little plump around the jowls, a grey military moustache which he kept brushing up with the knuckle of his right forefinger, and shrewd belligerent eyes. He would take not only the long view and the short view but the medium, too: he would be ready for any emergency.

But he was friendly: he got up and came round his desk, a small journey, to shake hands with Malone. 'Ah, Commissioner Leeds telephoned me and explained the situation. We have a problem, haven't we?' His English, like that of Goffi, was good. Since crime, and terrorism, had become international, police chiefs had had to improve their linguistic ability. Malone doubted that Leeds could speak anything but English, but that was his British heritage. It was the foreigners who had to broaden their languages. 'I have had dealings with the Vatican on many occasions. God's bureaucracy is far worse than any we have in the rest of Italy.'

'Did the Commissioner give you all the facts as we know them, General?'

'No, sit down and give them to me, Inspector.' He made the return trip to his chair behind the desk, sat down and stroked his moustache. He was wearing uniform, a sartorial splendour that added to his handsomeness; and he knew it. A braided cap lay on the desk, one that suggested, even at rest, that it would be worn at a jaunty angle. The General's vanity was often difficult for those who worked for him; what they didn't know was that it was difficult for him. He was that odd dichotomy, a vain man who wished he could be modest. 'Take notes, Captain Goffi.'

Malone gave them the history of the case, leaving out nothing; no Sydney newspapers or even Fingal Hourigan had a line into *carabinieri* headquarters. General della Porta listened without interrupting, something that Malone, with his small prejudices, had not expected from an Italian.

At last della Porta said, 'It is not going to be easy, Inspector. If the Vatican agreed to your taking the Archbishop back to Australia – indeed, if he agreed to go with you – it would be creating a precedent. And the Vatican hates to create a precedent, unless it holds a Vatican Council on it. It's the way with all religions. Are you a Catholic?'

'Sort of,' said Malone. 'I don't think they'd call me a *good* one.'

'We seem to be in the same mould, Inspector. But Captain Goffi here is a good Catholic, one of the best.' Malone would have had his doubts, but piety wasn't all pursed lips and steepled fingers. 'He's our conduit to the Vatican. He knows our contacts there and he'll lead you straight to them. I think you should talk to Monsignor Lindwall, he's English, before you approach Archbishop Hourigan. He works for the Archbishop in the Department for the Defence Against Subversive Religions.' He shook his head. 'What medieval titles they go in for! Sometimes I wonder that they don't drive around in chariots instead of their Mercedes-Benz.'

Malone, an iconoclast though a slightly reformed one, hadn't expected such disrespect for the Vatican so close to home. But then the Romans had had to live longer and closer with the Church than anyone else.

'Monsignor Lindwall was a missionary in Africa for thirty years. He has no time for bureaucracies, even though he works in one. He will tell you the best way to get over all the hurdles you are going to find over there.' He got up and motioned to Malone to follow him to the tall doors. They were open to the spring sunshine and he stood in the doorway and pointed across the city to the west. 'That's it, Inspector. The citadel, one of the smallest yet easily the most powerful city-state in the world. We Italians invented the city-state – well, perhaps the Greeks were ahead of us, but we developed it much further. That's the last survivor. Don't try storming it, that won't get you anywhere. The only way in is by trickery and subterfuge and burrowing. Monsignor Lindwall will tell you that – he's a Jesuit.'

Oh Christ, thought Malone in half a prayer, what have I got myself into? He looked out across Rome, across the old, pale-coloured buildings to the huge dome of St Peter's dominating the city as towering commercial buildings dominated the other cities he had known. Like most Australians he had little sense of ancient history, but a sediment of his Celtic heritage stirred in him, ghosts whispered to him out of long-ago mists that all men were connected by events. People had lived in this city for God knew how long, there had been voters and polling-booths here when Australia Felix was just a wilderness, there were buildings here far older than Australia as a nation or even a colony. And the Vatican, though its power was now limited by treaty, had ruled longer than any of those who had tried to challenge it. Now he, in a way, was challenging it again.

'We'll help you all we can, Inspector, but not in an obvious way. We have to live with them over there, but you can go back to Australia. So all our help will be unofficial and, as they say, under the lap. We Italians,' he smiled, showing what looked like more than the usual complement of teeth, 'are very good at under the lap. Good luck, Inspector. Please come back and see me before you return home, with or without the Archbishop.'

Malone thanked him and left, saying to Goffi as they went down the stairs and out of the building, 'I think he's on our side.'

'Up to a point, Inspector. Nobody at the top in Italy is ever fully committed to one side or the other. Except, of course, the Pope.'

'And Archbishop Hourigan.'

'Ah, but he's not Italian.'

There was another hair-raising drive down the Via Maggio XXIV, along the Corso Vittorio Emmanuel, over the Tiber and up the Via delle Conciliazone to St Peter's Square. Malone saw only sidelong flashes of what they passed and he vowed he would walk back to the *pensione*, wherever it might be. Better to be lost in the city than laid out in the morgue.

The Department for the Defence Against Subversive Religions was in a building across a small garden from the tower that housed Vatican Radio. It was a small department; evidently subversive religions were not as big a problem as Archbishop Hourigan made out. Or perhaps the Vatican, like the rest of the world, was cost-cutting.

Monsignor Guy Lindwall was a small man; indeed, he was tiny. All his life he had been plagued by his lack of inches. Amongst the extraordinarily tall Denka tribesmen in the southern Sudan, he had been only head-high to their navels. It had seemed to him that he had spent years preaching St Paul's Epistles to the Genitalia. A midget of the cloth, he just hoped to God that when he reached Heaven that God was not tall. But he had a sense of humour, was voluble as a fishwife in a gale, talked a blue streak but with only the occasional blue word. He would, however, never preach cant.

He listened attentively, if impatient to say something, while Malone told him something, but not all, of the case. When Malone had finished the little man ran his fingers through his unruly white hair and shook his head.

'I don't believe Kerry would have anything to do with a murder, not a nun and particularly his niece. He's a decent man at heart, a moral man. He just has this obsession with Communism. We call him Archbishop Rambo and around here we're all scared of what he's going to do next. Every time he opens his mouth, the Sacred Heart fibrillates.' He pointed to a religious print hung on the wall of his tiny office. 'You can see the glass is already cracked. Does anyone in the Curia know you're here?'

'I don't know. The Archbishop's father has friends and spies everywhere. I wouldn't be surprised if someone isn't whispering in the Pope's ear right now.'

'The Holy Father only got back from China last night – he has more on his mind than the Archbishop. No, it's the cardinals in the Curia we have to be careful of. If Kerry goes to them and complains about you harassing him, nothing short of a miracle will get him out of here. You can take out all the warrants you can think of, he won't be moved from here.'

'Maybe he won't broadcast too much. He's got plenty of reasons for keeping all this quiet.'

'True, true. None of us here in the Department knew he'd been in Nicaragua. His Holiness wouldn't like that.'

'Does anyone in the Curia back him on the Contras?'

'One or two. They're divided over there, just like Washington is. There are some of us here in the Department who think that some day, perhaps soon, Islam will be as big a threat to Christianity as Communism – it may even threaten both of them. But all Rambo can see is the Red menace.'

'How did he feel about the Pope going to China?'

'Oh, he was dead against it.' Lindwall smiled, showing badly fitting false teeth. He had lost his own years ago while surviving on a poor diet in Africa. He still suffered from malaria and there were traces of bilharzia in his bloodstream that had to be checked regularly. He had suffered for Christ, but none of it had left him bitter; he had a true vocation. In the next day or two, as he got to know him better, Malone would come to have the highest regard for the tiny priest: he was the best sort of advertisement for the Church, a priest who understood and did not just condemn sinners. 'He preaches that one should never get into bed with a Red, especially in his own country. His Holiness, I think, prefers not to know too much about what we get up to. Or what our Archbishop gets up to.'

'So all we have to watch out for are the cardinals in the Curia?' Malone had had some opponents in the past, but never a battalion of cardinals.

'They are enough. Captain Goffi will tell you how powerful

they are. Even the Holy Father has trouble with some of them.'

'Where's Archbishop Hourigan now? Does he live in the Vatican?'

'No, he lives across the river, in a riverside apartment.' He gave Malone the address. 'Do you want to telephone him?'

'No.' That would only be a warning. Kerry Hourigan would have Zara Kersey there waiting for him. 'He might call out the Swiss Guards.'

'I shouldn't be surprised. He's a loose cannon, as the Americans here in the Department say.' Lindwall escorted Malone and Goffi to the door. 'Have you seen the Basilica, Inspector? Come back this evening at six, you'll see it at its best. His Holiness is saying Mass to celebrate his trip to China.'

'What'll we have at communion – rice wine?'

'Tell that to Archbishop Hourigan. He'll probably agree with you.'

Out in St Peter's Square Malone gently but politely declined Goffi's offer to drive him to the Archbishop's apartment. 'I need the exercise, Captain. And I think it's better that I see him on my own. He may just shut up shop altogether if he knows you're involved, unofficially or not.'

Goffi looked disappointed, but nodded. 'I understand, Inspector. But take care. Rome isn't as safe as it used to be.'

Malone walked down the Via delle Conciliazone, passed under the shadow of the Castle of St Angelo, crossed the bridge and walked along the eastern bank of the Tiber. He could feel the city brushing against his consciousness; he began to wonder at the history of Rome, though he knew none of it. What secrets had been dreamed up behind these sun-drenched walls he was now passing? The sun beat off them as if the stone were alive. He touched one of the walls, felt the warmth of it; when he took his hand away, there were flakes of paint on his fingertips. I've left my prints on Rome, he smiled, being literary. Maybe the city did that to you, though he didn't know the name of a single Roman poet.

Archbishop Hourigan's apartment was on the third floor of a *palazzo* that had once been the home of one of Rome's richest and most powerful families. The grandeur was shabby now: paint peeled, dust floated, the busts on the wide marble staircase were chipped, like experiments in cosmetic surgery that had gone wrong. Malone passed several big doors, glanced at the names: Contessa This, Principessa That. The *palazzo* was a crypt for the past and Malone wondered what the Archbishop was doing here.

When he came to the Hourigan door he saw at once that it was new; or refurbished. The thick oak was polished, the brass door-knobs were bright. There was no title on the brass name-plate beside the door, just the name *Hourigan*. Perhaps clerical rank had no rating on this side of the river.

A butler in black uniform with white gloves answered Malone's ring. He was an elderly man with a rugged face that reminded Malone of that of a Mafia boss he had once arrested back in Australia who, true to the form of the period, had been acquitted. The butler showed no surprise when Malone introduced himself, but stepped back and gestured for him to enter.

Then Kerry Hourigan, dressed in street clothes (Why did I expect him to be in full regalia? Malone wondered. Did Rome do that to you?), came into the entrance hall, his heels clack-clacking on the black-and-white marble.

He put out his hand. 'I've been expecting you, Inspector. I was told you were in Rome. Come on in.'

He led the way into a high-ceilinged room too big to be called a living-room; Malone guessed this was what was called a *salon*. There was no seedy grandeur here; though nothing looked new, everything was stylish and expensive. The paintings on the walls were Old Masters, for all Malone knew: to his inexpert eye, they looked it. He noticed there were no religious paintings, no agonized saints sitting on red-hot pokers or Madonnas airborne by the Renaissance equivalent of Alitalia; perhaps the Archbishop got enough of that sort of art on the other side of the river. Hourigan waved Malone to a silk-covered chair.

'I never thought you'd have the persistence to follow me all the way here to Rome.' He appeared friendly enough; or anyway relaxed. He's at home, Malone thought: Rome is home. 'I understand there's been another murder.'

'Yes. Father Marquez – you met him that evening in St Mary's.' It seemed a year ago. Did jet lag and 10,000 miles do that to you? Or was it because he was in another world altogether? 'They tried to kill me, too.'

That upset the Archbishop's composure. 'They? Who are *they*?'

Malone decided to be blunt. 'I was hoping you might give me a clue, Your Grace. I tried my luck with Mr Paredes and Mr Domecq – they suggested I try you.'

Hourigan shook his head. 'You're bluffing, Inspector.'

'That's what your father's lawyer said – Mrs Kersey. Why does everyone think I'm bluffing? You're connected to these murders, Your Grace, whether you know it or admit it or whatever. All of you are bluffing much more than I am. Or lying.'

The Archbishop flushed at that. 'That's insulting! Dammit, man, who do you think you are? I've told you – I know nothing about the murders! Good God, don't you think I've felt *something* about my niece's death, some grief, horror? I feel for that young priest, too, though I never knew him. I have no connection with the murders – they are as much a mystery to me as they are to you!'

'They may be a mystery to you, but I'm still convinced you're connected to them. We want all of you brought together for questioning – you, your father, Paredes and Domecq. We can't bring Paredes and Domecq here to Rome, but we can stop them leaving Australia –'

'How?' The Archbishop was almost too quick with his query.

Malone grinned. 'You're in a bureaucracy – you know there

are ways and means. Come back with me, Your Grace. It'll cause less of a stink.'

'You mean you'll cause a – a stink if I don't?'

'It's on the cards.'

The Archbishop sat silent, his chin on his chest. His hands were folded, but he was not praying. The Lord, for Whom he was working, had let him down; the murders were accidents which should never have been allowed to happen. The Lord had made a mistake in allowing man his free will.

At last he looked up. 'If I come back, if all your investigations prove I had absolutely nothing to do with this, can you keep it quiet? Out of the newspapers? I have work to do, Inspector – it's God's will –' There was a glint of passion in his eyes, almost of fanaticism. 'I don't want it ruined!'

'I can't promise anything, but I'll do my best. Can you leave tomorrow night?'

'No,' said Fingal Hourigan from the doorway. 'He won't be leaving Rome at all.'

He did not look out of place in this *salon*. With his white hair, thin aquiline face, dark suit and silver walking-stick, he could have been a Roman aristocrat; only the bright Irish eyes gave him away. There were still rumours of power and intrigue in the corners of the big room; he looked as if he intended to revive them. It suddenly struck Malone that this was *his* apartment, which explained the name without rank on the door-plate; the Archbishop was living here as a rich man's son, not through some indulgence by the Church. Once again he wondered what had happened to vows of poverty. But he would get nowhere asking such a question of the Hourigans. The Archbishop probably looked upon luxury as one of God's casual gifts; Fingal would look upon it as a deal with the Almighty. He sounded at the moment as if Rome itself was part of the deal.

'My son belongs here, Inspector.' He came into the room, moving a little cautiously on the marble tiles; the silver walking-stick tapped bone-like on them. 'He's outside your domain altogether.'

'Not entirely, Mr Hourigan.' Malone had stood up, not wanting to be dominated by the old man. 'I can ask the *carabinieri* to arrest him and hold him. He's outside Vatican City.'

The Hourigans looked at each other quickly, as if this possibility had not crossed their minds. Then Fingal coughed a small dry laugh. 'You don't know Italy, son. When did the *carabinieri* last arrest an archbishop? One from the Vatican? I'm not without influence here, Inspector.'

'The Mafia?' It was a stupid remark and Malone knew it as soon as he uttered it; but he was becoming frustrated. 'Forget that. You'd be further up the scale than them.'

'I'm glad you think so. You're not that dumb – I don't do business with hoodlums. I don't do business with murderers, either.' He had once, long ago, but it never troubled his conscience. 'Neither does my son.'

'Paredes and Domecq have both been charged with murder in Nicaragua.'

'Charged and acquitted.'

'No, not acquitted. Never brought to trial. There's a difference.' He looked at Kerry Hourigan, who had remained in his chair, silent and with his hands still clasped together. 'You must have known their record?'

'They were fighting Communists,' said the Archbishop. 'There was a war ...' But he sounded as if he were trying to forgive sins that were beyond his comprehension. 'They are the leaders of an honourable army.'

'Bullshit, Your Grace,' said Malone. 'With all due respect. The FBI have them also tagged as being the leaders of a drug ring, tied up with some mob in Colombia. You're dealing with crims and you're a bloody fool if you don't face up to it!'

The Archbishop stood up, drawing some dignity into himself. 'I think you'd better leave, Inspector. I'll take my chances on my own judgement.'

Malone knew when to retreat. He was too experienced a policeman to go plunging on; there were other ways of going forward than by a direct line. At the moment, however, he wasn't quite sure where he was going. He felt the loss of back-up that could be relied upon. He had been like this twice before, in London and in New York; and he felt a recurrence of the same lack of confidence. But he didn't let it show.

'Then you'd better move back into the Vatican. A *cara-binieri* captain told me less than an hour ago, Rome isn't safe any more. You'd better believe it.'

As he went out into the entrance hall he heard a sound that gave him some small comfort. It was the nervous tap-tap of Fingal Hourigan's stick on the marble tiles.

## 2

Malone was both weary and tired; which can be two different conditions. Jet lag was catching up with him: he felt like falling into bed and sleeping for a week. But the weariness was greater: the weight of this case was exhausting him. Sitting here in a side pew in St Peter's he wanted both to fall asleep and throw in the case. Then, like the apparitions that sometimes appear in the moment before one falls asleep, the faces of Sister Mary Magdalene and Father Marquez, the one dead and serene, the other alive and afraid, would jerk him awake. Perhaps it was the setting. Both of them, the religious, would have been thrilled to be sitting where he was, to be so close to what was going on.

Once inside the great basilica he had been amazed at the size and splendour of it. He was not to know it, but a philosopher, Giovanni Papini, had once written, 'It is like the hall of an imperial palace designed for splendid gathering, rather than the mausoleum of a martyr intended for the public appearance of the Vicar of Christ.' Russ Clements's old

Congregationalist mum would have sneered at it and retreated to her tin-roofed chapel, but Malone, against the grain of his nature, found himself impressed.

The Pope had made a modest entrance; if popes, surrounded by a regiment of cardinals, archbishops, bishops, liveried laity and Swiss Guards, could ever move modestly in the huge basilica. He had not been carried in on the *sedia gestatoria*, the chair usually used during his public appearances; perhaps he, too, was suffering from jet lag and did not want a reminder of his long flight *from* Beijing. Newspapers had reported that, crossing the Muslim countries, the Alitalia flight had been subjected to intense air buffeting. The *sedia gestatoria* was rarely on an even keel: carried by Italians, it always tended to list to the right or left, depending on the current government in power outside the Vatican. Popes never looked more uneasy than when in the shoulder-borne chair.

'I'm glad you came,' Monsignor Lindwall had said when Malone had presented himself back at the Department for the Defence Against Subversive Religions. 'A lot of people may sneer at all the panoply of a papal Mass, but honest human nature needs panoply occasionally. The Communists go in for it on May Day. The Presbyterians are dour in church, but they get carried away by their pipe bands at the Edinburgh Tattoo – so do I, I must confess. I missed all the panoply during those years in Africa. I made up for it by going to watch the tribal dances, dreadfully pagan occasions, and enjoying them. A papal Mass is extravagant and I sometimes wonder what Christ would have thought of it, but the soul needs the occasional circus, even if it's a solemn one. It doesn't make one a better Christian to attend one, but it beats the hell out of self-flagellation.'

Malone had grinned at the little man. 'Who hears your confession?'

'Oh, I have a friend, another retired missionary. We try to out-do each other in imaginary sins. How did you fare with our Archbishop?'

'I think he's winning on points at the moment. But it's a long way from over. I think he may retreat into the Vatican, but he can't hide here for ever.'

'How much time have you got? There are over ten thousand rooms in the Vatican. There are nine hundred and ninety-seven staircases you may have to run up and down. Thirty of the staircases are secret – the Vatican has had more experience at hiding people than any other organization on earth. I sometimes think the CIA and the KGB and MI5 come here for instruction in safe houses, or whatever they call them. If Kerry goes to His Holiness or the Tardella –'

'What's that?'

'The Pope's inner cabinet. If he goes to one of the senior cardinals in the Tardella, you've had it, my son. You may just as well go back to the Colonies.'

'The Colonies? You're eighty-seven years out of date as far as Australia is concerned. I didn't think you'd be an imperialist Pom.'

'A figure of speech, Scobie. I was thinking in Roman terms. Everywhere outside of Rome is the Colonies.'

'How does a cynic like you last in a place like this?'

Monsignor Lindwall smiled. 'Better to have me inside, shooting my mouth off, than outside. Shall we go to Mass?'

Despite his lack of liking for panoply, Malone was impressed by the papal Mass. He could see that this could be part of the Church's seduction of converts; they expected Heaven to be even better. The basilica was packed; it seemed to him that people were even squeezed into niches in the walls, like flesh-coloured effigies. There was constant movement, even during the Consecration; Italian congregations evidently didn't consider it rude to wander around in The Lord's presence. One item did thrill Malone: the singing. This was *real* music: if The Lord could listen to guitars and banal hymns after this feast, He was straining His charity or had a tin ear. Then he found himself dozing off again.

Guy Lindwall woke him with a digging elbow. 'It's over.

Do you see who is on the other side of the altar?'

Malone shook his head, opened his eyes wide to get them working again. During Mass there had been so many people between him and the opposite pews that he had been able to see no one. Now, amongst the chromatopsia of cardinals, he saw the two Hourigans, Zara Kersey and General della Porta standing together in a group. With them were two elderly cardinals, one white-headed, the other bald, both of them looking like the princes they knew they were.

'You see?' said Lindwall. 'He's already with the Tardella.'

'And the *carabinieri*, too, it seems,' said Malone and all at once wanted to give up, to fall into bed and wake up in Randwick with Lisa beside him and the case wiped from his memory.

But it wasn't to be. As they began to move out of the basilica, Zara Kersey looked across and saw Malone. She smiled at him, then turned and said something to Fingal Hourigan. The old man shook his head, then he turned and stared across at Malone. He said something to his son, then the two of them pushed through the crowd to Malone and Monsignor Lindwall. Only when they had come through the throng did Archbishop Hourigan look down and see the little man.

'Hello, Guy, do you two know each other?'

'He's my spiritual adviser,' said Malone.

'I've been explaining the difficult ways to Heaven,' said the Monsignor. 'He's a stubborn man.'

'Don't we know it!' said the Archbishop.

'Inspector –' Fingal Hourigan had barely glanced at Lindwall. 'Mrs Kersey has suggested we get together for one last conference. She thinks we may be able to work something out. I doubt it, but I don't pay her to give me advice I ignore. Can you have dinner with us?'

'I'm bushed, Mr Hourigan – I have jet lag –'

'So have I,' said the old man. 'How do you think I got here? By transubstantiation, changing one body for another?'

'I wouldn't be surprised,' said Malone, dredging up some reserves that he thought he had lost; this old bastard acted like a battery charger on him. 'Where will we have dinner?'

'The Hassler. Nine-thirty. Is that too late for you? These Eyeties evidently can't cook anything before nine o'clock.'

That would give him time for at least an hour's nap. 'I'll be there. Will General della Porta be there? He didn't tell me he knew you.'

'He's an old friend,' said Archbishop Hourigan.

'I might have guessed it. What about the Pope?'

He left them on that, clearing a way through the crowd, with Monsignor Lindwall following in his wake. He walked quickly, almost hurling people out of his way and Lindwall had to run to keep up with him. Once outside, however, in the cool air of the spring evening, he slowed down, took a deep breath.

'I'll pray for you,' said the Monsignor as he said good-night.

'Will it help?'

'I don't know. I prayed every night in Africa, asking for something better of The Lord. Look where He landed me. But if we don't keep hoping and praying, what's the point of anything? Good luck.'

'Luck isn't a Christian symbol, is it?'

Lindwall smiled. 'I told you – I used to go to those pagan celebrations and enjoy them. Not all pagan things are bad.'

Malone went back to the *pensione*, asked Signor Pirelli to call him at nine o'clock, went up to his room and was asleep as soon as his head hit the pillow. It seemed only a moment later that Pirelli was shaking him awake. He got up, had a quick shower, dressed and, after getting directions from Pirelli, walked up to the Hotel Hassler at the top of the Spanish Steps. He was ten minutes late, but, usually a most punctual man, it didn't worry him. The Hourigan party had not arrived and he was shown to their reserved table. It was a window table with a view over the city. This was one of the perks of the rich, he guessed, and felt the natural envy of a poorer man.

The Hourigans and Zara Kersey arrived fifteen minutes later. Fingal made no apology and his son and Zara Kersey said nothing about their tardiness. Perhaps they felt that in Italy one did not need to.

'I thought you might not have waited,' said Fingal.

Malone had had two cups of the strong Italian coffee, felt more awake. 'General della Porta didn't come with you? I only stayed because I wanted to talk to him.'

'We'll keep the Eyetalians out of this,' said Fingal. 'What do you want to eat?'

Malone had already glanced at the menu and was glad that he was not paying; eating out in Rome was expensive. He ordered fish; judging by its price it had been landed in a Bulgari gold-mesh net. While he was eating it he could taste money; but he enjoyed it. It was Fingal Hourigan's money and it might be the only thing he would get out of the family. The Archbishop ate extravagantly; Malone tipped he might have asked for seconds at the Last Supper had he been there. Both Fingal and Zara Kersey ate sparingly. Nothing much was said during the meal, though Zara did try to keep some conversation going.

'You should have brought your wife to Rome with you, Inspector. Rome is a city for women.'

'Better than Paris?'

'Any city where they can spend money is a city for women,' said Fingal. 'Do you want dessert?'

'Yes,' said Malone. 'If you don't mind spending the money.'

Fingal grinned. 'It's a pity you're a cop, Malone. I could have found a place for you. I still could,' he added without the grin.

'Are you trying to bribe me? In front of your lawyer, an honest lady?'

'Let's not get into that,' said Zara. 'The bribery, I mean, not my honesty. If Mr Hourigan meant it, it was meant only as a joke.' She gave Fingal a hard stare. 'Right?'

He stared back at her, then retreated behind his menu. Kerry Hourigan said from behind his menu, 'I'll have the stuffed peaches. I think it's time Mrs Kersey put our case to you, Inspector.'

Zara put a cigarette in a holder and lit it. Fingal put down his menu and said, 'I don't like smoking at the table.' Zara put out the cigarette, made no apology and looked at Malone. This is like family, he thought. Fingal treats her as he does his daughter and he gets about as far with her as he does with Brigid.

'Inspector, the Archbishop tells me you have threatened to create a stink back in Sydney if he doesn't return with you.'

'That's about it,' said Malone. 'It's time I started playing dirty.'

'Where will you create the stink, exactly? Mr Hourigan is a major shareholder in two of our biggest newspapers, through one of his subsidiary companies.'

'There's the ABC – something like *Four Corners* or *The 7.30 Report*. You seem to forget, Mrs Kersey. Most of the journos in Sydney are left-wing or that way inclined. And I don't think any of them are particularly religious, probably the opposite. I don't think we'd have any trouble creating a stink.'

'We?'

He almost said *Me and the Commissioner*; but he knew just how far he could go in taking the Commissioner's name in vain. 'The Police Department. We're all pretty tired of people saying we're corrupt – we're looking for chances to show we're not. What was it you wanted to put to me?'

'I don't think this is the place.' She looked at Fingal. 'Can we go back to your apartment, Mr Hourigan?'

'I don't like entertaining cops in my home.' But then he nodded. 'Okay. We'll have dessert and coffee first. We don't want to disappoint my son.'

Kerry laughed. 'Gluttony is my only constant sin.'

Malone forbore to ask him what his occasional sins were.

They rode back to the Hourigan apartment in a Mercedes limousine driven by the elderly butler, who evidently doubled as chauffeur. Once inside the apartment he did a quick change, appeared again in his black livery and white gloves and served them liqueurs and more coffee.

'This is a forty-year-old Grande Fine Champagne,' said Kerry, sniffing his brandy glass. 'One of the best cognacs, another of my sinful indulgences. A religious war, or rather the end of one, was responsible for the creation of cognac. Did you know that, Inspector? Henri the Fourth of France stopped the war between the Huguenots and the Catholics in whenever-it-was, Fifteen – something. The Huguenots had learned about "burned wine" from the Dutch . . .'

He trailed off when he saw his father looking stonily at him. He had drunk too much wine at dinner; but something else had undermined him. Is he afraid? Malone wondered.

When the butler had retired, Malone said, 'Well, what do we have to talk about?'

Zara Kersey looked at Kerry Hourigan. 'I think you'd better speak for yourself now, Your Grace.'

'Be careful,' warned Fingal.

The Archbishop, replete and seemingly at ease now, as if a full stomach were some sort of assurance, sat back in his chair, re-gathering himself. It was a high-backed chair covered in rich red velvet; he looked cardinalate in it, almost papal.

'I have the strongest possible alibi for myself and Señor Paredes for last Saturday night. We were in Moss Vale, some hundred and forty or hundred and fifty kilometres from Sydney. We didn't leave there to return to Sydney by car till three-thirty in the morning.'

'Where were you? At Austarm?'

'You know about Austarm?' He seemed surprised.

'We've done some homework.'

'H'm.' Kerry Hourigan looked at his father. 'Do I tell him everything?'

'I wouldn't tell him anything. But now you've started ...'

'Only as much as you have to,' Zara Kersey advised.

Fingal suddenly changed his mind. 'Tell him everything. Otherwise we'll never get rid of him.'

Malone, tiredness all at once hitting him like a bilious attack, grinned. 'Thanks.'

'Well –' Kerry Hourigan seemed a little less assured now, as if he had expected to get away with telling much less. 'Señor Paredes and I were there to buy arms. You must understand, this is in the strictest confidence. If this got out, it would be a bigger scandal than the Irangate affair in the United States. Do I have your word on that?'

'No,' said Malone. 'This isn't the confessional. You know I have to put in a report. I can see that it goes to the Commissioner and nobody else, but I can't guarantee what he'll do with it.'

The two Hourigans looked at each other again and Fingal said, 'Leave that with me.'

I know the Commissioner isn't in your pocket, thought Malone; but maybe the Premier was and the Premier was the Minister for Police. All at once he felt unutterably weary. The world was full of conspiracy, of connections, of payments made and favours done. Why did he think he could beat it all?

'The Vatican doesn't know I'm involved in our programme in Nicaragua – the Contras' programme, that is.'

'Some people in the Vatican know you're involved. You mean the Pope doesn't know.'

'Well, yes ...'

Out of the corner of his eye Malone saw that Zara was disturbed by the Archbishop's frankness, reluctant though it might be. Or perhaps she had been shocked by what she had been told beforehand, whatever it might have been.

'When it comes off, when it is successful – as it will be –' Again there was that glint of passion (of fanaticism?) in the eyes. 'When it happens, I'll be a hero. Not a public one, but

230

here in the Vatican – yes. A success against the Communists –
one that will wipe out that canker in Latin America – is what
we want here in Rome. But there are ways it has to be done –
well, ways Rome would rather not know about. The Lord
understands, but Man sometimes doesn't –'

'Don't get too pious,' said the Archbishop's father, who
would never be that.

Kerry smiled, not offended: the zealot can never be insulted.
Malone understood that. Archbishop Hourigan was no
foam-mouthed raver, but he was a zealot or a fanatic, all
right.

'Señor Paredes and I went to Moss Vale to buy arms –'

'On a Saturday night? In the middle of the night?'

'We didn't want any of Austarm's staff to know about us.
We dealt only with their two top executives.'

'What was the order?'

'Ten thousand rifles –'

'What sort? Old ones or new?'

'Austarm's newest – it's based on the Belgian 7.62 rifle. Do
you know it?'

'I've seen it.' He was surprised that the Archbishop should
know one rifle from another; he was a Rambo, all right. 'We
confiscated half a dozen from a gang of bikies. They're pretty
lethal.'

'Rifles are supposed to be – you know that.' He could see
himself at the head of an army, another Julius II, that most
war-like of popes. 'We also ordered a thousand machine guns
and I've forgotten how many gross of grenades and land-
mines.'

*Just something to fill up the shopping basket.* Malone
looked at Zara, seemingly the only sane one besides himself
in the room. Fingal seemed unperturbed by his son's bizarre
militarism.

'Do you believe all this?'

'Yes.' But he recognized the reluctance in her voice; or was
there a hint of outrage, of disgust? 'It's all true, Inspector.

That's why I didn't want this conversation held in the restaurant.'

Malone looked back at the Archbishop. 'An order like that – how are the Austarm executives going to explain that to the factory production manager? What would it be worth?'

'Including the ammunition, shipping, everything – just on ten million dollars.'

'And you expected nobody to ask questions about an order like that?'

'It was being arranged.'

'That's not good enough. I want to know everything or I'm on my way back to Sydney, with or without you, and I'll start work again on Paredes and Domecq.' He looked at Fingal. 'You'd better tell him, Mr Hourigan – I'm a bastard for persistence.' He just wished he were not so exhausted.

'The end justifies the means, Inspector.'

'Hitler said that.' Had he? It seemed something that all the fanatics of history would have said. But, as he was honest enough to admit to himself, probably a host of honest men had also said it. 'Go on, Your Grace.'

Kerry Hourigan hesitated, then went on. 'The bill of sale says they are for Saudi Arabia. The export order will say the same.'

'Does anyone in Canberra know about that?'

Again the hesitation; then: 'Yes.'

'Do the Saudi Arabians know?'

'Yes.'

'Who's paying for it? Them?'

'No.'

'Who, then?'

'I am,' said Fingal Hourigan.

Malone kept his surprise to himself; then after the initial reaction, there was no surprise. Ten million was nothing to a man of Fingal's wealth; some profligate playboys spent that much on a yacht or a plane. But Fingal had never had a public profile as a rabid anti-Communist. Was he being just an indulgent father? It was hard to believe such a proposition. Fingal, he would have thought, was the sort of father because of whom charity would have left home.

'Do the Saudis know that?'

'No,' said Fingal. 'They don't need to know. They're willing to put their name to the order in support of a good cause.'

'That's a great combination – the Saudis and the Catholic Church. How ecumenical can you get? All that, just to get rid of the Sandinistas in Nicaragua? Okay, you've told me all that and that explains where the Archbishop and Mr Paredes were Saturday night. It doesn't explain where Domecq was after he left the brothel. It would take only one man to kill your niece, Your Grace.'

He said it brutally and it had its effect on the Archbishop. The big man seemed to slump in his chair: he had been hit by conscience, against which even a full stomach is no defence.

'When was my – my granddaughter murdered?' said Fingal.

'The medical examiner put it between ten p.m. and two a.m., give or take an hour or so.'

'Then it couldn't have been Señor Domecq. He was with Mrs Mosman, Tilly Mosman, till seven in the morning.'

'How do you know?'

'I checked with him and then with Mrs Mosman. He didn't leave the brothel, as I gather she told you. He was upstairs in her private suite.'

*Who isn't in your pay?* But Malone didn't ask that question. That would mean laying his cards on the table and Fingal would see that it was a dead hand.

'How do you know Tilly Mosman?'

'I don't.' He knew she could be trusted. 'I had someone visit her. I'm investing money in these two men. I investigate everybody I back. It's just plain business sense.'

Malone suddenly felt light-headed. He wanted to adjourn the interrogation. But that would mean losing his grip on the whip-handle; it was tenuous enough already. He sat up, held out his cup and Zara, the closest he had to an ally in this room, poured him more coffee from the silver pot. He gulped it down, forced himself at least to sound alert, if not to feel so. How did statesmen, shuttling across the world, keep wide awake when bargaining for peace? Would historians in the future take into account the effects of jet lag as now, writing of the past, they took into account those of syphilis and porphyria and a dozen other maladies of the past? He finished the coffee and put down the cup.

'Righto, that's Saturday night accounted for. Now we have Tuesday night, when Father Marquez was murdered and someone tried to do me in, too.'

'I was at the airport, waiting to board the plane for here,' said Kerry Hourigan.

'And Señor Paredes and Domecq were at my home,' said Fingal Hourigan. 'You have my word for that, Inspector.'

*What's that worth? Ten million?* But insults would never get him anywhere, not even if he were wide awake and on top of the situation. They might arouse the unintelligent, who might lose their tempers; but Fingal would never lose his, any rage would be instantly under control. He stood up, knowing he had lost this round.

'I'll sleep on what you've told me. I'll be back again tomorrow.'

'I'll have Paolo drive you home,' said Fingal, not bothering to rise. He had the smug look of a manager who, with his boxer, had just scored a knock-out. In his own eyes, though, he would never have given himself such a lowly image. He was a king-maker; or anyway a pope-maker. He was looking for a throne, not a champion's title belt.

'No, thanks, I'll walk,' said Malone curtly and left.

Outside in the night air he breathed deeply, trying to clear his lungs and his head, trying to stay awake. He knew that if he had accepted the lift back to the *pensione* he would have been asleep in the car before they reached there and Paolo, and probably Pirelli, would have had to carry him up to bed.

It was still early by what he guessed were Rome's standards;

234

the streets had none of the deserted look of midnight Sydney. He felt less light-headed, but he knew that if he had to break into a run for any reason he would just stumble and fall headlong. He walked carefully; how did modern cricketers turn out for net practice only a day after a twenty-four hour flight? He'd better have a check-up when he got back to Sydney; maybe there was something wrong with his blood pressure. Maybe the Hourigans were a health hazard.

He passed the ruins of the Forum, where the ghosts of ancient assassins lurked, and turned into the street where the Pensione Pirelli was, glad that he had only a few yards to go to his bed. Then he heard the footsteps behind him, heard them quicken into a run and he turned. The quick turn-round, with his light-headedness dizzied him and at the same time saved him; he fell against the man as the latter came at him with the knife. The fall saved him: he hit the man in the midriff with his shoulder, a thumping tackle. The man staggered back, hacked at him with the knife; Malone felt the blade hit the bone in his shoulder and he gasped. He fell away, kicking at the man as he came at him again, rolled over and came up on his feet and saw the attacker coming at him with the knife thrusting up for the kill. Then a gun went off right beside his ear.

The attacker stopped in his tracks, a gaping wound in his throat. He stood upright for a moment, his mouth open as if in surprise, then he toppled backwards. Malone turned and saw Captain Goffi, his gun still held for a second shot. Then the last thirty-six hours caught up with him in a black wave and he fell in a limp heap beside the man who had tried to kill him.

# 3

'He was a Mafia hit-man named Morello, brought in from Milan,' said General della Porta. 'Captain Goffi has identified him.'

'I don't believe the Mafia are involved in this,' said Malone.

'Of course not.' The General sounded as if he wanted no Italians involved, not even the Mafia. 'Morello was a contract man, he did outside work if the pay was good enough.'

They were in della Porta's office. After Goffi's shot had rung out in the quiet side street it had been only a moment or two before an excited crowd had gathered. Goffi had been kneeling beside Malone when the latter had regained consciousness. He had leaned down and whispered in Malone's ear, 'Don't say a word, just keep quiet.'

Then Signor Pirelli, in pyjamas, dressing-gown and a state of high concern, had appeared. 'Signor Malone! What have they done?'

Goffi had taken over at once, giving Malone no chance to reply. 'Get back to your phone, Dino, and call the ambulance.'

'And the police?'

'I am the police!' Goffi snapped, not wanting the city police to poke their noses into this affair. 'Start running!'

The ambulance had arrived within five minutes. Malone, his shoulder numb, had remained dumb. He had got shakily to his feet and leaned against the wall behind him. He had looked down at the dead thug, but someone had thrown a sheet or curtain over him and he was now just an anonymous lump. When the ambulance arrived the body had been lifted in and then Goffi, who had disappeared for a few moments to talk to his cousin, had come back and helped Malone into the ambulance.

'I've told them to take us to *carabinieri* headquarters first. We'll have a police surgeon look at your shoulder. If it's bad, we'll have to take you to a hospital. If it's not, then we can keep this to ourselves. I've told my cousin not to speak to the newspapers.'

'I don't care who knows,' said Malone. 'I was bloody near killed tonight! If it hadn't been for you . . .'

236

'You'll think differently in the morning.'

'I wouldn't bet on it.'

But this morning, after ten hours' sleep, he had felt differently. The police surgeon had said last night that the wound would heal without any serious consequences; the knife had skidded off his shoulder-blade and plunged down without much damage to the muscles. The shoulder was still sore and hurt when he moved his arm; but it was his left arm and he was right-handed. When he had woken he had had a bath instead of a shower, keeping the wound dry; the long sleep and the bath had made him feel much better. When Goffi had picked him up and brought him here to *carabinieri* headquarters he had been prepared to listen to what General della Porta had to say.

On the way across town he had said to Goffi, 'Were you tailing me?'

'Yes,' said Goffi. 'The General told me I wasn't to let you out of my sight.'

'Was that bloke tailing me, too?'

'No, he was waiting for you in a doorway. He knew where you were staying –'

'Nobody else did but you and the General.'

Goffi smiled, unoffended. 'Are you suspecting me or the General?'

'No. Sorry. Yes, there was someone else – Monsignor Lindwall.'

'Don't be too suspicious, Inspector. I think you may have been tailed from the moment you landed at Fiumicino. You were fortunate I was right behind you. Otherwise I think you would have been dead.'

'He used a knife, the same way they killed the nun back in Sydney.'

'There may be a connection, but I don't think so. Knives are just quieter than guns.'

'You can say that again.' Malone could still feel, rather than hear, the roar of Goffi's gun beside his ear.

Now, in della Porta's office, he said, 'Had Morello been in Australia?'

'No,' said the General. 'We checked with Milan – he was seen twice there last week. He didn't commit your Sydney murders, Inspector.'

'Have you interviewed Archbishop Hourigan or his father?'

'No.'

Malone wanted to ask why not, but managed to bite on the question. His concern, however, must have been apparent, because the General said, 'Is something worrying you, Inspector?'

Well, here I go for the high dive, Malone thought, and not for the first time: 'General, how well do you know Mr Hourigan and his son?'

Della Porta stared at him coldly, all the friendliness suddenly gone from his plump handsome face, bone seeming to show through the jowls. 'You dare to ask me a question like that in front of one of my junior officers? You may go, Captain.'

Goffi rose. 'Yes, General.' As he turned away, with his back to della Porta, he shot a warning glance at Malone.

When they were alone the General said, 'I have been trying to help you, Inspector. I don't like to be rewarded by that sort of insult, especially in front of a junior officer.'

Malone had had to eat crow before, but it had never been his favourite dish and it had never tasted worse than now. 'I apologize, General. Twice in the past week someone has tried to murder me. I think I'm becoming desperate . . .'

Della Porta's face didn't soften. 'You're an experienced man, Inspector. Commissioner Leeds said he had the highest regard for you. You should know that someone in my position can't always choose his bedfellows. I have to be a politician as much as a policeman – and sometimes a priest, too, since I have to deal with the Vatican. I was very good friends with Signor Berlingeur when he was chief of the Italian Communist Party, but that didn't make me a Communist. I sat beside

Licio Gelli, the head of P2, at dinners, but that never made me a Fascist. I'm sure it happens back in your own country, Inspector. Archbishop Hourigan, whom I've known for several years, telephoned me and asked me to join him and his father at the papal Mass. Perhaps they were using me as window-dressing – I don't know. I may have been in the window, Inspector, but I assure you – I am not a store dummy!'

Malone could see the genuine anger in the man, even though he was holding it in control. He felt a sudden shame at his suspicions; and a quick stab of apprehension. If Commissioner Leeds got to hear of this, he would be reduced in rank and bound for Tibooburra.

'I'll try biting my tongue, General, when I get out of here – *if* I get out –'

Della Porta's stern face abruptly broke into a smile. 'I accept your apology, Inspector. You just needed to be taught a lesson. I'm not sitting in this chair because I scratched people's backs and genuflected in the right direction. I occasionally have to do that, but it's not the reason I hold the job. Corruption is endemic in public life in Italy, but nobody has ever offered me money – they know they would be in prison before they could put their hand back in their pocket. I hope you are the same way. Now what are we going to do about Archbishop Hourigan?'

'I want to take him back to Sydney. I think if I leaked something of the story to the media –'

'No.' The *carabinieri* chief stroked his moustache with his knuckle. He had once cultivated the media: he had thought of himself as unique, an honest civil servant, but the media, made cynical by local history, hadn't believed him. 'Let's keep it between ourselves and the Vatican. Perhaps if Monsignor Lindwall could be persuaded to drop a few hints to those who run the Curia . . .'

Malone was driven across the Tiber with the General; the driver this time was a man who had had no Mille Miglia

239

ambitions. 'I like a stately progress,' said della Porta and in a moment of frank immodesty added, 'I think I was a king in a previous existence. What were you, Inspector?'

'I've never considered the possibility, General. Whatever I was, I don't think I was on the side of the angels. If I was, the buggers have let me down in this life.'

General della Porta smiled. He had never thought of himself as on the side of the angels, even in a fanciful existence as a king. They, he thought as they crossed the river, were with those on this side of the Tiber.

Monsignor Lindwall's white eyebrows rose when he saw Malone's arm in its sling. 'What happened? Has the General been twisting your arm?'

'No, Monsignor,' said della Porta, smiling at the little man; these two had a great deal of respect for each other, they were real friends, not political ones. He told Lindwall what had happened, then said, 'We need your help, Guy.'

'What happened to the man who tried to kill Inspector Malone?'

'He committed suicide,' said della Porta blandly, ignoring Malone's quick glance.

'Voluntarily or involuntarily?'

'Don't ask too many questions, Guy. It's not your mission to straighten out the truth, not on our side of the river. Now what can you do for Inspector Malone to get the Archbishop on a plane for Australia?'

'Can you leave the Inspector with me? Let's see what can be done with the truth on this side of the river.'

General della Porta stroked his moustache, left them with a wink and a nod and went back across the Tiber, into the country of poets, plotters and lions that, before they turned to stone, had once had a fundamental way of dealing with those in the Church. Perhaps, he thought, I was an emperor and more than a king . . .

Guy Lindwall took Malone for a walk in the Vatican gardens. The spring sunshine was warming up; the statuary looked as if sap might begin to flow in it. Staff were coming and going, all carrying folders, like good civil servants, all looking preoccupied if not busy: bureaucrats are the same the world over, Malone thought. Two cardinals passed, neither carrying a folder: Permanent Secretaries who had to do nothing to justify their employment.

'Cardinals Fellari and Lupi,' said Lindwall. 'Two men we might talk to if it's necessary ... They, too, dream of being Pope some day.'

'Too? Who else?'

'Why, our own Archbishop, of course. He'll be a cardinal before long and then it's just another step ... He thinks we don't know about it, but we do, at least those of us in our Department. But we never discuss it. Who knows – he might make it. And who wouldn't want to be on the Pope's personal staff? On the periphery of the centre of attention, the trips abroad ... And, of course, guaranteed entry into Heaven.'

'Not you, I'll bet.'

The little man grinned, looked like a white-headed mischievous boy. 'Think of the chaos I could cause!' Then he sobered. 'I think we should go and see His Grace now.'

Malone put his free hand on his arm. 'Guy, wait a minute ... I don't want you shoving your neck out on this. You have to live with this man. If I don't nail him on some charge back home, he'll be back here. And where will that leave you?'

'My dear boy –' Guy Lindwall suddenly sounded very English, more so than at any time since Malone had met him. The public school, the manor house in the Cumbrian dales, Oxford: all of it was a long way behind him. He was, if anything, more colonial than Cumbrian; but three centuries of influential family can't be wiped out in a lifetime spent in foreign climes. Malone knew the feeling: sometimes he felt he pissed Irish bog-water. 'My dear boy, at my age there are no risks, only whims. Detective stories are my favourite reading. Conan Doyle, Freeman Wills Croft, the American, Raymond Chandler – they were my salvation out in Africa, not my breviary. If I can help you solve who murdered your young nun and the priest, The Lord will take care of me. He always has up till now.'

Malone grinned. 'If ever I go to Confession again, I think I'll wait till you're in the confessional.'

'Glad to be of service. Now let's see how much service I can be in this other matter.'

Archbishop Hourigan was in his office, a room small enough to have compacted his conceits. He started up in surprise when he saw Malone. 'Inspector! What happened? An accident?'

'No, Your Grace, it was no accident. Someone tried to kill me again. With a knife this time.'

Hourigan looked at Lindwall as if he expected the latter to explain. The little man just shrugged and Hourigan turned back to Malone. 'So you've come to say goodbye.'

It was a statement, not a question. Malone said, 'Not quite. I've been putting pressure on the Monsignor here ...'

The Archbishop looked at the Monsignor again. 'How did you get into this, Guy?'

'Kerry, I don't have any conflict with the police. Inspector Malone asked me some questions and I answered them.'

'Questions such as what?'

'Did the Curia know what you are doing in Nicaragua, do they know you've been there –'

'Who told you that?'

'I did, of course,' said Malone.

'Go on, Guy. What did you tell him about the Curia?'

'Kerry –'

Lindwall had sat down; he didn't like being overshadowed by two tall men. He had adopted the same tactic in the Sudan; the six-feet-six Denka tribesmen had spent more time on their haunches, listening to him, than at any other time in tribal history. Malone and Hourigan remained standing for a moment, then the Archbishop sat down and gestured for Malone to do the same.

'Kerry –' The Monsignor might have been talking to a novice seminarian. 'If certain cardinals got to hear what you've been up to ... You have your rivals, you know that as well as I do. His Holiness listens to them more than he does to you –'

'He knows my dedication to what we're trying to do.'

'We all know it, Kerry, none of us better than I. But buying rifles and machine-guns?'

Hourigan looked angrily at Malone. 'You told him everything?'

'Everything,' said Malone. 'Just like in the confessional.'

The Archbishop's lip curled. 'Go on, Guy.'

'What he told me won't go outside this room. Except –'

'Except what?'

'Kerry, if what you have done ever got out, if *L'Unita* ever got hold of it and spread it across their front page, all our good work would be undone.'

'You're wrong!' The Archbishop hit his desk with his fist. 'With the Holy Father behind me –'

'How do you know he would be? He's trying to build bridges.'

'He's as anti-Communist as I am!'

'I haven't heard of him using Peter's Pence to buy rifles and machine-guns. Be sensible, Kerry – just take a cool look at the bomb you're putting together. Being over-zealous has helped the Church in the past –'

'I'm not some wild fanatic!' But he looked it at the moment, sitting tensed in his chair, his eyes hard and bright.

'No,' said Lindwall, half-conciliatorily, half-sarcastically. 'It's always the other chaps who are the fanatics.'

Malone sat watching the small battle between the two clerics. There was long-standing antagonism between the two. There was the resentment of the old man, who had paid his dues in the field, towards the younger man who had come to Rome on a much easier, more comfortable road. Equally, there was the impatience of the crusader with a tired old man who wanted to show tolerance towards the enemy. There was no real hatred, just a clash of temperament. Which, as he knew, could produce just as long and fierce a battle. He didn't, however, want this one to go on: Guy Lindwall deserved better than that.

'Don't blame the Monsignor for any of this,' he said. 'I bailed him up against a wall. I said if he wouldn't talk to you, try and persuade you to come home with me, I'd go straight to the Curia cardinals myself.'

'They'd never let you in the door,' said Hourigan scornfully.

'They would if General della Porta pushed me in.'

'Is he on your side, too?'

'Everyone's on my side.' There were no titles of rank between them now: they were man to man. 'I'm not bluffing any more. I'll go to the cardinals and lay the whole lot on the table for them. They may tell me to go to hell, but none of it will do you much good. I think you'd be out of this Department before you could say Hail Mary ... They'd find some backwater for you ...'

'I can recommend the southern Sudan,' said Lindwall with an impish grin and some malice. 'Or Ethiopia. No comfort there, but it's full of Communists. Your map shows that.'

He nodded at the map of the world on the wall behind the Archbishop. Great patches of it were coloured red. It reminded Malone of old school maps he had seen, before all the colour ran out of the British Empire. Now there was a new empire, one that had to be conquered by any means: rifles, machine-guns, possibly even prayer.

Hourigan sat silent and stiff-faced for a long moment; then abruptly he smiled. It was a weak, slightly puzzled smile, but it was genuine. 'Why can't you and I get on together, Guy?'

'God knows, I've tried, Kerry. But I'm too old for your sort of – enthusiasm.' There was just a faint pause before the last word.

Hourigan hadn't missed it. 'My fanaticism, you mean? I *believe* in what I'm doing, Guy. If I sometimes get carried away ... The end justifies the means.' For the moment he believed what he was saying. The end, of course, was something different from what they thought. When he was Pope there would be so much he could do ... But you never confessed your ambition to be Pope, certainly not to someone who, if he had the vote at all, would never vote for you. He looked at Malone. 'I'd like to talk to my father before I make a decision. And I'll want some sort of guarantee that if I come back to Sydney, there won't be any publicity.'

'I'll do my best, but I can't guarantee anything. Paredes and Domecq may shoot their mouths off.'

'I don't think so,' said Archbishop Hourigan, and his voice had a threat to it that didn't go with his smile.

# 4

Captain Goffi drove Malone to the airport, Monsignor Lindwall going with them. There had been a quick farewell of General della Porta in his office. 'It is a pity you did not have an opportunity to see our city, Inspector. The externals of it are very attractive.'

'I'll try and come back, General. And stay on this side of the river.'

'We can't promise you Heaven on this side, but they don't make it any easier for you over there ...' He waved towards the tall doors and the distant dominating dome. 'There was an English writer, a convert, who once wrote that anyone who could spend a year in the shadow of the Vatican walls and still retain his faith, need have no fear that the gates of Heaven would be closed against him. I hope he was right.' Then he blessed himself, smiled when he saw Malone's blink of surprise. 'I told you, I have to play both sides. Good luck, Inspector.'

On the way out to the airport Guy Lindwall said, 'I hope you can keep all this out of the newspapers.'

'Don't tell me you're now on the Archbishop's side?'

'Not at all, old chap. I just don't enjoy seeing the Church taking the bumps for what its zealots do. You must feel the same way about your police force. Even democracy gets a bad name when certain Americans think they are the only defenders of it.'

Malone nodded. 'How will you feel if he comes back here lily-white and takes up where he's left off?'

'Ah, then I think I shall play dirty,' said the one-time missionary. 'I didn't waste my time out there amongst the pagan, unsporting Denka.'

When he got out of the car Malone shook hands with two old friends; or so it seemed they were. One had saved his life and the other had saved his morale. He felt a gratitude that he could only express with the firmness of his grip. The other men understood and their handshakes were as sincere as his.

'Take care, Scobie,' said Goffi. 'The third time you may not be so lucky.'

Malone left them and walked across to the three-engined Dassault Falcon 900. He had hesitated when Fingal Hourigain had insisted that they return to Australia in his private aircraft – 'It's the only way to ensure we land there without publicity. I came over in my own plane and I'm going back that way. What's the matter, Inspector? Are you afraid I'll have you tossed out from thirty thousand feet?'

'I'd take someone with me if you did.'

Fingal had smiled. 'I think you would, too. But not me, Inspector – I'd be standing well back.'

So now Malone climbed the steps to the aircraft, stood at the top and waved to Lindwall and Goffi, then went into the forward cabin. It was the first time he had been aboard a private jet and he was impressed by the luxury and comfort of it. In the forward cabin deep lie-back chairs faced each other across console tables. In the middle section there was a similar set-up for dining. In the rear cabin there was a work-station and a lounge that could be converted into a bed. The furnishings were luxurious: Fingal Hourigan's caravan was designed to make him feel at home even above the clouds. But then, Malone mused, he probably has options on air space all over the world.

The two Hourigans were already aboard and so was Zara Kersey. A uniformed steward took Malone's bag and went aft with it. Then he came back with coffee and biscuits.

'I employ only male stewards,' said Fingal. 'Women are a distraction.'

'Thank you,' said Zara Kersey.

'You too,' said Fingal. 'But you're smart and that makes up for it.'

'I don't think I'll last this journey,' said Zara to Malone. 'I think I'll be getting off somewhere about half-way.'

Archbishop Hourigan had remained silent, greeting Malone only with a nod. Malone sat down opposite him, the console table separating them. Fingal and Zara were on the other side of the aisle and Malone was aware that both of them were watching him.

'I think we'd better declare a truce till we get home,' he said.

Kerry Hourigan looked stonily at him. 'You're interrupting my work.'

'You interrupted mine, when I had to chase you here to Rome. I'm only doing my job. I'm not going to get any promotion out of this. I stand a good chance of things going the other way for me.'

'I can promise that,' said Fingal from the other side of the aisle.

Malone buckled his seat-belt, sat back as the plane taxied out on to the runway. He looked at Zara and smiled wearily. 'It's going to be a long twenty-four hours.'

'I hope the movie is a good one,' she said. 'What's on?'

'*The Untouchables*,' said Fingal. 'I didn't choose it. It's about a cop who's a pain in the arse.'

'My autobiography,' said Malone and felt a glimmer of

relief when he saw the glimmer of a smile on the Archbishop's lips.

They flew by way of Dubai and Singapore, stopping at each landing for only two hours while the aircraft was refuelled. At Dubai and Singapore men came to the airport to confer with Fingal. He made no mention to Zara and Malone of who the men were, but Kerry, who by now appeared to be his old confident self, explained: 'My father never loses an opportunity to do business. He would consider it a waste of time to pass through these places and not make money.'

'I might have guessed he wasn't just picking up duty-free grog,' said Malone.

He was no longer amazed by human behaviour; but he had not become impervious to it. Hate and anger, jealousy and revenge, all those he could understand, though at times it was difficult to forgive the results of those emotions. Greed was the hardest instinct to swallow: it was not his meal at all. He wondered what the Archbishop thought of his father's greed, but did not ask. The truce was fragile, but he wanted it to last till they reached Sydney. Truces are often no more than a blind for the worst of intentions, but they are the best currency for buying time.

At Singapore he went to one of the duty-free stores and bought perfume. As he walked back to board the plane Zara joined him.

'I thought you didn't like shopping?'

'It's perfume for the wife. Arpège.'

'Is that her favourite?'

'I don't think so. But she wouldn't have liked it if I'd brought back that one of yours. I saw it in the store – Poison.' He pronounced it English style. 'I didn't get anything for the kids. I didn't know what to buy them. I'm a dead loss as a father.'

'I doubt that, Scobie.'

When they got back on board the plane he was moving up and down it, inspecting it again, when he saw Kerry Hourigan looking at him with amusement. He said, 'If it's not a rude question, how much does a plane like this cost?'

'It is a rude question, but I suppose you're used to asking them.'

'We're taught to ask them. Just like lawyers,' he said, smiling at Zara, certain now that she was as much his ally as an adviser to the Hourigans.

'Eighteen million dollars,' said the Archbishop. 'US dollars, that is. Are you shocked?'

'Stunned, I think would be closer. It's a lot of cash for convenience.' It was – what? Thirty times more than he would have earned by the time he retired? He would sit down on the way home and work it out. Whatever *he* earned, no one could say it had bought him convenience.

'It's also for security, Inspector. My father is worth enough to be the target of kidnappers. How would you feel as an ordinary passenger on Qantas if some terrorist, or even ordinary gangsters, took over the plane and held my father to ransom? This isn't just an indulgence, though I suppose that's how it looks. In any event, it's his own money, not his shareholders'. That's more than can be said for a lot of other barons.'

And what happens to all the money, and to this aircraft, when your old man dies and it all comes to you and your sister? But that, of course, would have been a really rude question.

Then Fingal came back on board showing, as much as he ever could, some pleasure. 'I've just given some Chinese a lesson in patience. We've been two years on that deal, trying to out-sit each other. I lasted longer than they did. How much patience do you have, Inspector.'

'Not much.'

Fingal sat down opposite this time as the plane took off. 'You will never out-last me.'

'I didn't know the competition was between you and me.'

'Oh, it is, Malone, it is. I'm not going to let you ruin my

son's career. You're a Communist.'

Malone laughed at the other man's prejudice. 'Your son accused me of that a week ago. I don't have any politics. If it turned out Gorbachev murdered your granddaughter, I'd be down on him like a ton of bricks. The same goes for our Prime Minister. Or the President of the United States.'

'That's fantasy. Top men never pull the trigger.' He knew: Capone hadn't pulled any trigger in the St Valentine's Day Massacre. Of course the Big Fella had killed people himself, but those murders had been personal. Which was different and understandable.

He sat back and stared at Malone across the cabin, the pale-blue eyes suddenly almost opaque. Malone stared back at him and all at once, with a tight feeling in his stomach, was certain he knew who had paid for the murders of Sister Mary Magdalene and Father Marquez. And for the attempted murder of himself in Rome.

Fingal at last turned his head away and looked out of the window. He had just had another moment of self-questioning, a disturbing weakness that had begun to occur too frequently. Why so many enemies? Brigid had asked him that back – when?

# ELEVEN

### I

'Why do you have so many enemies, Dad?'

Brigid had asked him the question on one of her few visits home to Sydney, back in the Sixties. She had also wanted to ask him why he had no friends, but one cruel question was enough.

He had smiled and shaken his head, 'Nobody loves a rich man, not in this country.'

'You're talking about the poor, the workers. Other rich men might love you.'

The smile remained. 'You don't know the rich. You see, I'm the *richest*. It's the same with a group of beautiful women. One of them's got to be the most beautiful and she's the one who'll always be the most envied.'

It was a cynical answer, but Brigid knew she should never have expected any more from her father.

She went back to England, where she saw the Swinging Sixties go out without any regret on her part. They would remain vivid only in the memories of those who would not go on to much better; there had been a spuriousness about those years that had never convinced Brigid they were something special. She had believed in free love and free thought long before those pursuits became wildly fashionable; mini-skirts, which didn't suit her legs, and rock music, which, like her brother, she had now grown to hate, were minor manifestations to which she turned a blind eye and a deaf ear.

She slipped into the next decade with relief, found at last her true *métier* as a painter.

Her natural irreverence, her sceptical opinion of her brother's vocation, led her to look at religious paintings with a suddenly discovered new eye. She began to paint religious subjects as they might have been viewed by a tabloid news photographer, a biblical *paparazza*. They stopped short of being sacrilegious, but they raised comment. One or two of the more progressive Anglican bishops, those who didn't believe in God, praised them; more conservative clerics, including her own brother, condemned them, though Kerry only did so privately. Museums and private collectors bought them and all at once she was no longer a part-time painter, a talented dilettante, but a working professional artist.

Teresa was now nine years old, a replica of her mother at that age. Brigid, caught up in her painting, sent her to boarding school and the nuns took over the raising of the bright, opinionated child. Brigid, without realizing it, was creating the same situation that had separated her from her father.

In Rome Kerry had already come to the notice of certain influential members of the Curia. He knew now that he was safe from pastoral work in Australia; his administrative brain was not going to be wasted totting up parish funds and throwing holy water on the heads of indifferent infants. He not only had an excellent administrative brain, he was financially clever, an inheritance from his father; he also had something his father did not have, a gift for public rhetoric, an ability to fire an audience or congregation. He was now attached to the Congregation of the Council, a body which administered, among other affairs, ecclesiastical properties and revenues. It had been founded by Pius IV, a sixteenth-century Medici pope who knew the value of ecclesiastical favours: he sold cardinals' hats as if they were summer straw bonnets. He raised taxes in the Papal State by 40 per cent and let rich defendants, who should have been imprisoned, buy their freedom with exorbitant fines. Kerry, not without some irreverence of his own, thought of Pius as his father's patron saint.

In 1976 he was made a monsignor and in 1980 became a bishop. It was then that Fingal, coming to Rome to celebrate the occasion, for the first time raised the subject of Kerry's becoming Pope.

'Now don't say it's a crazy dream –'

'I wasn't going to, Dad. Don't you think I've dreamed of it myself?'

'Is it possible?'

'It's a lottery. All you can do is buy as many tickets as you can.'

'You mean the cardinals can be bought, just like the pollies back home?' Even Fingal was surprised at the thought.

'No, not like that. You just make opportunities to be noticed. But I have a long way to go yet, two more steps. I have to make cardinal first.'

'How long will that take?' He was impatient now, he was seventy-five years old and occasionally he caught a whiff of the grave on the wind.

Kerry shrugged. 'Who knows? There are eighty-year-old cardinals over there in the Curia still hoping they'll get the vote.'

'Then we'll have to see you get noticed. Do they vote for saints as Pope these days?'

'I wouldn't fit the image, Dad.' He knew his limitations. 'No, I know my road. Communism is the enemy – if I can beat that wherever it's making inroads, then I'll be noticed. We'll just have to be patient.'

In 1983, by which time he had engineered his own small congregation, the Department for the Defence Against Subversive Religions, he was made an archbishop, one of the youngest in the Church. Fingal once more came to Rome to celebrate the elevation and to buy the apartment in the *palazzo* on the Tiber.

'It won't be out of character for an archbishop, you living

there. You can get a better car, too. What's the going model for an archbishop?'

'A Mercedes.'

Fingal shook his now white head. 'You haven't changed.'

'Have you?' said Kerry.

'What does that mean?'

'Isn't it time, Dad, you told me who you really are? You're – what? – seventy-eight this year. I think it's time you told me – and Brigid – who you were before we were born. The newspapers have already been on to me, they're already writing your obituary.'

'Who cares about the newspapers?'

'All right, forget the newspapers. What about Brigid and me? We have a right to know who you were. What have you got to hide?'

'Are you wanting to hear my confession?'

'In a way, yes.'

Fingal sat in a chair which had once seated a pope. This room, the main salon of the *palazzo*, held more secrets than he could ever divulge. He had at last begun to feel *old*: every road from here on was downhill, even though he sometimes felt he was *climbing* them. Winter (memories of Chicago) had begun to assail him once more. He spent his year now in perpetual summer, coming to Europe for it, going home for it. Like most old men he was beyond surprise but not beyond feeling. It both pleased and hurt him to learn that Kerry (and Brigid: it was always an effort to think of her these days) wanted to know who he really was. He had forgotten, if he had ever known, that a father owed more to his children than just their well-being.

Chicago and its ghosts were safely behind him now, though he had never been back there. O'Banion, Drucci and Moran were almost forgotten names; minor ghosts are kept alive only by discussing them and there had been no one with whom to discuss them. He still remembered Capone. He could close his eyes and see the Big Fella as clearly as on those days when he had faced him in the suite of the Metropolitan Hotel or in the back room of 2145 South Michigan, in Dr Alphonse Brown's surgery. But Capone was long dead and so was everyone who might have sought revenge for him; no dynasties die out so quickly as gangland ones. It was safe to kneel in the confessional:

'This is just between you and me. Brigid isn't to be told – I don't know she can be trusted to keep her mouth shut. You know what artists can be like.'

Kerry nodded, wondering what sort of sins he was about to hear. 'I shan't tell her, at least not till you're dead.'

Fingal hesitated, then accepted that. It might be a joke, if there were any jokes in the grave, to know how shocked some people would be to learn that Australia's richest man had begun life as a con man. Or maybe they would not be: Ned Kelly, the bushranger, was still a national hero.

'I was born in Ireland, in a village called Ballyseanduff, but I was taken to Chicago when I was six months old and I grew up there. I worked for Dion O'Banion and Al Capone –'

'You were a *gangster*?' It was Kerry who was shocked. He knew all about venality and skulduggery, but he was an innocent, though an archbishop, to real sin.

'No, I was not.' Fingal had his pride. 'I dealt in bootleg liquor, but I never belonged to any gang.'

'You said you worked for Al Capone –' His father had worked for one of history's worst villains, a latterday, low-class Borgia. He could see his whole career going up in smoke, but not the white smoke that signalled the election of a new Pope.

'Only as a consultant.' Fingal smiled: it was a joke that had lasted almost sixty years. 'I never carried a gun. Nor ordered anyone killed.' *Not till I came to Australia.* And that, now, was forty years behind him. 'I lived by my wits, the same as I've done in Australia. Only in Chicago I had to deal with gangsters.'

'Why?'

'Because in Chicago in those days a poor boy from a poor family got nowhere unless he worked for those with influence. And the gangsters had the influence. They ran the city. You've never seen corruption like it, not even here in Italy. If I wanted to get uptown, I had to forget everything my mother tried to tell me – she was a good Catholic woman, always praying for me, even took her rosary beads into the bath with her in case she had a seizure and drowned. I had to stop listening to her and listen to my father, who knew what the score was.' He sounded sincerely regretful, an honest moral boy who had had to bend his standards to survive. Old men have a tendency to colour not only their youth but their intentions. 'It wasn't easy.'

'Why did you leave Chicago?' Kerry was not taken in by his father's penitent tone.

Honesty, even towards one's son, could be taken too far: 'I could see myself getting too involved with Capone and the others.'

'Why did you choose Sydney, of all places?'

'I read it was warm.' That, at least, was the truth. He sat waiting for absolution; but none seemed forthcoming. At last he said, 'Well?'

'I don't know what to say,' said Kerry, never lost for a word. 'I always suspected you must have had something to hide. I thought you might have had another wife before Mother, that you'd run away from her ... But Chicago in the Nineteen-Twenties! With Al Capone! God, if it should ever get out ...!'

'It won't. That's why I don't think you should say anything to Brigid – you know what women are like.' Women and artists, the blabbermouths of the world. 'Well, maybe you don't know ...' He sometimes forgot that his son was celibate. 'You've come this far. Nothing must spoil it now.'

Kerry nodded, still absorbed in what his father had told him; and what he had not told him. For he knew that only half the truth had been told. He had lived too long with his father not to recognize that he was a consummate liar. He didn't feel disappointed that he had been lied to: perhaps it was better not to know the whole truth.

Later, over dinner in the apartment's big dining-room, with the newly acquired staff hovering over them in black-and-white livery, like trained magpies, Kerry said, 'Are you thinking of retiring?'

'What would I do? I'll retire when you become Pope. I'll come here and live, maybe I'll become a born-again Catholic. Just for appearance's sake.' He knew The Lord would never accept him.

'You may be ninety years old before that happens.'

'I'll live that long, if it's necessary.' He would do his best, would get up-wind from the grave.

'You're not going to keep on with the day-to-day running of Ballyduff?'

'Why not? I'm still two streets ahead of anyone who works for me.'

'Give it away, Dad. Ease up. Let Jonathan take over.'

'Not a chance.'

He chewed carefully on *scaloppina al marsala*. He still had most of his own teeth, preserved at great expense by Sydney's best dentist, but he had a small bridge that occasionally caused him trouble. He usually solved the problem by taking out the bridge and wrapping it in his handkerchief, no matter what company he was in; the very rich and the very old have their own rules of etiquette. He took out the bridge now and a manservant, accustomed to either the habits of the rich or just ordinary sensible Italians, appeared at his elbow with a fresh napkin. Fingal, impressed, took it and wrapped his bridge in it and put it on the table beside his plate. He had always thought the Italians had plenty of imagination but no common sense; maybe he had been wrong. Al Capone had had both, but then he had gone to America.

'You don't mean it.' Kerry was surprised. He had never interfered in the affairs of Ballyduff, never ventured an opinion. He had, however, never missed a line of the annual reports, never failed to check the stock prices of the holding company and its myriad subsidiaries. 'I thought it was taken for granted that he'd . . .'

'No. It's never been in my mind that he would.'

'Who, then?'

'Bob Borsolino.'

'Does Jonathan know that?'

'No. Neither does Borsolino. They work better together if they're kept guessing.'

'Jonathan is the better of the two of them, I think that's generally recognized. When he got his knighthood, I thought you'd arranged that.'

Fingal shook his head. 'Not me. He arranged it himself.'

'I've often wondered why you didn't get one yourself.'

'What would Sir Fingal be beside Pope Kerry? People would always say you'd upstaged me.'

'But what about Jonathan? Why are you so against him? The board and the shareholders won't agree with you.'

'I have my reasons for not wanting him to take over.' It was difficult to explain enmity born out of plain hatred, so he didn't bother. Wars have been started for simpler reasons. 'That's where you and Brigid will come in. She has no time for him, no more than I have. When I go, you two and your trusts will have 51 per cent of the holding company – and the holding company has the preferential voting shares in the subsidiaries. I've seen to all that in my will. All you have to do is vote against him.' He looked up and across the table at the son to whom he had given so much. 'That's all you owe me.'

## 2

Four years passed before Jonathan Tewsday learned that he was never going to have the top job at Ballyduff.

He was within touching distance of his target in the business and social firmament. He was equal No. 2 in what was now the nation's largest and richest corporation, above even BHP and the other, more recently arrived high-flyers. He had a wife who was one of Sydney's leading hostesses, a charity Queen Bee, and three bright daughters who, he suspected, didn't think as much of him as he did himself. He had a sixty-foot cruiser, the Rolls-Royce and a BMW for Fiona, his knighthood, a country property outside Bowral and a mansion at Pymble on the North Shore. Pymble reeked of respectability, like the smell of old mouldering money; he had arrived in the land he had promised himself. It was not Israel; for some reason, there were few Jews in Pymble. He and Fiona were both anti-Semitic, though they would never admit it. Some of their best friends were Jews, but they didn't want to live amongst them. To do him justice, Tewsday didn't dislike Jews as much as he did the Irish. Or anyway the Hourigans.

In the Pymble house he now had a library: Fiona had introduced him to books. He was now known as a collector of antique books, though he had to rely on an antiquarian bookseller to guide him; it did, however, give him a certain cachet, it set him apart from other newly rich men who collected paintings. He did not read the antique books; they were for show. His reading consisted of what he called 'solid' books: biographies, English sagas by long-dead authors and books about business chicanery, which he enjoyed the most. He never read 'modern' authors, certainly not women authors, and still had never ventured into poetry.

When they moved into the big home in Pymble, Fiona decided she wanted live-in staff. Up till then she had got by with a cleaning woman coming in every day and a cook coming in late on the afternoons when they were having dinner parties. Tewsday had had a company chauffeur for several years, but he had been available only during business hours; Fingal had insisted that he and Bob Borsolino had to drive themselves in their own time. Now, Fiona said, it was time they engaged other people to look after them.

They advertised for a couple. They chose Gary Gawler and his wife Sally, the only couple to apply whose native tongue was English. No Australians applied: to be 'in service' was against the native grain. Gawler, however, was an American and his wife English, each from a country where helots could still be found if the price was right.

They were a couple obviously in love, a pair who looked as if they might have arrived at true love rather late and for the first time. He was in his early forties and she in her late thirties, he quiet and controlled, she jovial and outgoing. Each was good at his or her job and the Tewsdays were glad to have them.

Yet Tewsday never felt entirely at ease with Gawler. It was not because he lacked the confidence, so endemic amongst the newly rich, to handle personal staff. It was just that Gawler was always slightly distant, a superior slave; it was as if he carried with him an invisible screen to match the one that had been specially fitted between the driver's seat and that of the passengers in the Rolls-Royce. He never ventured any information about himself other than what had been in his references: that he was Chicago-born, had served in the US Army in Vietnam, had worked as chauffeur for retired widows in Missouri and Kansas. He was polite, a hard worker, never complained; but as enigmatic as one of the Chinese jade statuettes that Fiona was always buying. Nothing, it seemed, could disturb his cold equanimity except the sight of the cheerful Sally waiting for him when he drove Tewsday home each evening.

On one occasion the Rolls-Royce ran over a dog. The fox terrier sprinted out into the middle of the road; Tewsday, later, thought there would have been time for Gawler to brake. He didn't: he just went straight over the dog. He did draw in then to the side of the road and went back to see if the dog was dead.

When he came back Tewsday said, 'You could have avoided that, Garry.'

'Yes, sir.' Gawler was unperturbed; he might just have run over a road marker. 'But the car behind me would have run into us. I think humans are worth more than a dog, sir.'

There was no answer to that, unless you were an animal welfare enthusiast; which Tewsday was not. 'Is the dog dead?'

'Yes, sir. There doesn't seem to be anyone coming to claim it. Shall we drive on?'

Tewsday, feeling a little sick, nodded. He was upset more by Gawler's apparent callousness than by the death of the dog. The screen between them had thickened.

He tried to sound out Sally Gawler on her husband, but Sally, though loquacious, told him nothing. 'That's just him, Sir Jonathan. He's kindness itself to me, the best thing that's ever happened to me. He doesn't say much, unlike me, but that's the way some people are. It'd be a pretty noisy world, wouldn't it, if everyone was like me.'

Then, one night, Tewsday worked back in his office. His secretary had gone home and when he finally left the office there was no one in the building but the cleaners, the security men and the two caretakers. He went down in the lift on his own, from the sixty-eighth floor to the basement garage.

He stepped out of the lift into the half-lit garage. Most of the cars had gone; there were no more than half a dozen parked in the vast cave. His mind was still occupied by the desk work he had just left; Ballyduff had made a raid on one of its smaller competitors. His wits were not about him as he got out of the lift and turned towards where the Rolls-Royce was always parked. The youth, long-haired, unshaven and grubby, wielding a long-bladed knife, seemed to materialize out of nowhere.

'Okay, shit-head, gimme everything you got on you!'

Tewsday was pushed hard against the wall; the long-bladed knife was pricking the skin between his first and second chin. He was paralysed by fear; physical courage had never been one of his attributes. He was on the verge of fainting; he knew his legs were going to fold under him at any moment. He could do nothing with his hands to give the mugger what he wanted; he just stood with his mouth and eyes wide open, an animal whimpering coming from him. The youth, with his free hand, began to rip at Tewsday's pockets.

Then Tewsday saw Gawler come out from behind the Rolls-Royce. He moved so silently, on the balls of his feet, that he was on the mugger before the latter saw him. Tewsday, closer to a killing, his own or anyone else's, than he would ever again be in his life, saw everything in frightening close-up. He saw Gawler take the youth from behind, wrapping a muscular arm round the scrawny neck. The knife flicked away from Tewsday's chins, cutting the top one; it went backwards to swipe at Gawler, but the American grabbed the wrist of the hand that held the knife, twisted, and the wrist was broken. The youth tried to scream with the pain, but the arm round his neck was pressing too tightly. Only a foot from him, watching the agony and the fear in the wide, drug-crazed eyes, Tewsday saw the youth die. Gawler gave a last savage jerk that broke the youth's neck, then let him drop to the floor.

'Come on, sir, let's get out of here!' Gawler was breathing heavily, but there was no sign of any emotion. He picked up the mugger's knife and put it in his pocket. 'I'll get rid of him. Pull yourself together!'

He grabbed the corpse's shoulders and dragged it across into a corner at the side of the lift. Tewsday was still leaning against the wall beside the lift door. His bladder had abruptly given way on him; he could feel the piss running down his legs. He gestured weakly as Gawler came back.

'What about the police?'

'We don't want any involvement, sir. Come on, sir!' Now Gawler sounded angry. He grabbed Tewsday by the arm and began to drag him towards the Rolls-Royce. 'Come on, for Christ's sake!'

Tewsday was a limp wreck, sodden from the crotch down. He was both terrified and embarrassed; he was certain the mugger had intended to kill him. He could not think straight; his mind, too, might have been full of piss. He made no effort to argue with Gawler. He let himself be dragged into the car, heard the door slammed behind him. Then Gawler was in the front seat, starting up the car without fuss or panic and a moment later the Rolls-Royce moved sedately up the ramp and out into the street. Tewsday twisted round and looked back. The garage was still deserted.

He said nothing all the way home to Pymble, just sat uncomfortably in his sodden trousers. Ever careful of his possessions, he had, however, picked up the floor mat, turned it over to its rubber side and put it between his wet behind and the leather of the car's seat. He knew that the acid in the urine could stain the leather and he did not want to have to explain it.

When they drew up in front of the house he got out at once, standing with his legs apart. The cut on his chin had stopped bleeding, but his handkerchief was blood-stained. He had regained some of his composure, but not much. 'I think we should have reported it, Gary.'

'No, sir. You would have been upset by the publicity, once it started.'

The shocking incident hadn't entirely dulled Tewsday's perceptions. 'I don't think you wanted publicity, either. Am I right?'

'If you say so, sir. This is just between you and me, okay?' He looked down at Tewsday standing with his legs apart, then back up at the big strained face. This was man to man, not servant to master. 'Nobody else is to know, not even Lady Tewsday or my wife, okay?'

Tewsday hesitated, then nodded. 'All right. Where did you learn to kill a man like that?'

'In Vietnam. Good-night sir. I'd get out of those trousers before you see Lady Tewsday.'

'What will you do with the knife?'

Gawler took the knife out of his pocket, looked at it as if he had forgotten it. 'I think I'll keep it as a souvenir. Good-night, sir.'

Usually, when a servant saves a master's life, a bond is established; or so some classical tales would have us believe. It usually is a sense of debt on the master's part. Tewsday, however, was not allowed to feel any such thing; for which he was glad. Gawler made no mention of the incident again, not even the next morning. Tewsday, still embarrassed by his own abject behaviour, still shocked by the cold-blooded way Gawler had disposed of the mugger, could find no way of broaching the subject. He had not even thanked Gawler for saving his life, yet he felt it was already too late to do that. The killing of the junkie seemed as inconsequential as the running down of the dog. Gawler was colder and more distant than ever.

Tewsday managed to hide his stained trousers from Fiona, but she was intrigued by the cut on his chin. 'Been duelling with Fingal?'

'That's not funny,' he said and gave her no explanation.

The youth's body had been discovered later that night by one of the security men. A Sergeant Clements from Homicide came to interview Tewsday, but he could tell the detective nothing – 'Yes, I worked late last night, but I saw nothing when I went down into the garage. I gather my driver saw nothing.'

'I've already talked to him,' said Clements. 'Nobody seems to have seen anything.'

Was the big lumbering oaf being sarcastic? 'You sound as if you don't believe us, Sergeant.'

'Why would I do that?' said Clements and went away. Nothing more was heard from the police. The case, it appeared, was closed. The mugger, a known junkie with a record, was expendable.

Gawler continued to trouble Tewsday. He had always

prided himself on knowing what made people tick; he told himself that even Fingal Hourigan was no secret to him. Knowing who Gawler really was, what was behind that cool façade, became an obsession with him. He finally phoned a man he had not spoken to in thirty years, someone he had hoped never to see again.

Jack Paxit came to the offices of Ballyduff. He had long ago given up bouncing at night-clubs and now ran the best-known private detective agency in the city. He was in his early sixties now, as beefy as ever but smoother, someone who would talk a man out of a situation rather than throw him out. He had once had a cauliflower ear, but had had cosmetic surgery done on it and it now looked like a white eggplant. He wore an expensive navy-blue suit, but he somehow looked out of place in it, as if he had only borrowed it for the occasion.

'Sir Jonathan, long time no see. You're still the Invisible Man, remember? But I hope it's not that old case, is it? I'm respectable now.'

'Who isn't?' said Tewsday, regretting now that he had sent for Paxit; but it was done and so must be gone through with. 'I want you to trace the background of someone who works for me. Do you have access to computer systems?'

'If the price is right, you can have access to anything you care to name. It's the Freedom of Information Act.' He was the sort of man who had to grin to tell you he was joking.

*If the price is right*: how many times had he heard that? 'Overseas systems? The US Army, the FBI, systems like that?'

'Computer systems don't know any boundaries.' Paxit screwed up his blunt face. 'This guy must be special?'

'I don't know,' Tewsday confessed. 'My suspicions may add up to nothing. He's my chauffeur – he and his wife live in at our place. I want to know more about him than he's prepared to tell me.'

'If he's just your driver, why not get rid of him if he worries you?'

'There's more to it than that.' Though he would never be

265

able to explain it. 'This is strictly between you and me – it's not a company matter. I'd like the information as soon as possible, but be thorough. Name your own price.'

'My price is reasonable, Sir Jonathan – you must remember that from the old days. It's what the others will charge that will cost.'

'The others? Will others need to know?' He was technically, or anyway technologically, ignorant. He appreciated the worth of computers, but he could not work one. He had grown up in an age when sums were done on scraps of paper; he was a brilliant mental mathematician, faster than the whiz kids with their calculators, but was an idiot in front of a computer. 'Can't you do it?'

'Sir Jonathan, in computer exercises there's always someone who has to know. The systems don't work on their own. It's the human beings who make it dangerous, not the machines. You still want me to go ahead?'

'Can it be traced back to me? I mean the line of enquiry?'

'It'll be traced back to me. I'm a private enquiry agent, that's what my licence says. They won't want to waste their time going past me. Not if the price is right. There's a certain honesty about computer hackers.'

'Really?' said Tewsday, who always doubted anyone who claimed to be honest. They were like those who claimed to have a sense of humour, jokers who found it hard to take a joke against themselves.

Paxit came back with the information on Gawler in two weeks: the price must have been right. He put down the envelope on Tewsday's desk. 'It's all in there, Sir Jonathan. Everything you need to know. I'd be careful of him.'

'Is that your comment or the computer's?'

'Computers don't have opinions, only facts. Would you care to pay me in cash?'

'I thought you were respectable now?'

Paxit smiled. 'Taxation makes it difficult. There are limits a man can go to. If only cash changes hands between us, who's to know we've done any business? You can be the Invisible Man again. Or was it me?'

'Twenty-five thousand – I don't have that much on hand. I'll send it by courier tomorrow.'

'No receipt, no pack drill – okay? Good luck, Sir Jonathan.' He looked around the big elegant office. 'You've come a long way.'

*There's an even bigger, more elegant office one floor above: I haven't finished climbing.*

Paxit went back to his agency, to his flexible respectability, and Tewsday looked at the record of Gawler's life. He had indeed been born in Chicago, as he had said, but his name had not been Gary Gawler. It was Alphonse Brown and he was the son of a petty crook with a long list of convictions. He had served in Vietnam, but with a counter-terrorist unit run by the CIA; he had been credited (credited? Tewsday wondered) with no fewer than seventeen killings and probably more. After the end of the Vietnam war he had stayed on in South-east Asia, moving to Bangkok, where he had worked freelance for the CIA; the report had nothing specific on what he had done for the agency. His contract had been abruptly terminated, no reason given, and he had moved on to Hong Kong. He had worked there for a year; again there were no details. He had gone back to the United States, had various jobs, no specific details, and had served three years in Joliet Prison, Illinois, for manslaughter: he had killed a man in a bar-room brawl. When he had been released he had changed his name to Ray Karr and had disappeared, at least from the computer records, for three years. When he surfaced again he was back in Bangkok, working for an American drug smuggler (here, a reference code was given). He was suspected of three more killings, but they were expendable victims, other drug smugglers, and the Thai police had not bothered following up the murders. It was in Bangkok in early 1986 that Ray Karr had met Sally Heston, spinster, on holiday on an organized tour. He had followed her to Hong Kong and they had been married there; he had signed the register as Gary Gawler, business consultant. The information ended there, except for the Australian immigration records that the Gawlers, man and wife, had arrived back in Australia in June 1986. If there was any further information in the Australian system it had not been accessible or the price had not been right. No matter: Tewsday knew all he wanted to know. Possibly more: he felt a deepening sense of fear.

He said nothing to Gawler of what he had learned. As he was driven to the office each morning he studied the chauffeur from the back: I'm employing a professional killer, he told himself with horror and wonder. Yet he made no attempt to dismiss Gawler; it was a week or two before he admitted to himself that he was afraid to. Gawler, for his part, seemed unaware of the deeper scrutiny to which he was being subjected. He was as coolly self-contained as ever; the killing of the junkie might never have taken place. He drove Tewsday home each evening and only then did his composure show the slightest crack. His face would light up at the sight of Sally waiting for him. Tewsday, angry with himself, would envy him; there was none of that feeling left between him and Fiona. He wondered how much Sally knew about her husband's past life, but he knew he would never again attempt to question her. He was afraid of what Gawler might do to him.

So the odd situation continued and after a while Tewsday grew to live with it. The Rolls-Royce became a merry-go-round, though he felt no merriment: he rode behind Gawler on a carousel from which he couldn't alight.

# 3

Brigid Hourigan came back to Australia in the spring of 1986, bringing with her a young handsome Italian who, quite obviously, was her houseman in more ways than one. Though not an alcoholic, she had become a regular drinker, another characteristic which set her apart from her father, the tee-totaller. She bought a waterfront house on Pittwater, twenty-five miles north of Sydney, set up a studio but painted only spasmodically. With her salaried lover, her daughter the nun now in Nicaragua, her father and brother more estranged from her than ever, she had become bitterly aware of the gaping holes in her life. She blamed no one, but that didn't help: she might have done better to have had a focus for her bitterness.

Fingal was glad to have his daughter at least within driving distance; but he could not bring himself to tell her so. He had never feared loneliness before; he had always found a certain safety in it. Now, however, safe at last beyond all danger and worry, he had begun to hanker for company and (yes, though he found it hard to believe) love. Kerry loved him, or so he made himself believe; but Kerry now spent all his time in Rome. Fingal went there every northern summer, but as soon as the cold winds came down the spine of the Apennines he would leave and return to Sydney. There the loneliness would creep in on him again, another kind of winter.

Sometimes he even thought of calling up Tilly Mosman and asking her to visit him. He had not seen her in twelve years, not since he had had the property division buy up the whole street in Surry Hills and then told Tilly to take up a long lease on the two big terrace houses. He had given her the money to pay the first three years of the lease, then bade her goodbye. To his chagrin and embarrassment, the lead had started to slip out of his pencil; too often Tilly, for all her tricks, failed to arouse his erection. To his further embarrassment, because he had always prided himself on his appearance, his body, if not his face, had become an old man's, stringy and wrinkled. He had never been one for making love in the dark: Sheila had liked it best in broad daylight. Now he had turned out the light for ever on love-making and Tilly had become only a memory, occasionally revived.

Jonathan Tewsday revived the memory on one occasion when they were alone after a board meeting. 'Did you know we own the lease on the Quality Couch?' Fingal looked at him feigning puzzlement and Tewsday explained. 'The top brothel in town.'

'Are you visiting brothels now?'

'Don't be sanctimonious, Fingal. Yes, I've been there a couple of times. Fiona and I are not the best of friends, well, not *that* way.'

Fingal was embarrassed; he did not like people to confess their bedroom problems. 'You're taking a risk, aren't you? You'd be recognized.'

'I went twice, that was all. Some of our Japanese clients had heard of it and when –' he named a top Japanese industrialist '– came out here, our PR man put on a party there. I went along.'

'That was once. Why twice?'

'I enjoyed myself, if you want the truth. I don't think being recognized would cause any harm – you'd be surprised who I saw there, girls as well as clients. Even two of our best-known girls-about-town work there.'

He waited as if he expected Fingal to show interest; but the latter had never been interested in gossip, not even when Tilly had been coming to his bed in the flat in Macquarie Street. 'Is it a good house?'

'The best. Five star.'

'They ever troubled by the police?'

'Not as far as I know.'

Good: it seemed that Tilly had taken care of herself. He felt pleased for her: she had made him happy at one time. 'So long as they pay the lease, leave 'em alone. We'd only get bad publicity if we closed them down.'

'Are you thinking of your son the Archbishop?' said Tewsday shrewdly.

'No. He's never been a customer there,' said Fingal. 'I was thinking of you.'

Tewsday left him then, angry that he had raised the subject of the Quality Couch. The old bastard could never resist scoring points.

He went downstairs and into Bob Borsolino's office. The other managing director looked up in annoyance; he was a workaholic, a man who hated wasting a minute of office time. Tewsday sat down uninvited and Borsolino sighed and leaned back in his chair.

'Bob, you ran the properties division ten or twelve years ago, right? Who recommended we buy up the whole of Sandhill Street, Surry Hills?'

Borsolino frowned. He had a narrow bony face that seemed to be continually frowning, as if he were deep in some financial problem, an accountant squeezed thin by heavy ledgers. 'Hell, I don't know, Jonathan – no, wait a minute. Is that the street where they have that brothel, what's it called?' He was a highly moral man, except when it came to creative accounting.

'The Quality Couch.'

'What a name!' He shook his head, his lank hair falling down over his brow. He had none of Tewsday's smoothness, tailored or otherwise, but then he had never aspired to appearances. He had other aspirations, though he had never confessed them to anyone, not even his wife. 'It was the boss who told me to buy up that street. I can't remember if he said anyone had recommended it to him. We looked it up and thought it was a good buy for the future, in case it was re-zoned. It's still residential and I guess we've just hung on to it.'

'Did Fingal recommend the lease to the brothel owner, Tilly Mosman?'

Borsolino frowned again, then laughed. 'Jonathan, d'you think the old man's been making money on the side out of a brothel? I don't know who recommended the owner, or if anyone did. When she took out the lease, she certainly wouldn't have said she wanted it for a brothel. All I can remember is that she wanted a long lease, renewable every five years, and the old man okayed it. Those were the days, you remember them, when he poked his finger in every pie.'

'An unfortunate phrase, but thanks, Bob.' And Tewsday went back to his own office satisfied that, even if not now, there had once been a connection between Fingal and Tilly Mosman.

Then he heard that Fingal's granddaughter, the nun Sister Mary Magdalene, had come to Sydney from Nicaragua. He discovered the fact by accident when he rang Fingal at home one Sunday and Mrs Kelly, the housekeeper, said she didn't want to interrupt Himself because he was entertaining his granddaughter – 'A lovely young nun, she's just come home from one of them South American places, Mick or Nick something-or-other.'

Tewsday hung up, then called Brigid. 'Your daughter's home, I hear. Congratulations.'

Brigid was cool. 'Thank you, Jonathan. But we're keeping it as quiet as possible, if you don't mind. She's a nun, she doesn't want to be bothered by the Hourigan name.'

'Of course not. It must be nice to have her so close to you again.'

He told Fiona and she, being a society hostess, which meant not missing the opportunity to examine any newcomer with the proper connections, even if she was a nun, suggested a dinner party for the Hourigans.

'You must be out of your head!' said Tewsday, though the idea intrigued him. 'Nuns don't go to dinner parties, do they? And Fingal would never come. Neither would Brigid, for that matter.'

'Leave it to me,' said Fiona. 'It's time I met Brigid. I'm told you once had a yen for her.'

'Who told you that?'

'I heard it at the bottom of a football scrum.' She had never forgotten her All Black heritage. Her approach to her society hostess competitors was said to be as rugged as that of her rugby compatriots.

Tewsday never learned how she did it, but she brought the three Hourigans to dinner at the house in Pymble. Twelve sat down at the table, all well mixed: the Tewsdays, the Hourigans, a politician, a businessman, a lawyer and their respective wives and a young gallery owner looking for buyers. The two older Hourigans, father and daughter, were quiet, as if uncomfortable with each other's company as with that of the other guests. Only the granddaughter, the nun whom everyone expected to be mum, was voluble and gay.

'I was teaching some girls in Year Twelve the other day and I mentioned adultery. What's adultery? said one of them. Some sort of kinky sex, said another one of them. I'm not even sure they were pulling my leg. The kids of today are way out, I can't keep up with them.'

'I suppose it's much different in Nicaragua?' said Fiona.

'Where is it?' said the businessman's wife, brain as feathery as her teased-out hair. 'I keep seeing it in the headlines, but I've never tried to find it on the map.'

Mary Magdalene stopped being gay, gave her a withering look. 'Oh, it's on the map, all right. I'd like to come and talk to you some time about it, Grandpa.'

Grandpa Fingal took a moment to recover from being so addressed. 'You should talk to your uncle, the Archbishop. He knows more about that part of the world than I do.'

'Oh, I have talked to him,' said Mary Magdalene, and Brigid, sitting beside her, looked at her sharply. 'I want to talk to lots of people about Nicaragua, now I'm here in Sydney.'

'We have our own problems, my dear,' said the politician, whose party was not in power and didn't look like winning it.

'I'd love to go there,' said the gallery owner. 'I just adore Aztec art. It's so *knowing*.' Whatever that meant.

'I tried to talk Mother into coming there to paint.'

'We'll go there together!' exclaimed the gallery owner.

'I'd love that,' said Brigid without enthusiasm.

Fingal contributed little to the dinner conversation, but at least he succeeded in not being ungracious. He was fascinated by his granddaughter, still finding it hard to believe that his blood ran in her veins. His mother, whom he had not thought of in a long time, would have been in a fit of religious ecstasy: a grandson an archbishop and a great-granddaughter a nun. He was covertly gazing at the young nun, looking for signs of himself in her, a hopeless search, when Fiona touched his arm. 'Fingal?'

He blinked, then looked at her. 'Eh?'

'You seemed miles away.'

'I was.' He had always tolerated Fiona, neither liking nor disliking her. Sometimes he wondered what she had ever seen in her husband. 'I'm just getting used to the idea of having a grandchild. It's a shock to a man of my age.'

'I'm looking forward to having mine, when my daughters get around to it. I like the idea of the continuum of the family – I've traced my own family back three hundred and fifty years in Scotland. The present and the past, the now and the then, they are always connected, don't you think?'

'The now and the then,' he repeated. 'Yes, I guess you're right. Which do you prefer?'

'Oh, the now,' she said. 'The present. At least we know that, don't we?'

'I guess so.' But he had an old man's memory and the past was clearer for him than it was for her.

At the other end of the table Tewsday had been studying Sister Mary Magdalene. He could see something of Brigid in her; they were both iconoclasts; the young nun had already made some joking remarks about Big Business, though she had been polite enough to make out she was referring to the Americans. There was something in her, however, that suggested something more passionate in her beliefs than Brigid had ever shown. He had the feeling that Sister Mary Magdalene, for all of her mother's statement that she wanted to be divorced from the Hourigan name, would some day look for publicity for whatever causes she adopted.

When dinner was over and the guests were leaving, Fingal offered his granddaughter a lift back to her convent in Randwick, but Brigid intervened. 'She's coming home with me, Dad. She has the weekend off.'

He was disappointed, but didn't show it. 'Well, come and see me some time, Teresa.'

'Oh, I'll do that, Grandpa. I want you on my side.'

He looked at Brigid, who had never been on his side; then back at his granddaughter. 'What side is that?'

'I'll tell you when I come to visit you.'

But she did not come to the castle in Vaucluse till Kerry arrived home unexpectedly with the two Nicaraguans, Paredes and Domecq. Fingal had already had hints of what was expected of him in the way of financial support; he had looked at his fortune and knew the money wouldn't be missed. He was just unprepared for the sudden arrival of Kerry and the two Nicaraguans and the speed with which they wanted the arms deal done.

It was the day after Kerry's return that Teresa (Fingal could not bring himself to call her Mary Magdalene or even Mary) came to Vaucluse. For the first time Fingal saw the passion in her when she confronted her uncle; she was even more of a zealot than he because she had no control over her temper. There was a stand-up fight in the big drawing-room, a substitute set for the Nicaraguan mountains; she hurled threats and insults at Kerry and he responded with heated rage. Fingal suddenly turned against his granddaughter; she was his daughter's daughter and more. The threats, he saw, were a real danger: she could throw Kerry's progress right off the rails. She knew too much and she would use that knowledge in her cause. It didn't matter whether she was a Marxist or not, he had no time for labels; she was a threat to Kerry and that was enough. So Fingal turned against her and, as always when opposed, became implacable.

He was sitting in his office next day, a Friday, his mind still

275

stewing with yesterday's fight, when Tewsday, unannounced, walked in. 'I think we'd better have a talk, Fingal.'

Fingal stared at him a moment, then he pressed the button on his intercom. 'We're not to be interrupted. No calls, nothing.' Then he settled back in his high-backed chair. 'Shoot.'

'An appropriate word,' said Tewsday, who had never been noted for his humour, 'in the circumstances. Austarm, where we make things that shoot.'

'Don't be a comic, Jonathan. What's biting you?'

'This deal that Kerry is trying to put through with his Nicaraguan mates. You're out of your head, Fingal, if you think the board will let you get away with that. Not to mention what Canberra will say.'

'Who told you about the deal?'

'It doesn't matter who told me.' It had been the managing director of Austarm, a man stunned by the size of the foreign orders. So many Australians, Tewsday knew from experience, were frightened by bigness. 'I *know*.'

'It's none of your business. Ballyduff won't be paying for the arms. It's a deal between Austarm and the Saudis.'

'Oh, come off it! The Saudis have nothing to do with it. Jesus, Fingal, what's the matter with you? Has Kerry got you wrapped round his little finger with all that anti-Communism stuff he's been peddling? Is he running for Pope or something?' It was a random remark, but Tewsday saw at once that there was a target he had never suspected. The discovery stopped him in his tracks for a moment; he was not religious, but he had just been confronted with a vision. 'Good Christ! He's really thinking about that, isn't he?'

'You're the one who's out of his head,' said Fingal, wondering how much had shown in his face; nothing showed now but cold hatred of this man across the desk from him. 'Go on.'

Tewsday sat a moment, heady with his discovery. He had no idea how the Catholic Church worked; he was a money man and he assumed that money, as in every other field, could buy position in the Church. *If the price was right* ... And Kerry, more than any other cleric in the world, would have the cash behind him. He could see now why Fingal was taking risks that he would never have otherwise contemplated.

'Your secret's safe with me, Fingal.' He all at once felt confident, in control here in this office that, some day soon, would be his. 'It doesn't concern me. But Ballyduff's name does. If this gets out, have you thought about what will go down the drain? We are up for renewal of our mining leases in Western Australia – the State Government there would be glad to kick us out and give the leases to their local boys. We're just about to sign that Federal ship-building contract for our yards in South Australia – 280 million dollars' worth. Canberra would cancel that without a moment's notice. For Christ's sake, Fingal, you're going to walk all over the people we have to cultivate – and for what? So your son can give arms to a bunch of right-wing nuts in some Central American jungle!'

'I always thought you were a right-wing nut. You bent your knee every time you mentioned that nut up in Queensland.'

'That's in my own country. And I wasn't supplying him with arms, busting up Ballyduff's contracts to do it! It's not on, Fingal. I'm seeing Bob Borsolino when he gets back from Melbourne and we'll call a board meeting for Monday afternoon. You're not going to take Ballyduff down the gurgler because your son has some crazy idea about being Pope!'

'Sit down, Jonathan.' Tewsday had risen, but he sat down again as Fingal waved a stiff hand at him. 'First, you're wrong about the Pope bit – you just don't know how the system works. If Kerry wants to be Pope, that's his ambition, not mine.'

'You're a liar, Fingal – I saw it in your face when I first mentioned it.'

'You're wearing out your welcome,' said Fingal softly. Tewsday found himself leaning across the desk to hear him.

'Second, *I* run this corporation, not you, not Borsolino and not the board. Third, you're finished!'

'*Finished?*'

Fingal nodded. He could not have imagined that he would enjoy this moment so much; but there was no outward sign of his enjoyment. His voice was still soft, but every word had a hard edge to it. 'You can go back downstairs and write out your resignation. Say anything you like, so long as you say it in two lines.' He sat back, raised his voice a little. 'I've already worked out your golden handshake. I'll have Miss Stevens type it out and it'll be on your desk in ten minutes.'

Tewsday was still leaning across the desk, but now he needed its support under his stiff arms. 'You really are out of your head! You think I'm going to *resign*? Just because you've told me to? I'm not the office boy, Hourigan – I'm the joint managing director! I'm lined up to be executive chairman when we finally push you out of here!'

'You couldn't be more wrong, Jonathan. It was never on the cards that you'd sit in this chair ...' He had had power for years, but he had never felt as powerful as at this moment. He wondered if Capone had felt like this when he had ordered Moran and the others eliminated. Holding a man's fate in your hands was the ultimate power, he told himself. But, as Tewsday had said, he was out of his head, though he would never have admitted to any madness.

'You'll have to fire me! You'll have to get the board to back you – and that'll never happen! You'll be the one to go!'

Fingal shook his head. 'You're being stupid, Jonathan. You know who has the voting stock. *I've* got it – and it doesn't matter a bugger what the board says or does. Goodbye, Jonathan. Try and say it all in two lines.'

He swung his chair round and faced the window. When he turned back a minute later Tewsday had gone. Then the reaction set in. What if Tewsday went downstairs and called a press conference, brought everything out into the open? A vindictive man knows what another vindictive man can do.

All at once he felt the vertigo that can affect old men. Here on the sixty-ninth floor, at the top of this most tangible monument to himself, he suddenly felt Ballyduff House begin to tremble beneath him.

# 4

Tewsday did not call a press conference. His rage almost blinded him; but not quite. Ballyduff had to be saved, not destroyed; which was what Fingal was going to do. He didn't write out his resignation; how can one resign in two lines after thirty-three years? Kings could, perhaps; but not he. He would spend the weekend marshalling his forces.

He went to bed that Friday night with his mind in turmoil. He and Fiona now slept in separate rooms; occasionally they met for love-making, like a senior citizens' wing-ding. He could not have slept beside her that night; he was an open book to her and she would have read every page of him. He tossed and turned all night, his rage increasing. All the years of enmity turned him mad, though, like the other madman, he did not recognize the madness.

In the morning Fiona, their daughters and Sally Gawler left for the Bowral property for the weekend. 'Will you be down this evening?' Fiona said.

'No. I've got too much to do.'

'Are you all right? You look as if you've spent the whole night at the bottom of a ruck.'

Christ, why did she have to drag up these bloody rugby similes? 'I'm all right. Get on your way or you'll be caught up in the traffic.'

She and the girls and Sally Gawler drove off in the BMW. He stood for a moment, abruptly lost; Fiona, for all their disagreements and the growing distance between them, was his only support. Maybe he should have confided in her . . .

'I don't think I'll wash the car, sir.' He became aware of Gawler standing in the driveway between the house and the garages. 'It's going to rain. Will you be needing me today?'

'I'm not sure, Gary. Stay around.'

He went back inside, tried to phone Bob Borsolino at his hotel in Melbourne and missed him. He did not want to contact the other board members until he had talked to Borsolino. He spent the rest of the day planning his attack at Monday's board meeting. By Monday evening Fingal would be cut out and he would be executive chairman. Tomorrow he would go down to Pittwater and woo Brigid. Hers would be the deciding voting stock.

He did not believe in fate; yet it was fate, he appreciated, that brought the phone call from Fingal's granddaughter that Saturday afternoon. 'Sir Jonathan, may I come to see you? It's important.'

'What's it about?' His voice was sharp. Had her grandfather arranged this, was this some cunning ploy on Fingal's part?

'It's about a company called Austarm, one of my grandfather's subsidiaries.'

'Does he know you're calling me?'

'Heavens, no! Don't mention it to him – he'd kill me! Please, Sir Jonathan, let me see you – it's important! I can come to your house this afternoon –'

'No!' He had never felt like this before, his nerves worn ragged. Well, yes, he had: the night the junkie had threatened to kill him. But this was worse: his whole life was threatening to crash down around him, yet he would still be alive. 'I'll – wait a minute. You've caught me by surprise. Come – can you come at eight o'clock this evening?'

'That's later than I'd like –'

'Eight o'clock,' he said firmly. 'Do you know how to get here?'

'Sir Jonathan, I found my way around the mountains of

280

Nicaragua for two years. I don't think I'm likely to get lost in Pymble.'

She arrived on time. She was wearing a grey raincoat against the rain that had started to fall in mid-afternoon; only a sharp-eyed observer would have noticed her as a nun. Tewsday, always a man with an eye for what other people wore, thought she looked smart and not too obvious. Nuns were not regular visitors to this house.

'Does anyone know you've come to see me?'

She gave him a quizzical look, one of her grandfather's. 'Does it matter? No, Sir Jonathan, nobody knows. At the convent they think I've gone to stay with – with a friend.'

'Have you had dinner?' He was ambivalent towards her: he wanted to be rid of her as soon as possible, yet he wanted to know more about her. She was the only Hourigan towards whom he had no antagonism.

'Yes, I had supper before I left.'

'I hope they feed you well at the convent?'

'Bread and water.' She smiled, but he could see that she was nervous and highly strung.

He took her into his library. Gawler, playing houseman for the evening, brought them drinks: a Scotch for Tewsday, vodka on the rocks for Mary Magdalene. 'I need a little strength,' she said when she ordered it. 'I'm trying to be Joan of Arc or something and it's a little scary.'

He had only a smattering of knowledge of European history, but he had seen the movie. 'Didn't she take on the archbishops?'

'Oh, she took on everyone. I'm not going to do that. Though I'm taking on *one* archbishop.'

'I shouldn't imagine you'd be scared of anything,' said Tewsday. 'Not if you've been in Nicaragua amongst all that's going on there. Pymble is considered pretty safe. Even for socialists,' he added tentatively and she smiled, humouring him.

She sipped her vodka: a Russian drink, Tewsday noted. But then it was also the favourite drink of Fiona, a Presbyterian and female All Black. 'I think you should know about Austarm and what my Uncle Kerry and those two Contra men are trying to do . . .'

Then she proceeded to tell him what he already knew; but more. He said nothing, listening to her without expression. At last he said, 'What do you want me to do?'

'You're the managing director of Austarm – you should be able to stop it!'

'It isn't that easy –' He couldn't tell her how powerless he was, that her grandfather held all the cards and all the voting stock.

'Nothing's easy! God, don't you think I know that?' She was beginning to boil beneath the surface, but she was still in control of herself. 'You have to do *something*! That's why I've come to you – you're my last hope. Well, almost . . .'

'What do you mean by that? Almost . . . ?'

She took a deep breath; all at once there was a look of despair on her pretty face. 'I'm going to tell it all to the newspapers and to television, to *Four Corners* or some pro-gramme like that. I was hoping I wouldn't have to do that – that you would help me – you're one of the managing direc-tors. I tried to get in touch with Mr Borsolino – I've never met him – but he's away somewhere –'

'He's down in Melbourne, he'll be back tomorrow night . . . I don't think you need to see him. I don't think you need to talk to the newspapers, either.'

'Oh, I'm going to talk to them!' She took a long gulp at her drink; it took a moment for her to recover. 'Grandpa threw me out of his house – even my uncle threatened me. They're mad, you know. They've got to be stopped. The only way to do it is to give the story to the newspapers.'

'That will have more effect than you realize. It could bring down a whole corporation, the biggest in the country, drop its prices on the stock exchange –'

'Does it matter?'

Oh Christ, he thought, she's mad, too, the whole bloody

Hourigan lot are mad. 'I think your vows of poverty have warped your vision, my dear ...'

He sounded patronizing, episcopalic. She saw her uncle in him and began to bridle.

'There are hundreds of thousands of people who depend on Ballyduff for their jobs and income ...' He really didn't care about Ballyduff shareholders and employees. The *hoi polloi* always survived: there was always the dole.

'There are hundreds of thousands of people in Nicaragua who could be killed if a full scale war breaks out there. Do the Ballyduff people want their jobs and income to come from that?'

'You're exaggerating everything. You're cockeyed with your Marxism –'

She laughed, a harsh sound in such a young throat. 'God, you sound just like my uncle! I'm not a Marxist – I've never read a political pamphlet in my life – all I'm concerned about is the people I lived amongst ... Are you in favour of selling the arms to my uncle and his friends?'

'No, I'm not. I'm trying to prevent it. But it shouldn't be done by going to the newspapers. There are left-wing journalists here in Sydney who'd make hay out of that –'

'They're the ones I'm looking for, someone who'll make a big splash ... I'm going to them, Sir Jonathan. I don't trust anyone any more. I thought you might back me up – from what I understand, you run the corporation from day to day ... But you've known about this all along, haven't you? I'm telling you nothing new.'

'No, I found out about it only yesterday. And I'm telling you – I'll do my best to stop it. But I'll do it my way!'

'No, you won't – not if you won't go to the newspapers. You'll hide it all there in the boardroom – my grandfather will find some other way of getting those arms to the Contras. You won't stand up to him – nobody does. I've only known him for a few months and I can see he rules everyone – he's a despot! I should have known – all you people care about is making money! You may not have any time for the Contras, but if it'll make you money, you don't care!'

He didn't know if it was the drink; not just one glass of vodka on the rocks, surely. She was drunk on something else: zeal, fervour, whatever it was that drove these religious cranks beyond reason.

'Sister, sit down – listen to me –'

She had risen, was heading for the door. He plunged after her, got between her and the door. 'Get out of my way!'

He put out a hand, grabbed the lapel of her raincoat. 'Listen to me! You can't go to the newspapers – that will ruin everything! I can stop the arms sale – I can beat your grandfather! Listen to me –'

All at once she was beyond listening, there was something in her (a madness? fanaticism?) that had turned her deaf. She saw her friend Rose Caracas, dead and buried now, the frightened José Caracas and his children, the unconscious figure of Audrey Burke lying in the dusty village street, Sister Carmel torn between neutrality and beliefs ... She hit at Tewsday with her fist: he was a dozen men: her grandfather, her uncle, the Contra lieutenant, everyone who had to be fought. Her fist struck him on his plump cheek. Without thinking, he hit back. The heel of his hand caught her beneath the jaw. Her eyes abruptly rolled back in their sockets, she moaned, then fell in a heap at his feet. Just as the junkie had done ...

The door was pushed against his back. He fell forward, just managing to avoid stepping on the unconscious girl, grabbed the back of a chair and spun round to see Gawler standing in the doorway. 'You all right, Sir Jonathan?'

All he could do was nod. He was trembling, his legs shaking under him. Was he going to piss himself again?

'I heard most of that, sir. You want me to get rid of her?'

Tewsday looked at him, uncomprehending.

'It'll be easy, sir, no trouble. She's a Commie, isn't she? I saw her kind in 'Nam ...'

'*Kill* her?'

Good Christ, was murder this easy? He had no memory of how he had felt thirty years before when he had purchased that other murder. That had been a hands-off affair, the victim had not been lying at his feet. He looked at Gawler – was he another fanatic, a Commie killer? No: he was just a plain killer. *It'll be easy, sir, no trouble . . .*

'How?' he croaked.

'Leave it to me. I'll dump her somewhere –'

'No, not anywhere. Dump – put her –' He was still trembling, even his voice; the plummy tone had gone, it was the flat voice of his youth, the barren country he had escaped from. 'Do you know the Quality Couch?'

'The brothel, the one in Surry Hills? Sure, sir.'

'Yes, yes. Put her there – on the doorstep –'

Gawler smiled as he picked up the still unconscious Mary Magdalene. 'A nun on a brothel's doorstep. You got a nice sense of humour, Sir Jonathan.'

Tewsday's mind had always been a calculator; it had stopped working for a while, but now it was in gear again. It was only his nerves that were not under control. He began to giggle, but it was from hysteria, not humour. He was going to avenge himself on the Hourigans with one deed.

Gawler took Teresa Hourigan across to the garage. There he put the junkie's long-bladed knife into her heart. He laid the body out on the garage floor on sheets of newspaper till the wound had stopped bleeding. Then he buttoned up the raincoat and put the body in the boot of the second-hand Toyota that was his and Sally's own car. He then got into the front seat of the car and slept till three a.m. when his wrist-alarm woke him. Ten minutes later he drove out of the grounds and headed for the south side of the city and Surry Hills. He felt a certain excitement being back on the job he did best. He was glad, however, that Sally had not been home.

Fingal Hourigan was deeply shocked by the murder of his granddaughter. He did not show it when Inspector Malone and Sergeant Clements came to the Vaucluse mansion on the Sunday morning; he acted the opposite to what he felt, because it was natural for him to resent any invasion of his privacy. When the two detectives had gone, he said 'I'll stay home. You go, Kerry, and say Mass.'

Kerry, equally shocked, said, 'I'll say it for her.'

'Keep it to yourself. Don't announce it publicly.'

'You're not going to be able to keep this out of the papers. They'll be here as soon as they know who Teresa was.' When she had called him and asked could she see him again yesterday, he had unhesitatingly agreed. The urge to convert is an appetite; but it worked both ways. She had arrived with all her arguments still intact and after a while he had replied with the same anger. But she had not deserved to die, not in such a way.

'They'll never get past the gates.'

'You'd better call Brigid.'

'Not yet.' The old man had sat down. 'I – I've got to get myself together. I'll call her soon.'

Kerry had never seen his father like this before; not since Sheila, his mother, had died. 'I'll be back as soon as Mass is finished.'

He left and Fingal sat alone in the big drawing-room. Mrs Kelly came in to ask if he wanted anything, a drink or coffee, but he just shook his head and sent her away. He sat on there for another half-hour, the silver stick occasionally tapping the carpet like an extension of a nervous tic. He had never been repelled by violence, though he had never physically indulged in it himself: it was a fact of life and he accepted it. He had, however, never been able to accept or understand violence against women. His granddaughter had been a major aggravation, provoking temper in him and Kerry; but he had recognized something of himself, and even of Sheila, in her. She had the courage of her convictions, wrong as they were, and she had been admirably, if irritatingly, persistent. She should not have been murdered and all at once he was angry.

He rang the White Sails Motel in Rose Bay and spoke to Paredes. 'You'd better check out of there at once. Bring your stuff over here to the house.'

'Is something wrong, Señor Hourigan?'

'A bloody lot's wrong! Get over here!'

Paredes and Domecq arrived at the same time as Kerry returned from saying Mass. The two Nicaraguans came in rather tentatively; it had occurred to them that Fingal Hourigan saw them as no more than minions. That offended their pride, especially Paredes', but this was the man with the money and certain concessions had to be made. He was obviously angry and their first thought was that he was going to cut off their funds, that the Austarm deal would be stopped before it had begun.

'My granddaughter has been murdered,' said Fingal bluntly and looked at them accusingly.

Paredes was the first to recover. Though he spoke English well, his mind could be slow in it. He was genuinely shocked, at the murder and at what seemed to be the accusation that he and Domecq might be responsible. 'What can I say? She was an enemy –' That was the wrong word, he saw at once. 'No, not an enemy. An opponent? But to be murdered for what she believed ...?' It was a good performance. He had murdered others, including a woman, for what they believed. 'We know nothing about it, Señor Hourigan, believe me.'

'Nothing,' said Domecq, shaking his head.

Fingal stared at them for a moment, then said, 'Then who did it?'

Domecq spread his hands and Paredes said, 'Where did it happen?'

'They found her outside a brothel in the inner city, in Surry Hills.'

Domecq's face closed up, but he said nothing. Paredes said, 'Outside a brothel? Then perhaps it could have been anyone who killed her? The brothel area in Miami, no one goes there alone, certainly not a woman.'

'Maybe.' But Fingal was certain Teresa had not been murdered by some casual stranger. These men, he was sure, had something to do with her murder, no matter how remotely. 'Anyhow, we have to keep you away from the police. They're getting nosey.'

'Would your granddaughter have told the police anything before she was — she was killed?' said Domecq, face still closed up.

'Why would she?'

Domecq shrugged. 'She never made any secret about how she felt about us. Isn't that right, Your Grace?'

Kerry had been silent up till now, sitting stiffly in a chair as if still in a state of shock. He looked up now, took a moment to catch the drift of Domecq's question. 'What? Oh, yes. Yes, she's been talking to groups around the universities.'

'There's a young priest,' said Paredes, 'a Nicaraguan. He's been encouraging her. Perhaps he will talk to the police.'

'How much does he know?' said Fingal.

'Who knows?'

'Have you spoken to him?'

'No.'

'Maybe someone should.'

'Dad —' Kerry looked anxiously at his father. 'This could get out of hand. Don't let's get any more involved ... It's bad enough Teresa being murdered. I never ...' He looked as if he might break down if he went on.

'Go upstairs and lie down.' Fingal spoke as he might have to a six-year-old; but his voice was tender. 'I'll call Brigid.'

Without another word Kerry got up and left the room. All at once it seemed that God had turned His back; Teresa's murder was a warning. But was it a warning of disapproval or just one that the road ahead would always have such tragedies, that the victory would not be easy? He would pray for an answer, but he didn't really believe in the efficacy of prayer. That required another sort of faith.

When his son had left the room Fingal said, 'You'd better have a look at that priest. What's his name?'

'Father Marquez.'

'Get someone to have a word with him.'

'I can do it over the telephone,' said Domecq. 'A few words ... It has worked in Miami when we have found people causing trouble.'

'That's all it needs sometimes,' said Paredes, the voice of experience.

Fingal looked at them, understanding them; it had been like that in Chicago all those years ago. 'Okay, do it then. But go to a public phone box, don't do it from here. Then have someone keep an eye on him, see if he takes the warning. You have someone here in Sydney can do that?'

'Oh yes, we have our supporters. It can be done.'

Then Fingal left them, went into his study and called his daughter. In the best of circumstances it would not have been an easy call for him to make; this was the worst of circumstances. He was surprised how sorry he felt for her.

'I have some bad news –'

'The police have already been here.' Her voice was calm and cool, almost cold.

'I – I'm sorry, Brigid.' Father and daughter, he thought, and we're strangers talking to each other. *And whose fault is that?* That sounded like Sheila, her voice coming out of the grave.

'If this happened, Dad, because of you and Kerry –'

'No,' he said sharply. 'No, Brigid. Kerry is shattered ... Would you care to come here? I think we need to be together.' It was the closest he could come to expressing love.

There was silence at the other end of the line; he thought she had just walked away from the phone. Then she said, 'I'll be there in an hour,' and hung up.

289

She arrived an hour later, as promised. Grief, however, did not reunite them. Kerry tried, but Brigid had retired behind an invisible wall. 'I only came to find out how much you were responsible for her death.'

'Bridie –' He tried to take her hand, but she moved it away from him. 'Do you really think I'd have my own niece *killed*? I saw her in Nicaragua –'

'She told me.'

'A Contra lieutenant there wanted to kill her. I prevented it.'

'No, I don't think either of you would be capable of killing her. I should hope not,' she said, looking at her father as if she had doubts about *him*. 'But those men you're dealing with – Paredes and Domecq. She told me about them. Are they here?'

'They're staying with us,' said Fingal. 'They had nothing to do with the murder. I swear that.'

She smiled cynically, 'Dad, your oath has never been worth a spit in the wind. But I'll believe you . . . I *want* to,' she said and her voice was full of despair, as if she had suffered enough and she wanted it all behind her.

*Oh Sheila*, cried Fingal silently, *where did it all go wrong?* But he knew the answer. Long ago in Chicago, when what few scruples he had inherited from his own mother had been smothered, like fragile flowers, beneath his father's corrupt advice and his own ambition. It was too late now.

# 6

The war with Jonathan Tewsday had been put aside for the moment. Tewsday's resignation did not arrive on his desk Monday morning and he did not send downstairs for it. The newspapers now had the full story on Sister Mary Magdalene, Teresa Hourigan; Ballyduff House and the castle at Vaucluse had been besieged by the media jackals. Brigid had not gone back to Stokes Point, but had remained at the house, occupying the room she had slept in as a child. The reporters and cameramen had looked as if they were about to camp outside the high gates, but Fingal called Chief Superintendent Danforth. The police arrived and within ten minutes the street had been cleared. The media men and women went away, complaining loudly about the violation of the freedom of the press, and the police agreed with them and gave them another kick up the bum. Both sides knew that democracy could sometimes be a comedy.

'Kerry and I won't go to the funeral,' Fingal said on Monday evening. 'The press would just turn it into a stampede. You don't want that.'

'No,' said Brigid, but it was impossible to tell whether she was grateful or hurt. In truth, she did not want either of them at the burial. If it could have been arranged, she would have wanted no one there but herself. She had to ask the dead Teresa, her one and only child, for forgiveness.

Late Tuesday afternoon Paredes knocked on the door of Fingal's study and came in. 'Did you watch the funeral on TV this morning, señor? The eleven-thirty news.'

'Yes.' He had watched it only till the coffin was lowered into the grave and then it had been too much for him and Kerry. They had switched off the set. 'What happened? You've got something to tell me.'

'The camera remained on Señorita Brigid. In the background were Father Marquez and the detective who came here Sunday morning, Inspector Malone. The priest gave Malone a letter. Father Marquez looked very worried.'

'Has Domecq spoken to him, given him a warning?'

'Twice. He also spoke to Inspector Malone.'

'Jesus!' Fingal raised his silver stick and for a moment Paredes thought the old man was going to hurl it at him. 'Why, for Christ's sake, did he do that? Of all the fucking stupid –' It was the first time he had heard the old man swear. 'This isn't fucking Nicaragua – you don't threaten our police!

You talk to them – you bribe them –'

Paredes spread a hand, as respectful as ever. The cause must not be lost, the money must still be promised. 'I'm sorry, señor, we all make mistakes –'

It took Fingal a moment or two to come off the boil. 'You'd better keep him under control. Christ knows what he's likely to do next. Where is he now?'

Paredes hesitated, 'He – he's gone out.'

'Where?'

Again the hesitation; then, 'He's gone to dispose of Father Hourigan.'

'*Who?*'

It had been a slip of the tongue; this old man was fast turning into another enemy in his mind. 'Sorry. Father Marquez.'

Fingal opened his mouth, but nothing came out but a coughing gasp; it was as if he were beyond words. He stood up abruptly, grabbed his walking stick and came round the desk. Paredes stepped aside, throwing up an arm to ward off the expected blow; but Fingal went right by him and out of the study, hurrying with surprising agility for such an old man. He went up the curving staircase in the big entrance hall, suddenly pausing half-way up as if he were about to collapse. He drew a deep breath, looked down at Paredes with a terrible expression of rage on his face, then went on up to the landing and disappeared.

Brigid, an empty glass in her hand, came to the doorway of the drawing-room. 'Do you know where the liquor's kept, Mr Paredes?'

'No.' He was still staring up at the empty landing.

She followed the direction of his gaze. 'Something wrong with my father?'

'I don't know, señorita. He'll tell you, I suppose.'

'I doubt it,' said Brigid and went back into the drawing-room.

Upstairs in Kerry's bedroom Fingal was explaining what

Domecq had gone to do. 'Get packed! We've got to get you out of here! *Now!* Do you hear me, for Christ's sake – *now!* Get back to Rome tonight –'

'I can't leave just like *that*! How can I get on a plane at such short notice? Planes don't leave for Rome every hour –'

'Just get out to the airport – I'll have the Falcon ready for you. If you can't get Qantas or Alitalia or one of the others for Rome, I'll have our crew fly you to Perth. You can pick up something there and change at Singapore. But you've got to get out *now*! You hear me?'

'I can't believe it –' Kerry, in this bedroom where he had harboured all the doubts and fears of boyhood, was nothing like the confident, arrogant man he presented to the world. He was still suffering from the shock of Teresa's death; and now this. The Lord was deserting him; he felt both hollow and angry. His devotion had always been narrow, a thin rod of sustenance; now it threatened to break. 'God, it's not worth it –'

'What's not worth it? Of course it's worth it! It's just bloody stupid, that's all, the way they've gone about it. Get packed! I'll have the car round the front in ten minutes. You're going back to Rome!'

It was an order. Or a coronation: Fingal was not going to be denied his ambition.

# TWELVE

When the Falcon 900 landed at Kingsford Smith airport Malone said a brisk goodbye to Fingal and Kerry Hourigan and walked quickly across the tarmac to the main building. He had had enough of the Hourigans for the moment; he breathed in the crisp autumn air as if it were smelling salts. He would not even think about them for at least twenty-four hours. He knew, however, that thoughts could be as slippery as criminals.

He stopped at the duty-free store on his way out to Immigration. Zara Kersey, looking as fresh as if she were about to begin a journey instead of just finishing one, came in after him. 'I'm buying something for my children.'

'So am I,' he said, conscience-stricken that he hadn't bought something in Rome or Singapore. 'But what? Kids today are so choosey. My thirteen-year-old actually reads *Choice* magazine. A thirteen-year-old consumer!'

She helped him choose: Italian boat shoes for the girls, a model airplane for Tom. 'Boat shoes? I don't own a boat.'

'It doesn't matter. Believe me, Scobie, those shoes are going to be the *in* thing for kids next summer. If I know anything about something, it's fashion.'

He grinned. 'You know more than that, Zara.'

She nodded. 'I've learned a few things on this trip. Good luck, Scobie. This case is a long way from over. Don't get in the way of any more knives.'

Lisa was waiting for him outside Customs. He had discarded his sling, hoping that they would be home before she discovered another attempt had been made on his life. But she rushed at him, embraced him; he let out a gasp of pain as she flung an arm round his wounded shoulder. She drew back in alarm.

'What's the matter? Have you been hurt?'

'Not here – I'll tell you about it in the car –'

She seethed with concern all the way to the car-park. Six overseas airliners had arrived within twenty minutes of each other; the path from the terminal to the car-park was a United Nations reunion. A party of Greeks blocked the Malones' way; Lisa pushed through them with discriminatory prejudice. A large family of white natives, back from a holiday in the tropics, shivering in their thongs and shorts, got the same treatment. She had only one nationality this morning, that of her family and him in particular.

Once in the car she demanded, 'What's the matter? Have you been hurt?'

'Not here – wait till we get home –'

'*Tell me!*'

He did, flatly and in as few words as possible. 'I'm okay. They got the cove who tried it –'

'They arrested him? You've got to go back to Rome?'

'No-o. They – they shot him.'

'Oh Jesus!' She rarely, if ever, swore. She slumped back in the seat of the car, stared at him as if she didn't believe what he was telling her. '*Twice!* Twice they've tried to kill you!'

'It won't happen again –'

'How do you know?' He couldn't remember when he had last seen her so angry.

'I don't. Darl – Please . . .'

He looked and sounded unutterably weary and abruptly she relented. 'I'm sorry. I'm selfish – all I think about is myself and the kids.'

'No. No, you're not selfish.' He put his arm round her and

kissed her again. 'I'm just in the wrong job for a family man.'

They drove home and he was reunited with the children when they came home from school. Zara Kersey had been right: the girls were delighted with their boat shoes ('Daddy, how did you *know?*') and Tom wanted to take off at once in his airplane for the moon ('Planes don't go to the moon.' ... 'Mine does.'). As numerous times before, he rediscovered God and was grateful to Him: his family was his harbour. Sunday he would go to Mass with them, suffer the boring sermon and the banal hymns and the monotonous guitar music, and say a heartfelt prayer of thanks. It suddenly occurred to him that he could not remember saying a single prayer while at Mass in St Peter's.

Clements came to the house at six o'clock. 'I guess you're ready for bed, eh? The Commissioner told me to ask how you were. Rome rang to tell him about the guy knifing you. You okay? Who paid for the job? Domecq and Paredes?'

'I don't think so.'

Clements bit his lip. 'Not the Archbishop?'

'No. It might have been his old man. I just don't know.'

Clements sat chewing on his lip. Then he said, 'Well, that's another tiger snake out of the can. If we bust this case, I hate to think where you and I are going to finish up. Still, that's all to come. I'd better brief you before you come in tomorrow. I've got them all together tomorrow morning at ten – the Archbishop and Paredes and Domecq. Mrs Kersey will be there, too, I guess. You want me to bring in old man Hourigan?'

'No. You made any progress with Domecq?'

'A little. I've found out how he could have known about you and Father Marquez and the letter. I went around all the TV stations checking if they had any Nicaraguans working in their crews.' He shook his big head. 'None. But a guy at Channel 8, Hourigan's own station, said they'd run a piece on the funeral on their eleven-thirty news last Tuesday morning. He got out the tape and ran it for me. You and

Father Marquez are there plain as day – he's giving you the letter and you're reading it. There's a second shot and you're saying something to him and he's looking pretty worried. If Domecq saw that clip, he could put two and two together.'

'We've got no proof that he did.'

Clements grinned. 'Don't be obstructive, mate. We have to hit him over the head with anything we can. How'd you go with the Archbishop?'

Malone shrugged. 'I don't know. How much resilience have martyrs got?'

'He's a martyr? You could have fooled me. Go to bed, Scobie, get a good night's sleep. I'll see you in the morning.'

On his way out he said to Lisa, 'Take care of him. He looks beat.'

'So am I,' she said, but good-humouredly. 'Who's taking care of me?'

'Uncle Russ,' he said and put his arms round her, the first time he had ever done that.

Next morning when Malone went into Homicide, Kerry Hourigan, Paredes and Domecq were waiting for him. Clements had procured a separate room for the interrogation; it was small and the five big men made it smaller. When Zara Kersey arrived, looking much fresher than Malone felt, she looked around and smiled. 'Whose lap do I sit on?'

Clements squeezed in a chair for her between the Archbishop and Domecq. The two detectives sat on the opposite side of the narrow table with Paredes beside them. It looked more like a conspiracy than an interrogation.

'We're taking Mr Domecq into custody on suspicion of murder and attempted murder,' Malone said without pre-liminary. 'Specifically, the murder of Father Luis Marquez and the attempted murder of myself at Randwick.' He turned his head and looked at Paredes. 'Someone also tried to kill me in Rome. Did you know that?'

Paredes showed no surprise or concern. 'How would I know it, Inspector?'

'I thought His Grace might have told you.'

Kerry Hourigan flushed, but said nothing.

'Have you any evidence against Mr Domecq?' said Zara Kersey. 'Any witnesses?'

'We'll be calling Archbishop Hourigan as a witness for the prosecution.'

It seemed for a moment as if the room were going to burst; the walls, Malone was sure, were pushed back. The Archbishop grew bigger with shock and indignation; beside him Malone felt Paredes swell. Domecq pushed his chair back, half-rose as if he were about to bolt through the door. Only Zara remained calm.

'You can't do that, Inspector.'

'Oh, yes, I can.' It was a gamble, but he had been mulling it over in his mind since four o'clock this morning when, his body still out of rhythm with Sydney time, he had woken. 'If he doesn't tell the truth, we're going to leak all we know about his work for the Contras. Rome will be interested in that.' He looked at Kerry Hourigan. 'There's another thing, Your Grace. You've told enough lies – but so far they've only been to me and Sergeant Clements and we're used to them. If I get you into the witness box, you can act as a hostile witness, but you're going to be no advertisement for the Church. People, even the non-believers, expect archbishops to tell the truth. Your father once told me that truth is a dangerous weapon. You'll have your chance to prove it.'

Paredes and Domecq looked at the Archbishop. He avoided their gaze, unable to suffer their anger and contempt if he showed that he might go against them. How could he explain to them his ambition? They would laugh, even though they had ambitions of their own. They were Catholics, but in name only: it was a good cover in Latin America. They would never understand the ambition of a man to be head of all the Catholics in the world, or the ambition of the father of that man to make him so. He had discovered in the months he had known them that they were men of little imagination, especially Domecq. Paredes *might* understand, but he was not the one who would be sacrificed.

'We didn't come here to be betrayed,' said Paredes and there was no mistaking the threat in his voice. He showed no surprise, it would not be the first time he and his fellow Contras had been betrayed. 'Especially if you have to lie.'

Kerry Hourigan's own voice was just a rumble in his throat. 'I didn't come home to see my niece murdered. Nor that young priest . . .'

'We had nothing to do with your niece's murder – you know that!'

'We're not charging Mr Domecq with that murder,' said Malone quietly.

Paredes saw his mistake, looked quickly across the table at Zara Kersey. 'Do something, señora. They are trying to rail-road Señor Domecq!'

She stood up. 'May I see you outside, Inspector? You too, Your Grace.'

Outside in the corridor people were coming and going busily; homicide, it seemed, was on the rise today. Oh, for a nice simple homicide, Malone thought, an open-and-shut case with the murderer still standing over the victim yelling that he had done it. But those were usually domestic murders and sometimes they could be worse, far worse, especially when the children had to be told what daddy had done to mummy or vice versa. At least there were no kids in this one.

'Will you be a witness against Mr Domecq?' Zara Kersey said.

Archbishop Hourigan was going through agony. 'If I do, I'm going to crucify him –'

'Don't let's get too religious,' said Malone. 'I know who threatened me and Father Marquez over the phone. I know who shot at us – I can *feel* it every time I'm near him –'

'That would never be accepted in court, Scobie,' said Zara, but she sounded sympathetic. She was out of her depth in a murder case, especially this one; her pool was white-collar crime where only money and not blood was spilt. Fingal Hourigan had made a mistake in calling her in on this and when she left here she would call him and tell him she was withdrawing from the case.

Malone said, 'Was Domecq still at your father's house at Vaucluse before you left for the airport that evening?'

Kerry hesitated, then shook his head. 'No.'

'Where had he gone?'

'I don't know.' Then he thought better of the answer: 'My father said he had gone looking for Father Marquez.'

'Did he have a gun?'

'He – yes, I suppose so.'

'What do you mean, you suppose so?'

Kerry hesitated again. 'When we were down at Austarm, at Moss Vale, he told the men we were talking to that he often went hunting in the States. He said he wanted to go pig-shooting while he was here – he'd seen it in some travel movie, he said. They presented him with the gun. It was a heavy, pump-action shotgun.'

'The sort they use for security?'

'I wouldn't know, Inspector. We don't go in for that sort of security in the Church.'

'You were going in for 7.62 rifles, ten thousand of them.' The Archbishop made no answer to the jibe and Malone went on, 'So he had the shotgun with him at your father's house?'

'I saw him showing it to Paredes. He'd confessed to me on the way back from Moss Vale that he really wasn't interested in pig-shooting, he just collected guns. He's the sort of man who likes people to give him things.'

'Will you testify in court that Domecq had the shotgun at your father's house?'

'God, do I have to?' There was real anguish in his voice. Pope Judas – would it be worth it? 'Do I have to, Mrs Kersey? Isn't there some way out?'

'You can refuse to answer any questions.' She showed him no sympathy.

'If I testify against him, he'll bring everything out into the open. I can't risk that!'

'You should have thought of that before you got yourself involved with them,' said Malone, equally unsympathetic. 'I don't know about the other Contras, they may be honest patriots, but these two are gangsters. You should have looked into their credentials, Your Grace. Well?'

The Archbishop looked at Zara Kersey again, but now he could see he would receive no help from her. He felt no bitterness towards her, though life itself had never tasted more bitter. He sighed, gave himself up to God, Who also might offer no help. 'I'll testify.'

## 2

Fingal Hourigan fell headlong into a terrible rage when Kerry went home and told him what he intended doing. 'Holy shit, do you know what you're doing?'

'Of course I do,' said Kerry gloomily, offended by his father's language as much as his rage.

'You're throwing everything out of the window! Years of effort, God knows how much goddam money –'

'Do you want me to pay you back?' A spark of rebellion showed. 'With interest?'

Fingal ignored that. He stomped up and down his study, swearing and yelling till Brigid opened the door and came in. 'I think every window in Vaucluse is open and listening to you. What's the hullabaloo?'

'Tell her!' Fingal stormed; the silver stick threshed the air like streaks of lightning. 'Tell her!'

Kerry told her, leaving out only that he was throwing away his ambition to be Pope. It was bad enough to be raged at; he could not bear to be laughed at. And he knew Brigid would laugh. 'I'll probably be asked to leave Rome.'

'Not necessarily,' said Brigid. She was the only calm one of the three of them. She had lived in Italy and she knew the Italian talent for accommodation. And the Vatican, after all, was still Italian, or almost. 'Doesn't The Lord look after His own? They'll probably make you a papal knight or whatever they do to cover up your mistakes.'

'They only do that in the civil service.' Fingal was simmering down. His eye was not so filled with fury that he missed his daughter's reaction to the crisis. But, of course, she did not know of the real prize that had been sacrificed. He looked at Kerry. 'What are the police going to do with Domecq?'

'They're holding him,' said Kerry. 'They're going to oppose bail. Paredes has stayed with him for the time being. He says he'll move out of here.'

'He won't be missed,' said Fingal. 'I never liked either of them.'

'Did Domecq kill Father Marquez?' Brigid asked, still calm. 'Yes.'

'Did he kill Teresa?' Icily calm now. 'If he did, I'll have him killed.'

She's like me, Fingal thought with wonder. She *would* have Domecq killed; just as I tried to have Malone killed in Rome. He had no conscience about that; it had been a mistake to have commissioned the contract. Brigid would have a conscience: he recognized enough of Sheila in her to see that.

'No. No, he didn't kill her. It wasn't Domecq. Nor Paredes, either.'

'Who was it then?'

All at once, unaccountably, he wanted to save her from herself. If she tried to have anyone killed, she would never cover her tracks as he could.

'We don't know. Unless . . .'

'Unless what?'

She was staring at him, and so was Kerry. The latter said, 'Be careful, Dad, If you have no proof . . .'

'You're thinking the same as I am.' He had not even thought of the possibility up till now.

'*Who?*' demanded Brigid.

'I'll tell you when I've done a little more checking.'

'No, tell me now!' She had lost her calm, was standing opposite him, pounding his desk. 'Dad, I have to know!'

'You will know,' he promised her and meant it. But she mustn't be allowed to endanger herself with her own revenge. 'But let the police do it. Let Inspector Malone do it – he owes it to us.'

She stared at him, not trusting him; yet suddenly wanting to. Blood bound the three of them here in this room; she was caught in it, as in a whirlpool. She looked into the once-bright blue eyes, now dimmed by age and pain and loss, and saw something she had never seen before: an effort at love.

She could find no words for him. She turned abruptly and went out of the room. She was running by the time she reached the stairs, stumbling as the tears blinded her.

Fingal reached for the phone book, then dialled Police Centre. They put him through to Inspector Malone at Homicide. 'This is Fingal Hourigan. You're holding Mr Domecq.'

'That's right, Mr Hourigan. We're going to oppose bail, if that's what you're calling about.'

'No, I'm not. I'm calling about something else. How far have you got on the murder of my granddaughter?'

'We're still working on it.'

'Which means you haven't got anywhere. Ask Sir Jonathan Tewsday what he knows about it.'

'Are you accusing him of it, Mr Hourigan?'

'You know better than that,' said Fingal and hung up. He looked across his desk at Kerry. 'There, it's done.'

'It's malicious,' said his son. 'You have no proof whatsoever.'

'None at all. But who else is there left to suspect? Tilly Mosman? She wouldn't dump the body on her own doorstep.'

'How do you know anything about the brothel-owner?'

'I set her up in business. We were – friends, once upon a time. Don't look shocked. Fornication is an everyday – or everynight occasion.' He was feeling better. In his inflamed imagination he could see the police cars screaming towards Tewsday. 'Jonathan knew about it. He hates me, Kerry, always has. I sacked him – he'd do anything to get back at me. We've hated each other for years. I've enjoyed it. He never did.'

Kerry had always suspected this uglier side of his father; it shocked him now to see it so openly displayed. 'But why poor Teresa? An innocent –'

'I don't know. He wouldn't have killed her himself – he's pure yellow all through. But he would have paid someone. Once, long ago, he did that ...' But then he stopped. Too much confession was not good for the soul; or the neck. 'If he did have Teresa murdered, Malone will nail him.'

At Homicide Malone had looked at the dead phone, then also hung up. He believed in the law of coincidence, though it was rarely recognized in a court of law. In the hours he had been awake in bed at home the murder of Teresa Hourigan had been as much on his mind as that of Father Marquez; one could not be thought of without thinking of the other. He had run down a list of everyone remotely connected with the dead nun; Tewsday's name had been there only because he had been at the funeral and there was no explanation for that. He was also connected with Ballyduff and Austarm; on top of that he had been less than forthcoming on the ride back from the funeral. Perhaps Tewsday *should* be asked a few more questions. But why had Fingal Hourigan suggested it?

'What do we know about Sir Jonathan Tewsday?' he asked Clements.

'I don't think there's a file on him, is there?'

'There's probably one over in Fraud. When I was on the squad over there, oh, I dunno, fifteen or twenty years ago, we thought we had a case against him. Bill Zanuch was in charge of it.'

'What happened?'

'I don't know. They just suddenly shut up shop on it.'

'I interviewed him a couple of years ago, him and a few others at Ballyduff. That Pommy junkie they found with his neck broken in the garage at Ballyduff House.'

'What happened on that one?'

'Nothing. We couldn't trace any of the junkie's relatives. He was better off dead, anyway.' Clements was not callous; he just had his own ideas of justice. But he never voiced them to anyone but Malone. 'We just put the file in a drawer and turned the key on it.'

'Whom else did you interview?'

'*Whom*? I'd have to look up the file. The only one I remember was Tewsday's driver, a Yank, I can't remember his name.'

'Gawler. Why did you remember him?'

'Yeah, Gary or Larry Gawler. I dunno, he just wasn't – forthcoming?'

'That's a good word. Put an enquiry on the telex to the FBI in Washington, see if they have anything on him. Do the same with Immigration here. In the meantime, let's go and have a word with him. And Tewsday, too.'

'Mind if I ask – who put this bee in your bonnet?'

'Fingal Hourigan.'

Clements bit his lip. 'This mob, they really love each other, don't they?'

Clements sent off the telex to the FBI, then he and Malone went to see Gary Gawler, Tewsday's unforthcoming chauffeur. 'Where do drivers hang out when their bosses are in their offices?'

Their first call hit the jackpot: Gawler was in the Ballyduff House garage. He had the bonnet of the Rolls-Royce up and was tinkering with the engine when Malone said, 'I didn't think anything ever went wrong with Rolls-Royces.'

Gawler put down the bonnet, wiped his hands on a clean rag. 'Hello, Inspector. Just a battery connection, that's all. Nothing is perfect.'

'So they tell me. Mr Gawler, can you remember where Sir Jonathan was last Saturday week, the night of the fifteenth?'

'I'd have to look up my book. Sir Jonathan has me write down every trip. He's very meticulous like that, with the fringe benefits tax.'

'I didn't think you'd have to look this up. It was the night Sister Mary Magdalene was murdered.'

Gawler was still wiping his hands, but now suddenly they were still, the rag held tightly between his fingers. A car went out of the garage, its tyres screeching a little as it went up the ramp into the street. At the far end of the garage a radio was playing: a talkback guru was listening to the woes of housewives whose husbands wouldn't listen to them. It was cold here in this concrete cavern and Gawler seemed to be feeling it. He abruptly dropped the rag and reached for his uniform jacket hanging on the car door.

'Yes, I remember. Sir Jonathan was home all day that day. The night, too. His family had gone down to their place at Bowral. He had a lot of paperwork to do. I cooked the evening meal for him.'

'He never went out? He doesn't drive himself?'

'I sleep over the garages, my wife and I have our flat there. I'd have heard him if he'd taken the car out.'

'You didn't go out yourself?'

'No. I was on my own. My wife had gone down to Bowral with Lady Tewsday and the girls.'

'And I suppose you watched television?'

'Maybe an hour or so, I can't remember. I don't watch much TV.'

'You read?'

'No, I watch videos.'

'What sort?'

'Anything with action in it. Sylvester Stallone, Arnold Schwarzenegger. It relaxes me.'

'It bores me,' said Malone. 'Is Sir Jonathan up in his office now?'

'Yes.' Gawler looked at his watch. He seemed warmer now that he had his jacket on, more at ease. But he hadn't liked Malone's remark about the action videos. 'I have to take him out in twenty-five minutes. He's always punctual.'

'We'd better get a move on, then. Thanks, Mr Gawler. We may be talking to you. What floor is Sir Jonathan on?'

'The sixty-eighth.'

As they walked across to the lift Malone said, 'What did you think?'

'He's used to being questioned,' said Clements.

'Yeah, not a stutter or a stammer. I wonder where he got the practice?' Malone pressed the floor button in the lift. 'Sixty-eight. I've never been this high before.'

'Getting into a lift is the only way I'm going to go up in the world.'

'Don't put yourself down. If we solve this case, they may make you inspector.'

Clements grinned. 'I got the feeling, we solve this case we're both going to end up out at Tibooburra.'

Sir Jonathan's secretary said he was *terribly* busy. 'So are we,' said Malone. 'We've got homicides piling up like those letters in your *In* basket.'

She gave him a look that said she didn't think either he or his remark was funny. But she spoke to Tewsday on her intercom, then stood up and ushered them into his office. 'You have your Reserve Bank appointment in twenty minutes, Sir Jonathan,' she said pointedly.

Malone smiled at her. 'We'll see he's not late.'

She nodded coldly and closed the door. Tewsday remained seated at his desk, but waved a hand to the two chairs opposite him. Malone, aware as ever of his surroundings, remarked the quiet elegance of the office; he guessed that more money

307

had been spent on this one room than on all the rooms in the Malone house at Randwick. He was not to know that the man sitting behind the big antique desk was spending his last day in the office.

'I won't waste time, Sir Jonathan, since your secretary made a point of telling us how busy you are. Where were you last Saturday week, the fifteenth, from say eight o'clock in the evening till two o'clock Sunday morning?'

'Last Saturday week?'

'The night Sister Mary Magdalene was murdered.'

A flush darkened the pink marbled face. 'Are you saying – are you saying I'm some sort of suspect?'

'I haven't said you're anything. I'm just asking a question.'

'You're *implying*.'

'Only if you want to take it that way, Sir Jonathan. Sergeant Clements has been doing a lot of leg-work on the case. Nobody has been able to tell us where Sister Mary Magdalene went between leaving the convent at Randwick at six-thirty that evening and when she was found next morning outside the Quality Couch. She rang her mother at seven o'clock – what did she say, Russ?'

Clements had his notebook open, saving Tewsday's precious time. 'She didn't say where she was ringing from or where she was going. They had a date to go to the opera, but she said she'd have to put it off. Her mother was at the Regent Hotel – they were booked in there for the night.' He glanced at Malone. 'Under the Hourigan name. We didn't think to ask when we were looking for her that Sunday morning. We were looking for Miss O'Keefe, remember?'

'I remember,' said Malone, but he had forgotten.

Clements looked back at Tewsday. 'She said she'd see her mother out at Stokes Point on the Sunday. She didn't turn up, as you know.'

Tewsday was solid jelly; but at any moment he would begin to quake. He had been expecting just such a call as this; yet he was unprepared for it. In a desk drawer, hastily put away when Malone and Clements had been announced, was a note from Fingal sent down half an hour before. It told him what his golden handshake was to be and it demanded his delayed resignation by 5 p.m. today. Fingal was back in business, no longer put off by mourning. Tewsday's mind had been full of further threats against Fingal, but he knew now they were as empty and lethal as party balloons. *He* was the one under threat and he had no proper answer.

'I think I was home. Yes, I was. I had work to do.'

'Your wife or your family can corroborate that?'

'Yes. No. No, they were down at Bowral. I have a property down there.'

'Your driver, Gawler – what about him?'

'He was at home with me.'

'So he'd be your only witness if –' Malone let the sentence dangle in the air like a looped rope.

'If what?' Tewsday was moving his opal ring round and round as if trying to unscrew his finger.

Malone stood up. 'You'll be relieved to know, Sir Jonathan, you and your driver have told the same story.'

'You've already seen him? You have a lot of gall!'

'It's one of my few talents,' said Malone. 'That and persistence. Goodbye, Sir Jonathan. I don't think we've kept the Reserve Bank waiting.'

'Give them my regards,' said Clements, who had great respect for banks, even though so many of them were being held up these days. He wondered what sort of crim it would take to hold up the Reserve Bank. Someone like Sir Jonathan Tewsday? No.

Going down in the lift he said, 'He was as nervous as an old-fashioned virgin.'

'I didn't know there were any left. You're right, though. I thought he had piles, he was moving around in his chair so much. But why would he kill Sister Mary? Unless he's tied up in this Austarm deal more than we know. How'd you like to drive out to Pymble and talk to the Tewsdays' neighbours?

309

They might give you morning tea – they're very keen on morning tea up that way. Check if any of them heard him drive out during the night. Or if he had any visitors.'

'Now? Okay. You want me to drive you back to the office?'

'No, thanks. I'll have a think walk.'

'What's that?'

'Ask Arnold Bennett.'

He left Clements bemused and walked back to Liverpool Street; but the think walk produced no solutions. The telex to the FBI did. When Clements returned from Pymble, Malone, smiling with satisfaction, laid the telex in front of him. 'Get a load of that. We're getting somewhere.'

Clements read the report, sucking on his bottom lip as he did so. Then he looked up. 'That tells us he has a police record. But what do they mean – check with CIA? Don't they know the CIA never tells foreign police anything? We're not in the spy business, we're low life.'

'I'll get on to Joe Nagler over at Special Branch. He's got contacts at ASIO.' ASIO was the Australian Security Intelligence Organization. 'They work with the CIA. In the meantime, what did you get?'

'Morning tea.' Clements brushed imaginary crumbs from his lapel. 'They're just like the rest of us up in Pymble – stickybeaks. Or anyway the Tewsdays' neighbour is, Mrs Prunello. I think she must spend all her weekend at the front window. Someone did go out on the Saturday night – or rather, Sunday morning early. She was awake. She doesn't know what time it was, but she heard a car go out of the Tewsdays' drive. Not the Rolls, she thought it was a smaller car. I had a peek in the Tewsdays' garages – the doors were open. They have a BMW and what looked like a Toyota.'

'Will Mrs Whatever-her-name-is keep her mouth shut?'

'I doubt it, though I don't think she'll talk to the Tewsdays. She didn't seem to have much time for them, thought they were uppity.'

'What's she doing living in Pymble then? I thought everyone

up there was uppity.' He sounded like his father, the worker from the south side of the harbour. 'You learn anything else?'

'This is the bit I've been saving. Tewsday had a visitor Saturday night, a young woman. Mrs Prunello saw the taxi arrive there about eight o'clock. It dropped whoever it was out in the street, then drove off. I've got the cab companies checking with their drivers. They're going to ring me when they find out who had the fare.'

There is always something where they slip up, Malone thought. He had known so many criminals who had overlooked the small, inconsequential links that bound the world together: a forgotten phone call, a taxi ride, an inquisitive neighbour. There was no proof yet that Tewsday had done anything criminal; but yes, now he was a suspect. There was a gleam of hope in Malone's eye. We all like to have our suspicions confirmed, no matter what prejudices they arise from. The truth of the matter was, he didn't like Sir Jonathan. Cops, after all, are human.

He reached for his phone, called Detective Inspector Joe Nagler at Special Branch, told him what he wanted, then hung up. 'Joe'll see what he can do.'

'What do we do now?'

'Wait. And put a stake-out on the Tewsday house.'

'What about Domecq?'

'He's been refused bail.'

'Paredes?'

'I've got Andy Graham tailing him. He's safe.'

'The Archbishop?'

'I guess he's out at Vaucluse praying hard. He's more a politician than a priest. And now he's going to find out that politicians can't fall back on the privilege of the confessional.'

'You Tykes,' said Clements. 'You make life so bloody complicated for yourselves. It's never like that with the Congregationalists.'

# 3

The meeting between Tewsday and Fingal was short and bitter.

'You've got your handshake – six times your salary. You own six hundred thousand shares – if you sell those at today's prices you'll have another twelve million. If you want to go on working, there'll be head-hunters rushing to offer you another job. You won't starve.'

Tewsday hadn't sat down when he entered Fingal's office. He stood on trembling legs, wanting to leap at the smug old man behind the desk but knowing he could never bring himself to that peak of violence. Cowardice is a good self-defence. 'I'll get you, Hourigan! I'll break this corporation –'

'If I owned a bakery, you couldn't break a piece of stale cake. You've only got as far as you have because I've let you. You're a number two man, Jonathan, you always will be ... Goodbye!'

He swung his chair round, disappearing from Tewsday's view behind the high back of his chair. Tewsday stood a moment longer, fury making him ugly; but there was no one to see it, not even the man at whom it was directed. He was full of words, but they were incoherent, even in his head; it takes a cool mind to be properly abusive. He spun round, almost toppling over on his unsteady legs, and galloped out of the office. This was the highest office in the land, the peak where he had always dreamed of sitting, and he had just been kicked out for ever. He felt he was falling from a great height.

Going home to Pymble he sat in sullen silence in the back of the Rolls-Royce. Gawler said nothing till they were held up in stalled traffic on the Pacific Highway. Then, without looking round, he said, 'Have the police been back to see you, Sir Jonathan?'

'Eh?' Tewsday came back to the back seat. He had been miles away in the past, a region he hadn't visited in years. 'You mean this afternoon? No. Why?'

'I didn't like the sound of their questions this morning.' There had been time for only a brief discussion on the short ride up to the Reserve Bank that morning. 'That Inspector Malone, I don't think he'd ever take maybe for an answer.'

'No,' Tewsday agreed. 'But we have to sit tight.'

'Yeah,' said Gawler, but for once he sounded less than cool and distant.

Tewsday had not mentioned to Fiona the ultimatum Fingal had given him; till five o'clock this afternoon he had refused to admit, even to himself, that his career with Ballyduff was finished. Injustice had been done; which is more soul-destroying than justice being done. Though no one had ever accused Tewsday of having a soul, not even Fiona.

'What are you going to do?' she said when he told her he had resigned. She didn't believe his resignation had been voluntary, but she did not want to humble him. He looked sick and she felt a certain pity for him; love had finished up as pity, but the latter was still a genuine feeling. 'Why don't you retire? Don't look for another position.'

'No, I'm too young –' Though he felt older than he had ever dreamed he would be. 'I have to see Fingal go first –'

'Don't get too worked up.' She recognized the signs. He had never told her of his hatred for Fingal Hourigan, but he had never been able to hide it from her. She was still a good wife in that respect, keeping a husband's secrets, even though he had not revealed them to her. 'We'll go away on a holiday. Somewhere on the Barrier Reef, Lizard Island, perhaps –'

'No, I can't go now.' An earthquake was about to happen and he wanted to be there when the victims were counted. Including, he hoped, Fingal Hourigan. Then he said, 'Can I sleep with you tonight?'

'It's still a double bed.' She said it kindly, almost with some of the old love.

# 4

In the morning he was half-dressed for the office when he remembered he would not be going to Ballyduff any more. After breakfast, which he only nibbled at, he wandered about the house, getting in the way of Sally Gawler, till finally he was told by her would he mind going into his library and staying there. There is no one so demanding of the territorial imperative as a woman doing housework. Fiona went off in the BMW to one of her charity meetings; his daughters, as usual, were at their weekly boarding school. At last he went out into the garden where Gawler was cutting back a big camellia bush.

Gawler said at once, 'I'm worried, Sir Jonathan. There's a car parked up the street with two guys in it. It was there early this morning when I went down to the gate to pick up the papers. It's still there.'

'Police or someone else?' But who else? Fingal no longer had any interest in him.

'I'd lay money it's police.' He snipped at the bush with the big sharp secateurs. 'I think I'd like to take a vacation.'

'You had your holidays only – oh, I see.' He shivered with the cold; or so he thought. A south-west wind was blowing, bringing hints of an early winter; a brown snow of leaves blew across the lawns. 'It'd be foolish to start running away, Gary. That would only raise suspicion.'

'It's already raised.' Gawler knew an ill-wind when it blew, warm or cold; he had been chased in all climes. 'Those guys aren't sitting out there just because they like the neighbourhood.'

'Have you said anything to Sally?'

'No. She's right outside this, okay?' There was a threat in his voice.

'Of course, of course. We mustn't panic. Let things take their course.' But he really didn't know how the police worked. They were in a different business altogether.

He watched Gawler cutting the camellia bush; the secateurs sounded as if they were slicing through bone. He said, poised ready to run if necessary, 'I know all about you, Gary.'

Gawler paused, the blades open round a branch. 'You know what?'

'About what you did in Vietnam, in Bangkok, back in the United States. Everything. Alphonse Brown, Ray Karr. Everything.'

Gawler lowered the secateurs, held them like a dagger for an upward thrust. 'How long have you known?'

'Since about a month after you killed that junkie who attacked me.'

'Who told you?'

'It doesn't matter. Your secret's safe with me.'

'Is it safe with the guy who told you?'

'Yes. Alphonse Brown. *Alphonse?* Did you have a French mother or something?'

Gawler smiled; the secateurs were hanging loosely in his hand now. 'No. My daddy worked for Al Capone, *Alphonse* Capone, when he first come up to Chicago from the Kentucky hills. He was only small-time, the old man, but he thought Capone was the greatest. Capone used to call himself Al Brown one time, I dunno why. My daddy thought he was doing me an honour, y'know? What kid would want to be called Alphonse?' Then he raised the secateurs again. 'So what are we gonna do?'

The wind had dropped; the cold seemed more deadening now. In the garden next door Tewsday could hear Mrs Prunello calling to her cat: like to like, as Fiona would say. He wondered if she had heard any of their conversation. Fiona had warned him that she had ears like satellite dishes; gossip was her energy current. He lowered his voice, which in his own ears sounded as if it had a shiver in it.

'We just trust each other, Gary.'

Gawler looked at him, cool and distant again. 'We better, Sir Jonathan. We better.'

Malone and Clements arrived at lunchtime. Tewsday was not surprised to see them; just depressed and afraid. He had had home-made pea soup and hamhocks for lunch; they curdled in his stomach when he opened the door to the two detectives. 'Why, Inspector Malone!'

'Sir Jonathan,' said Malone, too tired for preliminaries; jet lag had started to catch up with him again, 'we'd like to talk to you about your driver Gary Gawler.'

Tewsday hesitated, then stood aside. 'Come in.' He led them into the library, closing the door so that Sally Gawler would not hear what he knew was about to be said. 'What's all this about, Inspector?'

'We went to Ballyduff House, but they told us there that you resigned yesterday afternoon. A bit sudden, wasn't it?'

'It's going to be announced today, after a board meeting. My health has not been good. Blood-pressure, heart – I've been advised to take a long break.' He felt ready for intensive care. 'What about Gawler?'

'We've got two reports on him, one from the FBI in Washington, the other from the CIA.' Joe Nagler's contact in ASIO had used his contact in the CIA; even in the world of spooks, Malone had remarked to Clements, it was not what you knew but whom you knew that counted. 'Maybe you'd like to see them?'

Tewsday glanced at them, making a pretence of his surprise. 'I never knew ... His references were excellent!'

Malone took back the telexes. 'I think these are more reliable. Where is he?'

'Over – over in his flat.' He was trapped; Gawler would not take the rap on his own. 'Is – do you think he'll be dangerous?'

'I hope not.' But Malone looked at Clements. 'You'd better get the two fellers from out in the street, Russ. Just in case.' Clements hurried out and Malone turned back to Tewsday. 'Why did Sister Mary Magdalene, *Teresa Hourigan*, come to see you the night she was murdered?'

'Eh?' He put out a hand to steady himself, it fell on the big antique globe beside his desk; the world spun round, giving him no support at all. 'The Archbishop's niece? She wasn't here! Where did you get that –?'

'We've traced the cab driver who brought her here from Pymble station. We have another witness who saw her arrive.' But he did not name Mrs Prunello; he didn't want to start a neighbourhood war. 'Why did she come?'

The earthquake had started and he was to be the first victim. He had never been philosophical; there wasn't a philosopher on the surrounding library shelves who could help him. The 'good solid reads' were full of men like himself, successes who were flawed. But he had learned nothing from them.

'She – she called me, said she wanted to talk to me about her uncle and a deal he was trying to put through with one of our companies . . .'

'Austarm.'

'Yes, yes! I agreed to see her because I wanted to stop the deal – it was bad for the corporation, bad for Australia –' He was babbling, wrapping the flag, anything, round him. 'We were on the same side, she and I –'

Then Clements came bursting back into the room. 'He's gone, Scobie – bolted! Raudonikis and Harris have been out in the drive, in front of the flat, ever since we came in here. But he's not there – he must have scooted over the back fence.' He looked at Tewsday. 'What's at the back of your garden?'

'A small reserve – a park. He can't have – *bolted*!' He felt a prick of hope: with Gawler gone there would be no one to testify against him.

'Get a call out!' Malone snapped. 'Stay here, Sir Jonathan – don't *you* try to bolt!'

Malone and Clements left the room on the run; but Malone was back within a minute. Tewsday had slumped down in his chair and Sally Gawler, who had come in from the back of the big house, was standing beside him. She looked in

317

bewilderment at Malone as he came back in.

'What's going on? I can't get a word out of Sir Jonathan –
who are you?'

'Police. Who are you – Mrs Gawler? Where's your husband?'

'Gary? He's, I dunno, over in the flat. I was just going to
call him for his lunch – why do you want him?' Suddenly she
looked even more worried.

Malone took the telexes out of his pocket. 'Did you know
any of this, Mrs Gawler?'

She read the dispatches, then shook her head dazedly. 'The
FBI? The CIA? My Gary?'

'I think you'd both better come with me. I'll take you into
Homicide.'

Tewsday at last regained his voice. 'I'll have to call my
wife.'

'Of course. I think you'd better call your lawyer, too.'

'Does Mrs Gawler need to come?' He was not totally taken
up with himself: he saw how shattered she was.

'Just for her own protection.'

Sally Gawler was shocked at the suggestion. 'Gary would
never hurt *me*!'

'I'm afraid he's already done that,' said Malone and wondered again at the number of women who fell in love with
the bastards of the world.


# 5

Malone managed, on one pretext or another, to keep Tewsday
at Homicide and then at Police Centre for almost five hours.
He wanted to hold him till Gawler had been picked up, but
he spent the afternoon battling Fiona Tewsday, two lawyers,
a State Member of Parliament and finally Commissioner
Leeds himself.

'You'll have to let him go, Inspector,' Leeds said on the phone. 'The Premier himself has been on the line.' *And on my back*: Malone heard the unspoken words. 'If you can't lay charges, let him go.'

'Yes, sir,' Malone agreed reluctantly. 'I was just hoping we'd pick up this other feller Gawler, put them up against each other.'

'You can do that when you do pick him up. Tewsday's not going to skip the country. I think you'd better come and see me when all this is over.'

'When do you think that will be, sir?'

'That's enough, Inspector.' But the Commissioner's voice sounded more sympathetic than sharp.

Tewsday was released at six o'clock. He and Sally Gawler were driven back to Pymble by Fiona in the BMW. Fiona, a true All Black, drove straight at the assembled reporters and cameramen gathered outside the Police Centre, and the media crowd had to scatter for their lives. Accusations of mayhem, it seemed, bred thoughts of mayhem. Or maybe all the latent Kiwi antagonism towards Australians had come to her blue-rinsed surface.

On their way back to Homicide Malone said to Clements, 'I want a tail kept on Tewsday around the clock.'

'Is the Commissioner still on our side?'

Malone shook his head. 'I think he's had enough of me. It's better that we go on our own on this one.'

Clements gave him a quizzical look. 'Tibooburra's getting closer and closer. I can already hear the flies buzzing and the kangaroos bouncing up and down.'

The phone was ringing in the house at Pymble when the Tewsdays arrived home at 6.50. Tewsday was first into the house and picked up the receiver. It was Gawler ringing from a public call-box.

'Just a minute,' said Tewsday as Fiona and Sally Gawler came in the front door. 'I'll take it in the library. It's one of the newspapers about my resignation.'

'Tell them to get stuffed,' said Fiona, though her vowels were still rounded.

He switched the connection, hung up and went through into the library and closed the door. 'Where are you?'

'I'm not telling. Listen – what did the cops want?'

'You. They've been questioning me in the city for the last five hours. It's bloody embarrassing.'

Gawler laughed. 'Embarrassing? You dunno what embarrassing is. Listen, I need money.'

He had guessed that the demand would come some time. 'How much?'

'I want enough to get out of the country, get me set up again. I'll go somewhere where there's no extradition treaty. I'll get my wife to meet me there. Fifty thousand, how does that sound?'

'Are you trying to blackmail me?' He had expected a demand of pehaps ten thousand; he had lost track of the price of murder. 'You don't want to forget, she was still alive when you took her out of this house.'

'Don't bullshit me, Tewsday!' It was the first time he had ever heard Gawler raise his voice. 'You knew what was gonna happen to her! The same will happen to you –'

'Calm down,' said Tewsday, anything but calm. 'I just can't produce that sort of money out of the blue –'

'You're still bullshitting. I've seen the evening papers, they got it all about you resigning from Ballyduff. You got a big golden handshake, they said. What was it? A million, a coupla million? You owe me one, Tewsday, a golden handshake.'

Tewsday had seen the papers; Sally Gawler had gone out at one point in the afternoon and brought them back. It had been the lead story on the financial pages: BOARD-ROOM WAR? one headline had asked. Suddenly he heard himself say, 'Would you like a handshake of a hundred thousand?'

There was a moment of silence, then: 'Doing what?'

'Getting rid of someone else.' In for a penny, in for a hundred thousand. 'Fingal Hourigan.'

'You're outa your fucking head, you know that?'

'No.' But maybe he was; madness, after all, was just another state of mind. 'Do you want to earn the money or not?'

There was another silence; then: 'It's not enough. Two hundred and fifty thousand.'

'Don't be ridiculous!'

'You're the one being ridiculous. More than that, you're crazy. You want me to be crazy, too, that's the price.'

He sighed; he hated parting with his own money, even to win back a hundred times as much. Which he could do so, if Fingal was gone. 'You're a hard man, Gawler.'

'You got to be in my trade. Is Sally there?'

'I don't think you should speak to her now. She's pretty upset. I'll tell her you called and you'll talk to her tomorrow. Get the job done first.'

'Payment first. Give Sally ten thousand in cash, just for starters. Tell her it's my redundancy pay. The rest of it cable to my account in Switzerland. Take it down.' He gave an account number and a bank in Zurich. Tewsday was not surprised that Gawler should have such an account; there was still so much he didn't know, and would never know, about the American. 'If it's not there within forty-eight hours, I'll be back to take it out of your hide. You know what I mean?' He was cool and distant again, the professional killer. Tewsday felt weak, wondering that he should be dealing with such a man. 'Where do I find Hourigan? At home or in the office?'

Tewsday thought a moment. 'At Ballyduff House. I'll have him there at eight o'clock, in his office on the sixty-ninth floor. You be waiting for him.'

He hung up, sat staring at his desk. He *was* mad, he knew that; but it was not much to live with if it brought him vengeance. He had lived for thirty-two years with ambition: perhaps that had been a madness, too, but he had weathered

321

it, indeed thrived on it. Fingal Hourigan could not be allowed to win. He had to go.

He picked up the phone, dialled the number at Vaucluse.

# 6

'You'd better come with me, Kerry,' Fingal said as he hung up the phone.' That was Jonathan. He says he's got something that concerns you. He wants to see me in my office.'

'Why there?'

'At eight o'clock at night he thinks that's the last place we'll see any reporters hanging about. Are they still camped outside our gates?'

'No.' The Archbishop, for whom publicity had once been like another state of grace, was tired, even afraid, of it now. 'They've given up. They'll be back as soon as something else starts up. What's Jonathan got on me this time?'

'He didn't say.' Fingal went out to the entrance hall, put on his topcoat and hat, picked up the silver walking-stick. He looked over his shoulder as Brigid came down the stairs. 'Kerry and I are going out for a while. Jonathan wants to see us at the office.'

'You businessmen – why can't you keep business hours?'

'This is different sort of business.' He paused as he opened the front door. 'All of a sudden I feel tired.'

'Stay home,' said Brigid gently.

'No, not that sort of tired. Just as if ...' But he couldn't explain the weariness that had abruptly overtaken him. 'Come on, Kerry. Wait dinner for us, Bridie. We'll have it together.'

*Bridie*. Oh Dad, why did you leave it so late?

In the car going into the city Kerry said, 'Why didn't you tell Jonathan to go to hell? You're bone-tired ...'

Fingal looked out at the drizzling rain. The roadway was a black mirror patterned with moving white, amber and red lights; he was dazzled by it and had to shut his eyes. Small things were beginning to defeat him; this was the way healthy old men died, bit by bit. Was there any point to anything any more? Maybe he should have told Jonathan Tewsday to go to hell. But he had not been able to resist the opportunity to give the screw one last turn. He had no fear that Tewsday could do any more damage to himself or Kerry; the man was beaten. Still . . .

'I'm trying to protect you,' he said 'We don't know what the sonofabitch might do.'

'It doesn't matter any more. I'm finished with Paredes and Domecq.'

'There are others. You can't give up now!' He had to whip up the protest, though with a tired hand.

'I'll wait and see. I'm still young – they don't elect young popes any more. I still have to make cardinal.' But he had begun to lose hope; or ambition. Someone (Galen?) had once said that the temperaments of the body led the faculties of the soul. If so, his body was winning out, leading him to resignation. He had been running towards Rome for years and now he was suddenly as tired as his father. He had been caught up in the greatest sin of all, murder, and he could not give himself absolution. Especially since one of the victims had been his own sister's child.

'Don't give up,' Fingal insisted, but he knew in his heart that it really didn't matter any more. He would not live long enough to see the dream.

The Phantom V pulled into the basement garage of Bally-duff House, gliding in like a royal barge. There were half a dozen other cars in the garage, plus two vans; the contract cleaners were at work. As the chauffeur opened the door for Fingal to get out, the old man paused and looked around the garage.

'I can't see Jonathan's car.'

'It would be like him to keep us waiting.' The Archbishop decided this was no time for Christian charity. He began to look forward to being a sonofabitch, though he was not sure how one went about it. Then he reasoned that all he had to do was mimic Jonathan Tewsday. Up till now he had not realized how much he disliked the man. He might even come to hate him, as his father did.

They rode up in the lift to the sixty-ninth floor. As they got out, a thin balding man in white overalls was waiting to go down. He was carrying a heavy vacuum cleaner, the long cord rolled in loops over his shoulder.

'You finished on this floor?' said Fingal.

'Not quite. You're Mr Hourigan, right?' There was no touching the forelock, even if he'd had one; he didn't work for this big shot, he worked for his own boss. 'There's a guy waiting in your office. He told me to come back later. I like to keep me routine, you know what I mean? Start at the top and work down.'

'You'll never get anywhere that way,' said Fingal.

He walked on down the wide corridor, unbuttoning his topcoat but not taking it off; the meeting with Tewsday would be short. Kerry followed him, wondering what lay ahead. He was tired of scenes, he who had dreamed of a coronation.

Fingal opened the door into his secretary's office, crossed the room unhurriedly and opened the door into his own office.

'Tewsday?'

The man at the big window turned, Sydney brightly lit at his back. 'Sir Jonathan couldn't make it, Mr Hourigan.' Then he saw Kerry standing in the doorway behind his father. 'Ah shit!'

Fingal stepped into the room and, after a moment's hesitation, Kerry followed him. 'Gawler? What the hell are you doing in my office?'

Gawler moved quickly and lightly away from the window; before the Hourigans could move, he was between them and the door. He closed the door, took out a long-bladed knife.

'Two for the price of one. It wasn't in the contract, but I guess you're out of luck, Your Grace.' It was a black joke, but he didn't smile.

'Why?' Kerry was shocked, but, to his own surprise, he was not frightened.

'I don't even know,' said Gawler. 'With me, I got problems and I need the money. It's an old story – for me, anyway. Ever since I was a kid in Chicago.' He wasn't about to reminisce. He had come prepared for one killing, now he had to adjust himself to two.

'You're from Chicago?' Fingal was the coolest of the three of them. Or maybe just the most tired. After all these years he recognized fate when it was in the same room with him.

'Yeah, Chicago originally. What's that got to do with it?'

Fingal nodded. 'I might have guessed. Now and then.'

'What?' But puzzlement wasn't going to stop Gawler. He stepped towards Fingal, the knife blade sweeping upwards.

# 7

'Where's Paredes now?' said Malone.

'He's in the Crest Hotel up at the Cross,' said Clements. 'Andy Graham's in the lobby and he's got someone watching out the back. It looks as if Paredes isn't going to do a bunk, not yet.'

'He's a cool bastard. I thought he'd be on the first plane out of Sydney as soon as we charged Domecq. I was hoping he'd try it. Then we could have picked him up on suspicion.'

'We still could.'

Malone shook his head. 'We had no luck with Tewsday. He's free till we pick up Gawler.'

'Are the two murders connected?'

'I still don't know. The bloke in the middle of it all is the Archbishop and it seems he's the only innocent one, excepting for getting all these buggers together.'

'Him or his old man,' said Clements. 'There's someone else we never really questioned. Brigid Hourigan.'

Malone pondered the suggestion; then he looked in his

notebook for a number. He rang the house at Stokes Point and the phone was picked up almost immediately. '*Pronto?* Is that you, signorina?'

'No, it's Inspector Malone. Where is Signorina Hourigan?'

'She is at her father's house –'

Malone hung up in Michele's ear, quickly dialled the Vaucluse house before the houseman could call his mistress and warn her that the police wanted to speak to her again. Mrs Kelly, another keeper of the flame, answered this time. 'Miss Brigid? Yes, she's here. Who's calling? Oh, it's *you*.' Malone felt like the Devil himself. 'You don't give a soul any peace, do you? I'll get her.'

Brigid Hourigan came to the phone. 'No, Inspector, I really don't have anything further to say. Perhaps when you've caught whoever murdered my daughter –'

'We're still trying to do that, Miss Hourigan. That's why I want to ask you some questions. About Sir Jonathan Tewsday, for a start –'

'You should ask my father about him, not me.'

'We'll do that, too. Is your father at home now?'

'No.'

'Where is he?'

'Do I have to answer that? He's not under house arrest or anything –'

'*Where is he?*'

'He – he's gone into his office with my brother. Sir Jonathan called him, asked him to meet him there.'

'How long ago did they leave?'

'Not more than ten minutes –'

Malone hung up, was on his feet, dragging on his jacket. 'Ballyduff House, as fast as we can make it!'

'What's going on?' Clements was running after him down the aisle between the desks.

'I don't know! But I bet we're going to find the answer to everything in the next ten minutes!'

# 8

Fingal died instantly as the knife went in under his ribs and upwards. It was not an easy stab for Gawler; he had to drive in through the thickness of the topcoat. Fingal said something that sounded like *Now and Then, Amen*, but it was indistinct in what also sounded like a laugh, though there was no mirth in his face or the wide blue eyes. He stepped away from Gawler and, the fugitive from Chicago winters of long ago, fell into the coldest, darkest winter of all.

Gawler withdrew the knife and spun round as Kerry, a huge black figure of terrible rage, came at him with a roar. He swung with the knife, but Kerry took it on his left arm. He fell on Gawler, crashing him to the floor. The killer went down, but he had no hope under the bulk on top of him. The Archbishop was astride him, smashing at his face with a bloodied fist, when the door burst open and Malone and Clements came in. It took their combined strength to drag him off the unconscious Gawler.

'That's enough, Your Grace,' said Malone. 'That's the last of it.'

# THIRTEEN

## I

'We'll give him a State funeral,' Premier Hans Vanderberg told his Cabinet colleagues.

'Y-y-you c-c-can't do th-that!' The Minister for Culture had a shaky voice and an even shakier department.

'All the unions will go out on strike,' said the Minister for Industrial Relations, an ex-union man. 'A State funeral for a boss! You must be joking.'

'He gave the Party over a million dollars at one time or another,' said the Treasurer.

'H-he g-g-gave the other side tw-twice as m-much,' said the Minister for Culture.

'You'd like a State funeral when you go, wouldn't you?' said the Premier.

'I-I wasn't th-thinking of g-g-going,' said the Minister for Culture, but felt the knife already in his back.

So Fingal Hourigan had a State funeral. The country's richest man could not be buried without a salute in a country where wealth, till something better was recognized, was the main yardstick. Fingal, a clear-eyed cynic, would have understood. The obituaries put his fortune at between two and four billion dollars, but they were only guessing. Obituaries are never meant to be truly accurate: the laws of libel are too strict, something for which the heirs are always watching. Nobody would ever know the full truth about Fingal Hourigan. Which was the one thing he had in common with the rest of us.

Domecq, Gawler and Jonathan Tewsday were all sentenced to life imprisonment; the judges marked them all eligible for parole at the turn of the century, an appropriate time to start all over again. Paredes, against whom no charges were laid in New South Wales, went back to Miami, where the FBI picked him up at once; the law, with that talent it has for eventually finding the right charge, sent him to Federal prison for ten years for tax evasion, a crime that, as a Latin American, he had always thought was a joke. Fiona Tewsday sold up the house in Pymble, the property at Bowral, the sixty-foot cruiser and took her three daughters, Sally Gawler and the Rolls-Royce back to New Zealand, where the All Blacks turned out and did a *haka* for her on Eden Park. She was forgiven eventually for marrying an Australian.

Archbishop Hourigan went back to Rome, where he is still head of the Department for the Defence Against Subversive Religions. On his return he had a private audience of the Pope and came out looking like an elderly choirboy, as Monsignor Lindwall wrote to Malone. 'We forgive our sinners, Scobie. If they didn't, what church, of any persuasion, would last even a decade, let alone two thousand years?'

Brigid Hourigan sent her Italian houseman back to Italy. Then, unexpectedly revealing to the world that she was more her father's daughter than it had suspected, she became non-executive chairwoman of Ballyduff Holdings. Kerry, at last succumbing, after a great deal of soul-searching, to vows of poverty (well, almost; he still lived in the *palazzo* apartment), turned over the bulk of his inherited trust to Brigid. She thus became Australia's richest person and the land was loud with feminist hallelujahs. She was, however, still poor in spirit, though she hid it well. Part of her had died with Teresa, the young nun who might have taught them all true love.

One night at the end of winter Malone was sitting in the living-room in the house in Randwick. It had been a dull day at Homicide, just as he liked it; nobody dead, no attempts at murder. The front door was open, letting in the cold night air, but he hadn't the heart to yell at the children to come in and close it. He could hear them:

'Look at the stars!' said Tom. 'Tens of 'em!'

'Millions!' said Maureen. 'There are *millions* of 'em!'

'I can't count that much,' said Tom. 'Tens is good enough for me.'

On television an old, old man was being interviewed on *The 7.30 Report*. It was his hundredth birthday, but he looked much older, his face blotched and pinched and wrinkled by centuries. Malone turned up the sound:

'And what do you think is the secret of your great age?'

'No sex.'

'You mean you have been celibate all your life?'

'No, I mean I aint (*beeped*) a woman since I was ninety!'

The wrinkled old face broke into a wicked grin, then disintegrated as the toothless old mouth opened up and a happy, happy cackle came up out of a hundred years' of memories. Malone switched off the sound and fell back laughing.

Lisa came in from the kitchen. 'What's the matter?'

'Nothing! Nothing.' He reached for her, pulled her down on to the couch beside him as the children came in from the front veranda, slamming the door behind them. 'Everything's normal!'

'What's normal?' said Tom.

'We are,' said Claire, and her father looked at her gratefully. That was something she had worked out for herself, *Choice* hadn't had to tell her.

Then the phone rang. Lisa got up, went out to the hallway and answered it. Then she put her head in the doorway, sighed. 'It's Russ Clements. Normal?'